JEAN JOHNSON AND THE SONS OF DESTINY

"Jean Johnson's writing is fabulously fresh, thoroughly romantic, and wildly entertaining. Terrific—fast, sexy, charming, and utterly engaging. I loved it!"

—Jayne Ann Krentz, *New York Times* bestselling author

"Cursed brothers, fated mates, prophecies, yum! A fresh new voice in fantasy romance, Jean Johnson spins an intriguing tale of destiny and magic."   —Robin D. Owens, RITA Award–winning author

"What a debut! I have to say it is a must-read for those who enjoy fantasy and romance. I so thoroughly enjoyed [*The Sword*] and eagerly look forward to each of the other brothers' stories. Jean Johnson can't write them fast enough for me!"   —*The Best Reviews*

"Enchan   tching
woman   magical . . .   *Review*

"A par   DEC   2009   l historical   eated
a myst   ktales
we lov   **Richton Park**   ts the
Knigh   **Public Library District**   ng to
happe   **4045 Sauk Trail**   with
old-w   **Richton Park, Illinois 60471**   mage
for yo   *unkies*

"An intriguing new fantasy romance series . . . A welcome addition to the genre. *The Sword* is a unique combination of magic, time travel, and fantasy that will have readers looking toward the next book. Think *Seven Brides for Seven Brothers*, but add one more and give them magic, with curses and fantasy thrown in for fun. Cunning . . . Creative . . . Lovers of magic and fantasy will enjoy this fun, fresh, and very romantic offering."　　　　　*—Time Travel Romance Writers*

"I love *The Sword*. The writing is sharp and witty and the story is charming. [Johnson] makes everything perfectly believable. She has created an enchanting situation and characters that are irascible at times and loveable at others. Jean Johnson . . . is off to a flying start. She tells her story with a lively zest that transports a reader to the place of action. I can hardly wait for the next one. It is a must-read."
　　　　　　　　　　　　　　　　　　—Romance Reviews Today

"A fun story. I look forward to seeing how these alpha males find their soul mates in the remaining books."　　　　　*—The Eternal Night*

"An intriguing world . . . An enjoyable hero . . . An enjoyable showcase for an inventive new author. Jean Johnson brings a welcome voice to the romance genre, and she's assured of a warm welcome."
　　　　　　　　　　　　　　　　　　　—The Romance Reader

"An intriguing and entertaining tale of another dimension . . . Quite entertaining. It will be fun to see how the prophecy turns out for the rest of the brothers."　　　　　　　　　　*—Fresh Fiction*

SHIFTING PLAINS

JEAN JOHNSON

BERKLEY SENSATION, NEW YORK

THE BERKLEY PUBLISHING GROUP
Published by the Penguin Group
Penguin Group (USA) Inc.
375 Hudson Street, New York, New York 10014, USA
Penguin Group (Canada), 90 Eglinton Avenue East, Suite 700, Toronto, Ontario M4P 2Y3, Canada
(a division of Pearson Penguin Canada Inc.)
Penguin Books Ltd., 80 Strand, London WC2R 0RL, England
Penguin Group Ireland, 25 St. Stephen's Green, Dublin 2, Ireland (a division of Penguin Books Ltd.)
Penguin Group (Australia), 250 Camberwell Road, Camberwell, Victoria 3124, Australia
(a division of Pearson Australia Group Pty. Ltd.)
Penguin Books India Pvt. Ltd., 11 Community Centre, Panchsheel Park, New Delhi—110 017, India
Penguin Group (NZ), 67 Apollo Drive, Rosedale, North Shore 0632, New Zealand
(a division of Pearson New Zealand Ltd.)
Penguin Books (South Africa) (Pty.) Ltd., 24 Sturdee Avenue, Rosebank, Johannesburg 2196,
South Africa

Penguin Books Ltd., Registered Offices: 80 Strand, London WC2R 0RL, England

This book is an original publication of The Berkley Publishing Group.

PRINTING HISTORY
Berkley Sensation trade paperback edition / November 2009

Library of Congress Cataloging-in-Publication Data

Johnson, Jean, 1972–
    Shifting plains / Jean Johnson.—Berkley Sensation trade paperback ed.
        p. cm.
    ISBN 978-0-425-23086-2
    1. Young woman—Fiction.   2. Metamorphosis—Fiction.   3. Prophecies—Fiction.   I. Title.
    PS3610.O355.S55   2009
    813'.6—dc22
                                        2009029841

PRINTED IN THE UNITED STATES OF AMERICA

10 9 8 7 6 5 4 3 2 1

ACKNOWLEDGMENTS

In the midst of thanking wonderful people like Alexandra, Alienor, NotSoSaintly, and Stormi, all of whom help polish my prose (and Stormi again for managing my website), on top of giving thanks to friends and family for putting up with me, and others such as my accountant for her wonderful services that free me from the worry and hassle and pain of having to wade through tax code, et cetera, ad nauseam . . . there is one other group of people I should thank. The Concepts Crew. *Thank you* for keeping my computer running, my monitor functioning, and my laptops in good shape.

Some people have asked me why I spend so much money on my computer and laptops, and I tell them it's quite simple: My entire office is my computer. Without it . . . well, I've had hospital nurses and pharmacists alike complain how they can't read my handwriting; it's that much worse than a doctor's scribble. (Trust me, typing is the only way for me to go.) And if my computer breaks down (which it did a couple of times during the editing stages of this book, eep!), I have to have a laptop on hand to keep working . . . and if *that* laptop also breaks down . . . well, that's why I have two. So it's very important to have a good technoguru crew on standby, and they're it.

As always, you can visit my website at www.JeanJohnson.net to see what's coming out next, or even chat with me on the forum boards. And if you're 18 or older, you can drop by the Mob of Irate Torch-Wielding Fans and join in the benign insanity . . . er, I mean, fun. (E-mail me at my website for the address!)

~Jean

ONE

❧

*S*eventeen of them.

Tava closed her eyes. Seventeen bandits were too many for her to fight. It was one thing when she had been tracking just five of them. Five, she could handle, since she could have separated one or two from the others. But not seventeen.

Six was the number that had ambushed her father. Varamon Vel Tith had defended himself, slaying one of them with his dagger. The normally gentle scribe had fought hard and well. But two of the cowards had hidden in the bushes and shot him with arrows; Tava had seen that for herself in the tracks and debris they had left.

If I had gone with him, pressed the matter, he would be alive. Six would have been no match for him and me, not even with bows and arrows. Father . . . Father, I'm sorry. I should have insisted. I should have been more forward, even in front of the Aldeman. They already consider me strange enough, so why shouldn't I have also been unfeminine enough to have argued?

Opening her eyes again, she blinked, adjusting her vision. Despite her skills, the underbrush was thick enough in the foothills of the Correda Mountains that it wasn't easy to see all of the bandits at once. She counted them carefully as they moved through their encampment, marking them by the clothes they wore, the color of their hair, the weapons they bore. Still, most were visible, bartering over the loot they had stolen, gambling for each piece and laughing or groaning at each toss of the gaming sticks.

Her father was not the only one who had been ambushed by this group. From the looks of things, they had struck a cloth trader's wagon, one filled with bolts of brightly dyed linen, cheerful ribbons, spools of thread, and a chest filled with buttons and buckles and clasps, most made from pewter and brass. Apparently these brigands had encountered her father after disposing of the trader and purloining his goods, for they were still dividing the wagon's contents.

Her father was dead. The only parent she could even remember. Dead, because of these cowardly, dishonorable thieves. She wanted to strike them all, to tear into them, to spill their blood as they had spilled Varamon's . . . but seventeen was too many.

Too many.

Think! she chided herself. *You don't have time for grief right now, so think. Father always said that if you have the time to think, do so, for thinking is what separates failure from success. So think, Tava. How do I separate out one or two at a time, and how do I take them out quietly without drawing the attention of the rest?*

She shifted on the stout branch she had selected for her spying perch, considering her options. She wasn't about to go down there as herself, a single, young woman with no resources whatsoever. Luring them with the sight of a game animal wandering too close to their encampment was equally dangerous. Noises might be a good strategy, since they would need to investigate to keep their camp safe, but that was something best attempted after nightfall, and this was mid-morning.

Tava could see better in the dark than anyone she knew, and it would be child's play to lead a few of them around, separating and then attacking them in the deepest shadows of the night. The sounds of battle might even unnerve the rest into following and then getting lost in the dark. But she would have to be quick with each strike and flee into the shadows before she could be spotted by the rest.

. . . Yes. An attack at night. Or even over several nights, she decided. *Whittle down their numbers. That, I can do.*

She clutched at the branch supporting her weight, wishing it was their necks being throttled in her grasp. Mornai women were supposed to be gentle, docile, polite, and pleasant. They weren't supposed to argue in public, and they definitely weren't supposed to fight. Most wouldn't even think of leaving their homes to track down their father's absence, and most certainly wouldn't have chosen to travel alone. But something fiercer than the blood of the River People coursed through her own veins. Sometimes she was ashamed of that foreign blood, but not right now. Not when these filth had to be stopped before they could attack anyone else.

Maybe if I rigged a deadfall and led some of them to it? Or some other sort of trap? It would have to be some distance away, so they wouldn't hear or see me building it. I don't have any tools, but it's not that far to the Plains from here; I could make some braided rope from grass and rig a log to swing down at them, bashing into them . . .

Movement to the side made her twist her head that way, peering through the trees for the source. *Another bandit? A new raiding party returning home? A . . . tiger?*

That was odd. It wasn't unusual, since tigers hunted all along the fringes of the Morning River, particularly near the Shifting Plains. They even ranged up into the mountains on the south side of the Plains. But they were wild creatures; they disliked fire, and they were wary of men. They did not creep up to the edge of a bandit encampment, and they certainly would not do so on the downwind side, where the smoke from the three fires tended by the bandits would sting the striped cat's sensitive nose, arousing the instinct to flee. A tiger might approach from the side, but not from fully downwind of a campfire.

Tava searched the rest of the wooded slope that flanked the small vale the bandits occupied. The tiger was acting unnaturally; there had to be a reason. Unless there was something she was missing, something prompting it to be there, stalking slowly, warily, through the underbrush—there, another anomaly. *But . . . what is a* bear *doing there? And so close to the tiger?*

Confused, Tava kept searching the underbrush, narrowing her gaze to help sharpen her vision. A third bit of movement, soft and gray brown. She didn't know what it was, either another bear or maybe a wolf, but so many predators so close together was unnatural. Or at least not normal. There *was* a possible explanation, but it was one that unnerved her.

Morna! So many predators in such a small area can only mean one thing: Shifterai. This is a Shifterai warband, no doubt hired by some village, either Mornai or Corredai. If so, they're here to wipe out these brigands . . .

On the one hand, her father would be more than adequately avenged. Shifterai were shapechangers—at least, the men were—and they often formed warbands that traveled into the lands surrounding the Plains, looking for work. When they did so, when they traveled on foreign soil, they were usually trustworthy, sticking to the letter of any contract they made . . . unless they crossed paths with a lone female. Like her mother.

She had seen Shifterai twice before. Both times, her father had written the contract between the warband and a village to the Five Springs, where she and her father lived. He had acted as the scribe for at least eight other Shifterai contracts in the last twenty years, but had traveled to the other villages in order to do so. Few Mornai were well versed enough in the written arts to draw up a contract, so the Aldemen of no less than six villages had relied on Varamon for their business transactions.

Those same village leaders had also accepted Tava to a lesser extent, but only when her father wasn't available and the matter was time sensitive. Mornai females weren't allowed to negotiate important contracts; recording one was bad enough. Varamon had argued that in the larger Mornai cities, ladies of good education were often preferred as scribes for the neatness of their penmanship, but there weren't any large cities near Five Springs and the other villages. Nor even a modest-sized town for a full three days' barge-travel in either direction. The Aldemen refused to bend their minds to an unfamiliar way.

A scrabbling, yowling hiss snared her attention. Tava craned her neck carefully, peering through the boughs. She saw movement among the bandits, watched them snatch up their weapons and head to the right, toward the bear's position. Voices shouted in command, then yelled in pain. She had a brief, nerve-racking glimpse of the bear bowling over a yellow-shirted bandit with the swipe of a paw, and of the yellow tunic quickly staining red as the man tumbled heels over shoulder into the underbrush. Other bandits darted around the clearing, either grabbing for weapons or drawn to the attacks of the other predators . . . or fleeing their approach.

She was in the wrong spot to see anything after a few moments. A good one for seeing the scattered loot lying throughout the hastily abandoned encampment, but not for the war being waged beneath the layers of the forest canopy. Lifting her head to try to find a better vantage point, again she spotted movement through the trees. This time, it was the stealthy movement of two, maybe three men. One of them with brown trousers and a shirt that was dyed half in dull blue, half in sun-faded purple.

That was one of the bandits she had tracked; his boots had a distinctive crack across each sole. He and the other two men that she could see were picking their way uphill, sneaking away from battle. It was a wise course, provided they could get up and over the hill before the warband realized they were missing. There was a stream on the other side of the ridge, something they could lose their scent in . . . but only if they made it that far unnoticed.

Which they would do if the warband didn't realize they had left. Most of the battle noises were off to her right, toward the mouth of the little vale. Not toward the hillside. The hill wasn't tall, either; it wouldn't be long before the bandits were out of sight.

Thrusting off of her leafy perch, leaping fearlessly from branch to branch, Tava followed them, sticking to the higher gaps between the branches for cover. She *would* have justice for her father, and for the wagon's owner. A death for a death. And, most important, an end to these bandits' continued predations. They *had* to be stopped.

If you ever have to fight someone, she remembered her father instructing her, *make sure it is done swiftly. If they offer you violence, end it quickly and decisively. If they are neighbors—if Josan gets too much stout in him and he starts swinging at anything that looks twice at him—then you end it without killing or maiming him. If they are enemies, and they are trying to kill you, end it any way you can, but end the fighting quickly. You will be as much a target as they are, when you fight.*

The bandits crested the hill; she could now see that there were four of them, not just three. Two carried bows, arrows nocked on the strings. The other two carried axes and knives. They moved cautiously, but quickly, their attention behind and ahead. Not above.

Diving down between the branches, Tava concentrated as she fell, swelling her muscles, her mass, until she was as large and furry as that bear she had seen. Hitting the first man on the shoulders, she *crunched* him under her excessive weight. Thick fur and thicker muscles padded her from a bad bruising as she tumbled free. Those same muscles also allowed her to launch herself at the next man as soon as she completed her somersault.

Paws shifted into claws when she pounced onto his back. They raked down his spine, slamming him into the ground. Ribs cracked under her weight; blood flung in hot, wet droplets from her claws when she leaped again. It took two bounds to get to the next man, who had whirled at the noise of his companions being brought down. Pain blossomed in her shoulder, but it was too late to stop her lunge. She shifted shape as she passed his dodging body, shoving the arrow shaft out of her flesh by sheer force of will.

Now vaguely human, but fur-clad and three times her normal size, Tava used her uninjured arm to grab the wrist holding the offending bow. She used her forward momentum to spin herself around, yanking the bandit off his feet. A yell escaped him as she slung him around and released him, sending him flying through the woods. A *thump* ended all further noise, save for the crackling of branches, as his body landed limply on the bushes at the base of a tree.

Whirling to face the last bandit with the momentum of her throw, she shifted again, leaping at the ax-wielder with a feral, feline snarl. Bears had power for brute strength, but she wanted the claws of a stripe-cat to make this murderer pay. Something else slammed into him from the side, knocking him out of her way. Or rather, someone else. Striped and tigerish, the other shapeshifter tore into the bandit even more brutally than she had treated his three comrades. She skidded to a stop, not wanting to get involved in the fierce, brief battle between the two males.

For a moment, Tava allowed herself to feel a feral satisfaction, even though her aborted target was the one with the blue and purple patchwork tunic, *her* rightful prey. Still, at least one of the five who had survived her father's ambush was now thoroughly dead, one of the few she had been able to identify as one of his attackers. She let herself feel satisfied for a moment.

Backing off of his bloodied prey, the other tiger looked up at her, tawny, light brown eyes narrowing in wary puzzlement. Realization dawned as he met her gaze.

Shifterai male. Lone female. Oh . . . muck!

Spinning, she launched herself downhill, sprinting for the same stream the bandits would have used to hide their scent and their tracks. When she glanced behind her and saw the other tiger giving chase, Tava threw herself and her attention forward. She raced as hard as she could, ignoring the pain in her shoulder and the stitch in her abdomen. Unfortunately, tigers weren't built for long sprints; they could dash after prey, but usually only in short bursts. Mostly, they traveled great distances at a steady lope. Time for another change.

Limbs lengthening, spine bunching and flexing, she bounded over bushes and rocks, dodged trees, and crossed the wending stream in her nearly straight flight. A few minutes later, another glance showed no further signs of pursuit; Tava slowed just enough to catch some of her breath, but she didn't stop running and didn't lower her guard. Shapeshifters could become almost anything and hide almost anywhere.

There was only one place safe for her, and it was at least an hour's run from here. The Morning River. She had heard of Shifterai warbands taking the shapes of eagles, but she had never heard of them taking the shape of a river eel. As soon as she reached the great river, she would be relatively safe, provided she avoided any barge nets and made herself too large to be swallowed by another fish.

Father, I have avenged you. At least in part. And, Goddess save me . . . the Shifterai have avenged the other part. I never thought I'd be grateful to their kind for anything, not after what they did to my mother! But as you taught me, I must acknowledge the truth, and the truth is, they have done me a favor. I could not have taken on all seventeen bandits, not so swiftly, and not on my own.

But Father, I wish it hadn't been necessary! How I wish you were still alive!

A tigress . . . *That was a* tigress.

Still a little stunned by the discovery, Kodan padded back toward the bodies of the fallen bandits, nose to the trail. Tigerish, humanish, bearish pawprints reeked of nervous sweat and battle adrenaline.

A bloodstained arrow discarded on the ground smelled of pain and injury. And all of it smelled *female*. There was no lying to a Shifterai nose.

Noise up on the top of the ridge made him tense, then hurry away from the four corpses. *I have to keep the others away.* He didn't question the possessive urge; it was a cautious one, and caution usually saved lives. *Her* life, whoever she was.

But that's the problem, isn't it? Shifter females don't usually leave the Plains. Not without an escort; they're too important. If the others got a whiff of her, they'd act impulsively, scaring her farther away . . .

Whoever she is, I haven't smelled her before. Either she's someone from a far-flung Family, exploring on her own, or . . . Well, I don't think there has ever been a case of a Centarai cross-kin being a female. This could be an exception, but if she is cross-kin, where is her escort? Even cross-kin males ride from their Plains to ours with an escort of some sort.

"Did hyu get de last of dem?" the bear pausing at the top of the ridge asked, peering down through the bushes and trees.

"Hyez." Talking with a tiger's mouth was about as comfortable as talking with a bear's, but it was less tiring than shifting into something more human. And more courteous; Manolo wasn't a *multerai*, but he might still feel compelled to shift back to a humanoid form if Kodan did. Better for the older, less skillful man to conserve his energies until they were absolutely sure the battle was over. "Fhour crozzed de ridge, and fhour are dead. De odders?"

"Dead." Twisting his head back over the ridge, Manolo indicated the vale. "I help gadder tings from dem?"

"No, I be fine. Go help de odders," Kodan directed him.

Nodding, Manolo loped over the top of the hill, heading back down toward the others.

Normally he would have suggested the other way around, that Manolo strip the corpses while he returned to the others. He had been voted the warlord for this expedition, and it was his duty to direct their group efforts. However, the scent of that female shifter still lingered near these corpses. Until he knew what to do about her—if anything, given how fast she had fled from him—Kodan would keep her existence to himself.

He retreated back to the four corpses. Two had crushed rib cages and one had a broken neck, thanks to the woman shifter. The fourth, he himself had disemboweled. Her kills were cleaner than his, with mostly minimal damage to the brigands' clothes. Much of it could be salvaged. Keeping enough fur on his body to preserve his dignity, he shifted to his natural form and started tugging off the nearest set of boots.

Whatever he and his men didn't want for themselves would go to the villagers that had hired their warband. It was only fair to reclaim such things; most of whatever these bandits owned had been stolen from others in the first place. He had his duties to perform, in spite of her tantalizing, fading scent and the unpleasantness of handling dead and bloodied bodies.

If I wasn't in charge of the warband, I would have given further chase. Whoever she is, I'm fairly certain she's not Shifterai. A Princess of the People wouldn't have run from a fellow shapeshifter. A thought made him pause as he stuffed a pair of brown, Mornai-style britches into a yellow tunic. *Unless perhaps she's a spellshifter? An actual mage? If so, she's a long way from lands where mages are born. Possibly from the head or the mouth of the Morning River, or possibly from somewhere to the east?*

But she doesn't really smell like a mage. I've only been close to three, all of them priestesses, but they all stung my nose like fresh-ground pepper. Adding the boots and the worn leather belt, he moved on to the next corpse. *It's a question I may never get answered.*

When he was finished stuffing tunics with garments and using the last of the belts to lash the weapons together, he bundled the salvaged belongings over his shoulder and headed back across the ridge. The others had been equally industrious; not only were the bodies stripped, but the buttons and buckles the bandits had been gambling over had been gathered back into their storage chest, and the bolts of fabric were being reloaded onto the wagon.

That'll be a good haul to bring back home, Kodan acknowledged, satisfied. *The Aldeman can send word back along the trader's route of the poor man's loss . . . though I wouldn't give the Aldeman the bolts and buckles to send back as well, not without knowing exactly who should inherit them. He'd be more likely to "tax" the whole amount and keep it for himself and his fellow Alders.*

These remote village leaders are often greedy, even power-hungry. Full of themselves. And we don't have a written contract with them, just a verbal one. They wouldn't accept me as the scribe, and they were too cheap to send for the local man.

"You've snagged a fine haul for us, Brother." Kenyen came up and took the bundle of weapons from Kodan. Like his elder sibling, he was clad in fur from waist to knees, his feet bare of all but self-toughened skin on their soles. The younger shifter lifted his chin at the wagon. "Such bright colors and finespun threads will be worth quite a lot when we get to the City."

"Yes, when we get to the City," their father stated, limping up. He, too, was mostly naked, though he had chosen to clothe himself in feathers from hip to thigh. At Kodan's concerned look, Siinar lifted his hand. "Just a stab wound to my calf. It's half-shifted whole and no longer bleeding. I'll be fine by tomorrow—*don't* tell your mother. She worries too much. I am *not* too old for the warband, whatever she says."

Kenyen snorted, and Kodan grinned. Sinya had been worrying over Siinar Sid Quen for as long as they could remember, despite how often he came home alive and well. She wasn't a princess, but she did rule over their family whenever her menfolk were home.

Siinar eyed his sons, then the wagon again. "A fine prize indeed. That just might be enough to retire for the winter . . . though we could always seek out more. Only a few of us were injured. Even

Torei, the least-shifted of us, should be healed within a few days. So, do we head back to the Plains, Warlord, or do we seek out more work?"

It wasn't the prospect of more wealth that occupied Kodan's thoughts. It was the sight of a tigress bounding downstream as fast as she could. Work would be a good excuse to linger in the area. *If she gets over her fright, she* might *seek us out. She's not Shifterai, and she's not a Centarai cross-kin. The Centarai are warriors in their own right, but even they don't travel alone when they leave their Plains. No, it's slightly possible that she's a by-blow from some shapeshifter's visit to a local village. If so, she may be local-born.*

"We'll stay and seek more work," he decided. "These bandits were attacking whoever they could. We'll head upriver to the next village after we've collected our fee from Muddy Ferns, and see if they, too, will be suitably grateful . . . though we won't tell them immediately why they should be grateful."

Siinar chuckled and clasped his eldest son on the shoulder. "You've learned your bargaining at your mother's knee. I feel pity for these Mornai."

Kenyen laughed outright at that, heading to the wagon to add the weapons to its load. Someone was bringing over the pair of horses that had drawn it, preparing to hitch the geldings to the traces. The bodies of the bandits would be left where they had fallen. Kodan followed his younger brother, adding the bundle of clothes to the items piled under the wagon's canopy. They would have time to wash and sort everything on the journey north, since Muddy Ferns was roughly a day away.

Manolo came over, tying the drawstring of his *breiks* around his waist. The older man had draped more than his own tunic over his naked shoulder; he had also fetched Kodan's clothes. "Here. I'm off to fetch the rest for the others. Did I hear right, just now? We're going to look for more work?"

Kodan nodded, accepting his *breiks*, *chamak*, and boots. A check of the lattermost showed his socks were still stuffed inside. "It's a good haul, with no one other than the Alders of Muddy Ferns likely to try to claim the wagon's goods, but we have enough time left in the season to do a little better. Family Tiger is strong because of its wealth, not because of its numbers."

"I think there's a village just south of here, within a day's walk. Five Springs, Aldeman Tronnen, if he's still in charge. It's been a while since I was in a warband this far south along the Border." The older shifter shrugged. "We'd have been here long before, if Clan Dog hadn't claimed this corner of the Border for themselves."

Kodan shook his head, glancing at the forest around them. "Claimed it, but not sent any warbands into it. I hate to say it, but . . . Clan Dog has grown strange over the years. There's something . . . unfamiliar in the way its Families have behaved."

"Well, the land down here is still somewhat familiar to me." What Manolo lacked in shifting ability, he made up for with his long memory. Kodan listened as he continued, rubbing his chin. "There was also a scribe living in the village of Five Springs . . . Vanamon, I think. A good man with a neat hand and a little girl. Though I suppose she's all grown by now. I haven't seen any of them in years."

"We *all* grow up," Kodan said, shaking out and stepping into his *breiks*. "And I picked this far south because no one has been down here in years. If the Aldeman of Muddy Ferns gives us trouble, we'll go find this scribe of yours. They usually have Truth Stones and Truth Wands as part of their business."

"T-T-Truth St-stone?" Torei asked, limping up to the two men. "Sc-sc-sc-scribe?"

The youth was barely eighteen summers old and could take only three shapes, but he was a good enough fighter to qualify for a warband. Of course, not good enough yet to avoid getting injured, Kodan noted. Torei's thigh wound was bandaged to prevent further seeping of blood, though it did show some signs of shifter-fast healing. A few more shapeshifts and the wound would be fully closed, though it would be an effort for the young man to heal himself that way.

He wasn't like Kodan, who had learned seven shapes within his first year as a young shifter. At the age of eighteen, Torei had mastered only three shapes and would likely never become a *multerai*. His stutter didn't help him to appear strong and powerful, either. But there was nothing stunted about his ears or his mind. "You mean, th-this?"

He dug into a bag slung over his naked shoulder and fished out a handful of quills, a scrap of parchment, and a smooth, white, marble disc.

"Why would bandits have a Truth Stone?" Manolo asked, frowning slightly.

"Why would they have a bag full of parchment and quills?" Kodan countered, plucking one of the altered, ink-stained feathers from Torei's grasp. He gave Manolo a grim look. "I suspect the scribe you just mentioned may have also fallen victim to these brigands. If so, it is our duty to tell his fellow villagers what may have happened to him. Particularly if they do not already know. I think these *curs* may have been killing their victims, not just robbing them."

Nodding, Torei handed him the disc and the bag, leaving it a matter for his warlord to deal with. Accepting the bag, Kodan tucked the feathers gently back inside, along with the disc. Lifting his hand when he was done, he rubbed at an itch on the side of his nose . . . and smelled something faintly familiar.

Brow pinching in a frown, he lifted the bag, examining it. Oiled canvas on the outside to shed the rain, leather lining the inside for sturdiness. Dyed threads stitched along the canvas in interweaving bands of wool. The embroidery smelled of sheep, making his nose itch, but other parts smelled of that same familiar something. It took burying his nose along the fabric covering the leather shoulder strap to figure out what that elusive scent was: something very similar to *her*.

The tigress . . . she's touched this bag. Not just once, but several times.

It's an old scent, the kind that has become one with an object. Nothing too recent, and definitely not with adrenaline or fear. There's no stink of either in her scent on this strap, nor any hints of pepper in her scent. He eyed Manolo, who was studying him curiously. Lowering the bag, Kodan slung the strap over his head.

"I smelled spices." It wasn't really a lie; there were faint hints of herbs and spices imbued into the canvas along with the scents of a male and a female. "Maybe this Five Springs village has some for trade?"

"It's more likely for them to have tea this close to the Corredai Border than foreign spices," Manolo said. "Don't hold your breath on finding exotic foods this far from outlander cities, Kodan. Not in quantities they'd be willing to trade. We wouldn't be that lucky."

"Good luck only happens if you're quick enough to grasp an opportunity, Mano," Kodan returned, thinking of his own missed opportunity in letting that tigress flee. The older man shrugged and moved away, letting him dress in peace.

By the time he had his *breiks* tucked into his boots and his tunic settled over his chest, Kodan knew he would have to go looking for that tigress. Somehow. Even if it meant sending the warband home without him, since he had no idea which way she had fled once she had vanished downstream.

But she is Shifterai, and I will find her. We don't abandon our own.

Both Tava's and her father's horses were tired by the time they reached home the next day. She had spent too many hours yesterday obscuring her backtrail and hadn't been able to hitch up the cart until this morning. Driving to the place on the trail where she had found him, she had wrapped Varamon's body in a sheet and lifted it into the wagon. It was a task made physically less difficult from the way she could flex her muscles bigger, but a task made emotionally harder from the tears that kept blurring her vision.

Even now, with the sun playing shine-and-shadow games with the drifting clouds overhead, it wasn't easy to keep her grief at bay. Her father was gone. The only parent she had ever known. The one person who had accepted all of her, from her occasional stubborn streaks to the outlander magic she had inherited.

Varamon had loved her, encouraged her, cared for her, even when the rest of the village had declared her an improper disgrace. She wasn't docile enough, she was too forward and bold, and she didn't heed her rightful place. Her father hadn't cared that she couldn't stitch as neat a seam as the other village maidens, so long as she could pen a neat line. He hadn't limited her education to the needs of household and garden, but had encouraged her to study as much about the world as she could, given their limited resources. He would debate with her in the evenings, discussing motives for people's deeds, the balance of politics versus profit, and the way the events of the past echoed into the future.

But that was all gone. *No more debates on the King's decision to rebuild the levees this far up the river next spring, no more mutual sympathies for having to weed the garden when we'd both rather be reading ... no more seeking out and studying new kinds of animals together, to see if I can transform myself into some new creature ...*

"*Where* have you been?!"

The strident demand startled both Tava and Tender. The gelding tried to rear in the traces, forcing her to deal with the reins. With a voice that could erode iron, the Aldeman's wife attacked her again.

"You ungrateful child! Unnatural girl! You've been gone all day long, and with your father off on business, there's been no one to chaperone you!" Abigan Zin Tua grabbed at Tender's halter, yanking the nervous horse still. "You were gone yesterday, and you were gone today—for all I know, you've been tossing your skirts for the boys in the next village! Is that why you're on the path to the priest? Are you finally going to confess all of your hidden sins?"

The urge to growl like a beast rose up within her. Tava swallowed it down, even though she knew they were alone at the moment. Abigan was a *proper* Mornai woman; she never raised her voice this stridently in the presence of a man . . . but there weren't any men around at the moment. *Hypocritical to the last,* Tava thought sourly. She didn't fight with the reins for control, not wanting to give the gelding a sore mouth.

"Tender came home alone, yesterday," she managed to say, only to be cut off before she could add more.

"Alone? What do you mean, *alone?*" the middle-aged woman demanded. "Alone, like *you* were alone? Where is your father, girl?"

"I went searching for Father . . . and I found him, yesterday. But I couldn't bring him home until I came back for the cart. That is where I have *been* all day. Bringing my father home . . . and taking him to the priest."

Abigan choked back her next demand, face coloring. She quickly released the gelding's harness, hurrying to the back of the cart. No doubt she intended to apologize profusely for being so forward in his presence, but she stumbled to a stop, peering at the shrouded shape in the bed of the small wagon.

"He . . . he . . ."

"He's dead," Tava confirmed.

Abigan's mouth opened and closed soundlessly a few times before she managed to ask, *"How?"*

"He was ambushed by bandits."

Shrieking, Abigan snatched up the hem of her skirt and pelted up the path, gasping something about warning the village's Alders, and something else about invaders on the way and everyone being murdered in their beds.

Depression warred with disgust. Gently shaking the reins, Tava nudged Tender into plodding forward again. She wasn't going to the priest to confess her supposed sins; she was going to the priest to deliver her father's body. After that . . . she didn't know what she would do.

I used to ask Father why he stayed among such small-minded people . . . and he always said that they needed someone with a bigger mind to watch over them, even if they didn't appreciate it. But what you did, Father, putting up with these people . . . I don't think I can do it. I don't think I want to do it. Not for these people.

I can't stay here in Five Springs, Father. Not without you to buffer and protect me from these people . . . and not without you here to protect them from me. Because the next person who calls me unnatural and accuses me of . . . of . . . with men, I might not confine the urge to growl and bare my teeth at them.

I don't have you to protect me anymore, Father. All I have is myself. I must protect myself. Somehow.

If Tender hadn't been waiting for her, if the goats hadn't needed milking and the ducks and chickens feeding, Tava wouldn't have returned home. Not that sitting outside all night had been pleasant; the edge of the great Morning River was a prime breeding ground for mosquitoes, midges, and other insects. She had hardened her skin to keep them from biting her all night long and wrapped herself in a wool cloak to keep warm against the cool night air, but they had still buzzed around her eyes.

She sat vigil long after the other villagers returned to their homes for the night, stoically watching the flames on Pyre Rock until there was nothing left but smoldering ashes and bits of bone. Varamon's soul had fled to the Dark at his death, to make its journey to the Afterlife; the body that burned was nothing more than a shell. Yet she couldn't quite tear herself away from her vigil, couldn't quite contemplate going to bed without remembering that her father wouldn't be waiting for her.

It was hard to grasp. Not until she heard a horse nickering in the distance, the sound joining the twitterings of birds welcoming the dawn, did she think of her father's horse. She had returned the gelding to its paddock, had made sure there was water in the troughs for him and the other animals to drink, but hadn't done much more than that to see to her animals' basic comforts. She certainly hadn't seen to her own, other than the cloak.

But that whicker from one of the village horses reminded her of Tender and the fact that he would need her. That his stall needed sweeping, his water needed changing, his coat needed grooming. Thinking of that made her realize that she needed water, and grooming, and a bit of food herself.

The village priest had laid out her father's body for a day so that mourners could pay their respects. The second day had been spent purifying it with prayers for Varamon's departed soul and wrapping it in fat-soaked linens woven in the rippling blues, greens, and browns of the river that gave the Mornai their sense of identity. On the third day, it had been carried by the village Alders to Pyre Rock, which the men of the village had stacked with bundles of wood to ensure a full, clean burning.

In all that time, she had eaten and drunk whatever had been pressed upon her by the more sympathetic wives in the village, but nothing had passed her lips once the funeral pyre had been lit. Now, contrary beast that her body was, it dared to feel hungry. To protest that it was alive and wanted something to eat and drink. Life and death flowed like the river; even after a terrible flood, some plants continued to live, and some animals continued to survive. She was alive, and her body reminded her that she needed to stay that way.

Mindful of her duty to both the gelding and herself, Tava uncurled her body from her seat on the stones of Mourning Rock, erected on the edge of the river across from the matching stone platform of Pyre Rock where the remains of countless villagers had been burned over the years. Giving the smoldering cinders one last, long look, she picked her way down the rough-hewn steps and headed inland, following the path that skirted the village.

The sun rose as she mounted the first embankment, golden pale as it peeked through the trees around her. Some of the golden rays lit up small, bluish, acorn-shaped fruits lurking among the leaves of the salal bushes. *Father loves . . . these.*

Closing her eyes for a moment, Tava fought back the sting of association. When she opened them again, she harvested several of the pea-sized berries. *Father is dead, passed into the Afterlife where he will be offered the holy fruits of the Gods and the best of history's finest feasts. I am alive and am required to earn my food, either by growing and gathering it myself, or trading for it through some craft or skill. I do not dishonor his memory by being hungry for the same fruits he loved.*

They were tart-sweet, puckering her mouth and reminding her of her thirst. Still, they were food, and they were good. Picking and eating as she moved, she slowly made her way toward the second embankment. The path joined the road not far from where it crossed one of the two streams that flanked the village. Detouring when she reached the brook, she knelt and cupped her hand, drinking her fill from the one, and nibbling on a few of the berries cradled in the other.

Closing her eyes, she rested on the mossy bank next to the road. Tender could wait a few moments more; he had water and grass. She had water and berries. A simple, meager repast, but at least she was able to focus on it. *It certainly shows the recent state of my mind, how I cannot remember what I've been eating over the last few days . . .*

I am alive, and I will live, she thought, eyes closed as she accepted her father's fate. *I must decide how to live. I know farming and animal-tending, but I've seen how the Aldemen treat their servants. Particularly the female ones. I will not take up a life where I am ordered about like that, with no say in anything I do, or when I can do it. I am a scribe, a good one . . . but these villagers hesitated to take me on even with Father's reassurances.*

He did say women scribes were preferred in the cities, and he came from the cities himself, so he would know. I should go downriver to the next city and see what kind of work a wandering scribe can acquire. It was a daunting thought, but a necessary one. She could guess what life here in Five Springs would be like if she didn't go. *Staying here is not a pleasant thought. At least I'm of age, and the sole heir to Father's belongings.*

Alder Bludod has always wanted to annex Father's property. I can sell the land to him for a good price, pack up all the things I need on the cart, and drive Tender south along the road—I know it'll be safe to travel on the road because the bandits are gone. Warbands are vicious and frightening, but they are thorough. That was the only thought that spoiled her imaginings: running into the warband again. *No, not drive downriver. I'll take the next barge, instead. Even if it's headed upriver.*

There are large towns upriver as well as down. There are even other kingdoms I could visit, if I'm brave enough to leave the valley. Surely someone, somewhere, will need a scribe, and won't mind if it's a woman. Father always said these little villages were very conservative, compared to other places.

Footsteps on the road brought her out of her thoughts. Opening her eyes, Tava twisted to peer behind her. The sight of Alder Bludod and Aldeman Tronnen coming up the path made her scramble to her feet, almost tripping on her skirts in her haste. It was rather early in the morning for both men to be up and about, particularly when she knew from village gossip that the elderly Bludod preferred being served his breakfast while he still lay abed.

It was even odder to see both men headed her way. Either they were leaving the village to go somewhere—which was unlikely, given Bludod's age—or they intended to come and see her, since the side path that led to her home wasn't that far ahead. Dusting off her skirts, Tava firmed her resolve. She would speak to Alder Bludod about selling the farm and its animals to him, save only for her belongings, the cart, and Tender to pull it.

Having the Aldeman on hand made the moment a little awkward, since she knew Alder Bludod was reasonable enough when on his own, but the other man was a bit too status conscious for her tastes. Then again, the sight of the village leader stiffened her resolve to leave. *Father put up with these small-minded men for his own reasons, none of which is mine. I know I'll lead a happier life as a traveler, even with all its uncertainties, than I would if I remained here.*

"There you are." Aldeman Tronnen didn't wait for her to greet him. He jerked his head back, indicating the road behind him. "Go to my house. Abigan is expecting you, so do not dawdle."

His terse words confused her. Stepping onto the road, Tava blocked both men. "I don't understand. Why is she expecting me?"

"To tell you what to do, of course. Now step out of our way," he said.

To tell me what to . . . ? That sounded like he expected her to take orders from his wife, like some sort of servant. Tava didn't move. "I'm sorry, but I have other things to do today. Including speaking to you, Alder Bludod. I know my father refused you several times over the years, but now that he is gone, I would like to discuss selling our farm to you, since I know you've always been interested in it."

"*Sell* the farm?" Aldeman Tronnen scoffed. "You do not have any rights to *sell* that farm, girl! Get to my wife, and do not waste any more time."

He moved to step around her and cross the low, wooden bridge spanning the brook, but Tava shifted, blocking him. "What do you mean, I don't have any rights? With . . . with my father dead, all that was his now belongs to *me* as his sole heir. And as I am of age by three full years, the property is mine to do with as I please. To keep or to sell."

"That is a lie," Tronnen said.

"That is the *law*," she countered.

He frowned at her for arguing, but Tava didn't back down. Hands going to his hips, the Aldeman addressed her. "You, woman, are no heir of Varamon Vel Tith. You are not of his blood, you did not come from his loins, and you are *not* his inheritor. You are nothing more than a landless bastard—and you will be *grateful* I am giving you a roof over your head!"

"Varamon bathed me in the waters of the river and accepted me as his own child. My name is scribed in the priest's book of names and lineages. I *am* his daughter, by the writings of the law!"

The middle-aged Aldeman smirked. "Funny, I don't recall *reading* your name in the priest's book."

Barely in time, Tava bit back the retort, *That's because you're too ignorant to know how to read.* Saying it would have been the truth, but it would not have helped her cause. Instead, she strove for logic.

"It is still the law, and my name is still in that book, written down as the sole surviving heir to Varamon the scribe. And you, as Alderman, are sworn to uphold the laws of the Mornai. Deny me my legal rights, and you will break the law," she warned him. "If you do so, you are nothing more than a greedy criminal. *Are* you a criminal? Or are you an Aldeman who follows the writ and the spirit of the laws you have sworn to uphold?"

For a moment, she almost backed him down. Noise on the road behind her distracted all three of them. Glancing behind herself, Tava spotted several riders coming into view through the trees. The winding nature of the road had cloaked their approach until now. Both the Alder and the Aldeman stepped around her, moving onto the bridge for a better look. Tava had to crane her neck to see the riders, with their loose-gathered, pale-dyed garments and the gleam of strange necklaces made from gold and polished stones draped over their collarbones.

Alder Bludod grunted. "That looks like a warband from the Plains. I haven't seen any Shifterai in a good three decades, but I do remember those pectorals they wear."

"Thank the Goddess," the Aldeman muttered back. "I've been worried about those bandits that killed the scribe—*you* will go to my wife," he ordered, turning to face Tava. "And you will learn your place, serving in my household. Count yourself *lucky* that you will have one. If you serve well and are obedient, I *might* grant you a small dowry so you may wed."

Tava felt her blood roil. Before her father's death, she had done her best to hold her tongue. She hadn't always succeeded, but she had tried, for *his* sake. But for all she was Varamon's legally accepted daughter, she wasn't enough of a Mornai to stay her tongue now. "I will do *no* such thing! That land is *mine*, and all that stands upon it!"

Stepping around him, she strode across the bridge, intending to angle through the woods to reach her home all the faster. It wasn't just about feeding and watering Tender now; it was about securing her few belongings and the cart, and getting ready to leave this place as soon as she could. Whether or not she was paid for the land. She was *not* going to stay in Five Springs just to be a servant to a pair of hypocrites. She knew she had caught the attention of the Shifterai men ahead of her, but if she just could get across the road and slip between the thickets—

—Pain exploded through her head as the back of the Aldeman's fist knocked her down.

TWO

Kodan spurred his horse forward. He had seen the trio talking, seen the young woman look like she was arguing with the two men, and had been curious. The Mornai who lived in cities weren't nearly as conservative as these far-flung villagers seemed to be, and the cultural expectation that females had to show respect toward men while in public often meant they had to be subservient as well. It was a foreign concept to the Shifterai, of course, but then, these Mornai were foreigners, outlanders with outlandish ways.

Striking a woman, however, was not something he would tolerate. Not when she had offered no visible violence of her own. His wasn't the only steed hurried forward; Manolo rode just behind him on his right and his brother Kenyen rode on the left. If there were others who followed faster than the rest, Kodan didn't take the time to look for them.

The girl, knocked off her balance by the blow, stumbled over the edge of the low, flat bridge and tumbled into the stream. Water splashed up around her as she landed; then she twisted and struggled to keep her head up. Seeing that she wasn't going to drown immediately reassured Kodan, allowing him to focus on the two Mornai men.

The pair stared at the approaching Shifterai in alarm. Kodan lifted his hand, slowing his fellow shapeshifters. His objective was to get the attention of these men off the girl, not to trample them—it was tempting to trample them for striking down a woman, but there could have been a legitimate reason by Mornai cultural standards. Warband members were reminded over and over again that the cultures of the lands they rode through had to be respected, or they could bring down more trouble on their heads than that warband could handle.

Both men wore the woven blue headbands of a Mornai Alder, and the younger of the two had a stone bound to the center of his headband. That meant he was the village Aldeman, the local leader. It galled Kodan to see the woman, with her brown hair plastered to her skin, her dark blouse, vest, and skirts all soaking wet, struggling to right herself, but if this was a matter of village discipline, he knew he should not interfere directly.

All he could do was distract them from her. Bringing his mare to a stop, Kodan leaned over the pommel. "You are the Aldeman of Five Springs?"

"I am Aldeman Tronnen, yes. This is Alder Bludod. You are a Shifterai warband, yes?" the middle-aged man asked as his elderly companion bowed, palms pressed flat together in homage. Both ignored the girl splashing up onto the bank.

"Yes. I am Warleader Kodan, *multerai* of Clan Cat, Family Tiger, South Paw Warband. We have business to discuss." Kodan started to say more, but two things stopped him. The morning wind that carried the young woman's damp scent, and the Alder's exclamation.

"You are a gift of the Goddess brought to us!" the white-bearded man praised, hands lifted in salute. "The River flows and delivers blessings to the land!"

"Our scribe was killed a handful of days ago by some bandits," the Aldeman explained quickly, forcing Kodan's thoughts back to the business at hand. "We are not fighters; we are farmers and fishermen. We are therefore willing to pay you and your fellow Shifterai an agreeable sum if you will track down the criminals responsible for this heinous crime and put an end to them."

Kenyen chuckled at that. Kodan couldn't blame his brother; he had told the others the details of his plan to squeeze extra money out of the village of Five Springs. It looked like the Aldeman was handing his very own plan to him, wrapped in a bow. Movement from the girl stopped him from agreeing with the village leader. She was edging her way around the far side of the bridge, trying to sneak off as unobtrusively as her dripping self could manage.

His gaze caught the attention of the Aldeman. Craning his neck, he scowled at the girl. "Get you to my wife, and learn your place!"

She lifted her chin, showing a defiance that was familiar on the Plains, but not something Kodan had ever seen in the women of the Valley. She looked a bit wild as she defied the startled Alders, but defy them she did. "*My* place is as a free woman and a scribe. I will *not* be your servant, and I will *not* let you steal from me! That land is *mine*, as my father's heir!—And I am *not* a bastard; my name is in the priest's book!"

Definitely the scribe's daughter . . . and definitely not *a Mornai,* Kodan thought, pleased by her show of spirit.

His amusement was cut abruptly short when the Aldeman lunged at her, fist upraised. "—*Defy* me in front of strangers? I will *beat* your place into you for this!"

The girl yanked up her sodden skirts and sprinted up the road, fleeing his wrath. Instinct drove Kodan's heels into the ribs of his mount. The startled mare bounded forward. Years of hunting his fellow humans told him where the woman would most likely try to dodge him . . . and within only a few moments, his outstretched arm snatched her off her feet as she sought to leap between two of the trees lining the dirt road. Just as he had calculated.

Tightening his legs around his steed, strengthening the muscles in his arm, he hauled the yelling, squirming, kicking woman onto his lap. She didn't go willingly; indeed, he barely had enough warning to thicken the skin of his throat, protecting the tender flesh from her thumping fist. Reining in his mare, who was made nervous by his squirming bundle, he guided the horse back toward the others.

A grunt escaped him when she switched from hitting to biting, twisting and sinking her teeth into his shoulder, but he endured. This close, her scent could not be denied; she was the same woman as the tigress, and the same one who had handled the scribe's satchel. He endured all of this, until she kicked his mount, making the mare rear.

Increasing the mass of his muscles, Kodan squeezed the breath out of her with his left arm, while his right fought the nervous mare back onto the ground. Once the mare was settled, he met the woman's scared green eyes with a low warning growl. "*Do not* kick my horse again."

As much as he wanted to reassure her that he wouldn't harm her, he had to put on a show for the two Mornai villagers. Easing his grip just enough to let her breathe, though not nearly enough to let her go, he nudged his mount forward once more, back toward the others.

"Bring her here!" the Aldeman ordered imperiously. He was unlacing his cuffs, no doubt intending to roll them up before thrashing her; his words confirmed Kodan's guess. "That demon-child is long past due for having the insolence beaten out of her."

With both villagers facing Kodan—or rather, the girl in his arms—neither of them saw the dark looks on the faces of the warband waiting on the other side of the brook. Kodan stopped his mare a few yards away. "Don't trouble yourself. We'll take her off your hands, as part of our payment for destroying the local bandits."

The woman in his arms sucked in a sharp breath. Not wanting her to reveal that the bandits were dead, Kodan squeezed her again in warning. She subsided. Both the Aldeman and the Alder looked troubled by Kodan's claim, but after a moment of brow-creasing thought, the village leader nodded curtly.

"You have a deal."

The elder of the two Mornai hurried to join his leader. Kodan sharpened his hearing as the white-haired man gripped the sleeve of the gray-haired one.

"Tronnen, you *know* what they're like," Alder Bludod muttered. "I wouldn't give a lame goat to the Shifterai, much less a girl!"

What the . . . ? Kodan glanced up at the others in the warband, but no one else looked like they had heard. Not that he could really tell, since they were still scowling over the physical threats that had been offered toward the girl. The younger Mornai's equally low-voiced response troubled him even further.

"Any *other* girl, I would agree, and protect her with my life," Tronnen muttered. "But *her* blood is as bad as her mother's. The River flows and washes away all debris; you know this as well as I do. We'll be well rid of her, and you'll finally have her land as part of your own. You can bless the Goddess for getting rid of the foreign trash in our midst, delivering these men in time for our need. I am merely Her servant, seeing the opportunity She has granted us."

The woman in Kodan's arms struggled again. Something odd was going on, but he didn't think now was the moment to ask questions. Any show of confusion on his part would weaken his bargaining stance in the eyes of these Valley men. But he couldn't let her frighten his mare again. Kodan tightened his grip a little, growling under his breath at her. "Cooperate, and you will be unharmed. Fight me . . . and I will give you back to *them*, and their *mercy*. Make your choice."

She stilled in his arms, letting him guide his steed back to the others with no further problems.

"Lead the way to your Aldehall," Kodan directed the two men. "We will write up a contract, decide on the rest of our payment, and settle the matter of your bandit problem."

The girl on his lap jerked and looked at him, green eyes wide. They narrowed after a second. Then she ducked her head, but not before Kodan saw the mirth tugging at the corner of her mouth. *She knows what my plan is. Good. That means she's quick-witted, as well as quick-tongued.* Pleased with that thought, Kodan led his warband in following the two Mornai men.

Manolo rode up next to him. "Your father is having a fit, Kodan. As am I. We do *not* trade in—"

Kodan shook his head, cutting him off. "—That is not a topic I want discussed right now. I have another task for you."

Quirking his brow, Manolo eyed the young warlord. "And what would *that* be?"

Lowering his voice, Kodan spoke below the hearing level of the two villagers. "I believe this woman is the late scribe's daughter. Find the priest's book of names. I want you to verify whether or not she has a legal claim to his lands—but don't let the Alders know what you're looking for."

Again, the young woman in his arms looked up at him, wonder and confusion in her stare. She shivered after a moment, looking away. The day wasn't yet warm enough to dry her clothes, but Kodan didn't think it was that cold. Nodding, Manolo let his own mare lag by a few paces, giving them a semblance of privacy.

The scribe's daughter frowned up at him. "Why . . . ?"

Her voice caught the attention of the Alder, who glanced over his shoulder. Kodan shook his head, silencing her. She squirmed a little in his grip; belatedly, he realized she was slipping off his lap and shifted his squeeze to a scoop, hitching her higher. She squirmed again, no doubt prodded by the saddlehorn, then settled in place without further fuss.

Relieved, Kodan held her a little more gently, though he didn't relax his vigil. This woman, whatever her name was, belonged with her own kind. *His* people, not these river-dwellers. Of all the wealth he had secured for his warband and the Family Tiger this year, she would be the richest.

He was not about to let this particular prize get away.

The Shifterai kept a hand on Tava even after they dismounted and entered the Aldehall. She wanted to bolt, but those fingers, their warmth radiating through the damp, baggy brown linen of her sleeve, were a tangible warning that she wouldn't get far right now. Her father had stressed over and over that it wasn't a good idea for her to reveal her shapeshifting abilities to anyone else in Five Springs. Even now, exposure could bring her far more problems than using her abilities might solve.

Of course, the reason was that the Alders would have exiled her to the Plains for being a shapeshifter, and here she was, about to be sold off to the shapeshifters in exchange for eradicating bandits who were already dead . . . but as much as the situation was ironic, the fact that these Shifterai were trying to dupe the Aldeman and his cronies pleased her in a twisted-about way. *Aldeman Tronnen is trying to trick me out of my land, and these Shifterai are trying to trick him out of his money . . . the River flows and does eventually level all the hills and valleys in the land . . .*

Alder Bludod hobbled off to blow the summoning horn. The man holding her arm, Kodan, ordered one of his fellow warriors to fetch some scraps of parchment, a quill, and an inkwell from one of the wagons they had brought with them. When the youth came back with the requested materials, half of the village Alders had gathered in the hall, and more were entering, filling the room with the babble of their voices, most of them praising the warband's presence in their midst and discussing the threat posed by the bandits that had slain their scribe.

With visible reluctance, Aldeman Tronnen gestured curtly for

Tava to take her place at the scribe's table, where the writing supplies had been settled. The leader of the warband released her, but he did follow her to the table, ensuring she couldn't slip out one of the side doors in the bench-lined hall.

Settling onto the stool behind the small table, Tava squared the pieces of parchment, examined the cut of the quill to make sure it would make an acceptable nib, and tested the ink in the small, tightly corked bottle. Then she set everything down and stretched out her hand, palm up. About to begin speaking, the Aldeman paused mid-breath, frowning at her.

". . . What are you doing, girl? Write this down!"

"Twelve scepterai, please." Only the force of habit, and a certain stubborn pride in her work, kept both her tone and her words polite.

Aldeman Tronnen wasn't the only one in the hall to choke. The other Alders, most of them graybeards, spluttered and muttered among themselves, frowning in disapproval at the still-damp girl sitting patiently in their midst. The Aldeman scowled at her, hands going to his hips.

"*Twelve* scepterai? You expect us to pay you, let alone that much?"

"I am the *only* scribe you have," Tava replied, keeping her voice calm, her words implacable. "These Shifterai want a written contract. You cannot read nor write, nor can anyone else in this village read and write well enough to make up a contract . . . and twelve scepterai is the price for writing a contract. Coin first, contract after—do not think you can force me to write," she added quickly, smoothly, as his fingers clenched into fists. "The only person in this village who can read besides myself is the priest . . . but he doesn't write well enough to scribe a contract, and he certainly doesn't read well enough to be able to know what *extra* clauses I might put into this contract, if you try to beat me into submission. You might end up with a contract giving away *your* land, if you tried.

"Twelve scepterai, for an honest contract. No more, no less. Of course, you *can* always do your best to convince these Shifterai to accept a *verbal* contract . . ." she offered, letting her voice trail into the quiet that filled the hall.

As she hoped—though she still wasn't sure of his motives—the warband leader, Kodan, folded his arms across his chest. "We want a *written* contract."

"Then *you* pay her," Tronnen ordered the warband leader.

Tava kept her hand out, shifting her attention to the younger man. "Twenty scepterai, for a written contract."

"You just said it was twelve!" the warleader protested, unfolding his arms.

"Twelve for my fellow Mornai. *Twenty* for outlanders."

Again, the Alders whispered among themselves, but with less scowling than before; her altered demand had amused the men of Five Springs, despite her unwomanly boldness. Tava waited, palm up on the writing desk. To her relief, the dark-haired Shifterai merely looked amused, not offended; he curled up the corner of his mouth as he studied her.

Digging into a pouch at his waist, he pulled out a small gold coin, worth far more than the score of copper she had requested. Holding it over her palm, he leaned close and murmured, "I—like most of my fellow Shifterai—can read and write well enough to follow a contract. You *will* earn this money honestly, with a fair and true accounting of our business transaction."

Closing her fingers around the small but heavy coin, Tava waited until he backed away. Tucking the precious money into her belt pouch, she picked up the quill, ready to dip it into the inkwell and begin scribing the terms of their agreement. Out of the corner of her eye, she saw one of the older Shifterai handing something to their dark-haired leader. Not just something, but the priest's book.

She couldn't pay closer attention to their actions, however, because Aldeman Tronnen had already begun his rambling, pompous version of a business discussion. That forced her to concentrate, so she could pick out the key points and write them on one of the scraps of parchment as a list of things to either include or discard from the coming agreement. *Pompous windbag . . . if he'd get off of the topic of how grateful Five Springs is for these beasts' presence, we could actually get this over with so I can plot how I'm going to make my escape . . .*

Behind her and to her left, the warleader muttered something to his men, gesturing briefly. Three of them separated from the rest, each one coming up to her side, stooping over her shoulder, and inhaling deeply. *Sniffing* her. Disconcerted, Tava edged away as much as she could, given her seated position. They didn't touch her, but they did sniff at her, deeply, audibly. No doubt they were getting a noseful of mud from her still-wet skirts, but she worried that they were smelling something different about her.

Even the village Aldeman thought their actions strange. Breaking off his speech, he eyed the trio of Shifterai warily. ". . . What are you doing?"

A flick of Kodan's hand dismissed the three collared men. They nodded and jogged out of the Aldehall without uttering a word. The warleader hooked his thumbs into his belt and smiled. "Surveying our payment, of course. Longwinded preambles of your thanks and appreciation can be saved for afterward. They do not belong in a contract negotiation. You have a problem, a group of renegades and outlaws to the south of Five Springs. These bandits have slain your scribe . . . Vanamon, yes?"

"His name was Varamon," Tava interjected, speaking firmly. "Varamon Vel Tith. My father."

"Silence, girl!" Tronnen ordered her. "Yes, Varamon was slain by some bandits; the girl brought his body home just a few days ago. We want you to eradicate them, so they will endanger no other travelers."

"So . . . if we have slain these bandits, you will pay us an agreed-upon sum, correct?" Kodan asked. The Aldeman nodded impatiently, flipping his hand. The warlord glanced around at the Alders seated on their benches, who nodded in turn, agreeing with their elected leader. Kodan nodded as well. "Good. Write this down, scribe:

"The Aldeman of Five Springs, with the acceptance of his fellow Alders, agrees to pay the South Paw Warband of Clan Cat, Family Tiger, after the slaughter of the criminals responsible for the death of the scribe Varamon Vel Tith, who was accosted by them on the roads south of Five Springs. This payment shall be rendered by the villagers of Five Springs upon Truth Stone–clarified proof that the South Paw Warband of Family Tiger has indeed slain the bandits responsible for the death of said scribe. Said payment shall be as follows . . ."

"Pardon, but we need to fetch a Truth Stone first," Tronnen interjected, cutting him off as the younger man paused for breath. "The one we had at the Aldehall faltered and cracked a turning of Sister Moon ago, and we have not yet bothered to replace it. Varamon owned two; he would have carried one with him, but the other should still be at his home."

The other Alders nodded, their beards waggling and bobbing in agreement.

"You are fortunate, in that I already have one with me," the warleader reassured the Alders. Fishing it out of the pouch strung on his belt, he wrapped his fingers around the marble disc. "To prove it works . . . my name is Tronnen, and I am the Aldeman of Five Springs."

Uncurling his fingers, he displayed the blackened marks of his fingers marring the otherwise pure-white, polished stone. The blemishes faded after a moment, and the Shifterai gripped the disc again. "I am Kodan Sin Siin, warlord of South Paw Warband, Family Tiger, Clan Cat."

A shift of his fingers showed the Stone was still white, supporting the truth of his claim. Tronnen nodded, accepting proof of the disc's accuracy. "Your Truth Stone is adequate for the task. Now, as to the payment . . ."

"The payment will be this woman, the daughter of Varamon Vel Tith, plus the contents of her father's home, stables, barns, outbuildings, any carts, any animals, and any other belongings she and her father can have claimed . . . *and* the full cost of the fair and reasonable sale of her father's property, to be paid in coin and goods by either a specific villager, or the village as a whole, for the right to keep that land as a part of Five Springs and its future prosperity," Kodan stated, causing an instant stir among the Alders. He raised his voice, though his tone remained calm. "In *other* words, her fully accounted dowry, as the sole inheritor of her family's property."

"The daughter of Varamon Vel Tith and her full, rightful dowry . . . shall be traded to the Shifterai in exchange for the eradication . . . of the bandits responsible for the slaughter of Varamon Vel Tith," Tava repeated, scratching the words on one of the scrap pieces of parchment. *Only I will* not *remain traded to the Shifterai . . . and I'll probably lose most of everything I own, in the need to run away as fast as I can . . . which means with as few belongings as I can manage. Which will make it difficult for me to make my living until I can do so as a scribe, but at least I can hunt and forage as I travel. Most Mornai women cannot say the same.*

On the other bank, if I leave them the majority of my worldly goods . . . maybe these beasts won't chase me down. It was a slim hope, and one she couldn't count on happening. Not after what had happened to her mother.

"Your proposal has a slight problem," Aldeman Tronnen said as his fellow Alders settled down. "This girl is *not* Varamon's true heir, but an orphan that has been taking shelter in his home. Now that he is gone, she has only the clothes on her back to her name. Varamon died without a true heir, and as such, all of his belongings revert to the village of Five Springs."

Tava quickly glanced around the Aldehall. None of the Alders protested their leader's claim. Most were men who had been friends with her father, the ones who had been kind to her over the years. Some of those men frowned, visibly uncomfortable at staying silent, but they stayed silent regardless. The riches implied in her father's belongings, the coin and goods that would have to be exchanged for the sale price of her father's lands, the thought of all that wealth leaving Five Springs and going into outlander hands did not please *them*, either.

Out of the corner of her eye, she saw the warleader stretch out his hand. The priest's book was placed into it. Raising his other hand, Truth Stone clenched in his fingers, Kodan spoke. "This is the book of names and lineages for the village of Five Springs, fetched straight from the hands of your own Mornai priest. It has not been tampered with in any way since the priest handed it over."

A flex of his fingers showed the whiteness of the disc.

"I read now the lineages written within its pages, and it lists a Tava Ell Var as the River-baptised daughter of Varamon Vel Tith. By the laws of the Mornai, any person that is washed in the waters of the Morning River and acknowledged as their own kin by the head of a particular household automatically becomes a member of that household, as surely as if they had been legitimately born to it. By your own laws, Tava Ell Var is the true and rightful heir of Varamon Vel Tith. Varamon was originally born in the city of . . . Kelsing's Landing," he read from the book, "but having subsequently moved to Five Springs to purchase his own land and establish his own household, was the head of that household while he lived here in Five Springs."

Displaying the Stone, the warleader turned and presented the disc to Tava.

"State your name and lineage, woman, so that the truth of your identity may be seen and confirmed."

Accepting the enchanted marble, Tava felt ambivalent about it. On the one hand, this man was going out of his way to prove her claim to her property, irrefutably securing her inheritance . . . yet on the other hand, he was doing so in order to claim it as the reward for slaying bandits that were already dead. Taking it from her as surely as Aldeman Tronnen wanted to himself. The Aldeman moved as she hesitated, stepping over to one of the village Alders and murmuring in the other man's ear.

Warlord Kodan stiffened, his brown eyes narrowing. The Alder stood, and Koden spoke quickly, curtly.

"—Do *not* follow through on that plan, Alders. I have already sent some of my men to find and secure the girl's property. You would *not* like their response, should you challenge their orders to protect the contents of her home and its fields. You are farmers and fishermen, after all," he added, returning his gaze to Aldeman Tronnen. "*Not* fighters."

He's thought of everything, Tava realized as the Alder sank slowly back onto his bench. *This warlord is cleverer than I thought. Clever enough, he might think to keep a close eye on me until we're well onto the Plains. The only thing in my favor is that they don't know I'm a shape-shifter, too,* she thought . . . then remembered how those three men had sniffed at her.

One of the Shifterai in this warband had seen her fighting. Whichever one it was, he might have caught enough of her scent to remember it even now. Unfortunately, she had been upwind of that shifter herself and hadn't caught the warrior's scent in the brief time she had been in his proximity, whoever it was. *Any* of these two-legged beasts could be able to identify her.

If I try to stay, the Alders might play along . . . but they'll strip everything away from me in their fury, once the Shifterai have gone. Beatings will be the best of my problems within the village. That's assuming the Shifterai leave without a fight, which I doubt . . . and he is right. We're farmers and fishermen, not fighters.

I have no feasible choice but to play along, for now.

Gripping the Stone, Tava spoke firmly. "I am Tava Ell Var. Vara-mon Vel Tith bathed me in the River when I was born, accepting me as his own daughter and making me his sole, rightful heir."

A flip of the Stone flashed the pure white on both sides. Aldeman Tronnen strode up to her desk, dropping his hands roughly on its surface. His voice was a growl as he glared at her. "I will beat you black and blue for this *insolence*."

Several voices growled in ragged, unpleasant unison. The Alde-man jerked back from the writing desk, staring warily at the Shifterai in the Aldehall.

"Lay your hand on her," the Shifterai who had fetched the priest's book growled, "harm one hair on her head, and your village will be stripped of *ten times* the value of her chattel and land."

"Count yourselves *lucky* that we are willing to barter fairly with you," another added, flexing his muscles. "You *do not* threaten a woman in the presence of the Shifterai."

That *is a very odd thing for a Shifterai to say*, Tava thought, con-fused. She warily eyed the collar-draped men who were shifting closer to her—not quite crowding her table, but definitely crowding the Aldeman. Intimidating him. Tronnen fell back a step, then an-other, as Kodan moved between him and her.

"This woman, all of her rightful belongings, her beasts, and a fair trade in coin and goods for the value of her land, in exchange for the deaths of the bandits who slew her father," the warlord repeated. "You *can* refuse to sign this fair and reasonable, mutually agreed-upon contract . . . but if you do, we shall take her and her belongings anyway, plus what *we* think is the dowry price of her land, culled in goods salvaged from the length and breadth of your village . . . and then we will leave you to hunt down the solution to your bandit problems yourselves.

"These are the only two options available to you," the broad-collared, smooth-chinned Shifterai told the bearded Aldeman.

Tava couldn't see his face, and he didn't speak loudly, but she could hear the implacable edge of steel in the warleader's tone. "Choose *wisely*."

The two men stared at each other for a long moment, until the Aldeman finally moved. Stepping around the Shifterai warlord, he braced his hands on the edge of the writing desk. Brown eyes bored into green with a mixture of disgust and dislike. Unlike the previous moment when he had leaned on her table, the village leader didn't raise his voice.

". . . Like mother, like daughter," Aldeman Tronnen told her, raking his gaze over her damp clothes, dismissing her worth in a glance. "The River flows and washes all of last year's debris away." Pulling back, he gave Warlord Kodan an equally dismissive look. "Twenty crownai for the land, and not a scepterai more."

The Shifterai leader twisted, craning his neck to look back at her. "Is that what the land is worth?"

"It is worth *five* times that, being up on the second embankment, with a wellspring that has never run foul, and never run dry," Tava stated coldly, hiding her anger at being reminded of her impending fate. *If* she couldn't escape. But she wasn't her mother. *She* had resources, skills, and knowledge that Ellet Sou Tred hadn't possessed. Gripping the Truth Stone still clutched in her hand, she added, "It never floods but once every fifty or sixty years, and the house was built high and dry to withstand even that. Even the barn is raised above the fifty-year waterline . . . though it does need a new roof."

Lifting the disc, she displayed the honesty of its unblemished sides. Tronnen narrowed his eyes, but did not refute her words. Instead, he countered the cost of her estimate.

"We don't *have* a hundred gold coins in Five Springs. As it is, we'd be hard-pressed to come up with twenty crownai . . . or beggar ourselves, scraping up the thronai and scepterai."

One of the older Shifterai moved closer, muttering something in his leader's ear. Kodan nodded. "Twenty crownai in solid gold and silver, and the rest in trade goods. In specific, we want a long-wagon and a team of six horses, with the wagon bed piled with straight lumber cut both from soft- and hardwood, at least half of it in hardwood and as long as can be carried. We also want a team of six horses hitched to a short-wagon full of iron and other ingots, and six barrels filled with birch-tar sticks . . ."

THREE

Tava scribbled the amount of the goods on the scrap parchment in front of her, even as the Alders started protesting. There were deposits of iron, copper, and other ores nearby, down in the mountainous kingdom of Correda, but metal was still expensive for such a small village to acquire. Twelve horses were also a steep price to pay, never mind the two wagons requested. Tronnen held up his hands, calming his fellow Mornai, then gestured at the white-bearded man who had the greatest stake in gaining Tava's property, deferring to Alder Bludod.

Bludod frowned, thinking, then counteroffered all the ingots one horse could pull, and two horses and a long-wagon of straight lumber . . . though he'd be willing to give up a four-horse harness, if the Shifterai provided the remaining two horses.

Kodan demanded four and four, plus a wagon piled with food supplies, albeit one to be pulled by their own horses. The bartering began in earnest, Bludod frowning and consulting with his fellow

Alders to see what he could get out of his neighbors without making the counteroffer too expensive overall. Given this was early autumn, in the brief pause between the early and late harvests, foodstuff was considered the barter of choice, not horses or metal.

It took a little while, but with Alder Bludod's approval, Aldeman Tronnen agreed to the final tally of the worth of Varamon's land: fifteen crownai, forty thronai, sixty scepterai for the cash portion; a four-horse team and a long-wagon stacked chest-high with lumber; and a second long-wagon with a four-horse harness and two horses to fill it, two to be provided by the Shifterai themselves; the second wagon bed to be filled all across the bottom in a single layer of metal ingots, half of which had to be iron, the rest copper, tin, brass, and such, and filled the rest of the way to the rails with oilcloth bags, four barrels of birch-tar sticks, and sealed clay pots filled with the sorts of dried fruits, herbs, and spices that grew all along the Valley and up into the nearby mountains, but not on the Plains.

The total value, Tava estimated, was probably close to seventy crownai, maybe seventy-five. It was not the hundred the land was worth in her opinion, but it was a reasonable deal. To have made it a truly fair one . . . the goods would have to belong to *her*, not to the men bartering for her so-called dowry. The Goddess knew she had no intention of staying long enough to be claimed by one of these brutish Shifterai, however.

Waiting impatiently as the village priest began his painfully slow reading of the final version of the contract she had scribed, Tava tried to plot out in her mind where these Shifterai would go next. Being forced into the subservient, polite mould of a Mornai woman had long ago meant learning not just how to keep her thoughts to herself, but how to think strategically. Forethought and subtlety were the only weapons a Mornai woman could successfully wield.

They want all the belongings from my home, and Tender, and the milk-goats—they might even want the chickens and the ducks. Who knows? Either way, it will take more than a day for me to pack everything. I know

Tronnen is expecting them to be gone for a handful of days at the very least, searching for the bandits, but I know the bandits are already dead.

In fact, I'd be surprised if this Kodan doesn't plan to use this Truth Stone to reveal that fact to the Alders. After all, the terms of the contract are ". . . in exchange for the deaths of the bandits responsible for slaying Varamon Vel Tith of Five Springs village . . ." and the odds are, this Truth Stone could be my father's Stone, liberated from the bandits' loot. So they could just go away for a short while, pretending to hunt and kill the bandits, then come back. Somewhere in there, I might actually have the chance to escape . . . though if he's as clever as he seems, I'll have to be twice as clever to slip away unnoticed long enough for a big enough lead to escape completely.

The only good part of this mess is how they'll be a buffer between me and the Aldeman, preventing him and his fellow Alders from stealing my goods. Of course, she thought, wincing as the priest badly mangled one of the words he was reading aloud, sounding it out three times before he got it right, *these Shifterai will just steal and keep my belongings for themselves. The only pleasure I can get from that fate is that they'll keep my things away from the Alders' greedy grasp.*

The River rises and falls every year, she reminded herself, *bringing fresh mud even as it washes away the old . . . I just have to get my hands on some of the coins that are a part of this trade and figure out a way to carry it as I run. Father once spoke of reading about strange animals that had pouches as a part of their bodies, some sort of mage-constructed species left over from before Aiar was Shattered all those years ago.*

It shouldn't be too difficult to shapeshift a pocket for storing a fistful of coins . . . though my clothes would be more problematic. I hope—ah, finally, they're done. Pay attention, Tava, or you'll not be alert enough when your opportunity for escape comes. Now is when they'll announce they're heading out, maybe leaving a couple of the warband behind to keep an eye on me and my property . . .

"Start packing the wagons," the warband leader instructed the Alders. "Bring them to the scribe's farm as soon as they're ready. We will secure her dowry immediately."

Aldeman Tronnen spluttered at that. "You will not pack her dowry immediately! You will go after those bandits first!"

Palming the Truth Stone he had set on the table, Kodan smiled tightly at the village leader. "We are not stupid. We will not leave and allow you time to steal away any of Scribe Tava's goods, or worse, burn everything she owns to the ground. We will not bother to split our forces in half, either. The sooner her dowry is packed for travel, the sooner your problems will be solved, after all.

"You have my word that we will not take a single scrap of that dowry or a single hair of this woman from the village of Five Springs until we have given you sufficient proof that the bandits that slew your previous scribe are indeed dead." Displaying the Stone's unblemished sides, he set it down on the table again with a soft *clack* of stone on wood. A flick of his hand indicated the scroll in the priest's hands. "Sign the contract, and we will sign as well, making our bargain binding and legal. Refuse to sign . . . and we will go straight to our other option in this matter. The choice of *which* path we will take, Aldeman Tronnen, is now yours to make."

Aldeman Tronnen snatched up Tava's quill and the contract and scribbled his mark on the parchment. Kodan followed it with his own. When he held out his hand, the Aldeman grimaced but clasped it, sealing their deal.

"Take the whore, and all of her filthy goods!" Tronnen growled as soon as their hands parted. "She's as worthless and deserving of her fate . . . as . . . her . . ."

The mass of growls from the shapeshifters startled not only the Aldeman into falling silent, but it shocked Tava as well. She glanced at the angry men arrayed around her. *Why . . . why would* they *be upset at him calling me a whore? They're Shifterai! I'm nothing but a* thing *to them, something to add to their pile of warband spoils!*

Hand raised, forestalling anything other than that strange growling from his men, Kodan addressed the Aldeman in a soft, dangerous tone. "This woman is now a member of Family Tiger. Any insult you give to her is an insult you give to the rest of us. Since I doubt you are man enough to apologize when you are so clearly wrong about someone, I strongly suggest you silence your tongue from here on out . . . or find it silenced for you. Pack those wagons, and do not delay. Come."

Tava blinked as he held out his hand to her. The warlord wasn't looking at her; instead, he kept his gaze on the Aldeman. *Like a hunter would keep his eyes on a venomous snake*, she realized. She also realized she *could* refuse his hand, but something about the way he offered his hand made it seem like he was indeed offering her his protection. A glance at the bearded faces of the Alders showed they were just as unhappy with the Shifterai in their midst as she was . . . but that they were also unhappy at her.

The enemy of my enemy . . . isn't my friend, and in this case will never be my friend, she acknowledged, remembering her father's advice on such matters. *But for now . . . these horrid shifters are the closest thing I have to an ally. Because I certainly cannot stay here any longer.*

Wary of the demonic bargain enfolding and ensnaring her, Tava slipped her hand into his. His flesh was softer than she expected, lacking the calluses common to most Mornai men's hands, but his fingers were strong. They didn't crush her palm, but they did help to pull her from her seat.

"Manolo, gather her things," Kodan directed one of the others. The older man complied, shuffling together her scraps of parchment, quill, ink jar, and Truth Stone. A gentle tug on Tava's hand drew her in the warband leader's wake, his men shifting to flank both of them. No doubt their closeness was as much to keep her from escaping as to keep the Alders from retaliating somehow, but Tava didn't resist. Surrounded by watchful, angry shapechangers wasn't the wisest moment to flee.

They made an odd procession, for none of them rode their horses; instead, they walked their beasts, save only for the three driving the wagons, including the trader's caravan she had seen back at the bandit camp. Tava had expected to be thrown over a saddle and carried off, but the warband leader seemed to be content with walking her away from the Aldehall.

It was clear that what he did, his men echoed. Glancing at him in snatches, she took in his somewhat young but full-grown face, his air of confidence and watchfulness, and compared that to the others in the group. Some were much older, many were only a little older, and a few looked to be younger than him. It made her wonder what power he had over the others, that *he* was their leader.

It wasn't long before one of the others spoke. He did so once they were beyond the heart of the village, out of the range of watchful Mornai eyes and straining Mornai ears. "Your actions are very puzzling, Brother."

Glancing at the speaker, Tava could make out some similarities in their features. His eyes were darker, his hair longer, his face younger. Actually, compared to the sun-wrinkled faces of the village men, all of them looked younger than they should have been, even the ones with gray hairs; it was their smooth chins and lack of heavy wrinkles on their tanned faces that made them seem youthful compared to the bearded Mornai men she was used to seeing. Every boy in Five Springs longed for the day when he could grow an Alder's beard. To see so many clean-shaven, fully grown men felt unnatural.

"Not as puzzling as you'd think. This woman is as welcome in this village as a blue jay is among vultures," Kodan pointed out. "We would do her a disservice to leave her here."

"That, too, but I meant your belligerence. It's not likely we'll be welcome in this corner of the borderlands again for some time."

You're not welcome here at all, Tava thought, surreptitiously trying to tug free her hand. The warlord Kodan shifted his grip, lacing their fingers together. She caught the quick glance of his unnamed brother, the pinching of his brows, and the raising of them in comprehension.

"*Ah*, now I know why. Just remember, we will *all* have our chance at her," the brother chuckled.

Tava stiffened, fear warring with rage, but there were still too many of them for her to break away. These were seasoned warriors, experienced shapeshifters. Unfortunately, both men sniffed, then twisted to look at her, frowning in confusion. Her anxiety spiked again, this time from the realization that they could *smell* her fear. Both exchanged quick looks, but neither said anything. The warleader didn't release her; if anything, he quickened his pace a little. Not enough to make her stumble, but enough that she had to concentrate on matching his lengthened stride.

". . . So much for your infamous charm, I see," the brother drawled, smirking a little.

"Be silent, Kenyen," Kodan ordered. "This is not the time nor the place to discuss such things."

"When *will* be the time?" the man who was carrying her things asked.

"At her home, where we can have some privacy. I don't want these Mornai interrupting us while we take care of business."

Oh, Goddess! Shock made her stumble. *They're not even going to wait to take me up onto the Plains!* That did it; she would run, as far and fast as she could, the moment he let go of her hand. *I don't need money, I don't need food, I don't even need clothes—I just need to get away from these beasts!*

Again their nostrils flexed, more than just the two brothers', but she couldn't stop her fear. All she could do was control it, forcing herself to walk along in their midst. Desperately thinking of how she would escape, and to where: namely, the River. No Shifterai she'd ever heard of could turn themselves into a river creature—not that she'd heard much, just whatever was written down in her mother's book. Nor could they learn fast enough to follow her. Even she had choked, the first few times she'd tried to grow gills.

Everything depended on getting herself away fast and far enough to fling herself into the river. Unfortunately, they were now on the second bank, moving farther away from the safety of the water with each step. Her anxiety rose with each stride, until all of the Shifertai men surrounding her were sniffing the air and giving her confused, concerned looks.

When they reached the bridge over the brook where all of them had first met, the warleader appeared to have had enough. Jerking her to a stop, fingers still firmly entwined with hers, he faced her.

"*Why* are you so afraid of us?" he demanded. His hand slashed out at the muddy bank, still bearing the marks of her fall and recovery. "Haven't you been paying attention? We've *rescued* you from those monsters! *And* we've saved your things from their greed."

Somehow, his bold confrontation gave her the strength to shift some of her fear into anger. She tried using her free hand to pry his fingers from hers, but they tightened their grip. "Ha! Only to have it snatched away by *your* greed—let go of me!"

"No! Not until you tell me why you're afraid of us," he repeated, shifting to grab at her with his free hand as she struggled harder to free herself. "Stop that!"

Tava quickly raised her free hand in a fist, glaring at him. "Don't you dare hit me! *I'm* not my mother! Hit me, and I'll hit back!"

That froze all of the Shifterai men. The looks of horror and disbelief on their faces confused Tava.

"*We* don't hit women," Kodan told her, speaking slowly and carefully. He didn't release her hand, but he didn't strike her, either. "Whatever you may have suffered at the hands of these Mornai, your suffering is now over."

"Ha! I know my suffering has only begun! I'd rather take a beating from the Alders than be beaten and raped by all of *you*! Let me go!" Taking advantage of his shocked, wide-eyed stillness, Tava kicked the warband leader in the shin. He hopped, not quite avoiding the blow, but her boot had only grazed him. She tried kicking again. "Let me *go!*"

"*Not* until we get a straight answer," Kodan countered. "What do you mean, *rape* you? We don't hurt women, and we *certainly* don't do that!" he asserted.

Several of the others nodded, though most were still eyeing her as if she had shapeshifted a second head. Tava shook her head, unwilling and unable to believe it. "I don't believe you."

The one holding her papers, Manolo, quickly shifted the bundle, separating out the Truth Stone. "I swear upon Father Sky and Mother Earth, Patrons of the Shifting Plains, that Shifterai men *do not* rape our women!"

Flipping the disc, the older warrior showed its unblemished sides.

"... I don't believe you—you said *your* women!" she added quickly. "You said nothing about outlander women!"

"We *don't* rape outlander women, either," Manolo asserted, gripping and releasing the Stone. "See?"

"Then it's broken," she countered. "Let go of me!" Tava argued, aiming another kick at her captor's leg. This time, he was more successful at dodging her blow. "You can have my things, you filthy thieves, but you're not taking *me!*"

Manolo gave her a dark look, gripped the Stone, and said, "I am the Aldeman of Five Springs." The marble disc showed a blackened imprint of his fingers when he shifted them. "*See?* We do not lie. I tell you that the Shifterai do not beat our women, nor do we beat outlander women. We *certainly* do not rape them, and we are *not* going to hurt you."

Tava peered at his upraised hand. The black marks had faded, leaving the Truth Stone white. A glance at the dozen or so men surrounding her showed a matching level of conviction in their expressions. One and all, they still looked disturbed at the thought of any of them hurting a woman, never mind her.

Confused—this clashed with everything she knew about the Shifterai—Tava peered at their leader.

"We are *not* thieves," Kodan told her. "Everything will be packed up and carted off in *your* name, solely for your use, save only for the one-fifth tithe to the Family of all the trade goods that have been added on top of your worldly goods. That's the same one-fifth all of us have to pay when riding in a warband—where did you get the asinine idea that we . . . that we rape and beat women?"

"From my *mother*, that's who!"

His brows lifted, his light brown eyes widening in comprehension. Tava had the sudden, instinctive impression that *he* knew she was that shapeshifter from the bandit battle. That she was one of *them*, despite her being a female. How many of the others knew, she didn't yet know. Her fear increased.

"Why w-w-would she th-think the Shift-t-terai would r-r-r-r . . . *you know* her?" the youngest man in the warband asked, stuttering his way through the words. He blinked twice under her scrutiny, but met Tava's gaze with the open confusion of someone undeniably innocent. "We hav-haven't c-c-come here in y-ye-years!"

"Yes; this is the first time in decades that a Shifting Family warband has been this far south and east," Manolo confirmed. Since he was still holding the Stone, she could see from the shifting of his fingers that his words were true. "We certainly wouldn't have raided the Mornai just to steal away one of their women!"

"She wasn't Mornai. She was Zanthenai, from the southwest border of the Plains. And she was kidnapped and brutalized for *two years* by you animals, before she finally had the chance to run away," Tava told them, lifting her chin. "She ran through a grass fire to get away from the hell your people put her through! My father found her while hunting for oak-galls up in the forests on the Corredai border and brought her back here. She was too badly burned to travel any farther, so he took care of her. *She* told him all about the way you beasts treated her—and my mother wasn't a liar! Nobody would run through a grass fire just to lie about why. And my father was a scribe, the *best* scribe, and *he* wrote down everything she said, word for word!"

"Your mother may have been brutalized by someone, but it *wasn't* a Shifterai," one of the older warband members told her. He had the same chin and nose as the warlord and his brother, probably some relative of theirs. "Such a thing is anathema to our people."

"She said they were shapeshifters. That's why she had to run through a grass fire just to get away. Every other time she tried to run, they shifted into dog shape and tracked her down!"

That caught their attention. Frowning, Kodan asked, "Dog shape? Did she ever say what Family held her, or what Clan, or even what warband?"

Tava lifted her chin. "Yes, she did. She said they referred to themselves as Family Mongrel."

"Family *Mongrel*?" Kenyen repeated. His confusion was echoed by the others as they all glanced at one another. "There's no such Family. Not even in Clan Dog."

"Did your mother mention a warband, like how we're the South Paw?" Kodan asked her.

"It was all one warband, as far as I know. She said there were other women, stolen from other outlying lands, though there weren't many of them. That's why they passed her and the others around—but *I'm* not my mother!" Tava swore, lifting her left hand in a fist once again. "If you try any of that with me, I'll hit you so hard, you'll wish you'd been born at the mouth of the River! Now, let me go!"

". . . No."

"Kodan!" the older, related man snapped. "Let her go!"

"*If* we leave her here, Father, the Mornai will confiscate her property and beat her senseless for what *they* would call her insolence. These Valley-dwelling idiots don't value her wit, her pride, or her spirit," Kodan said, ignoring the way Tava tugged again at their joined fingers. He caught the fist she aimed his way, subduing her struggles.

"If we let her go, she won't get far before they'd find out and come after her. The safest place for her right now is on the Plains with us." Turning, he looked at her. "Where you can see for yourself that *we're* telling the truth.

"I don't know who or what captured your mother, but they *weren't* Shifterai, I promise you. *We* don't do that sort of thing—the very thought of it is anathema!" he finished firmly.

"Really? Then why are you still holding me?" Tava challenged him, lifting her chin. She tugged on her arms for emphasis, since now he held both of them captive.

"Yes, Brother," the one named Kenyen echoed, folding his arms across his chest. "Why *are* you still holding her?"

He wasn't the only one who gave the warband leader a doubtful look. Kodan directed his answer to Tava.

"I'm holding you here because my instincts are saying you'll try to run away . . . and my instincts are also saying that would be a very bad idea. You have too many enemies here. Come and live with us, at least for a while," he coaxed as Tava stiffened. "Long enough to let the closed-minded men of this little village forget about you. Live with us for a year and a day, and see with your own eyes that whoever tormented your mother before she escaped, they *weren't* true Shifterai. Whatever wrongs you think our people have done . . . give us the chance to show you it wasn't us. Don't condemn us as a whole before you've sought the truth for yourself."

He seemed sincere. So did the others when she glanced at them. Tava had to admit that most of what she knew about the Shifterai, she had learned from her mother's book, dictated to her father before her mother had died from her lingering grass fire injuries. Worse, Warlord Kodan was right about the reaction of Aldeman Tronnen and the others; they would never forgive her the insolence of a female standing up for herself—never mind that she no longer had her father around to speak up for her. They wouldn't forget her boldly asserting her rights, contradicting them publicly in the Aldehall itself, the bastion of male Mornai authority.

But . . . to go with these shapeshifters? All I have is their word versus my mother's. She glanced at the Truth Stone still clasped in the hand of the one holding her other writing tools. *I can't stay here, but I can't take my belongings with me. Not by myself. Even I know it would be very hard to find a home for myself in one of the big cities up or down the River, not without the money and resources to support me as I seek out work as a scribe. I could do it, but . . . I just don't know!*

"How do I know this isn't a trick?" she challenged him. "You won't let me go right now, so how do I know you won't let me go in a year and a day? Why should I trust you?"

Holding her gaze a long moment, the warlord finally released her left hand, holding his palm out toward the one with the Truth Stone. As soon as it was in his hand, he spoke. "I swear upon this Stone that, if you agree to come and live among us for a year and a day, treated with the exact same courtesies, honors, and deferences as any other woman of the Shifterai should expect . . . if you choose to leave us after that year and a day, I will personally pay you five times the cost of the dowry we negotiated for you today and give you full escort to wherever on Aiar you wish to go. This I swear, Kodan Sin Siin, *multerai* of Clan Cat, Family Tiger."

Turning their entwined hands up, he placed the unmarked disc on her right palm and released her fingers, fully letting her go. Released from his grasp, Tava stared at the white marble Stone.

He *was* telling her the truth, but years of thinking one way about these shapeshifters, of doubting their humanity based on their treatment of Ellet Sou Tred, weren't so easy to shift out of their fearsome shape. She held out the Stone, looking up into his light brown eyes. "What if I don't want to stay the full year and a day? Will you drag me back if I try to escape?"

Those light brown eyes rolled in a pained gesture for self-patience.

Taking the Stone from her, the warband leader clasped it again, pausing between statements to show her his bargain was true. "I swear that if you want to leave before the year and a day is completed, you will be free to leave with all of your belongings and dowry . . . save only the one-fifth of the extra trade goods, as I mentioned before. I will also give you safe escort to whatever border kingdom of your choice you wish to travel to . . . though not all the way across Aiar, if that is what you'd prefer. And *not* for the first full turning of Brother Moon.

"*You* have to give *us* a chance," he explained as she frowned. "You've laid some very powerful and rather insulting accusations at our feet. Whoever mistreated your mother, they've slandered our people's name, and we deserve the right to prove it wasn't us. If you leave now, or within the first full turn of Brother Moon . . . you can take whatever you can carry, coin, goods, whatever, and a single horse from among your herds. But we'll take the rest back to the Plains with us and hold it for a year and a day, as surety of *our* good faith in our good natures. If you want it back before that point, you can come onto the Plains at any point and finish a full turning of Brother Moon among us.

"If you want it back after a year and a day have passed . . . we will find you and send it to you, and we will have nothing more to do with you. We wouldn't *want* to, if you'd be so closed-minded as to refuse to see for yourself whether or not we speak the truth." Pressing the unblemished Stone back into her hand, he folded his arms across his chest. Waiting for her to make up her mind.

My mother didn't lie. She was raped by the Shifterai—I'm living proof! But this man isn't lying . . . my heart wants to say he is lying, but the Stone says he isn't. I know the Stone works. There was too much doubt clouding her head. Turning to his brother, she held out the disc. "You swear that these things are the truth. That you'll let me go at any point I demand it. And swear to the truth of all the rest. *Then* I'll consider the offer."

"I am *not* going to swear to pay five times your dowry," Kenyen countered, though he took the Stone from her. "That is Kodan's bargain, and Kodan's burden. But I *will* swear, affirm, and avow that we will let you go at any point, as my brother has said. And give you escort at least as far as one of the border kingdoms around the Plains of your choice. And do all the rest that he says about your own goods—he doesn't always think along the same paths that the rest of us take, but my brother *is* scrupulous when it comes to upholding the letter of whatever contract he makes."

Displaying both sides, he tossed the white disc to the next-nearest shapeshifter, who stated simply, "Kodan *is* one who speaks the truth," before passing the enchanted slab of rock to the next one, who also agreed the bargain would be true.

The younger brother's choice of words pricked at Tava's sense of honor, and strangely, her sense of humor. No longer quite so terrified of enduring her mother's fate, though she was still uneasy inside, she acknowledged silently that this Kodan of Family Tiger *was* clever with his words. Clever enough that he'd managed to get the Alders of Five Springs to pay them, sort of, for killing bandits they had already slain.

Except they're not really getting a huge payment, save for that one-fifth thing of the trade goods they've bartered, if they all swear this barter is true. Which, if he holds to the letter of his words, won't include my personal wealth . . . I think. Goddess . . . everything I know, versus what they're telling me . . . I'm confused!

When the Truth Stone came back to Kodan, he lifted his brows. "Well? Do we have a bargain?"

"I . . ." She couldn't bring herself to say yes. There was still a knot of fear tied around her thoughts, bands of doubt and confusion. The presence of all these men—whether or not they were Truth-sworn not to harm her—pressed in on her senses. Crowded her. Expecting an answer. ". . . I need to think!"

The words came out of her harsher than she'd intended. Tava

cringed reflexively, expecting their rage at her unfeminine outburst. What she got instead were a couple of rolled eyes, and a grunt from the warleader's father.

"*Women,*" he muttered. "They're the same in any land . . . Lead us to your home, young maiden. You can *think* as we walk, and think as we pack."

Kodan held out one of his hands. Tava reached for it, expecting to be handed the Truth Stone, only to realize he hadn't offered that hand. Too late, she found their fingers clasped, though not twined as before. A gentle tug urged her into walking beside him. But it was hard to think when he touched her; all she could think about were the men surrounding her and the man touching her. The man determined to take her with him. She shivered as she walked, and not just from the slowly drying folds of her damp gown.

As they approached the path that turned off from the road and led to her home, Tava caught him sniffing deeply. "What are you doing?"

"Smelling the way to your home. It's off to the right, isn't it?" he asked, gesturing at the dirt lane angling off through the trees.

Tava recalled the other three shifters sniffing her, then being dismissed from the Aldehall. "That's why you sent away those other three. When you threatened the Alders with defending my property."

Kodan grinned. "That's right."

"That's because my brother *likes* you," Kenyen teased from the warlord's other side.

He received an elbow to the ribs. "Keep your tongue in your head!" Kodan ordered sharply. "Or find you'll have to regrow it. This woman is *frightened* of us, you son of Family Ass!"

A hand smacked into the back of his black hair. "Be respectful yourself," the father of the two said, "or I'll tell your mother what *both* of you just said."

Wide-eyed, Tava glanced back and forth between the three men, before flicking her gaze to the others walking behind them. Some were amused, some looked bored, and others were busy watching the sides of the trail as they turned toward her home. As much as Mornai women weren't allowed any public outbursts by custom, it was also rare for Mornai men to chastise one another in public. Such things were discouraged because it could be seen as undermining their all-important authority.

Yet these Shifterai discipline one another in front of me . . . and they do it like rowdy young boys who haven't yet become sober young men . . . Her mother's book did mention of the men of Family Mongrel fighting among themselves, but not in a friendly way. Their way was the way of the fist, of might making right. But the elbow and the hand had been applied more with exasperation than with true anger, as far as she could tell. Light baps, not hard bashings.

Unsure what to think, Tava approached her home with trepidation. It was the last time she'd look upon her home, and she studied the stilt-raised structures unhappily. The woodshed lay off to the south by the apple orchard and the birch trees composing most of the local forest; the fowl house sat to the north at the edge of the pasture. Between the two stood the house and the barn, both raised up on the stout stone pillars that most Mornai houses boasted. Even the fowl house was raised, with only the refreshing hut not built up on stilts.

The ducks had waddled off to the stream that wended through the pasture, where some previous owner had dug an artificial pond for them to float upon. The chickens were scratching and pecking in the dirt under the barn, looking for bugs to eat. She could see the gelding grazing contentedly not far from the pond and the dark shapes of the ducks rippling its waters, but the quartet of goats that her father . . . that *she* owned weren't in sight. Alarmed, she hurried forward, tugging to free her hand. Thankfully the warlord released it, though he followed closely as she headed for the barn.

A soft bleat reached her ears, which she instinctively sharpened; as soon as she did, she also heard the faint, familiar *hissss hissss hissss* of milk hitting the pail. Hurrying up the ramp, she found one of the three missing Shifterai seated on the milking stool, milking one of the three nanny goats. The other two, also munching on the fresh, thick hay he must have laid in their manger, looked like they had already been milked. Beside them, the one kid her father had chosen to keep, a young nanny goat, nibbled on the stray stalks of rye and alfalfa that had fallen to the barn floor. The other two, born billy goats, had been turned into smoked and jerked meat, and their hides turned into parchment not long ago.

Running his fingers along the nanny goat's udder, the shapeshifter gave her teats a few more downward squeezes, then untied her halter and left her to eat. Rising from the stool, the middle-aged man picked up the metal bucket, fetched a second one also filled with goat-milk, and gave her a questioning look. "What do you want done with these?"

At a loss for words, Tava stared at him. Milking her goats was not something she would have imagined these outlanders would willingly do. Seeing Kodan stop next to her, she tried to gather her scattered wits. Normally, she would set the milk aside to await either cooking it in her breakfast porridge or turning it into cheese, but the latter wasn't exactly an option, given how soon she would have to leave. That meant either drinking or cooking it.

That made her realize she had . . . twelve, fifteen Shifterai to feed? *I've never cooked for so many! I don't think I have that many plates and bowls in the whole of the house, let alone cups . . .*

"Take it to the house for now," Kodan instructed him as she stayed silent in her indecision. He touched her elbow. "Tava, have you had anything to eat yet?"

That brought her back to her long, overnight vigil, watching her father's pyre burn. Numbly, she shook her head. *Father's gone. I have to leave my home . . . and I'm being blackmailed into going with these Shift-*

erai, or take only what I and Tender can carry. I have no one and nothing anymore.

It was too many fears, too many emotions, too many surprises and changes, all too close to one another, all at once. She struggled to contain it, lungs tightening with grief, but it was too much. Too much. Vision blurring with tears, Tava covered her face with her hands, wanting to hide that she wept, but too overwrought to stop herself from shuddering with each breath.

FOUR

***

Dismayed by her strange, silent weeping, so different from the vocal wailing of Shifterai women, Kodan glanced quickly at the others. His brother looked disconcerted, Manolo looked confused, and Tedro, milk pails still dangling from his hands, looked distinctly uncomfortable. He himself felt an urge to comfort her, to take her in his arms and hold her. There was just one glaring problem.

She was a maiden. A Shifterai maiden, not just by her sudden adoption, but by birthright. Worse, she was a maiden with a distorted view of what his people were like. Spotting his father on the ramp, Kodan beckoned Siinar over. Married and trustworthy, he was the best choice for handling her.

"Take her to the house," Kodan told his father. "Make sure she has something to drink and something to eat, if she can. Tava, this is Siinar, my father. Go with him, and he will take care of you."

Siinar cupped his arm around Tava's shoulders, guiding the weeping young woman out of the barn. Shrugging, Tedro followed with the milk pails. A couple of the others had followed them to the barn, the others spreading out to check the other buildings. But there were enough within hearing distance for Kodan's needs.

"Alright, listen up. We'll need cages to transport the ducks and chickens, and leashes for the goats, since there are too few to make a herd. Check also for containers, baskets, chests, and sacks, as well as ropes, thongs, and such. Four of you, sort yourselves out and go scout the village. Make sure the Alders are indeed packing the bartered wagons."

The nanny kid, young and curious, meandered over to Kodan and stretched out her neck, nibbling at his trouser leg. Gently pinching the small, floppy ear, Kodan discouraged the young goat from damaging his clothes. He did it a second time, pinching a little harder, until the goat learned her lesson and wandered back to her mother's side.

"Torei, you and Manolo look over that wagon parked next to the barn. Make sure it's sound enough for traveling the Plains—I'll take her things," he added as Manolo glanced pointedly at the scribal satchel, which he had acquired at some point during their walk to put her quills, scraps of parchment, and ink jar into. Accepting the bag, Kodan slung it over his shoulder. "The priorities will be her personal belongings, her scribal effects, her animals, and her food.

"After that will come her household goods, and the last on the list, wood and hay, whatever can be fitted on the wagons without too much strain. The sooner we pack and leave, the less we'll have to deal with these uncivilized outlanders," he half muttered to himself.

The wry twist of Kenyen's mouth told Kodan that his brother agreed with his assessment of these uncouth Valley men.

After being offered a soft kerchief, sympathetic murmurs from the warlord's father, and warm food that she hadn't even had to cook for herself, Tava was left mostly alone. The Shifterai men bothered her only for the occasional polite inquiry into which of her personal goods she thought she would like immediate access to and which she didn't think she would need for a while. Had she been more accepted by the village of Five Springs, it would have been her fellow Mornai women bustling around her home following her father's cremation. Not a band of intimidating male strangers.

The comforts were strange, because they were being offered to her by these Shifterai men. Men in general were stoic creatures of authority and discipline; they did not offer comforting touches on her shoulder, nor a freshly exchanged kerchief when the previous one grew too damp and crumpled. That was something women did in the River Kingdom.

It was also rare for a man to cook, though her father had learned out of necessity, both as a bachelor and then more or less as a widower with a small child. Yet three of the Shifterai invaded the front room, where she sat numbly watching most of her life being packed up, and took over the half of it that was the kitchen. Together, they coordinated their efforts into making a simple yet satisfying midday meal of soup and porridge, before settling down to weave willow withes culled by the others from the nearby trees into makeshift baskets, in between plucking, drawing, and roasting a brace of wild geese brought in by one of the others.

More than that, they first muttered among themselves; then the three Shifterai men scrubbed and filled all the pots she had with water, but for the porridge one, which had been thinned with the soup and given more grain to cook for supper, turning it into a sort of pottage stew. Greens were brought in from the vegetable garden, mixed with crushed berries and a bit of vinegar-wine, and redistributed with meat from the geese and the pottage as their supper.

It was a good meal, if sparsely seasoned. Yet the approach of night made Tava nervous. They had *said* she would be safe . . . but they were men, and they outnumbered her by too many. Worse, as the sun colored the sky to the west, the warleader's father took down the washing tub from the rafters by unnaturally stretching his body thin and tall enough to bare his belly between the waistband of his trousers and the hem of his thigh-length tunic. Carrying it into the back room, which had been divided long ago by a pair of wooden screens into a sort of room for herself and a sort of room for her father, he directed the other three that had stayed in the house all day to take the pots of heated water into the bedchamber.

Tava stared at the doorway, listening to the sounds of water splashing into the large wooden tub. Uncomprehending, she stared at the older man as he reappeared. *Why are they preparing a bath back there?*

Crossing to her where she sat at her father's scribing table, he curled his fingers. "Come. It is time for you to retire."

They do *want to get me alone*, she thought for one uncomfortable, fearful moment. He must have seen her fear, or perhaps smelled it, for he lowered his hand, giving her a patient look.

"It is customary on the Plains for our unmarried women to retire to the maiden's *geome* at sunset, which means your sleeping quarters will have to do," he explained, though it wasn't much of an explanation, since Tava had no clue what a *geome* was. "It is now sunset, and thus time for you to retire. Since you have spent all day in muddied clothes, I have laid out a fresh set for you to wear tomorrow, and what I think is your nightdress, as well as changed the linens. These . . . Mornai fashions," he said, pausing to wrinkle his nose, eyeing her loosely cut brown dress dubiously, "don't differ much from day to night, as far as I can tell. But I thought you would like to bathe and sleep in fresh linens.

"From the rate at which my son is overseeing the packing, it is probable that we will leave by mid-morning, tomorrow. There won't be many opportunities to stop and bathe in leisure until we are well onto the Plains, probably not until we rejoin Family Tiger." He lifted the corner of his mouth in a wry smile. "Normally we would not leave someone who is grieving the loss of a loved one alone, but there are no women to attend you, and only women are allowed into the maiden's *geome* after dark. But you may rest assured that we will guard the house all night long, both here in this front room and around the outside, as well as the other buildings. No one will disturb your slumber, once you retire for the night."

Bemused by the thought that she *would* be alone, Tava rose from her father's desk and hesitantly entered the back room. The moment she stepped fully into the room, the warlord's father pulled the door shut behind her, firmly enough to make the latch *clank* into place. For a moment she felt trapped, then flushed with embarrassment, realizing that the latch-string could only be pulled through into *her* side of the house. He wasn't locking her in here, so much as giving her privacy.

In fact, when she returned her attention to the rest of the room, she realized either he or one of the others had not only closed the shutters, but draped sheets over them, ensuring that no one would be able to peek through the cracks. He had also lit the oil-soaked wicks of two of her father's four precious glass lamps, giving her plenty of light to see the tub sitting next to her father's bed . . . which had been stripped bare of everything, even the feather mattress. Not even the straw-stuffed tick remained on the wooden platform; only a length of toweling linen and one of her pots of softsoap lay on the planks, waiting to be used.

An unscented soap, she realized, recognizing the clay pot by its shape. *If I have no strong scent about me . . . maybe I'll have a better chance of escaping.*

Not completely sure she *would* be left alone, or even for how long, Tava dithered several minutes, pacing between the steaming tub, the door, and the two windows, one on her father's half of the room, the other on hers. She could see the Shifterai had spoken true; a folded set of clothes had been laid on the stool at the foot of her bed, and a plain linen nightdress laid on her pillow.

The encroaching chill in the air made up her mind for her. Tava hurried out of her clothes and into the still-warm water. With the door leading to the front half of the cottage shut, the heat of the fire could only radiate through the river stones separating the two chambers, which was worth only so much now that autumn was on its way. It was a luxury to have not only enough warm water in the tub to soak in, but two extra kettles besides for rinse water.

A nervous luxury, because she still didn't quite trust these Shifterai men. But even after she got out and dried herself with the toweling cloth, they left her alone, though she could hear sounds of the others settling down for the night. Not only inside the house, but outside as well.

A cautious shift of the sheet draped over one of the shuttered windows gave her enough of a glimpse through the cracks to see at least three members of the warband shifting into the shapes of strong, muscular stripe-cats, the tigers of their Family name. They settled down on the trampled grass next to the little piles of their clothes, pectoral necklaces, and belongings, stationing themselves at regular intervals within her awkward field of view.

Cats. Of course. The ideal animal to nap and rest, yet remain distinctly alert to anything unusual. Including my own attempt to escape, even if they're one and all facing outward, wary of an external threat.

Lowering the makeshift curtain back into place, Tava retired reluctantly to her bed. It looked like she wouldn't be going anywhere tonight. Or possibly any other night, if they continued such a cunning, careful plan for guarding their encampments once they left the Valley. Not without being spotted as a shapeshifter.

Tava didn't know what the Shifterai would do, how they would react, if they learned that there was a *female* shapeshifter in the world. All she had were her mother's words, of how the stronger and more multi-shaped the shifter was, the more powerful that shifter had been in the ranks of the so-called Family Mongrel that had captured her. Any shifter who could assume ten or more shapes was given the title of *multerai*, and there had been only three of them among the Mongrel men unwillingly observed by her mother.

It was a rank that permitted a man to lord over his fellow shapechangers, to the point where any *multerai* who wanted a particular woman could rape her, without regard for the wishes of the one who had actually claimed her as his war prize. *Multerai* were powerful, arrogant, and cruel; they reveled in their authority over the others and took whatever they wanted. By contrast, women had no rank whatsoever. No power, no authority, nothing but the status of a *thing*. If Tava had been born among them, if it had become known that she was a shapeshifter, it might have been seen by her mother's captors as the ultimate insolence. Worse than insolent, because Tava knew she could skillfully imitate a double handful of shapes.

Maybe these shapeshifters were different. Maybe they wouldn't beat her, or force her, or harm her directly . . . but they were still proud of their shapeshifting. They wore the same circular collars that their Mongrel brethren wore, with the same pride in how many rows each man's necklace boasted, each row of beads carved and painted and shaped like the animal forms they could make. That much was the same between these men and the monsters of her mother's captivity.

They might be nice to me because of some cultural difference in how they treat women, but I'm still a woman, and women are not shapeshifters, she worried, pulling the covers up over her nightgown-clad body. Curling up on her side, she tried to relax. *I don't think any of these shapeshifters recognized me after all. Surely if one had made the connection between the shifter that helped battle the bandits earlier and my own self now . . . surely he would have mentioned it to the others?*

The only reason to keep silent would be to blackmail me somehow . . . but I don't see what they could possibly want. They're already taking my worldly goods onto the Plains, whether or not I choose to come with them. Unless it's to put me in his power . . . but if their Truth-Stoned words are true, it wouldn't be to force me into their arms . . . as hard as that is to believe.

No. No, my secret is safe for now, she convinced herself, closing her eyes. *If I ride with them to the Plains, I can either leave at the end of the bartered month . . . or I can leave sooner, if I don't like how they treat me. All I'd need is an hour or two with their guard down, to give me enough time to flee . . .*

Her whirling thoughts slowed, settled, and stilled. Slumber crept up, dragging her into blissful, or at least restful, oblivion. For a while, Tava knew nothing more . . . until a pounding at the door woke her with a start.

"Tava?" she heard the older man, Siinar, calling out. "Tava, wake up! We need the washtub! I'm coming in, just for the tub!"

We need the . . . what? she wondered, automatically shifting her eyes to see in the dark. She heard the door open and caught a brief glimpse of the Shifterai entering the room. A moment later, she heard sloshing water and the creak of the floorboards . . . and saw a much stouter, heavily muscled version of the same man exit the chamber, carrying the washtub in his now-elongated arms like it was just an oversized bucket. Curious, she climbed out of bed and crossed to the door, but the front half of the house was empty. Tava shut the door, mindful of her nightdress.

The sound of voices shouting outside was joined by stripe-cats roaring and a frightened, masculine scream. Worried, she hurried to the nearest window. She saw nothing and crossed to the one on her father's side of the room. An orange glow off to one side gave her a clue, as did a crackling, rushing noise, though she couldn't actually see the site of the fire.

The ground shook, startling her with the *thud thud thud* of heavy footsteps. They ended after a few more moments, only to be punctuated by a roaring *hisssss* of water poured on the fire. The *thud thud thud thud* came back, and *now* she saw Siinar, stripped of clothes and clad only in a thick, dark brown pelt from waist to knees, barely preserving his modesty. He raced past the back of the house, shaking the ground with each step, for he was now nearly three times his normal size, and carried the washtub like it was nothing more than a large bowl, despite the fact that Tava could almost stretch out her legs when sitting in it.

A commotion to the other side, of the goats bleating and the ducks squawking, had her racing toward the other window. It was a strain to see two-legged figures chased by four-legged ones, even with night-shifted eyes. Clouds had moved in at some point during the night, obscuring what little light shone down from the moons and the stars.

A *sploosh* from the direction of the pond was quickly followed by the returning *thud*s of the enlarged Shifterai man racing back to pour more water on the fire. From the direction of it, the fire had probably been started among the logs and limbs stacked in the woodshed. Another long *hisssss* of pouring water extinguished the worst of the orange glow, though the enlarged Shifterai raced back to the pond for another load.

Comprehension dawned. *The Alders! They planned a diversion, to set the wood piles on fire in the hopes of making everyone dash for buckets to put it out . . . and while the shifters were busy with that emergency, they probably thought they could steal my animals!* Tava smothered a laugh behind her hand. *Foiled by the ability to shift their size as well as their shape! Oh, Father—why didn't I ever think of trying that myself?*

. . . It's just as well, she realized, lowering the makeshift curtain once again. *I would have been tempted to grow myself so large, I could have snatched up the Aldeman and threatened to drop him on his stupid, stubborn, self-righteous head. That would've given him every right to thrash me senseless . . .*

The sounds of the shouting seemed to be more directed at containing the would-be thieves than at trying to make sense of the attack. Even the sound of Siinar racing back to the woodshed ended with more splashing than hissing from drowning flames. Returning to her bed, she waited to see if the middle-aged Shifterai would return the washtub, but he didn't.

He did eventually return to the door, and knocked softly upon it. ". . . Tava? Are you still awake?"

"Yes," she called out.

"Some of the younger men of the village attacked. Two of them set fire to the woodshed, while the others tried to get into the barn. We're holding them captive in the barn for now. In the morning . . . the village will be dealt with."

That alarmed her. Biting her lip, Tava struggled between her dislike for the men of the village, versus the fact that they *were* her fellow villagers. "You're . . . you're not going to harm them, are you?"

"No. But they will be fined, and some of their goods confiscated. This is *not* the village some of us remember from our distant youth . . . and I think most of us will not be coming back for another visit anytime soon. Tava, one more thing," he cautioned her through the closed door. "My younger son overheard a couple of them talking as they approached, whispering about how they hoped they could steal *you* away. At least temporarily . . . and only to treat you like *you* thought we were going to treat you.

"My older son is very angry with them. Most of us are, but he is our leader on this trip. If he does not calm down by morning, this entire village will be lucky if he leaves them with enough food and clothes to see them through the winter—I do not tell you this to alarm you," he added quickly, as if he could sense her shock through the door, "but to show you that we consider you one of us now. We will keep careful watch while you sleep, so that you may sleep safely." He paused, then added gently, "Do try to sleep well, in spite of all this excitement. Good night."

"Good night," Tava replied reflexively, though she stared across the night-dark room for several moments more, trying to absorb his words. *They weren't just after the goats and the chickens . . . but after* me *as well? Intending to do me harm? And now the Shifterai are going to punish them for it in the morning?*

. . . Oh, Father, if I couldn't tolerate staying here before, I cannot stay

here now. I cannot stay, and I will never be able to return. Not if the younger men . . . no. No, I will never return. Better to take my chances among these Shifterai than to stay within the reach of men I used to be able to trust!

Shuddering at the thought of not just being beaten for her insolence by the men of the village, but forced as well, Tava huddled under the covers. Soft, padding footsteps a few minutes later alarmed her. Rising, she returned to the window and peered out through the cracks in the shutters, only to just barely see the source of the noise. Someone in the warband wasn't curled up taking a nap; instead, the tiger-shaped man was actively patrolling, furry head lifting and lungs sniffing the air at intervals, testing for foreign scents.

The sight of such diligence didn't bring the same disturbed disappointment it had earlier. Before, the thought of all the Shifterai on guard against any unexpected activities had felt cloying, even smothering. Now, it felt protective. Comforting, even. Retiring one last time to her bed, Tava curled up under the covers, deciding she *would* give these Shifterai and their offer a try.

The restrictive, constrictive life of the Valley wasn't very suitable for her anymore. The thought of subjugating herself to Alder rule for the rest of her life did not appeal, if it led them to discard all semblance of decency in selling her off to the Shifterai and permitting a destructive raid on her property and even her person. More to the point, the thought of submitting to their jurisdiction just because she was a woman definitely did not appeal.

Trying to make a life for herself in some Mornai city wouldn't be that much better, because she would still have to be a Mornai woman, bowing to the whims of Mornai men. She wasn't Mornai. She wasn't sure she wanted to be Shifterai, but she definitely wasn't Mornai.

I'm tired of being bound up by all these rules and expectations like . . . like a caterpillar trapped in the hardened shell of a cocoon, she thought as she slowly relaxed back toward sleep. *I'm not a caterpillar. I'm not content to grub along the ground. I'm not meant to be some farmer's wife, or some farmer's servant. I am far greater than that, meant for far greater things. I . . . I don't know what, yet, but I do know I will never know if I stay here in the Valley. Nor can I leave on my own, because I don't know where to go.*

Moving to the Shifting Plains isn't a direction I'd ever thought I'd go, but it is away from here. It's a start. And . . . if it isn't a good place to stay, I'll just move on again. Like a butterfly, if I don't like the flowers I find, I won't rest long in any one place.

I don't know how to be a butterfly yet, but I refuse to remain a caterpillar, she decided, yawning and tugging the covers just a little higher for warmth. *I'll just have to learn as I go . . .*

"They'll have to be dealt with, of course," Deian muttered. A fellow *multerai*, he was only three years older than Kodan and had looked upon Kodan as something of a younger brother, having only sisters for his own siblings. Deian didn't have to say who had to be dealt with; all of the Shifterai of the South Paw warband were upset with the vandals that had attacked the woodpile on one side of the farm and the barn on the other side.

Mindful of the young woman sleeping in the other half of the cottage, Kodan closed the book he had been reading in the light of one of the glass lamps they had found in the cottage, and kept his response equally quiet. "My brother almost castrated them on the spot. I'm sorely tempted myself."

"But?" Deian prompted him.

"I've been thinking."

Deian let out a mock-groan. "Again, with the thinking! What about, this time?"

"About this so-called Family Mongrel for one, and about the treatment of her mother. And the fear of the Shifterai that this village has because of it." Kodan glanced down at the brown leather and smooth-planed oak boards that formed the cover of the book he had found. A book filled with highly uncomfortable revelations. "Even by Plains standards, simply stating an intent to force a woman isn't enough to justify castration . . .

"*Punishment*, yes. But castration and banishment only if there's an ongoing threat for the foreseeable future. Or an actual hands-on attempt. Which they didn't get to do, and it could be argued that they spoke in the heat of their anger. That had they actually gotten their hands on her, they might not have followed through. But there's not an actual, ongoing threat to her, mostly because we're taking her away from here," Kodan pointed out. "I may not sit on the Sister Council, but I do know the law."

"You're right." Deian nodded slowly, then shook his head. "But we can't leave them unpunished. It's bad enough they fear us, but we can't let them think even tacitly that this kind of . . . *wrongness* . . . will be tolerated."

"Nor can we trample on their rights as citizens of another kingdom," Kodan reminded his friend. "Which castrating them certainly would do. Not to mention solidify the idea of the Shifterai being nothing more than violent brutes. I don't think our queen would be happy about that."

Deian winced. "No, she wouldn't. Ailundra wants to emphasize trade over trouble when it comes to the services we offer to the other nations."

"Precisely. Not to mention, I have to justify everything we do here to both the Sister Council *and* the Shifter Council." Dropping his head to his palm, elbow braced on the table, Kodan rubbed at his tired eyes. "I'll get a better idea of just how much damage they actually did in the morning, when there's enough light to see clearly. If they're lucky, or rather, their families, I'll only tax the village the equivalent in ruined lumber. Plus something extra for the trouble and the fright."

Bumping his elbow against Kodan's, Deian gave him a wry grin when the younger man glanced his way. "There are days when being a *multerai* is a real headache, isn't it?"

"Thank you," Kodan muttered. It wasn't a statement of gratitude.

Deian smiled again, rising from the bench. "Get some sleep. You'll need fresh wits in the morning. I'll sleep outside the front door, on the porch. You can join me if you want; there should be enough room, if we shift small."

Nodding to acknowledge the offer, Kodan didn't comply. Once the other shifter left, Kodan was alone. Or at least, the only one awake. The large, sleeping bodies of Manolo and his father covered part of the floor, both sprawled out in stripe-cat form, fuzzy ears flicking at the creak of the floorboards under Deian's feet and the *clank* of the latch as he left the cottage. Technically, Kodan shouldn't be in the same house at all with everyone else asleep, not if a bedchamber was considered the same as a maiden's *geome*. But it wasn't an iron-clad law, it was more like a strong cultural suggestion.

The book in front of him, unlabeled and unornamented, was too important not to read immediately. He knew it would give him nightmares if he weren't careful, but he had needed to know. This was the book Tava had mentioned, the one containing her mother's story, penned by her father the scribe. Or rather, by her next-father. Kodan had only skimmed it so far, and it wasn't arranged in chronological order by any means, but rather as a series of conversations and confessions.

But he had found the part where Ellet Sou Tred, the Zanthenai woman, spoke of realizing she was pregnant, after having endured two years of rapings and beatings, and seeing what happened to the children among this "Family Mongrel." How the boys were praised and indulged, and how the girls were punished and beaten. Ellet had spoken fervently to the scribe, Varamon, how she couldn't stand the thought of any child of hers being raised in such a way, even as she hated the men who had contributed to that child's impending existence. She had spoken of hiding her pregnancy, desperate to figure out a way to escape that would elude the shapeshifted noses of the curs keeping her in their camp.

The descriptions of how she had braved the grass fire, how she had stolen a pair of thick wool blankets and soaked them in the stream as the others fled on horses and in wagons, how she had hidden herself in the reeds before the shifters had given up trying to find her in favor of fleeing themselves, of how she had hunkered down in the stream under the blankets as the world itself seemed to burn— those gave him waking nightmares.

Grass fires were a very serious threat to his people. Late summer might be the season of harvest for wild-growing foods and grains, of scouring the scattered remnants of old orchards for fruit and enjoying the last warm days of the year, but it was also the season for a burning heat that parched the land. Everyone was extra-cautious of how they built and watched their fires, and kept watch well into autumn, which had only now just begun.

Men and beasts both might be able to outrun the flames of a grass fire, but their worldly goods would vanish in a carelessly sparked blaze. Family Tiger wasn't the largest of the tribes by sheer numbers, but it was one of the wealthiest. The thought of losing everything, of being impoverished and losing rank and status, was not something the warlord cared to contemplate for long. He was a *multerai*, one of the best in Clan Cat, and everyone in Family Tiger expected Kodan to be a great leader.

Which means contemplating how to increase our wealth, he reminded himself firmly, keeping the book closed. *I do need to read more of this book . . . and the others she has, none of which I know. New books are always a treat. But . . . not tonight. Tomorrow night, maybe, and her mother's book first. Somewhere in the words this Ellet spoke, in the words the scribe faithfully wrote down, might be the key to unveiling this mystery.*

Who or what were the men of this Family Mongrel? Why did they form in the first place? Where did they roam, if Zantha is all the way over to the southwest of the Plains and we're in the southeast, nearly a month's journey away by wagon? What happened to them after Ellet fled through the grass fire? And, most important, why have the rest of us never heard about them?

More to the point, Kodan acknowledged, looking at the door to the bedchamber half of the house, *what else can I do to reassure this Tava Ell Var that the real Shifterai are nothing like the monsters her mother describes? She is one of us by birthright, and she needs to become one of us. But I don't dare let it be known that she's a shapeshifter herself. Not before she understands us; not before she replaces this warped image she has of the Plains with the truth. Not if she's to have any chance of assimilating that truth and joining our culture of her own free will.*

Not just for her own sake, but for the sake of our people. If she doesn't have the time to learn and to think about what she learns, she'll react badly to the fame she'll garner as a female shifter. Plus there's that whole . . . well, I couldn't rightfully call it shyness, he acknowledged ruefully, the corner of his mouth quirking up, *but she is uncomfortable about the ways of men and women. The moment my fellow shifters realize she can change her shape, they'll overwhelm her with their attentions . . . and if this book is what she thinks of our courtship practices, she'll only resist all the harder.*

His father snorted and shifted in his sleep, stretching out one furry, tan-and-black-striped leg. A twist of his fuzzy, feline-shaped head tucked it more comfortably in place, using his foreleg as a pillow. It made Kodan think of a similar habit he had seen in his younger brother at night, disdaining a feather-stuffed pillow for his own bicep.

Kenyen teased me about wanting to court her . . . She's spirited, and not unattractive, Kodan acknowledged. *I definitely find her fascinating, though I'm not sure how much of it has to do with her for herself, or simply my curiosity about when she first realized she could shift her shape, or even how she managed her first successful shift, to have rolled through those different shapes so easily during that battle the other day. We encourage one another and offer all manner of suggestions and exercises to our young shapeshifters, but then, we know from past experience what to look for and how to make it work. I don't know how she managed on her own, here in another country . . .*

I think I will use the excuse of courting her to get to know her better, Kodan decided, still staring at the door. *I do need to gain her trust, to convince her of the true Shifterai way, and to prepare her for the mass of men who will want to court her, once her powers are known.*

He tried not to think of *why* so many Shifterai men would want to court her. Of how the rare shapeshifting woman was considered the most attractive kind of all, mutable, changing, strong-willed, fascinating . . . He certainly didn't think of how rare it was for him to show interest in any particular woman; *multerai* were encouraged to take their time picking the *right* woman to be their wife, because *multerai* automatically had a seat on the Shifter Council, and it was encouraged for them to wed the sort of strong, intelligent, thoughtful woman that was often asked to join the Sister Council.

A foreign-raised woman was *not* the sort usually considered as prime material for the Sister Council, he knew. Outlanders didn't always adapt to the ways of the Shifterai. *Which means I'll have to do my best to instruct Tava in the subtle, instinctive ways of my people, so that she'll be an asset rather than a burden, at least until I can get her to the priesthood for training in our ways . . . which brings me back to winning her trust, even in the face of the ugly facts written down in this book.*

A book whose facts were *very* ugly, based on the little he had managed to skim through so far. Deciding to pack it into his own saddlebags, Kodan shed his clothes and shifted into the shape of a small reed-cat, the wild equivalent of a housecat. Quietly, he made the short leap from the floor to the bench, and then to the tabletop. Curling up on the book cover, he tucked his head next to his feet and closed his eyes, determined to sleep.

Lumber for lumber would probably be a good trade, he thought as his body gradually relaxed. *They burned some of our wood, so we take away some of theirs. The City is always willing to pay well for good, long, straight*

timber, whether it's to maintain the various buildings, to split into geome
staves, or to turn into useful objects by various craftsmen . . .

It felt strange to wake up well after dawn to the sound of strange
voices and unfamiliar footsteps in the front room. At first the noises
from the other half of the house confused her; Tava knew she had to
rise and milk the goats, though she wasn't quite sure what time it was.
The sight of the sheet draped over the window at the head of her bed
equally befuddled her, until the events of the night came back. Cheeks
flushing, heart racing, she struggled with the turmoils of yesterday.

Some of her doubts from last night remained. It was more about
caution than fear or skepticism, though she felt those emotions, too.
Regardless, Tava knew she couldn't lie in bed all day. *I'm not a little
girl anymore, hiding under the bedcovers when a storm rolls through. I
have to make my way in the world. And . . . it's hard to believe, given all
that I thought I knew, but I owe these shapechangers a debt of gratitude.
Without them, I'd be fighting the Alders to salvage even a scrap of my own
things.*

Of course, to keep those things, I'll have to go with them onto the Plains.
It was an ironic thought. Kept in the village as a servant, or dragged
onto the Plains as a . . . a . . . *What* will *they expect of me?* Tava wondered, rising and changing out of her nightdress.

She grimaced at the sight of the gown laid out for her, her second-
best with its full skirts, bell sleeves, and carefully stitched zigzags of
blue and green on a field of brown, meant to be worn to River festivals. Not what she would have chosen to wear on a journey, but her
clothes chest wasn't even in the room anymore.

*What will they expect me to do on the Plains? Cook for them? Clean? I
know they live in tents since Mother's book described them as nomads, so
what am I supposed to do, sweep the grass?* Not that there would be grass
as a floor for long, she knew. It was now mid-harvest season, still
warm during the days, but increasingly cold at night. *Mother's book*

said they lived in caves in the winter, and it was always bitterly cold, with the men going around covered in so much fur that they looked like man-headed beasts.

I'm not sure I'd care to live in a cramped tent like my father and I used, traveling from village to village, nor would I care for a life spent herding animals all day . . . but I think I'd like living in a cave even less. The only caves she knew of were the muddy, undercut kind found on the steeper banks of the Morning River, and some narrow, boulder-tumbled niches on the foothills flanking the western edge of the Valley. Neither appealed to her. *Not to mention, these outlanders seem to know how to read; if they know how to read, they might know how to write, and where would be the need for a scribe's services then? What do they expect me to do, living for a year among them?*

She missed her father. The voices of the men talking in the front room were the wrong voices. They talked too quickly, laughed too boldly, trod too firmly on the floorboards of her home. Lacing her boots in place, she knew she couldn't dawdle any longer. Crossing to the door, she lifted the latch and pulled the heavy panel open.

She recognized the warlord's brother, and vaguely remembered his name from yesterday. Kenyen, that was it. The father was Siinar, and Kenyen looked a bit more like him than his older brother did, with darker brown eyes and a narrower face. With him was the youngest of the warband, the one who stuttered. Both men were seated at the table.

They broke off their conversation as soon as the stutterer spotted her and ceased talking. He fumbled his way off the bench and started toward her, then backtracked and snatched up a small clutch of wildflowers. Swallowing at least three times, he licked his lips, opened his mouth, closed it, started all over again, then finally managed to speak.

"F-F-For y-y-you. Pr-Pr . . . Lovely f-flowers for a l-l-l—"

A hand whapped him on the back of his head. Not hard, though the youth did flinch from the blow. "You're *not* supposed to court her until she's been through her initiation days—don't mind Torei," Kenyen added to Tava, giving her a charming smile. "He's still young."

"You're n-n-not that old, yours-s-self!" the younger shifter argued.

"But I'm less impetuous and more mindful of the rules," Kenyen pointed out.

The front door opened, and one of the older men leaned into the cottage. "Quit arguing and serve her the last of breakfast. Kodan wants us on our way within the hour."

Manolo; that was his name. Tava tried to memorize it, and the name of the stuttering youth, since it seemed she would be going with them to the Plains. At least for a while, providing they didn't try to harm her. She hadn't been jesting yesterday on the path; she *would* hit back, if anyone tried to hurt her. She would hit them hard enough to buy the time she needed for an escape at the very least.

But they didn't hurt her. Torei hurried toward the kitchen area, which Tava abruptly realized had been stripped bare of everything but a kettle, a bowl, a spoon, a pitcher, a cup, and a cloth-draped plate. Even the iron poker used to stir the fire under the soapstone cooking shelf that spanned the hearth was gone, though a stick with a charred end rested against the hearthstones.

There were no wooden barrels stuffed with salted or smoked meats, no strings strung across the ceiling between the rafters, nor sign of the herbs that had been drying upon them, no crates holding the bags of grain she took to the mill for grinding into flour. Not even a rag to wipe the counter had been left, nor a broom to sweep the floor, and only a few sticks of kindling remained in the wood box built next to the hearth.

Kenyen touched her elbow, making Tava start, but he merely smiled and gestured toward the chair he had been occupying. The table normally had two chairs and two longish benches, the chairs at the short ends, the benches along the sides. Varamon had sometimes entertained the other Alders of the village and had attempted to teach some of the ways of reading and writing to the other children, though most of them hadn't the patience or the aptitude for such learning. But one of the chairs and one of the benches were no longer there, nor was her father's book chest, his writing table, the tanning frame for the parchment, the pulping tub and costly silk screens for making paper—anything that had stood on the scribal half of the front room was now gone, just as almost everything was gone from the kitchen half.

The cottage looked rather bare and forlorn without any of those things. Tava glanced at the stout log angled in the corner, cut with steps that led up to the trapdoor of the attic. The hinged planks had been left open, making her wonder if there was even so much as a single dried pea left up there, if everything downstairs was so bare. She had culled and dried those peas herself, along with beans and other foods, and waited only for the rains of autumn to finish softening the ground so that she could dig out the late-harvest roots still waiting in the garden.

Torei laid a bowl of porridge thickened with eggs in front of her, a cup of goat's milk poured from the pitcher, and the covered plate, which held raw, scrubbed carrots arranged around slices of an odd flatbread covered in melted cheese. The porridge and the plate were both warm from sitting on the cooking shelf, but the milk was cold enough to let her know it had been at least an hour since the nannies had been milked, if not longer.

While she ate, both Kenyen and Torei had vanished into the back room. They came out a short while later carrying her mattress between them, stuffed with duck feathers and thus bulky and awkward, but they didn't seem to have much trouble navigating it over to the far end of the table. They came back for the straw-stuffed tick and carried that out the front door, then returned for the feather mattress. Then reentered the house for her pillows and bedding, including the linen sheets that had been draped over the shutters. Tava thought she saw a corner of her nightdress, tucked into the stack of blankets and sheets, but the young shifter moved quickly on his journey outside, barely even taking a moment to give her a shy smile.

He's not supposed to court me yet? Tava wondered. *Not until I've been through my "initiation" days? Mother's captors didn't even wait to drag her onto the Plains before they forced themselves on her. How different are these people, if they have such clearly defined rules about when a young man could start paying court to a woman?*

Kenyen came back, only to pick up the pitcher and drink straight from the lip. He caught her staring at him and quickly lowered the container, grinning unrepentantly. "What? It has to be washed, and if it's to be washed, it has to be emptied first, right?"

Bemused, she watched the warlord's younger brother drink the milk to the last drop, before picking up the porridge kettle as well, carrying both outside. The emptiness of the house reminded her that he would no doubt come back for the spoon, bowl, cup, and plate. Kenyen and Torei both came back as she finished; seeing that she was done, Kenyen took the dishes from her and carried them outside. Torei had brought in a pair of buckets and began carefully pouring water over the fire, gradually dousing the embers and flames. Reminding her of last night's events.

Drawn by her curiosity, Tava exited as well. She wanted to see how much damage the fire had done. Instead, she found herself stopping at the top of the porch steps.

The grassy field in front of the house was filled with wagons, carts, and horses. There were the three wagons the Shifterai had come with, the trader-wagon, her own cart and horse, plus the wagons they had bartered out of the Alders yesterday . . . and four more wains hitched with horses she recognized from the village, all of them packed with baskets, cages, bags, and arches made from willow withes on the topmost layers, and lumber down below. A handful of the shapeshifters was stretching lengths of cloth for covering over the arches, securing their contents against possible rain, using sturdy, oiled tarp-cloth on the uppermost sections where the rain would strike heaviest, and more colorful, less durable blankets and sheets down the sides.

It looked like a cross between a harvest-faire and a caravan had sprung up in her yard overnight. Slowly descending the steps, she glanced off to the side, toward her vegetable garden. Two dog-sized, striped, gray-furred shapes were digging in the dirt with zeal, followed by a third figure, that of a man who stooped and scooped things into the loose-woven basket balanced on his hip. It wasn't until he carried it back to the nearest cart that she saw it was filled with roots.

That means those overgrown badgers in my garden are actually a pair of Shifterai . . . no doubt using the most efficient form they have available for digging in the dry-packed ground. But where did these wagons come from? There aren't that many wagons to spare in the village! That was the point of yesterday's negotiations, after all.

The angle of the sun shining down through the drifting clouds told her she had slept quite late. And quite solidly, to not have heard the noise of all these wagons being assembled and loaded or the things in the house being removed. Tava wanted to ask questions about all these things, but wasn't sure how these Shifterai men would take her inquisitiveness. The men of the village put up with it to a point, but only to a point; even Tava's own father had displayed some annoyance at too many questions over the years, though he had been more patient about answering her curiosity than most Mornai men would have been.

"Ex-xcuse m-me," Torei muttered, detouring around her to hurry down the steps, buckets in hand.

Tava followed, descending slowly to the ground. A glance over her shoulder showed the space under the stilt-raised house had also been gleaned for worldly goods, though not much had been taken. Like most Mornai houses, the place underneath was more used for tossing broken objects in need of repair than for storing anything valuable, in case a flood came along. The River didn't reach this high very often, but it wasn't unknown.

This, however, was confusing. Too mysterious. Unable to stand the pressure of her curiosity regarding the extra wains, Tava hurried toward the shifter Manolo as soon as she spotted him. Torei might have done, if it weren't for his stutter. It would make answering her many questions awkward, even difficult for the tongue-twisted youth. Thankfully, the older shapeshifter gave her his attention politely when she approached, with no sign of impatience at being interrupted while loading wicker cages onto one of the wagons, cages filled with the quietly quacking, bobbing bodies of her ducks.

"Yes?" he asked, settling the cage in his hands on top of the bartered planks of lumber.

"Erm, these wagons . . . where did the extra ones come from?" she asked, hoping it wasn't too demanding a question. The men of the village hated it when women said things that sounded like demands.

"From the villagers, of course." Catching her confusion, he elaborated. "Kodan went to the Aldehall this morning to demand a cart and horse with harness culled from among the families that participated in last night's attack. He was going to have it loaded with wood not found on the Plains. But once we unbound the boys in the Aldehall, intending to set them free, one of them grabbed a knife and stabbed Kodan."

Shocked, Tava gasped, quickly covering her mouth to hide her unseemly gaping.

Seeming unconcerned at the violence, the middle-aged shifter continued, shrugging. "The Alders were upset at what they called the boy's public lack of control, and so the Aldeman agreed to pay a blood-price for the unprovoked attack. Four wagons, eight horses, harnesses, and lumber." Manolo gave her a quick smile. "It seems the Aldeman's wife has herself a new servant after all, though it's a young man and not a young lady."

"And . . . Kodan?" Tava asked, upset at the thought of the shape-shifter being hurt or worse, and a little confused by her dismay. The man *had* bartered her freedom away, even if it hadn't been much of a freedom. "Is he . . . ?"

"He's sleeping it off in the trader's wagon," Manolo dismissed. "That's why we decided to let you sleep, too, so that he could get his rest before we moved."

"Was it a bad wound?" Tava found herself asking, letting more of her curiosity spill out when it seemed Manolo was willing to an-swer her questions. "Where was he struck? How deep was the cut? He's a warlord, a fighter; why didn't he dodge it?"

Manolo held up his hand to stem the tide of her questions, though he smiled as he did so. "The boy stabbed him from behind, shaming himself that much more in front of the village elders, since it wasn't an honorable blow. Kodan says the knife pierced all the way to his lungs—but you must understand that Kodan is a *multerai*. That means he is a *very* strong, very fast shapeshifter.

"The moment after the knife pierced his ribs, he sealed the wound to keep it from bleeding. Then he turned to glare at his opponent." Manolo chuckled. "Seeing him still standing, apparently unharmed, the boy fainted at Kodan's feet. It also looked like the other boys and the village Alders were thinking, not twice, but four and five times again about the wisdom of protesting our warlord's quite rea-sonable demands for restitution on your behalf. That's when the Al-deman offered up four carts of lumber . . . but insisted we hurry on our way to destroy the bandits today."

"And *that* was when my dear brother delivered the other blow to their outlander egos," Kenyen stated, joining the two of them. He loaded another makeshift birdcage into the wagon, ignoring the way its two occupants quacked and fluttered their wings, upset at being relocated.

"Oh?" Tava asked, turning to face him.

Kenyen grinned. "You see, we had *already* encountered the bandits in question just a few days ago. In fact, we had been hired by another village to take care of them. That was where we got the Truth Stone he was using yesterday, from the scribe's bag we found among their loot. He used the Stone to prove their bandit problem had been taken care of . . . and by the wording of the contract, there was nothing in it stipulating we had to kill them *after* these outlanders handed over all the requested goods. With that knife still stuck in his back, not seeming to bother him, Kodan was a living reminder that they didn't dare protest."

"He *was* injured," Manolo stressed, reassuring Tava. "Wounds give us the same level of pain as anyone else, the same bruising and tears and trauma to the flesh. It's just that shapeshifters can heal ourselves by shifting that flesh whole."

"Those who are weak, with only a few shapes to their name like Torei," Kenyen informed her, "the healing shifts can take a day or two just to process the wound. The flesh heals more and more with each shift, which is why Torei isn't limping from the leg wound he took during the bandit fight a few days back—but it does take a great deal of energy and strength for Torei to shift his wounds whole. Someone like my brother . . ." Kenyen paused and shrugged. "Well, he merely needs to eat and rest for a while."

"Once everything is packed, we'll be heading out, so you'll want to take care of any last-moment needs before then," Manolo told her, lifting his chin at the refreshing hut. He ignored her blush at the implications, continuing by nodding at the oversized badgers in the vegetable garden off to the side. "We think we can get most of the roots onto the wagons without stressing the horses too much. The more food you can contribute to the Family upon your arrival, the more welcome your addition will be. Most worldly goods are easily shared, after all, whereas food cannot be, once eaten. Or at least, it shouldn't be."

His dry-voiced jest made Tava giggle, though she quickly muffled it out of habit, biting her lower lip.

"Since you haven't traveled with the Shifterai before, I should tell you a few things, so you'll know what to expect," Manolo added, gesturing for her to move out of the way as someone else approached with a caged chicken. Kenyen eyed the two of them, but at a gesture from the older shifter, he sighed and moved off to fetch something else to load onto the wagons. "When we travel, we travel from an hour after dawn until an hour before sunset, though we do stop to rest the horses and use the bushes a couple times, plus a pause for the midday meal.

"We usually set up a single tent for all of us to sleep in, save those who stand watch for a few hours in turn. Since we have so many goods, and of such value, Kodan has decided that we will put you in the trader's wagon, which will be yours alone to use from sundown to sunup. That is, once he's up and around, we'll move your bedding into that wagon for you to use and shift most of the goods that were in there into your wagon instead. The rest of us will shift shape and sleep around the other carts, to make it all the more difficult for anyone to attack the encampment, or attempt to pilfer anything," he told her. "Shifterai custom for traveling is very strict; when the sun sets, we're not allowed to be in the same enclosed space as you. Normally we would give you the tent to sleep in each night, but it's a very large space for just one person, and the trader's wagon is entirely enclosed, so all of us have agreed it should suffice."

Taken aback, Tava blinked at him. "The entire tent, just for myself?"

"Shifterai Law is very strict about how outlander women are welcomed into the Clans and Families," Manolo explained. "You are to be treated as a maiden for the whole of the trip—even if you came to us as a Centarai woman already married to a shapeshifter cross-kin, you would be expected to spend the entire journey into the Kingdom as a maiden and spend your first ten days with the priestesses before returning to your husband. If you had one. Otherwise you would be sent to one of the maiden's *geomes*.

"The *geome* is the special kind of tent we build," he said, answering her unspoken confusion. "It's round instead of square or wedge-shaped like most tents, and has a dome-shaped roof, which helps it stand up to the strong winds that can sometimes race across the Plains. The walls and roof are also made from oiled canvas and felted wool, so it stays cool in the summer and warm in the spring and fall—if a storm comes along, you will see for yourself how strong and sturdy it is. We'll put it up if it rains so that we can have a dry place to sleep."

His description sounded something like what her mother's captors had used, though they had also used wedge-tents as well as rounded ones, mainly for the members of Family Mongrel with the lowest status. But she couldn't picture it in her mind, other than something low and bulging at the top, and couldn't see how that could possibly be strong.

"Anyway," Manolo continued, "since we will have so much to take back with us, it is unlikely we'll stop anywhere else for one last commission. That, and we are far enough from the Family that we will want to make it back in time to rest for a little bit, before heading for the City to help with the final harvests and the task of settling into our winter homes."

"The City? Winter homes?" Tava asked, wondering why her mother's book had never mentioned anything of the sort. "I thought your people lived in tents and caves all year round."

The look the black-haired shifter gave her was a bemused one. "Hardly. Winter on the Plains is nothing to trifle with. Our *geomes* may be sturdy and can withstand a few storms, but like anyone else, we'd rather have stout wood and stone to shelter us from the snow and wind. We leave the City in the spring to graze our flocks on the rich grasses of the Plains and return each autumn to the City to take shelter.

"And, once every four to five years, we take our turns farming the fields and tending the orchards maintained by each Clan. Last year was Family Tiger's turn to stay on the farms. This year, it's

Family Lion's," he told her. "Which is a good thing, since barring bad weather, they're large enough in numbers to sow up to five times the fields that Family Tiger can, and cut as much hay. Everyone tries to get back in time to help with the harvest, and we usually stay for the earliest plantings, but not the interim ones. When we have a farm-year—Family Tiger—the Clan uses up most of the stores not set aside for planting, because we can't plant as much as the other Families. But that isn't a bad thing, for they do need to be used up."

Tava stared at him, wondering at how much information he was freely giving her. Without being asked, let alone acting as if her curiosity was bothersome to answer. Manolo lifted his hand and patted her upper arm.

"You'll learn. You'll have a whole year to learn, and hopefully a whole lifetime, too. If you want something to do, you can help Deian over there in the field, the one carrying the roots to the wagons," Manolo said, pointing at the covered vehicle in question. "Once Kodan leaves the trader's wagon, you can go there and settle your things however you may like. Mind you keep it tidy, though, since no one else will do it for you. Anything inside its four walls will be considered a part of maiden's territory, just like it is for the wagons the maidens travel in when we move from one pasture to the next on the Plains."

"From one pasture to the next?" Tava repeated, feeling stupid. "Aren't the Plains by definition one big pasture? A giant grassland?"

The smile he gave her was a wry, indulgent one. "Grass grows in abundance, yes, but *water* does not. 'Pasture' refers specifically to those areas of grass directly around the streams, ponds, wells, and cisterns scattered across the Plains. You will see what that means once we get up there. Now go on, either be useful or be restful—I suggest you enjoy the rest while you can. Once you've passed through your ten days of instruction with the priestesses, you'll be expected to become a part of life in a Shifterai Family and do your share.

"As I said, we'll probably head for the City in time to help with the last of Clan Cat's harvests shortly after we rejoin the rest of Family Tiger. No one rests at that point until all the beasts and bushels are settled to wait for winter. But once they *are* settled, the Waiting for Winter festival will begin."

Patting her once more on the shoulder, Manolo gave Tava a little push in the general direction of both wagon and field, leaving the choice up to her as to which to choose. Not accustomed to being all that idle, and not wanting to wander aimlessly through the emptied house and the no doubt emptied barn, Tava headed for the field. Her second-best festival dress wasn't one she would have chosen to wear for hauling beets, but it was better than just sitting in the back of a wagon with her books packed away and nothing else to occupy her mind until it was time to leave.

FIVE

◦⸰✣⸰◦

She kept peering at his back. There had been a little bit of teasing from the other men when he had emerged from the trader wagon only to climb up onto its bench and take up the reins, but Kodan had endured it stoically. What he wanted—or rather, needed— was enough time to begin his campaign of seducing Tava Ell Var into accepting her heritage, her need to live with her people on the Shifting Plains. But first, he had to break the silence between them. The way she kept leaning back and twisting a little, sneaking peeks at his back, gave him an opening.

"I take it you heard what happened?" he asked when she did it for the tenth or so time.

She quickly faced forward, hands in her lap, and nodded.

Kodan wondered if she would make some comment, or ask a question. When she didn't, he wondered why not. A Shifterai woman might have known he would recover from the wound since it hadn't killed him instantly, but she also would have asked questions, or at least given her opinion. *But that is how my people are raised,* he realized. *It's not just Shifterai ways she has to learn; I have to learn something of the people who raised her, the Mornai, to know better how to deal with her. More than the basics one needs to know for trading among them without giving insult or slight . . . at least, in a normal village.*

"I was very angry last night," he confessed, making her glance at him. "But I calmed myself down and reminded myself to think before I acted. The Shifterai tend to be a bit more passionate than the River folk. Possibly because, in shaping ourselves as beasts, echoing and copying them to blend in with nature, we learn the instincts and impulses of those beasts. For my own people, what that boy did would be understandable; he was upset, and he attacked on impulse."

That got a reaction from the young woman at his side. She gasped softly. *"Understandable?"*

"Understanding is *not* the same as forgiving," Kodan reminded her. "But it seemed to me the Alders were more shocked by him attacking me in public, than by him attacking at all. Both of our cultures frown upon attacking someone from behind, of course, but the other differences are still there. Perhaps you could enlighten me on why this is so?"

"Mornai men are supposed to exhibit self-control, in public. To be . . . figures of authority and to be worthy of being a figure of authority," she explained.

"And the women, in public?" he asked her, guiding the enclosed wagon up the switchback road that would take them up toward the Plains. The road was rutted more from weather than from use, and the late trader's cart wasn't sprung like a Plains cart; it rattled uncomfortably over the lumps of earth and rock.

"Women are to be obedient. And quiet."

Kodan glanced at her, amused. "Now, why do I get the feeling that you are inclined toward neither of those things?"

She blushed and ducked her head.

"Let me tell you about the Shifterai way," he said, still smiling.

"Because I think you will need time to get over the shock before actually experiencing it. We are *not* the Mornai. I suspect we are a lot less serious and sober than the Valley folk you're used to seeing. *All* of us have opinions, both men and women. And the women in particular like to air theirs. Since half our population are shape-shifters, with the ability to increase muscle strength, grow claws, or sharpen teeth, our *physical* self-control is very important. But in their wisdom, our ancestors knew that our inner energy had to be expressed somehow.

"So we tend to be vocal. Exaggeration and excess are discouraged, of course, since that leads to the temptation of acting physically as well as verbally. And talking just to hear your own voice is considered an annoyance just as it would be in any kingdom," he added, guiding the mares pulling the brightly painted wagon carefully around the next bend in the road. "But it is more unusual for a Shifterai to keep quiet than it is for them to speak. Man *or* woman. Since you didn't grow up among my people, I thought you should know this. You will *want* to ask a lot of questions, and not hesitate to ask them. Provided the person you are asking is not overly busy, of course. Common sense is highly valued, on the Plains."

He realized after both of them stayed silent for several seconds that his last comment sounded like an end to the conversation between them. Before he could think of something else to say, she ventured a question.

"Was the wound a . . . a bad one?"

"If I weren't a *multerai*, yes, it would have been bad." His back itched at the memory, though the flesh itself had healed. His ribs and muscles were still tender, since the Mornai youth had struck with enough force to break bone, but the wound itself was gone. "It might have been fatal for a non-shifter, too, since I did get a little blood in my lungs. But I have plenty of experience shifting my wounds in the middle of battle. Part of our training in learning to use our power is learning how to heal our injuries. We start with little ones, little cuts on our hands and arms, and all of it carefully supervised so that the weakest among us are not injured beyond our capacity to shift away."

"Oh." She stared down at her hands, as if contemplating deliberately injuring them to learn such a skill.

It was the best opening he would have. A quick glance showed the other wagons strung out along the tree-lined road, and the outriders picking their way through the underbrush far enough away to give the two of them an illusion of privacy. Not visual privacy, but enough distance to let them have a private conversation. Provided he kept his voice low, just in case anyone was straining with shapeshifted hearing to listen to the two of them.

"Regarding what happened the other day . . . I know it was you."

She jumped and stared at him, her green eyes wide.

"You do not know our people, and you do not know our ways. Until you come to understand us a lot better . . . I suggest you keep it a secret," Kodan told Tava, glancing at her. She continued to stare at him. "I tend to think more than my fellow Shifterai and have given this some consideration. I do not think the others will *think* about your situation. Even though they know you are coming among us as an adopted outlander, they will react as if you were born and raised on the Plains, which you clearly weren't.

"Because you weren't born among us and do not understand our ways, their reactions might confuse, alarm, or even frighten you— when that is *not* our intent," he quickly reassured her, seeing her biting her lower lip, visibly worried. "My advice is to keep your secrets to yourself at least for now, but to open up your mind to who and what we really are. Learning the difference between what happened to your mother versus the truth of a woman's life on the Plains is too important for anyone to confuse you with too many expectations and too much pressure applied to you too soon.

"Which leads me to the most important piece of information you need to know, and need to get set into your head as firmly as possible," Kodan continued, speaking quietly as one of the outrunners padded closer to the wagon to avoid a clump of vine-choked trees. "I do not know what the wedding customs are down in the Valley, but up on the Plains . . . a woman does not stand in front of an open fire and hold out her hand to any man standing across from her. Don't do it. Not until you're absolutely sure you want to marry that man."

She stiffened, her cheeks flushing, then paling. The brown dress she wore didn't flatter her coloring when she did that. "I *know*. That's how my mother was 'claimed' by the shapeshifter who won her as his war prize. I'll not let *any* man drag me through the flames. Like I said, *I'm* not my mother. *I'll* fight back."

Drag you through the . . . what? Kodan stared at her, appalled. The whickering of one of the mares warned him he had to pay attention to his driving, and he carefully guided horses and vehicle away from the bushes lining the curving road.

"Whatever your mother endured, *that* is not the way of the Plains, I can assure you. In fact, the more I learn about these curs, the more I hope they're long dead. And I'll make sure the Councils start looking for any sign of them, to make *sure* they're long dead. Or if they're not, to send them rapidly in that direction." Taking a moment to compose his thoughts, Kodan continued his explanations. "Because so many of our men are shapeshifters, taking the forms of beasts on the land, in the rivers, and through the skies, it is said that we tend three of the four elements, earth, water, and air. But since our women tend to our homes and our hearths, it is said that they are the keepers of the fourth element, fire.

"If a man wishes to court a maiden, he must be strong enough to brave the fourth element. It is the *man* who leaps through the flame to a woman. *Not* the other way around," Kodan emphasized. "But he is only supposed to do so when she holds out her hand to him, with some form of fire between them bigger than a candle or a torch, and witnesses to see it happening. Only then is it considered a true marriage.

"For this reason, our women are taught to hold their hands out to the side, or to walk around the firepit, the hearth, or the brazier-pan, before handing something to a man, or accepting it from him. And a man is taught to also walk around a fire before handing something to a woman—if *she* drags *him* through the flames to her, it is as shameful and invalid as it would be for a man to drag a woman to his side of the coals," he instructed her. "So be very, very careful that you do not hold out your hand to any man near a fire that can be leaped or crossed."

"Your brother . . . um . . ." She fell silent a long moment. Kodan waited patiently, until Tava finally asked, "Your brother suggested that *you* were going to court me. But . . . if this is so, you're saying I *shouldn't* hold out my hand to anyone, including you?"

"Not until you understand us. And *not* if you're not interested in me. Which you couldn't possibly be, just yet, since you don't really know me yet," he added honestly. "You *are* pretty, and you have an inner fire that I suspect has been smothered by life down in the Valley. You've shown your intelligence as well as your spirit, and I admire both in a woman. Most of us do. But while I admire you, I have also been trained to be practical, and until you understand who we really are, shedding the misconceptions wrought by your mother's terrible ordeal . . . you really shouldn't choose *any* of us. You need to know your own mind first, and you need to know our culture, so you'll know what to expect if you do wish to choose one of us as your mate.

"So ask as many questions as you like. Just keep certain subjects quiet, so that you aren't overwhelmed by expectations you do not yet understand. Because of your mother's ordeal, you'll probably misunderstand what those expectations are and misinterpret how the others would act toward you," he said. "Keep the others ignorant for now. You'll have a lot more time to explore and absorb Shifterai culture that way, and be able to do it at your own pace."

"You say this as if you expect the others to . . . to pressure me somehow, with what I can do," she muttered. "But what about you? Why shouldn't I fear you, since you know?"

Kodan made sure they were on a straight stretch of the road before giving her a long, pointed look. "Because you think you have to fear me, simply because I know. I told you; I think things through more than the average Shifterai—it is expected of a *multerai* to think broader thoughts, to think well into the future, and to consider all options carefully.

"*Multerai* are often made Clan and Family leaders and are expected to be worthy of the responsibility. We are expected to think before we act and speak. I *know* you don't understand us, and until you do, I will do my best to give you the time you need to absorb the truth of our people. I cannot say the same for the others, so it is best if you do not tell them just yet."

She absorbed his words in silence for a while, long enough for the trees to thin and open into a bush-strewn meadow. Up at the head of the caravan, Kodan's father raised his hand, swirled his fingers into a fist, then flicked them to the left and the right. The others stopped their wagons, so he did the same.

"I don't know if you saw it or not, but my father—Siinar—just signaled for a bush break," Kodan told the woman at his side. "This is one of those things our people don't think about, since they learn it as very young children. What it means is, when we are traveling, the men go into the bushes on the left to, well, *use* the bushes, and women go off to the right."

Tava glanced off to her right and frowned. "But, there are men to the right. Or at least some tigers."

"The outriders always stay out there. It's to ensure no wild beast stumbles upon us unawares. But you'll note their attention is turned outward, so if you need to use the bushes, you will still have some privacy," he told her. When she hesitated, Kodan added, "You'd better get used to it now. Until we reach the Family camp, there are no refreshing tents already set up, and no pits will be dug. I'll trust you know which of the local leaves are safe to use.

"Once we get up on the Plains, I'll show you which kind of grass is best for cleaning oneself. You don't want to pick the wrong kind. Sawgrass cuts all but the most callused of fingers, and you *really* do not want to get it near anything delicate. Even a shapeshifter isn't immune to sawgrass cuts, if we're not careful *and* mindful of what we're doing."

That made her giggle. She quickly raised her hand, muffling and subduing it, but her cheeks blushed and her eyes gleamed with humor. In that moment, Kodan realized his flattering words from earlier were indeed true: She *was* quite pretty. The dress was baggy and ugly, but the woman wearing it was lovely.

So far, he had seen her angry, scared, grieving, wary, and curious. Now he wondered what she would look like if and when she laughed heartily. Setting aside that thought for now, he nudged her with his elbow. "Go on. Use the bushes if you need to. I'll be using the ones to the left myself."

"Um . . . avoid the low vine-plant with narrow, four-lobed leaves and a red vein down the center of each lobe," Tava told him, biting her lower lip for a moment. Kodan didn't know whether she was suppressing a smile or not, before she added with another hint of humor, "Your sawgrass might be preferable, since you could shift-heal the cut, but the itchy oils of the redvein leaf are another matter entirely."

"I'll keep that in mind, and warn the others," Kodan acknowledged mock-gravely, pleased she had unfurled from her fears at least enough to advise him against potential woodlands harm.

Two days later, just as they were reaching the edge of the Plains, Tava had her first true glimpse of the Shifterai way of life. Or rather, her first glimpse of the Shifterai version of their summer homes, the mysterious *geome*. A light sprinkle had begun about mid-afternoon, picking up into a misting drizzle. Consulting with his father and Manolo, the two eldest men of the warband, Kodan had called for an early halt. The rain looked like it would be falling in earnest soon, and that meant setting up the tent for those not on patrol.

Sitting under the scant shelter of the forward-projecting roof of the trader's wagon, Tava watched its assembly, fascinated and yet puzzled. Rather than starting with a vertical pole at each end and a line pegged across them, forming the roof ridge, the start of the Shifterai tent was a series of latticework fences. Long staves had been drilled and fastened together by braided cord, making the framework both flexible and expandable.

There were five such sections taken from one of the wagons the Shifterai had brought with them, and they were assembled inside a circle marked by a long loop of knotted rope. More thongs lashed the fence together, save for one spot that was left empty. That spot was closed by an empty, rectangular frame and yet more strong, grass-woven cord.

It looked more like a goat pen to her, or maybe a place to put the ducks that were waddling around, eating the grass of the meadow the warband had chosen for the night. Not like the makings of a tent. As she watched, short, shallow arcs of wood were brought out of the wagon, their tongue-and-groove ends slotted together and pegged in place as soon as they were passed over the fence wall from one man to the next.

There were a series of slots carved into the giant assembled ring on the upper and the outer edge. A much smaller ring had similar holes, though it was attached to what looked like the bones of a conical-roofed doll's house attached to it, carved from carefully joined pieces of wood. It was brought into the center and held thigh-high by one of the shifters, while two others started slotting short staves between the innermost ring and the outer wooden circle. Torei—the one holding the little ring—finally let go and stepped away from

the smaller, hat-topped ring, allowing the others to finish filling in
the spokes of the odd wooden cone. As they did so, Tava saw the
shifter who had milked her goats, introduced during their travels as
Tedro, slipping the cord-woven handles of net bags onto four of the
spokes, spaced evenly around the ring.

Four long poles and three bundles of longer staves were brought
into the fence, distracting her from wondering what the nets were
for. Four odd pieces of wrought iron were brought in as well. They
were mostly straight and vertical, save for where they swirled in a
horizontal loop twice down their length, one near one end and the
other just past the halfway mark. The far end was pointed. Like the
net bags, she didn't know what these were meant for; all Tava could
do was watch and wonder.

Three of the Shifterai picked up the cone-braced ring. They
stretched themselves up, their belts and tunics rising up with their
torsos until the drawstring waistbands of their gathered pants hung
well below the hems of their shirts. Four more moved in to place the
poles, which had Y-shaped ends, under the ring. Tava thought it was
for support, until she saw the others who were standing on the outside picking up the longer staves and slotting them into the holes on
the outer edge of the large wooden ring, like they had done for the
shorter staves forming the cone.

These staves all had loops on their outer ends, which were hooked
over the crossed tops of the lattice fence. As soon as about five of the
staves were in place, stabilizing the ring, the men holding the forked
poles in place moved them out of the way, and Tedro quickly went
from spot to spot, hammering the looped iron into the ground. The
poles were dropped down through the double loops, the ring lifted
just a little higher by the shapeshifters still holding on to it, and settled
into the forks in the poles. The loops on the ends of the staves were
adjusted, and more staves were slotted into place, until the outer edge
of the ring resembled the inner one. These staves were set at a steeper
slope than the inner ones, though, forming a sort of angular dome.

Now the tent tarps came out and were dragged up and over the slanting roof sides. First came oiled canvas ones, three of them angled to drape over most of the roof and down the sides, overlapping, then thick felt, and then a final layer of canvas. These were all lashed around the sides by broad woven bands fastened to the frame. The final layer of canvas had been painted with animal shapes, worn from being handled and somewhat faded from the sun, but the predominant pattern was easy enough to see, for most of the animals depicted were tigers, many of them sitting on their haunches with their right hind legs stretched out in some way, each extended paw outlined by a light blue diamond.

Over the tiny, solid cone at the very top, a double-sided stripe-cat hide was pulled into place, attached by ropes that fastened to the bands looped around the walls. Two of the five ropes were pulled back, leaving just enough room for air to escape through the gap between the tiny cone-roof and the small ring supporting its struts. Those struts, not much longer than half her forearm, were just high enough to let air flow in. *Or rather*, Tava realized, *just high enough to let smoke out. That cone-tip is broad enough, it should keep all but the worst rain out of the tent. How very clever . . . and how very* large *the whole thing is, now that it's assembled.*

All of it had filled the bed of one wagon to the top of its rails. Tava thought it was a bit much to take when traveling, when a wedge-tent was far more compact and thus more practical in her opinion. It would have also taken less time to erect, though the practiced movements of the shapeshifters and the sheer number of helping hands had assembled the whole thing almost as fast as she and her father had ever set up their own travel tent . . . which was just big enough for the two of them. Not this massive structure that was at least as big as her whole house, if not bigger.

It was a good thing the *geome* was finally up and ready, she realized, squinting up at the overcast sky. The light rain had thickened. The droplets were still smallish, but far more of them were falling now, in the steady, earnest way that said it would most likely rain all night, if not longer.

Looking away from the *geome*, Tava saw Kenyen and Torei chasing down her ducks and hens, catching them and putting them back into their makeshift cages, which they tucked under the wagons for shelter. Enough meadow grass was available through the spaces in the cages that they should be able to forage. Even the horses were given some protection; felted blankets had been tied over the backs of the Shifterai ones, with makeshift blankets tied around the Mornai horses. Only her goats were left bare, but then, a goat would chew on just about anything in the often futile hope it would turn out to be something tasty.

Siinar approached her, holding up his hands to help her down. "Come; by custom, you are allowed into our tent until supper is finished."

Seeing a complicated bit of ironwork that looked like some sort of brazier and stand carried into the *geome*, Tava let him help her down from the wagon bench. The thought of being somewhere warm and dry appealed to her.

"After you have eaten and drunk your last," Kodan's father explained to her, "you must retire to your wagon for the rest of the night, since on the days when the sun cannot be seen, the end of supper is considered sundown for all the maidens out on the Plains. In the City, the customs are a little different for after supper or after sunset, but the priestesses will explain these things to you once we reach the Family."

He gestured for her to enter the doorway of the tent, and Tava realized it *was* a doorway. At some point in her distraction, someone had brought out a door-panel and hung it on the rectangular frame. It even had a latch with a pull-string, though it stood open at the moment. Once inside, the thickness of the layered walls was evident; she could hear the rain pattering on the outermost canvas, but it was muted and muffled by the intervening felt. The sounds of the men doing mysterious things with the brazier and with the net bags hanging from the ceiling, of them bringing in ground tarps and blankets from the other wagons, were all louder than the rain itself.

On the sloped sides of her father's wedge tent, the sound of rain falling was sharp and noisy, making conversation difficult. But her father had always planned for such things and usually brought along a book or two. Usually it was something small, such as a book of stories or of poetry, something that could be tucked into a saddlebag without much trouble

Tava couldn't remember which book her father had taken with him on his ill-fated, final journey, nor had she been in any shape to notice which one was missing when these Shifterai had packed up her home three days ago. She longed for a book now, as she had the last two nights, but they were packed under too many of her things in the other wagons to be easily extracted. Or at least, she would long for one once she had to retire to the trader's wagon.

The wagon had clever oil lamps fixed to its walls on the inside, but nothing worth reading other than the late trader's ledger of transactions as he had traveled up and down the length of the Valley. Dry reading suitable for putting one to sleep, but Tava was tired of sleeping once night fell.

A sudden, bright light startled her. Blinking, Tava squinted and looked up. A miniature white moon hung in one of the nets, glowing brightly. Stunned, she watched as Tedro, body stretched so that he could reach the net, tucked another translucent ball into the next loosely braided cord bag. The bag had a bone-carved hook, which he fastened in place, safely caging the head-sized orb. A sharp thump of his knuckles set the bag and ball swaying and brightened it into abrupt, glowing life.

Oh! Those are lightglobes! Eyes wide, Tava stared at the orbs. She had read about them in some of her father's books, but had never seen one before.

They were mage-made Artifacts, crafted by spellcasters from glass and mysterious, exotic ingredients, which the books hinted came from far-flung lands. Because of that distance, they were also incredibly expensive to own. Varamon had once told her that he knew of several houses in the larger cities of Mornai that had lightglobes, and that he himself had once owned a lightglobe in his youth, a gift from a very pleased city patron, but that he had sold it to make enough money to buy himself a farm in the village of Five Springs.

An oil lamp, made from brass and glass, could last its owner for decades, provided it was refilled on a frequent basis and the wicks occasionally replaced. River eels had a good oil for that, once their abdominal fat was rendered—though the smoke smelled like a mixture of burned fish and mud if the wick wasn't kept trimmed every few hours. It also took the oil rendered from twenty eels to fill just one of her father's four lamps.

Lightglobes lasted only a handful of years by comparison, but they never had to be refilled. The light they produced could also be adjusted. A soft tap produced a soft glow, while a harder rap brightened the globe. Two swift, sharp taps shut it off, conserving its magic. That these Shifterai had not one or two, but *four* of them—the last of which the shifter Tedro hooked into place and rapped into life before shrinking back down to his normal size and shape—spoke of just how wealthy these men were.

Someone touched her elbow. It was Torei, the stutterer. He gestured toward a canvas-slung chair, which had been assembled to one side of the brazier, indicating she should take it. No sooner did she sit in it, enjoying the comfort of the fabric seat and back as they bent under her weight, than someone else flicked a blanket over her legs, warding off some of the rain-brought chill in the air.

More light danced up, this time from the flames in the brazier pan. The two men tending to it added more slivers of wood and twists of dried grass, then increasingly thick sticks. The heat was nice, but they didn't add larger chunks of wood, as Tava might have done. Instead, they continued to add thin branches. The faint hiss of water sizzling told her why; thin branches were more likely to dry out and burn better than thicker, wetter limbs. Not until they had a full bed of bright-glowing embers did they add thick rounds of fallen branches to the edges of the fire. It cut off some of the heat from radiating into the rest of the tent, but concentrated that heat into the center of the broad iron pan.

They also fixed a metal grille over the brazier, supporting it on forked iron spikes. Someone else brought in another strange, wrought iron contraption, a pole with a zigzag near one end and tiny figure eight loops at the other. The man stepped on the horizontal part of the zigzag, embedding the pole in the ground. Dangling from his elbow were a pair of metal loops where the ends met and then stuck down perpendicularly like little tails. The little tails fitted into the figure eight loops, and someone else settled a pair of bowls into the broad hoops, then poured a bucket of water into both pans.

A strangely shaped bit of metal sort of like an arm was added between the two bowls, hooked and twisted into place somehow. The small hoop at its end was fitted with what looked like a pot of softsoap, while the arm itself was draped with a bit of linen, forming an instant, portable washstand. The last two nights, they had camped by streams and simply dipped their hands in the running waters to clean their fingers. Tava wanted to ask questions about the washstand and the other clever aspects of their constantly camping lifestyle, but there were male bodies moving all around the tent, still doing things to make it a temporary home. She wasn't sure if she had been gestured into this chair for her comfort, or simply so that it would get her out of their way.

Someone stretched up and hung a trio of sheets, stretching the middle sheet between two of the four poles and the two outer ones from the poles to the lattice walls. It formed a sort of room, behind which four of the twenty men in the warband vanished, carrying what looked like their bedrolls. Siinar came over then, pointing at the curtain as he stooped to murmur in Tava's ear.

"Those men have the middle-night watch. They will go to sleep now and will eat when they rise near midnight, scout and guard the camp for a few hours, then wake the early watch and return to their beds. Out of respect, we will try not to be too loud tonight, but as we have put up the tent, we will probably hold some entertainment while supper cooks. Since you likely do not know much about Father Sky and Mother Earth, our Patron God and Goddess, I will suggest the others choose the stories of how the world was created by Their love, and how Sister Moon and her two Brothers were created."

"*Two* Brothers?" Tava asked, confused. "But there are only two moons in the sky, not three. Just Brother Moon and Sister Moon, no less and no more."

Smiling, Siinar patted her shoulder. "A lot of people have forgotten there was once a second Brother Moon, but we have not. The story was found in one of the sub-basement ruins of the old Palace shortly after we reclaimed the City, following the Shattering of Aiar. While we do not worship Brother and Sister Moon directly, we do worship Their Parents, Mother Earth and Father Sky, so we do our best to remember *all* of Their Children as a way to further honor Them.

"Kodan," Siinar called out, catching the attention of his elder son, who was just entering the tent. "Come and tell Tava the story of the Murder of Elder Brother."

Caught with a bag of flour in his hands, Kodan looked around for a moment, then passed it to his brother, who gave him a dirty look. Ignoring it, Kodan dusted off his palms and approached Tava. "The tale of the Murder of Elder Brother?"

Siinar nodded. "She knows nothing of our legends, and you tell that one very well."

Setting the bag down on a table one of the others had assembled, Kenyen snorted audibly at that.

Kodan rolled his eyes at his brother. "My father exaggerates . . . but I will do my best."

Detouring, he fetched a rolled-up bundle of blankets, untied them, and arranged them as a sort of folded-up cushion. A gesture got Tava to stand, and he adjusted the chair so that it faced the cushion instead of the brazier. Once she had settled herself again, blanket re-draped across her lap, he dropped cross-legged onto his impromptu seat and began, giving Tava his full attention.

"As we have read, and so we were told," Kodan began, "a very, *very* long time ago, there were three moons in the sky. Elder Brother, Younger Brother, and Sister Moon. The one we know of as Brother Moon was Younger Brother Moon, and he was big and new and bright. Sister Moon was born the middle child, and was middle-sized, and middle-bright.

"Elder Brother was, strangely enough, the smallest and dimmest of the three," he explained, continuing. "This was because the astronomancers had determined that Elder Brother, being the eldest and given the most freedom, had roamed the farthest from Mother Earth, deep into the realm of Father Sky. And just as someone in the distance gets smaller the farther away they are, so it was with Elder Brother. The three siblings sailed through the heavens, with Elder Brother at a stately pace, surveying the skies once a year, Sister Moon four times a year, and Younger Brother twelve times a year."

"That's because the youngest child usually has a lot of energy to spend," Siinar interjected, pulling over another bedroll and turning it into a mat. "Just ask any parent which of their children is the most exhausting to tend."

"Yes, but now we must turn our attention from the Moons to the land of Fortuna," Kodan said. "You may or may not know about Fortuna, but it is the oldest continually ruled Empire in all the world. Even today, it is still going strong, at least according to all that we have heard from the various people we trade with. But the time of this story was many, many years ago. Maybe as many as four thousand years, maybe a little more."

"Four thousand?" Tava asked, bemused by the number of years Kodan was claiming.

"Around that many," Siinar confirmed for his son, nodding. "This was shortly after the First Convocation of the Gods, which took place a very long time before Aiar ever hosted it, let alone lost it. This, the scholars of Shifting City have managed to piece together over the years. When Aiar Shattered a hundred and eighty years ago, our ancestors lost most of what they used to know, and we have been slowly rebuilding that knowledge ever since."

Kodan cleared his throat, recapturing Tava's attention. "This is not a story about the Convocation. Not just yet. The story is set in Fortuna, yes, but it is about a group of mages, who called themselves the Dimensionars. They were exploring how to transport people instantly from one region to another. This was long before glass mirrors were invented, and so their experiments in creating Gates were not very controlled, and no one had yet figured out how to make the Portals that led to the destruction of most of Aiar."

"I know about the Portals being destroyed, laying waste to the lands around them for miles, and contributing their damage and chaos to the Shattering of Aiar," Tava said. She shivered a little. "I'd hate to think how much damage was wrought back when they were still figuring out such things."

"Not as much as you might think," Kodan pointed out, "since they clearly continued in their experiments . . . but I am told there is a difference between opening a tunnel between two points in this world and opening a tunnel between this world and the other universes that are out there. As you may know, we live in the world of Life. It is surrounded by the Dark, where the dead roam between the mortal realm and the immortal one, and beyond the Dark is the Afterlife, the home of the Gods. *But*, that is only in one direction.

"Now, I am not a mage, and what few we do have on the Plains are mage-priests, but from what I understand, there are as many different directions to open a Gate as there are directions in the world. To open one upward is to tap into the Dark, in the hopes of reaching the Afterlife. Only the Convocation of the Gods has ever managed that task," Kodan reminded her. "Opposite that direction, downward, opens a Gate to the Netherhells. To aim inward is to aim across the skin of Mother Earth, which is the kind of Gate you may have read about. And to aim outward is to tap into other universes with other worlds and skies and people of their own."

"A mage aims inward, to travel outward across the land?" Tava asked, confused by that idea.

Kodan shrugged expressively. "I am a shapeshifter, not a mage. This is just what I have been told."

"The directions are metaphysical, not physical," Siinar explained. "One does not literally dig down through the soil to get to the Netherhells. The only thing one finds when one digs down is earth, rock, and eventually magma at the hot heart of Mother Earth. And then one finds rock and earth and eventually the far side of the world, since we all know the world is a huge ball shaped by the hands of the Gods and set in the arms of the stars. From there, it flies around the heart of Father Sky every year, which is of course the sun."

"Am I telling this story, or are you?" Kodan challenged his father.

His tone was mild, but the look in his light brown eyes was pointed. Tava bit her lower lip, trying not to smile too obviously. Siinar lifted his hands, backing off from the tale.

"To continue," Kodan said, "these things are known today, but had not yet been discovered back then. And while the Dimensionars were careful as they could be in their experiments, other mages in a neighboring land had obtained some of their research and were not quite so cautious in following it. And *they* opened the Veil between this world and one of the Netherhells. This drew the attention of a powerful, clever demon-princess, who pretended to be the Goddess of this other realm. Through lies, trickery, and deceit, she managed to convince many of the people of this other land to worship her, and thus gained power in this realm. Enough power to act.

"Her intent was to destroy the other Gods and set herself up as the sole Patron of this world, to receive the faith of all the people and thus make herself into a terrible, unstoppable power," Kodan told Tava. "To do this, she used her mage-priests to open another hole in the Veil between worlds, this one set deep among the night stars, and launched a massive rock from her world to this one."

"It was a rock a thousand times bigger than the biggest boulder you may have ever seen," Siinar added.

Kodan gave his father a stern look at the interruption. Tava tried not to giggle, but some of it escaped as a soft snort. Between the noise of the rain on the tent roof and the sounds made by the men preparing what looked like biscuits, baked vegetables, and dried fish cooked in goat's milk, she hoped it hadn't been overheard. The dry look Kodan turned on her let her know her humor hadn't passed completely unnoticed, but he didn't seem angry at her mirth, unlike a Mornai man.

Sighing, he continued. "As I was saying, she caused a great, massive rock to be launched at the world. The astronomancers wrote in the records we found that, after painstaking observation, this giant boulder was set to aim straight at the heart of Fortuna and would land—or rather, crash catastrophically—in the middle of the great temple that hosted the Convocation of the Gods, just three days into the Convocation. Unfortunately . . . the astronomancers uncovered this news with less than a day to do anything about it. Mostly because the rock was obscured by a cloud of darkness, and they had been forced to track it as much by the way it blotted out the light of the stars at night as by any other means at their disposal.

"I must remind you at this point in the story that *no one* outside of her high priesthood knew that the Goddess Zundi had originally been a demon-princess from the Netherhells," Kodan told her, slashing his hand through the air. "In fact, she had grown so powerful in just the few years since her first appearance in this world, proclaiming herself a deity, and the start of the very next Convocation, that she managed to Manifest through the Gateway of Heaven during the Naming of the Gods."

"*Or* it could have been just an elaborate trick performed by her high priests," Siinar interjected. "No one actually knows."

"*Father,*" Kodan protested.

The gray-and-brown-haired shapeshifter shrugged eloquently. "I'm just saying, no one truly knows!"

"*Anyway,*" his eldest son stressed, returning his attention to Tava. "The usual homages were set aside by a hasty petition of all the priesthoods toward their Patrons to save the people of the world, and in particular the people of Fortuna, who would have been destroyed with as much certainty as the people of the capital of Aiar.

"Since the giant rock had been flung through the stars, it was determined that the three sibling Moons should catch it in a net of Their powers during the night, before it could get close enough to strike during the day. They would do this augmented by the energies of the other deities. The demoness Zundi, having been proclaimed the Goddess of Night, volunteered to track the rock's trajectory and guide the siblings in catching it, for it was dark and thus difficult to see in the depths of the sky.

"The only problem was, she used her powers to further obscure the rock from the astronomancers who were tracking it, and so she betrayed the Moon Gods as to the rock's exact location," Kodan said. "Equally unfortunate, the sibling Moons had to actually change Their paths and paces in the heavens to place themselves appropriately to cast Their net. And, rather than the rock missing the net and going on to smash into our planet . . . it smashed into Elder Brother instead, destroying the third moon. The only good that came from His death was that the rock itself was also destroyed by the impact.

"Younger Brother and Sister Moon scrambled to reshape Their net, catching most of the shards of Their slain sibling before those, too, could crash into the world and destroy it that way," Kodan told the raptly listening Tava. "Instead, They cast the pieces of Their sibling's corpse deep into the night, all the way into the Dark itself, since there was no way to repair the damage that had been done to

Elder Brother's physical, tangible anchor, that being the farthest-out moon."

"No doubt Zundi expected the worshippers of Elder Brother to falter and weaken, perhaps even for their kingdom to collapse, which bordered her own claimed lands. But the High Priestess of that land was said to not only have worshipped Elder Brother, but to have been in love with Him, too, and bound her soul to His, keeping Him alive for his people . . . after a fashion," Siinar amended. "He is the only Dead God in the whole pantheon of the world that we know about, and His high priestess is the only mortal made into a Goddess. His people's faith in both Him and His high priestess were so strong, she was made into a Goddess herself, since she had literally bound her life eternally to the existence of Elder Brother."

"It was this same high priestess who probed for the truth of the whole matter," Kodan continued, apparently giving up on quelling his father, though he did give his parent a somewhat annoyed look as he continued the tale. "It was she who discovered that Zundi was not a real goddess—an honest manifestation of the will and faith of her people—but was instead a power-thieving impostor from a Netherhell. And it was this same high priestess who uncovered the plot of Zundi and her followers to destroy the Gods by destroying the Convocation, with the intent to survive and proclaim herself High Goddess of the world by the right of having survived the cataclysm caused by her own secret attack.

"Once the Gods had dealt with her—destroying her powers, breaking her people's faith in her, and scattering her priesthood— they cast her back into her Netherhell and sealed the Veil. And with His people still worshipping Him firmly, and giving great honor unto His high priestess for her devotion to Him, the God of Elder Moon became the God of the Dead, and His priestess became the Goddess of Lost Souls . . . or so we have read, and so we were told," Kodan concluded.

Siinar wasn't the only man in the tent who clapped his hands as his son finished the tale, though all of them clapped softly, mindful of the men trying to sleep beyond the makeshift curtain. Enjoying the story, Tava joined them after only a moment of hesitation. It was more of a habit from the Mornai custom where women weren't supposed to draw undue attention to themselves, but when she patted her hands together, showing her pleasure in the tale, no one protested her actions. In fact, Kodan blushed a little, ducking his gaze.

"I liked that tale," she praised him, venturing to actually speak her opinion, as he had claimed Shifterai women were allowed to do. When neither he nor his father told her to be quiet, she added, "I've never heard anything like it before . . . but then, Five Springs doesn't have a lot of books. I think, now that my and my father's things are gone, if there are more than six books in the whole of the village, I would be surprised. Um . . ."

"Yes?" Siinar asked Tava when she hesitated.

"Do you know *where* my books are? At least some of them?" she asked, glancing between the two men. "This maiden's *geome* thing is, well . . . I don't mean to insult your customs, but . . ." At the encouraging look from father and son, she admitted, "It's boring. At night. There is only so much I can sleep at a stretch, and there's no one to talk to and nothing to do, and even if it's just one of my little books of poems, which I've read a hundred times before . . ."

Kodan's brows rose sharply, as if suddenly realizing something. "Ah. I see. Wait here."

Pushing to his feet, he left the tent, ducking out into the rain. Tava glanced at his father. Siinar shrugged.

"He's probably fetching one of your books. Or he might be fetching one of his own. I believe he brought three on this trip." The older Shifterai shook his head and *tsk*ed. "I don't know where Kodan got his bookishness from. All the children of the Plains are taught to read and to write, but his mother prefers to work with numbers over words, and I prefer to work with my hands, just like my other son. The boy brought only two changes of clothes, one of which you see today and the other of which now has a hole in the back, and yet I *know* he made room for at least three books in his saddlebags!"

Amused by such a strange yet clearly fatherly rant, Tava wondered at how different Siinar was from her own father. And at how similar Kodan was to Varamon. Her father would rather have read a book than done a more mundane task, such as washing their laundry. So would she. The only way Tava and her father had managed to keep such a neat home was by the trick Varamon had taught her, a trick he had learned in his own youth. By promising themselves a good read if they did a good and quick job with their chores, those chores got done. Usually first thing in the day, which meant their evenings were free for reading and for discussing whatever they read.

But traveling like this, there was nothing to read and nothing to do. She couldn't even discuss anything once the sun had set and she was packed off to the brightly painted hut-on-wheels that was the trader's wagon. And though the gray, rainy sky seen through the smallish gap in the roof was still somewhat light, she would have to retire to the wagon all too soon, with only the pattering of rain and the memory of her supper for company.

At least the fish soup simmering in the large kettle on the grill smelled good, as did the grass-wrapped roots baking in the embers of the brazier. Watching the men working to cook, she was puzzled by the long, ropy lumps of dough they were shaping. With a little fat and some of the milk from her goats, along with some salt and what looked like fresh-picked, minced herbs, they could have made the flatbread they had made previous times, but instead they picked up the heavily floured, thickened ropes of dough and tucked it around the base of the large pot, draping it over the mesh of the grill in three curving segments.

The men who had worked the dough, including Kenyen, washed their hands at the wrought iron stand, but only by dipping their hands into the one basin. From the other one, they carefully scooped up water with a dipper, pouring the liquid over their lathered fingers into the first pan. After the third man washed up in this manner, the dirty water was taken outside, where she heard it being tossed off into the meadow grass, and the pan brought back. The water from the second pan was poured into the emptied one, along with a bit more from a bucket to fill it up, and fresh, clean water was poured into the second pan to replace it.

They must do that to ensure they have clean rinse water each time, she decided, thinking about it. *It makes sense, since a little soap might drip from their lathered hands whenever they use the dipping cup. And of course they didn't lay any tarps over that corner of the ground, which means any water that splashes free will soak straight into the ground. It's also at the lowest point of the ground inside the tent, though they did pick the most even, bush-free patch of meadow they could find . . .*

Looking up, she studied the spokes of the tent. It was not unlike a house, though her house had planks over the rafters, making an attic-space for storage. Although it didn't have a fireplace, with that centermost, solid wooden cone sheltering the ventilation hole from the rain, the tent was warm and relatively smoke-free. The mid-ring was high enough that even the tallest of the shapeshifters didn't have to worry about banging his head on the lightglobes hanging in their woven bags, though the edges of the tent roof were a little short right next to the latticework.

Of course, it's possible that if they can make themselves taller, they can also make themselves shorter, she acknowledged, *and thus avoid hitting their heads on the costly Artifacts. I wonder how they support their torsos when they grow themselves that tall? Maybe a second spine for stability and strengh?*

The door opened, drawing her attention to the front of the *geome.* Kodan entered, his green tunic dark with rain, mostly across his broad shoulders. Held against his chest was a largish book, leather bound with a flap that could be tied shut. Bringing it to her, he checked it, brushed off a stray raindrop, and held it out to her.

"Here. This is a book on the plants of the Shifting Plains, what is poisonous, what is edible, and what is useful in other ways—it starts with the poisonous ones, so we can teach our children what to avoid, and goes all the way through to the seventeen kinds of grass and bush that can be made into cord, or even twisted into fuel for the fire, that sort of thing. The drawings are very good, and spell-copied straight from the original," Kodan said. "I brought it along to show to some herb-traders in one of the cities west of here, describing what we can grow in bulk for sale. I thought it would be useful as well as entertaining for you to read."

Pleased by his thoughtfulness, Tava smiled at him. Accepting the book, she cradled it in her lap. "Thank you. I will be very careful with your book."

"You are a scribe, after all," Kodan pointed out, smiling. "I have no fear on that matter."

The trio of cooks were busy stirring the soup, rotating the roots, and turning the crescents of half-cooked dough. The others—those not patrolling outside in the rain or asleep behind the curtains—brought their own blankets over, folding them into cushions. Tava found herself motioned to stand and turn her chair one more time, this time putting her back to the brazier so that she faced an audience of eight or nine men.

"T-Tell us a s-s-story of *your* peop-ple," Torei urged Tava, folding his legs and giving her an earnest, interested look. He braced his palms on the cushion between his crossed legs and leaned on his arms. "P-Pl-Please?"

Seeing so many men facing her, so many pairs of male eyes watching her, waiting for her to speak—*wanting* her to speak—was a very odd sensation. Mornai culture was such that if a woman wanted her opinion and thoughts shared, she either told them to her father, to her brother, or to her husband or son, who *might* share them with others, at his discretion. Only in the privacy of their home had Varamon encouraged his daughter to speak freely of her thoughts and opinions. Never mind ask her to tell stories.

Mind blank for a moment, she let her gaze fall to her lap. Tava saw the embroidered sleeves of her gown. It was a little dusty, though she had done her best to brush away the dirt that came with plucking turnips and beets from the ground. Two of her three summer-weight dresses had been kept readily available, along with a warmer wool gown and her nightdress, leaving her little choice of what to wear each day. Not that she had a lot of clothes, but it did remind her of a story regarding the River Goddess.

"A long time ago, there was no summer, no winter, no autumn, and no spring. All the days were mild, the rain fell lightly, the winds blew softly, and the sun frequently traded places with the clouds during the day, as did the moons with the clouds during the night. And Morna—the River Goddess—had only one dress to wear. It was clean and clear if you looked at it close, allowing you to see straight through to the bottom of the river, but from a distance, it was like a blue and green mirror, reflecting the bank, the trees, and even the sky.

"But then one day, the Sun thought the clouds were hogging more of the sky than was their fair share, and so it chased the clouds back, shining bright and hot. The heat not only parched all of the animals; it also shrunk Morna's dress, until the gravel and mud of Her shorelines began to show. Morna rebuked the Sun," Tava told her odd, male audience, "saying it was not his place to touch Her clothes . . . and the Sun sulked and let the clouds come back.

"Now, the clouds were so joyful at no longer being burned out of the sky, they gathered so thickly and puffed up their sky-wool so large that they jostled and bumped into one another, until they jostled and bumped the rain right out of their wool and down onto the ground. It rained like this for several days, and as the land could hold only a little rain at any given time, most of that rain ran down to the river. In its eagerness to go downhill," Tava continued, "the rainwater grabbed at the fallen leaves and the soil, dragging it along until it poured mud and debris all over Morna's pretty dress. No longer was it clean and clear straight through to the riverbed, nor did it reflect as clearly as a mirror, and the rain itself roughened the smoothness of the now muddy brown fabric of Her gown until it couldn't even reflect the light of day without great effort.

"Upset with the ruining of Her dress, Morna rebuked the clouds next. The clouds, being many in number and proud of their collective might, rebuked Her in turn," she told the Shifterai men. "They rained more heavily, and She argued more strongly, until the men-clouds blew a strong wind that ruffled Her gown and chilled the air with their censure. They stole the warmth from Her gown, turning it gray and cloudy, and then stiffened the fabric straight into ice. Morna was trapped into stillness by the cold breath of the clouds, though She could still move and speak deep within Her dress. But She longed for Her freedom of movement and spoke prettily to the clouds, gentling their anger and agreeing with their claims of magnificence, until they were satisfied and scattered to find a place to rest.

"And when the sun came out, taking the place of the clouds, Morna spoke gently to him, too, coaxing him into forgiving her. The sun relented and shone brightly, softening Her cage and warming Her clothes until She flowed free again. Off in the distance, the clouds pouted and wept rain, that She should even speak with the one who had started the feud, but though the runoff from their wrung-out protest muddied Her gown once more, Morna patiently endured it, speaking gently to the clouds once again . . . and within a short while, the mud had either settled or flowed down to the sea at the hem of Her gown, and once more Her dress was bright and clear, and as beautiful as a mirror whenever it reflected the trees and the sky.

"This is the story of the River's four seasons," Tava explained. "The dress you see me wearing is the one I wore to the spring and autumn festivals; the brown is the mud that enriches our fields, and the blue and green zigzags represent the water running off the land. My dress for winter is gray, which is my best dress; it has snowflakes embroidered all over it. And my dress for summer—"

"—Is clear?" one of the men interjected hopefully. He was immediately smacked by at least four hands from the men seated nearest him, but the speaker merely rubbed his bruises and chuckled, unrepentant.

"My dress for the summer is *blue*," Tava stressed, blushing. "Some of them are green, but I dyed mine blue."

"It's n-not very pr-pretty," Torei told her, and was whacked by two more hands for his trouble. Rubbing the back of his head, he protested, "Well, it isn't! It's t-t-oo baggy, and sh-sh-shhe would l-look better in p-pink!"

That earned him several more hits, until the young man scrambled free, retreating beyond the reach of the others. One of the middle-aged men started to lengthen his arm, clearly intending to give Torei one last whap, but the youth hissed exactly like an upset cat would have, bared teeth and all. In fact, if he could have flattened his human ears, Tava was sure he would have done that, too. The older man shortened his limb back to normal, leaving Torei alone.

There was a bustle of activity around the brazier, and Tava found herself urged to stand and rotate her chair one more quarter turn. At her puzzled look, Kodan—the one adjusting her chair—leaned in close and murmured, "This is a trick the Shifterai play for our guests who have been out in the rain; we dry each of your four sides in turn."

Kenyen reached up and whapped his brother on the leg with the back of his hand. "No courting her until she's been with the priestesses, Brother."

"I am not courting," Kodan returned, giving his brother a mildly annoyed look. "I am merely instructing. And for that, I charge *you* with telling the next tale."

"Not until the food's been handed out," Kenyen countered, nodding at the men still working to divide their meal.

Reseating herself in the chair, Tava was surprised to be handed the first bowl of fish soup and a bit of bread broken off one of the longish crescents. She murmured a puzzled thanks to the three.

Women were never handed the first tastings during communal meals, down in the Valley; that went to the village Alders, the eldest of the men. She was even more puzzled to be given a bowl so small, it was more of a cup. Lifting her gaze to Kodan's, she glanced between his eyes and her portion.

Kodan smiled, accepting a portion of baked root in a small bowl similar to hers and an equally small scrap of bread. "The size of your bowl ensures you'll take the time to have seconds, and even thirds. You don't retreat to the maiden's *geome*—or to your wagon, in this case—until your supper is *finished* . . . which means you'll be encouraged to eat very slowly, in many small portions."

"Ah! I have the perfect tale for you!" Kenyen exclaimed, rubbing his hands together before reaching for the larger bowl one of the two remaining cooks offered to him. "It's called The Maiden and the Whale, and it's about a young woman who was having so much fun staying outside the *geome* each stormy night, she sought for a way to make sure her evening meals would *never* end . . ."

SIX

◆━❂❂━◆

Squinting, Kodan adjusted his eyesight to eagle sharpness and back, then glanced at the woman riding on the wagon bench next to him. She had braced her feet on the kickboard, the better to brace the book spread open in her lap. Deep in her reading as she was, it took him two nudges of his elbow against her arm to get her to look up at him. As soon as he had her attention, he nodded at the specks in the distance.

"Do you see those dots out there?" he asked.

Distracted from learning the different ways—beautifully illustrated, as promised—one could weave Shifterai-style baskets—Tava looked in the indicated direction. At first, she didn't see anything as she scanned the horizon, then squinted a little, sharpening her eyesight. "Are those . . . tents?"

"*Geomes*," he patiently corrected her. "Outlanders use tents. We use *geomes*. Except for the refreshing tents, or trench tents if you want to be derogatory about them."

"Of which, I use the red ones, *not* the green ones," Tava recited, dutifully remembering her lessons over the last ten days of travel.

"Correct." Kodan checked to make sure the gently undulating grass held no immediate surprises to navigate around, then looked at her again. He smiled as he saw she was reading once again. "If you don't stop reading that, you won't have anything to read tonight."

Tava looked up again. "I thought you said you'd get me another new book to read once we reached Family Tiger."

Kodan grinned. The moment she had voiced her complaint about missing her books, he had known exactly how to reach her. His plan to seduce Tava's attention through his collection of books was working; she couldn't hide her anxiety at the thought of a new tome being delayed in reaching her eager hands.

"You're not used to gauging distances on the Plains," he told her. "We're still about five hours from the encampment, and we have only two or so hours of daylight left today. We'll reach Family Tiger tomorrow."

"Five hours?" Tava asked, surprised. She squinted at the dots in the distance. "It's that far away?"

"We actually have to detour to the west by about an hour, just to find the next stream to water the animals," he told her. "They wouldn't make it all the way to the Family without eating, drinking, and resting overnight anyway. Not without stressing them unnecessarily. And we Shifterai always . . . ?"

". . . We always take care of our animals first," Tava recited at the prompting. As much as she wanted to finish the book in her lap, she pulled the little ribbon marker into place and set it between the two of them. Nearly ten days of travel had taught her that questions were encouraged among these Shifterai men, and particularly with this one man. "Have they seen us approaching?"

"It's possible," Kodan admitted. "If one of them is circling up in the sky, they'll land, tell the others about a caravan approaching, and send a fast-flier to investigate. If not, we might sleep under the stars since it's a clear night, and one of the scouts might spot the light of our fire tonight. But they might not spot us for another half hour or more. Our caravan is small, after all, compared to the Family encampment."

Tava twisted in her seat, peering at the wagons in their train, wagons and horses which represented almost one in ten of all the horses and wains in the village of Five Springs.

"When we left at midsummer to try a second round of hire among the outlanders, an outland caravan of eighty-three wagons was in the middle of traveling west across the southern half of the Plains. The West Paw Warband offered to give them escort through Family Tiger territory—the Family was pasturing a lot more to the north-west than it is now," Kodan added, tugging gently on the reins.

The line of wagons, trampling a nearly uniform trail of wheel and hoof ruts in the grass, started aiming more to the left, away from the tiny dots on the gently sloping terrain. The subtle swell of the land shifted as well, as the South Paw Warband rattled and bumped their way downward until the tiny encampment could no longer be seen.

About to go back to her book, Tava found herself distracted by a green streak in the distance. Since most of the rest of the grass was a pale golden blond, bleached by the hot summer sun, the difference was eye-catching. It stretched to either side of the blanket-covered wagon in front of her, making her crane her neck to try to see more.

As they descended the gradual, slight hill, the green blotch grew broader and darker. It resolved itself into a field of some sort of tall, broad-bladed grass interspersed with fluffier-looking tufts of bushes. But rather than approach it, the caravan turned north well before it reached the vegetation that promised the water they were seeking.

"Why aren't we going closer?" Tava asked, craning to look past Kodan.

"The ground is boggy, down there. Anything heavier than a pony might snap a foreleg, not realizing it isn't solid enough ground, and the wagon wheels would lodge deeply in the mud. If you look ahead,

over there, you can see the edge of a small lake that forms the start
of the marsh, and the trail of the stream feeding it." He lifted his chin
in lieu of pointing, since his hands were holding the reins.

Unable to see past the wagon in front of them, yet impatient to
view the lake for herself, Tava leaned in front of him. The wagon
bumped over some lump hidden by the grass, as it had bumped many
times before. Caught in a precarious position, Tava quickly threw
down her left hand, bracing herself so that she wouldn't fall over
completely and land on the reins.

Kodan jerked and gasped, startled as much by the location of her
hand as by the unexpectedness of her touch. Her palm had landed
high on his thigh. High enough that her littlest finger had brushed
right over the linen-covered curve of his bollocks, before wedging in
the crease between it and his upper leg. Thankfully, her finger had
only brushed, not scraped or bruised. Part of the fire that had raced
instantly up through his nerves was an instinctive, masculine cringing
against that possibility.

Part of that burn came from an equally abrupt but completely
different problem. An utterly unexpected problem. *I am* not *going to
get aroused just because she fell against me*, Kodan ordered himself firmly.
She certainly wouldn't understand it's involuntary. I am not *aroused by her,
either. I'm courting her so I can get her to think more kindly of her rightful
people.*

His loins didn't seem to want to pay attention. The wagon jostled
again, pressing her hand against his flesh. *That*, his body noticed,
even as it continued to ignore his mental castigation. Kodan gave up.
Father Sky . . . I am aroused by her. I just hope she hasn't noticed!

Embarrassed by her clumsiness, Tava quickly glanced at Kodan
to make sure she hadn't offended him. His light brown eyes were
wide, enough to see hints of smoky blue rimming the edges of his
irises. He also didn't seem to be paying attention to where the wagon
was going, though the two mares assigned to pull it didn't seem to

mind following the wagon in front for the time being. They were slowing down a little, but were content to follow the trail broken by the caravan.

"Kodan?" she asked, confused by his blank, wide-eyed expression. "Are you all right?"

He blinked twice, sucked in a breath through his teeth, and hissed, "Remove . . . your hand. Please."

Glancing down, Tava saw where her fingers had fallen. Gasping, she sat up quickly, snatching her fingers away. "I'm sorry!"

Flinching a second time, Kodan dragged in a deep breath and let it out slowly. "That's alright," he said, reassuring himself as much as her. "You didn't realize, and no harm was done. But that is something you must *never* touch until you are married. Or unless you're defending yourself," he added, thinking of the things he had read in her mother's book.

The reminder of those things quelled some of his body's lingering interest in the touch of her fingers. Paying attention to the mares again, he flicked the reins, speeding them up a little so they caught up to the next wagon again.

"It is forbidden for men and maidens to touch such areas on each other outside of marriage, to discourage the chance of such touches getting out of hand." A glance to his side showed her cheeks pink, her green eyes wide. "But . . . as I said, no harm was done. You just . . . startled me. I know it wasn't deliberate."

"No. No, it wasn't," Tava agreed quickly, feeling as if she had gotten too much sun on her face. "It was an accident."

"I know. Because of your . . . misperceptions about the Shifterai, the subject of improper touches never really had to come up, before now," Kodan explained.

His loins still tingled a little, aroused by her inadvertent caress, but he did his best to ignore it. They would camp soon, giving him plenty of physical things to do to get his mind off the touch of her littlest finger, off the press of her palm against the muscles of his thigh. He struggled to get his thoughts as well off the memory, turning her accident into a teaching opportunity.

"These are some of the things the priestesses will teach you once we reach the Family tomorrow, as it is their task to teach all the children, young men, and maidens of the Shifterai. This is why you will continue to be considered unapproachable for courting for the first ten days you are with the Family, so that you may have plenty of time for proper instruction."

"I . . . see." Actually, Tava didn't completely see. She had placed her hand—however inadvertently—right against his manhood. The parts her mother's book had warned against touching, since it seemed to drive men either mad with pain or mad with desire. Yet aside from looking a bit dazed, Kodan didn't look or sound like he was mad in either direction.

Of course, it's not like I know how people court normally. My mother's troubles were horrible, and because I've never been particularly feminine, plus the stigma of being born of an outlander woman, the boys in the village never showed that much interest in me. Facing forward, she tucked her hands in her lap, her interest in the small lake forgotten. *Father told me that young men hold hands with a young woman, and that in private, the young man might try to give the girl a kiss, or even try to caress parts of her body. That it was all gentle and consensual, not violent and unwilling.*

Her fingers still tingled a little with the awareness of where they had landed. Tava reminded herself that Kodan wasn't going to leap on her, that these Shifterai men were honorable, that they seemed just as trustworthy as a Mornai man would in such matters. At least, where she was concerned. No one in her village had shown that sort of interest in her.

Too outspoken, too energetic, too educated, too curious, too . . . everything. At least for the Mornai, I was, Tava reminded herself. She snuck a look at the man sitting beside her, with only the width of his book of plants separating them from touching again, accidentally or otherwise. *Yet these Shifterai don't seem to mind me being, well . . . me. And here is one that actually wants to court me. Me, of all people!*

The worst heat of mid-afternoon was finally beginning to break, but it was still bright enough that she reached for one of the water-skins nestled at their feet. Sipping from it, she offered him the leather bag. Kodan carefully juggled the four leads of the reins, then took the bag, drinking from it. He left her the task of stoppering it, nodding his head in thanks as he resumed a two-handed control of the two mares pulling the wagon.

Tava wanted to ask another question, but wasn't sure if it was alright to bring up the question of *why* she shouldn't mention to the others that she was a shapeshifter herself. Deciding her discretion would have to continue, she looked past him again. The sun was now low enough, she had to shade her eyes to do so, both against its rays and against the glare of light coming off the curved strip of water. The small lake he mentioned had come into view on the left, and it was indeed small, more like a pond at most. There was also a snaking line of bushes marking the bottom of the low valley, barely a wrinkle in the landscape, that traced the course of the stream feeding it.

"I take it the ground at the mouth of the lake is also soggy?" she finally asked. "Is that why we're not approaching it?"

"Yes," he agreed. "Well, that, and when we set your ducks free to feed on the grass, none of us want to have to wade into the lake after them."

"But the day is hot, and we're covered in chaff from the dry grass," Tava pointed out. "That pond looks tempting."

"It also has mud, and leeches. Like sawgrass, leeches are best left alone, since a shifter isn't always aware of their painless bites. We're headed for a small retention pond, suitable for warbands and brief stops from caravans," Kodan added. "It should have enough water for our needs, based on the water level of the lake, but it won't be suitable for bathing, either. Not as our only source of water."

"What about where the Family is camped?" Tava asked.

"They're camped at the ruins of an old noble estate."

Tava shivered at the thought of the Shattering of Aiar. Everyone knew of the massive explosion that had devastated the old Imperial City, though no one alive knew why it had happened. With the loss of their central government, with its plethora of mages, communication mirrors, and great Portals that allowed instant travel from one side of Aiar to the other, had come the loss of a unified, continent-wide nation. Even now, almost two centuries later, many areas across the continent were still struggling to establish themselves as independent kingdoms. Or so she had heard the river merchants say whenever they had stopped on the docks of Five Springs to trade.

Kodan noticed her shudder. "Don't worry; our priesthood cleansed and blessed all such places long ago, and we still bless them each time we set up camp in such places. There won't be any bad energies lingering. The basements and cellars were all scoured, repaired, and fully lined with stones, turning them into water cisterns and retention pools. Every year around this time, when the water level gets very low, we reseal them with plaster shortly before leaving for the City. The autumn rains, the melting snows of winter, and the spring storms refill them in our absence, making them ready for our return in midsummer."

"So there isn't much water, then?" Tava asked, looking down at her faded, dusty green skirt. She grimaced a little. The one good thing about living in the Valley had been an abundance of water. At times, too much water, but certainly enough to bathe year-round, even if it was laborious to heat that water to anything above tepid in temperature. "Not enough to bathe?"

"There should be enough for a bath for everyone in the warband, though the priestesses may have you just wash from a basin until proper clothes can be made for you, so that you'll be clean when they're fitted and ready."

"What do you mean, proper clothes?" she asked, frowning at him. "I'm wearing proper clothes!"

"You're wearing Mornai clothes. They're fine for riding on a wagon bench, but you'll be expected to ride like a Shifterai, which means dress like a Shifterai woman. Don't worry," Kodan said, guiding the mares up the side of the low valley, "if you don't know how to ride, we'll teach you. Or even if you only think you know how to ride, we'll still teach you. The same with driving a wagon, shooting a bow and arrow, herding animals, twisting grass-logs for the braziers, and a host of other tasks that the Shifterai undertake each and every day here on the Plains. This is your home, and you have a lot to learn."

Tava wanted to argue that this *wasn't* her home. That he was holding her belongings ransom to ensure her ongoing presence on the Plains. But habit kept the words behind her teeth. Habit, and something more. Something somewhere between mere politeness and actual curiosity. While it was true she had often imagined running away to a Mornai city, where female scribes would be far more welcomed in such cosmopolitan places than they were in little backwater villages, she hadn't ever really considered traveling to other kingdoms, let alone that she might be welcomed in other lands.

She's thinking again. Kodan snuck glances at her as he guided the mares pulling the bright-painted trader's wagon. *She thinks so quietly, compared to our women. I want to know what she's thinking . . . but we're almost to the pond. Once we're there, we'll lose all semblance of privacy until we start out again tomorrow morning . . . and between now and then, I really should make sure the Family is warned that she's coming.*

If someone hadn't spotted them already, if they weren't visited by sundown, he would have to fly to Family Tiger himself to deliver the news. He did have a reasonably swift owl form, and the evening winds might be favorable for the return trip, but flying there and back would be exhausting. Kodan hoped someone flying over the Family pasture had spotted their caravan and was on his way; if someone was coming, he could send back one of his own men with news of their impending arrival, sparing their visitor the return trip.

Maybe his brother would like to go, to reassure their mother that her two eldest children and her husband had survived. *Or perhaps Manolo, or Deian . . . I'll have to think of who to send.*

His father might have more experience navigating the Plains than most of the warband, and was thus in the lead, but Kodan was still in charge of organizing and directing the score of men traveling around him. However interesting Tava Ell Var was turning out to be, he wasn't going to neglect his duties even this close to home.

There was just one problem. When he glanced at her again, she had lifted her left hand, scraping back a few strands of the soft brown hair blowing across her face. Looking at the deft movements of her fingers as she slid those strands back behind her ear made a normally ignored corner of his mind wonder what it would be like for her fingers to touch him like that. With purpose, instead of by accident. The thought sent a shiver through his blood.

Telling that corner of his mind to be quiet and to behave, and that it hadn't been *that* long since his last chance to visit with one of the earth-priestesses, Kodan focused his thoughts firmly on guiding the wagon toward the pond.

Their visitor came winging down out of the sky just as the warband was pulling the second of the three felts into place over the roof of the *geome*. Kodan had decided to erect the tent for shelter despite the currently clear skies so that it would be apparent to any distant watcher that this was a Shifterai caravan, not some group of outland traders. So when the hawk landed and transformed into the half-naked, half-feathered body of a shifter named Medred, the young man was already grinning in welcome.

"Welcome home, South Paw!" he called out cheerfully. "I see you went out with only a couple of wagons, and have come back with more than ten!"

"Medred!" Tedro shouted back. He pulled on the lead-rope, hauling the roof up into place, then passed it to one of the others and hurried to embrace his cousin. They hugged; then Tedro stepped back and gestured at Kodan, who had paused from his own work of helping to unfold the outer layers of oiled canvas in order to help greet their arrival. "Wait until you see the haul Kodan secured for us from the Mornai!"

"Eleven wagons, when you left with three?" Medred retorted. "I *do* have functional eyes, cousin."

"What Tedro means is that most of the wagons do not belong to *us*," Kodan said, joining the conversation.

He clasped forearms with the younger man in greeting. Medred glanced between him and Tedro, visibly confused. Tedro grinned, enjoying his cousin's confusion.

"Most of them, and most of their contents, belong to a Mornai woman we have brought back for adoption into the Family. Minus the Family's tithe, of course," Kodan explained. "I'll be sending Lakkan back to the Family tonight to explain our arrival—he volunteered for it."

Medred smirked. "Four years, and he still acts like he's newly leaped to his wife. I trust I'm welcome to stay with you overnight to rest and eat?"

"And to tell us the news of all that's happened while we were gone," Tedro added.

"Well, the first two pieces of news deal with *you*," Medred said, giving Kodan a significant look. "The first of which is, Rahala is gone."

"And this is important, how?" Kodan returned mildly. Inwardly, part of him sighed with relief. The other part was annoyed at the mere mention of the young woman's name. Annoying though she was, he didn't wish her ill; courtesy prompted him to ask, "Is she dead?"

"No. Or at least not as far as we know. She insisted on . . ." Medred trailed off, staring past his cousin's shoulder. The other two glanced that way as well, following the line of his stare.

That gaze had landed on Tava, who was emerging from the bushes lining the retention pond. Her baggy green dress, cut in the unflattering Mornai style, was damp in a few spots down the front, suggesting she had taken the time to fill herself as well as the two buckets she carried from the water. It pleased him to see her offering to help set up camp, giving him hope that she was beginning to accept the fact that she had a place waiting for her on the Shifting Plains, that she would fit in among her own kind far better than she had with the Valley folk.

"Is that her?" Medred asked, watching her hauling the heavy buckets with ease.

"Tava Ell Var," Kodan said, lifting his chin at the young woman. "She comes from a somewhat isolated and barbaric village. She's a bit shy because of their culture, but there is a fire banked inside of her, one worthy of the Plains."

". . . Kodan wants to court her," Tedro translated for his cousin.

"Ah. Well, once she gets out of that sack she's wearing, she might actually be quite pretty . . . but that only makes Rahala's absence all the better for you," Medred said, turning back to Kodan. "She could be as ugly as a toad, and Rahala would throw a fit, if you wanted to court her."

"You were telling us what happened to the girl?" Kodan prompted. "She insisted on . . . something?"

"Yes—she insisted on going with the West Paw when they escorted that caravan westward. It happened just after you left," Medred explained. "And then, when they passed the caravan on to Family Malamute just inside Clan Dog territory, she insisted on going farther west with *their* escort, too. From what the West Paw says, she spent a lot of her time driving the wagon of that really tall, old fellow, conversing with him."

"Wasn't that the one who claimed to be all the way from Mendhi, and was traveling to see as much of the world as he could before he died?" Tedro asked.

"That's the one," Medred agreed. "Apparently he's been telling tales every single night of the adventures he'd had in his youth with the caravan . . . and West Paw said he never once repeated any of his stories while they were giving escort. Anyway, Rahala went off with Family Malamute's escort, and nobody knows when she'll return. West Paw said her interest in the old man wasn't like her interest in you, exactly . . . but that it was a strong interest."

Kodan grunted. "She could hold out her hand to him from now until eternity, for all that I care . . . so long as she never holds out her hand to *me*."

"Too late," Tedro commiserated, giving Kodan a sympathetic pat on his shoulder. "For your sake, I hope Rahala stays away long enough for you to court Tava successfully . . . though I'll warn you, you're not the only one who'll try courting her, too, once her initiation days are through."

"If she does clean up pretty, you'll have a *lot* of competition, *multerai*," Medred teased Kodan, clapping his hand on the older man's other shoulder. "And if she's an outlander, it just might be she'll want a man with *fewer* shapes, rather than more, so she won't feel quite as uncomfortable around her husband. Outlander women are said to be backward, that way."

"In that case, you will have far more to fear from Torei than from Kodan," Tedro teased his cousin.

"What of the other news?" Kodan asked, dragging the conversation back to that. "You said there were two pieces that deal with me."

"The second piece of news," Medred stated, his expression turning somber and serious, "is that your great-father has gone to Mother Earth. I'm sorry."

Closing his eyes, Kodan absorbed the news for a long moment, then opened them again. Brushing the tears out of his eyes, he looked at Medred. "My mother? The rest of our kin? How are they faring?"

"She grieved a lot, as did your uncle and your aunts. But we all took comfort in that he passed peacefully in his sleep. There's already been one formal Grieving Day, but your mother suggested to both Councils that there should be another one, for both South Paw and for Tailtip to express their own sense of loss. They're the last warband besides yourselves to return to the Family," Medred told him. "The Council of Shifters pointed out at the Family meeting after the Grieving Day that *you* are now the strongest shifter in the Family, now that Chodan is gone. They want *you* to take up the Lordship of Tiger.

"With no princesses in the Family, the Council of Sisters has agreed. I thought I should warn you so that you'll be braced for it," Medred added, "because the Sister Council pointed out that you are twenty-eight. They think that's a bit old for a man to be unmated and added firmly that it's not always best for the leader of a Family to be mateless—you'll be happy to know they said those things *after* Rahala left," the younger shifter added lightly, attempting to leaven his news. "But they did agree that you're both mature and wise enough for the position, and both sides agreed that the intervening three weeks of trying to govern the Family strictly by the Councils hasn't worked very well.

"Given all of that," Medred continued wryly, "you being interested in *any* woman will be welcome news . . . but the fact that it's an outlander woman will be looked at sideways. Plus it's not just you that'll have competition for the outlander's hand, but how she'll have competition for *yours*. Rahala wasn't the only maiden interested in you, just the most persistent."

"Lovely," Kodan muttered. He had focused so much on preparing for taking on some position of responsibility, authority, and even leadership in his future that he hadn't spared much attention or time for things like courtship. A little bit of courting—he was an adult, and he did like women—but nothing serious.

The problem is, I don't want to pick a woman because it's expected of me. Or because she's simply there, convenient and available. And she needs to be my equal, he added silently, watching Tava coming out of the almost finished *geome*, the buckets dangling light and empty from her fingertips. She headed for the wagon she had fetched the buckets from, giving the trio of men a brief, curious look.

Not necessarily a shapeshifter, for all it's highly encouraged for multerai to court princesses, but I definitely want to find someone strong-willed, intelligent, courteous, and understanding. Someone who knows when to stand strong, and when to give way. And she definitely has to be intelligent enough to lead the Sister Council, wise enough to take good advice from others, kind enough to listen to the needs of others, and practical enough to know when to stand firm on a subject.

A hand clapped him on the shoulder, startling him. Tedro grinned. "Father Sky to Kodan, you'd better wake up before you get wet!"

"What?" Kodan asked, blinking and looking away from the green-garbed woman headed for the pond.

"You were wool-gathering in the rain of your thoughts," Medred told him. "While looking at the outlander woman, no less. You *must* be interested in her." The younger man grinned cheekily. "I do say, it's nice to finally see *you* losing your wits over a woman!"

Kodan narrowed his eyes, but let the teasing pass. "As there will be a maiden at supper, Medred, you'll not dine in just your feathers. Tedro, go find your cousin a pair of *breikas* to borrow."

Tava approached as Tedro moved off. She glanced at the newcomer, her expression curious, but when her gaze dipped down to the feathers forming a pair of shorts from his hips to his knees, she blushed and quickly looked away. Kodan gestured sharply, flicking his hand in a silent order to make Medred follow his kinsman. It took an additional whap of his hand on the younger man's arm to get him to move, since Medred was busy smiling at the flustered maiden, but he finally moved.

"Um . . . Deian asked me to tell you one of the felts is getting a little thin at the crease-point where the roof staves meet the lattices. He wanted to know if it should be, um, patch-felted when the warband gets back to the Family, or re-felted," Tava relayed. "What did he mean by that? Your father asked me to fetch water for the cookpot before I could ask."

"The felt wears thin from use, rubbing against the frame, being put up and taken down each time we move pasture or travel in bad weather," Kodan told her. "If the wear is just in a single, somewhat small spot, the thin spot can sometimes be thickened with additional wool. If it has several thin spots, it's far easier to just apply a new layer of wool all over, because of the different processes."

"What are the differences?" Tava asked, curious. "We never owned any sheep, and goat hair is meant only for spinning, so I never really paid much attention to how felt is made."

"Well, first you shear the sheep, removing the wool. The fleece is then picked clean, since the sheep picks up debris by roaming around, rolling on the ground to scratch or rubbing up against bushes and trees," he said. "Usually it's soaked in different changes of water if it's dirty, and the lanolin is skimmed off the wastewater to become part of softsoap and such. Some Families advocate cleaning it while it's still on the sheep, but that takes a large body of water, and can foul the water for drinking purposes.

"Once the wool is dry, then it's beaten with sticks until it fluffs up—if it's meant for spinning, it'll be carded and combed to straighten out the fibers, separating the long ones from the short. The short fibers get put into bags to either be turned into cushions, or to be used for felting, since they're useless for spinning—you've probably done the same with short goat hairs," he added.

Tava nodded, thinking of her own experience in such things. "When I comb those out, I put them into a bag to be turned into cushion stuffing. It works well when mixed with feathers, smoothing out the lumps of the quills. But three goats don't produce much fiber, and I usually ended up buying pre-carded wool from the other women in the village to mix with it."

"We do that, too. Anyway, after the fibers have been fluffed up, they're teased apart, to increase the fluff further. That helps make the felt work better," Kodan explained. "Good, thick felt, not too compressed but not too loose, can keep a *geome* cool when the weather is hot and warm when it's cold. If we're doing a full re-felting, the wool is laid out on one of the oiled over-covers to make sure we have enough."

"How much wool goes into the felt?" she asked, glancing at the nearly finished tent.

"That depends on the size of the *geome*. The warband *geome* is two to three times the size of the typical family one. A family-sized one needs anywhere from two hundred to three hundred fleeces." Nodding his head at the tent in front of them, which was having the tiger-skin pulled up over the smoke-hole cone, he added, "So you can see how something the size of this one requires more like seven to nine hundred fleeces. That makes patch-felting much more practical than re-felting. Re-felting is also usually done in the spring when the sheep are freshly sheared, so we only have to carry a few extra fleeces for mid-season patching.

"Once the fleece wool is teased and laid out on an oiled canvas cover to gauge the amount, the original felt—we call it the 'mother felt'—is dampened thoroughly, and the new wool laid out on top, paying attention to where the thinner spots are to make sure there will be extra wool to compensate. It takes several years of experience in both patching and re-felting to gauge such things," he warned her. "You might be asked to help lay down the wool, as it can take up to a score of people to work on the task, but you won't be placed in charge of where the wool goes for at least fifteen, maybe twenty years."

"I'm not sure I'd still be here in fifteen or twenty years," she muttered, thinking of his yearlong bargain, her presence on the Plains in exchange for getting to keep her household goods. He ignored it, choosing to continue his explanation.

"Once the new wool is laid on the mother felt, the new wool is also dampened with water. This will help it bind to the old felt. The oilcloth is then laid on top to tamp down the new wool and keep it from binding to the mother on that side, and we use a long, heavy pole to wrap it all up in a long bundle. The roll is then bound in hides and tied shut, the ends of the pole are fitted with a pivot-hitch, which is in turn tied to a pair of horses, and the whole thing is dragged off by the horses for several miles, until the wool is compressed into felt.

"Then we just take off the hides and peel it open, which the oil-cloth helps with in separating the rolled-up layers. But that's the way we re-felt. Patch-felting is a different process," he said.

"So how does patch-felting differ from re-felting?" Tava asked, drawn back into his explanation by her curiosity, and by his willingness to sate it.

"Well, first you look carefully at the old felt to find the thin spots. This is sometimes done by tossing it up on a *geome* frame when the sun is shining brightly, to see where the light glows through the thinnest bits," he admitted. "Of course, if the felt is that thin, it's often that thin in several spots and needs re-felting. Sometimes it just wears down in one particular spot, and you can often feel it just by laying it out on the ground and crawling over it. Obviously we don't do that when it's been raining, but the ground is mostly dry, even this close to the pond."

Tava nodded. A lot of the short-cropped grass farther out was the same late-summer yellow as the rest of the Plains, but the grass close to the oval pool was more green than golden. Cropped short by whatever herd animals had passed through here not that long ago, but close enough to the water in the pond to gradually regrow.

"Once you've found the thin spot, which is often worn in a curved line following the stake-ends where the roof meets the wall, you get a set of special brushes, some with wide teeth, some with narrow ones," Kodan told her. "You use them to brush the felt, teasing up the fibers so that they're very fuzzy and loose—not just over the weak, thin spot, but for at least two hand-spans all around the area in need of thickening, if not more. This is done so that the new felting binds firmly with the old.

"Once it's been dry-brushed, the mother felt is carefully wetted, the new fleeces are laid down over the area, with the wool piled thick-est in the weak spots and tapering out to the rest of the brushed-out area, and more water is sprinkled on top. An oiled cloth is laid over the top of the new fleece, and you get the children to twist-dance on top, which mashes the new wool into the old, matting the fibers to-gether and thickening the felt until it's no longer weak."

"Twist-dance?"

"Look at my feet, and I'll show you." Kodan demonstrated on the short-cropped grass that surrounded their campsite. He balanced on the balls of his feet, but with his knees bent so that he could twist them one way, then the other. His arms swung, too, counteracting the twisting of his lower limbs, and he swayed his weight from one leg to the other. The effect, when he stepped back, was a tangled, circular smear of yellow and green grass stems with hints of matted dirt where each boot had rested. "We have the children do it, because for one, it's fun, and for another, their weight is gentle enough that the fibers aren't smashed completely flat before they've had a chance to truly bind together during the felting process."

"I think I can see how that would matt everything together," she agreed. "That's kind of an odd way of dancing, though. In the Valley, we tend to dance in lines, holding on to each other by kerchiefs in our hands and stamping and skipping, or kicking our feet as we move, usually with the girls on one side, boys on the other. Do you hold hands when you twist?"

Kodan shook his head. "We have other dances where we do that."

SEVEN

The thump of the *geome* door closing drew their attention back to the others, and the fact that the domed tent was just about finished. Kenyen approached them, a basket in his hands. He pushed it at his brother, smirking. "Here, oh fearless warleader. Our dear father spotted some dried apples downstream and wants you to collect some for the fire. I'm to show our lovely guest how to find *rora* flowers when they're not in bloom, as well as teach her how to make grass-logs."

Hands going to his hips, Kodan didn't accept the basket. "*You* are going to gather the dried apples, and *I* will show Tava how to find *rora* flowers."

Kenyen opened his mouth to protest but, at Kodan's pointed stare, sighed and trudged toward the low sloping hill to the southeast.

"Dried apples?" Tava asked, confusion wrinkling her brow. "I didn't, see any apple trees on the way here."

He blushed. "It's a discreet term for, um . . . grass-eater droppings. In specific, dried, straw-filled droppings." At her horrified expression, Kodan spread his arms. "Do you see a lot of trees out here? Don't count these little bushes around the pond," he added as she glanced their way. "The Family is about eight hundred people strong. If eight people were to share a single cooking fire, that's one hundred fires to fuel every single day. We make grass-logs and we burn dried apples so that we don't strip away what few trees we *do* have on the Plains."

"But . . . *dung*?" She wrinkled her nose again.

"That's why we look for *rora* vines in the grass. Come, I'll show you," he urged, holding out his hand. As soon as she took it, he tugged her uphill. "*Rora* grows best on the south-facing slopes and along the tops of hills, where the sun shines the most. They also grow fast, but at this time of the year, we have to make sure to pick off and scatter the seed pods so more will grow next year.

"We throw them on the fire, vines, leaves, and especially the flowers if they can be found, because they contain an oil that changes the smell of the fire. Normally we'd make do with grass-logs—which I'll show you how to twist—but there isn't much in the way of long stalks around here, possibly because some of the herds have been pastured here recently. Which also explains the dried apples being available."

"So what do these vines look like?" Tava asked.

"They have small, heart-shaped leaves with serrated edges, and they grow in pairs from a common base at intervals, with the leaves often set at right angles to little branches of shorter vines that curl out among the grass-stalks. Sheep, goats, and horses won't eat the runners, though cattle will. But since it grows down at the base of the hay, we feed the cattle first, since they eat the higher ends of the stalks, then the horses and goats and the sheep after that—ah, here's some," Kodan said, tugging her toward a patch of green peeking through the yellowed stalks. "The vines are reddish brown at this time of year, though they can be quite red in the springtime."

"Should we go back for a basket?" Tava asked.

Kodan shook his head. "For a single fire, one that will be half grass, we only need about two body lengths. With the grass this short, it'll be easy tugging it up. Here, you start tugging, while I pull up some grass from over there—keep yourself in sight of the *geome*."

Turning, she looked around at the subtle, rolling hills. ". . . Why? I don't think I could get lost out here, not with that line of greenery from the stream and the marsh to orient me."

"I'm glad you realize you *can* get lost out here without familiar referents," Kodan praised her. "But, no, it's more a matter of custom. A young man and a young woman aren't allowed to go out of public sight together."

Tava gave him a thoughtful, sober look. "I don't . . . I *don't* think you'd ravish me, the moment we were alone." Her sober expression softened a little, allowing a shy hint of a smile. "I think you might even be trustworthy, Kodan Sin Siin."

He didn't stop the smile that curved his lips. "Thank you . . . but actually, it's *you* the custom is worried about. Since the customs you were raised under aren't the same as ours, the others might think you want to drag me into the next gully and have your wicked outlander way with me."

That made her laugh. The hearty sound pleased him, as did the way her green eyes gleamed with her amusement. Her mirth hardened after a moment, and she folded her arms across her chest. "I don't think you'll have to worry. Father explained that sort of thing isn't always about pain and suffering, but I'm not interested in 'doing my wifely duty' either. From the sound of it, gathering dried apples would be more fun. At least for the woman."

Kodan opened his lips, then closed them. *I see I'll have to have a word with the priestesses about that. She needs to learn that it is fun for her.* For a moment, he pictured her going beyond the lessons of the earth-priestesses, to the moment when she joined some future husband in their marriage bed. *Whoever he is, he'd have to understand, deep down, that she doesn't expect to enjoy the experience. Which means that, if she is to enjoy it, he'll have to be extra patient and extra careful to arouse her.*

If it were me, a corner of his mind mused, studying her as she turned her attention back to the grass, stooping and looking for the vines in question, *I'd spend days arousing her . . . That dress is ugly on her, but what a magnificent rump!*

Whoa—rein in your passion, Kodan. You're only supposed to seduce her into accepting her rightful place among us. She's a shapeshifter, and thus automatically desirable, but that doesn't mean she'll hold out her hand to you, he chided himself.

But he couldn't quite turn his attention toward looking for suitable stalks of straw for twisting. Instead, he found himself moving up next to her, watching her concentrate on the ground. Nor could he let her statement pass unchallenged; her resistance had to be plowed up, like breaking up sod for good farming ground.

"It's fun for *both*, Tava. Women and men. We Shifterai know we approach the matter differently than the people of most other lands. Because our courtship rules are so strict, we know that men *and* women need an outlet for our natural urges . . . and we *teach* that outlet.

"You will learn all these things for yourself in the first ten days of your life among the Family," he promised her, meeting her wide-eyed look. "Just as you will learn the customs for honoring Father Sky and Mother Earth in each turning of the seasons, how to dance and how to ride, and how to set up a *geome* and twist grass into logs for the fire. You will learn how to find pleasure in yourself, and how to find pleasure in a man. Self-control is *not* the same thing as ignorance among the Shifterai."

Flustered by his words, embarrassed by the topic, and unsure if there *was* any pleasure for a woman in such things, Tava didn't know what to say. All the things her mother had endured according to her book, they sounded horrible. Varamon had tried to tell her it was otherwise, but had admitted his own experience with women was limited. Yet the straightforward way this man spoke, the matter-of-fact look that Kodan gave her, suggested there was some truth to his words.

Her confusion and doubt manifested in a single word, one she wasn't even aware of saying until it was already out. "How?"

Somehow, he wasn't too surprised by her question. A little embarrassed to be asked so bluntly—even among his people, such things weren't asked between a maiden and an unmarried man—but Kodan knew enough about her by now to know that *being* able to ask, feeling free enough to ask, was important to her. *Damn those backward Mornai idiots. How are we ever to improve ourselves as a race, if people like* them *keep suppressing the natural curiosity of their children?*

"Let's grab some straw for twisting into logs, and I'll tell you what I can as we work," he bartered quietly. He felt a little twinge of guilt at what he was offering to do. "An earth-priestess will *show* you these things, demonstrating on her own body and, um, having you practice on your own flesh . . . but I *can* give you some knowledge in advance. Just don't tell the others I'm telling you these things.

"It's not entirely appropriate, since you are a maiden . . . but technically, you're *not* yet a Shifterai maiden," he hedged, more to soothe his own conscience than hers. "If you were born to the Plains, raised among us as you properly should have been, this would *definitely* be inappropriate. But . . . by the *letter* of the law . . . you're not yet one of us."

"You aren't going to *touch* me, are you?" Tava asked, unnerved by that possibility. The way his suntanned face paled, then flushed, reassured her as much as his quick reply did.

"No! Definitely not. That would be *far* beyond what I'm allowed to do," Kodan asserted. "No amount of justification could possibly . . . Look, let's just grab some of that grass over there."

Following him, Tava sat by an uneaten patch of longish, sun-dried grass, plucked up a handful, and did her best to copy his movements.

Settling himself at her side, Kodan showed her how to twist the stalks tightly, until they kinked and twisted up in the middle, forming a blunt sort of cord. Adding more stalks to lengthen the twisting ends was definitely a skill that would take practice. He did it by rolling the strands together on the knee-length flap of his tunic, which he spread over his thigh for a base. When she tried it on her skirt, the gathered folds kept trying to bunch up over the straw, forcing her to pull the material tight and tuck it under herself.

"You're getting it," he praised after a few more minutes. "Now make one of the 'legs' longer than the other by rolling more straw onto it, and then twist it into a roll, but before it can try to pinch itself into a cord-twist, wrap it *twice* around itself and the free end, then let it double back on itself."

Tava tried to follow his instructions, and failed. Bits of straw kept escaping her grasp.

"Twist and wrap it down to the loop at this end, but as you wrap, untwist the first two lengths a little and push the third one through, back and forth—adding more straw where necessary," he said, demonstrating with deft movements of his hands and wrists, "—and untwist this starting loop down here, just enough to tuck the ends of the third twist through. And there you have it: one grass-log, ready to be thrown on the brazier, replete with tinder-ends suitable for catching fire."

"Wrap twice around the free end . . . and push it back and forth . . ." Tava struggled to hold on to the twisted straw so it wouldn't unravel. It unraveled anyway, making her sigh and start again.

"You'll get it eventually," Kodan encouraged her. "But you'll need to roll in a little more . . . Watch your skirt!" he admonished as it started to tug free from under her hip. "You'll be glad to wear proper Shifterai clothes, soon. The panel of a *chamsa*—the women's version of the *chamak*, or tunic, which I'm wearing—is a lot less likely to get rolled up in your work than your skirts."

"But *your* pants are gathered," Tava pointed out. "They're just like my festival dress."

Unfolding one leg, Kodan tugged down the leather cuff of his boot. "My *breikas* may be gathered, but they're gathered at both ends, and tied at hip and ankle. My folds won't get very far, unlike your skirt—watch the free end!"

Dragging her attention back to her task, Tava twisted, rolled, pinched, and pushed, until she had an approximate version of his tidy, tufted log in her hands. A very approximate version. It kinked and listed to one side, and bits of hay stuck out here and there. She wrinkled her nose at it. "I'm not very good at this, am I?"

Kodan didn't see any reason to lie to her. "No, but you merely lack practice. For a first try . . . it *will* burn. But the twists are loose and it'll come unraveled more quickly in the fire. That *can* be a good thing if you want a lot of flames for light, but they won't last as long, and you won't have the longer sort of burn suitable for cooking. That's where the dried apples come in."

"I'm not sure I could eat anything that's been burned over a fire made of *dung*," Tava muttered, making a face. "Wouldn't it flavor the food?"

"Without *rora* flowers and a layer of grass-logs, yes. I'll show you another way to twist a log." Scooting over to another patch of grass, he stripped out a couple handfuls and started twisting and rolling. "Just like before . . . you do a two-strand twist . . . with one leg . . . longer than the other . . . but . . . when you get to the end . . . you bend *this* strand into a loop, wrap *both* strands twice around its base"—he demonstrated—"then pull *both* ends through the loop."

"Why didn't you teach me that one?" Tava asked, lifting the tufted lump in her hands. "It looks so much easier than this!"

"If you don't pull it tight enough, which takes practice, it will unravel itself and shed grass all over. To prevent that, you'd have to double-back around . . . and tuck through, and then twist the end under itself twice for further tension," Kodan explained, demonstrating with another bit of dried grass twisted onto the end. "It forms a lumpy knot at one end and doesn't stack very well—when we start migrating back toward the City, the whole Family will be stripping and twisting grass-logs as we go, to supplement the fuel everyone will need to survive the winter. The version you learned is more tolerant of loose twisting, and it holds together with greater cohesion when burned. This two-strand kind uncurls and spreads out when burned, and is best used in a kiln instead of a brazier. We *can* use it, but it'll have to be placed under others to weight it down."

"Oh, I see—if it uncurls and spreads out, it could uncurl itself right over the edge of the brazier and start burning the grass on the ground," Tava offered, thinking it through. "Or anything else lying inside a tent . . . a *geome*."

"Exactly. That's another reason why we burn dried apples with *rora* vine, mainly because we burn it after supper is through so that it heats the tent without fear of anything flying out of the brazier pan—as good as the vine is at changing the smell, we try to limit how much we use while actually cooking. We're not tasteless barbarians, you know," he teased her. "Literally or figuratively. Why don't you practice the three-strand twist?"

"Are you . . . um . . . going to demonstrate that thing you mentioned?" Tava asked. She could feel her cheeks heating, but kept her attention on the nearby stalks of grass, plucking out the ones that looked straight and unbent.

Kodan rolled a short twist of grass, knotting the end in the third way he had shown. With a smaller bit of grass, he twisted it and stuffed it through the loop opposite the knot just enough that it formed a bump. Scooting a little closer to Tava, he held it by the knot and pointed at the loop with its bump and the two twists between it and the knot. "These are the three parts of a woman's loins, the places of her privateness.

"You may have seen or felt this bump up here, which lies closest to the front of your body. You may have even rubbed it. The more you rub it, the better it feels, but you have to take care to rub gently . . . and a little moisture makes the rubbing all the nicer. Just below the nub is the tiny hole through which you pass water, and you have to be careful not to scrape it or treat it harshly."

Tava blushed at the mention of *that*, but he continued on, sliding his hands up to the lowest of the twists and gently prying them apart, forming a small gap in the grass-log next to the knot.

"This is the other spot to be careful, since it is where one passes, um . . . dried apples, I suppose you could call it. When it is caressed gently, it can feel good—"

"—Ew!" Tava protested, embarrassed and disgusted.

"Such things are best only done after one has thoroughly bathed and that area is very clean, since as you said . . . ew," Kodan agreed. "But it can be quite pleasant—it actually isn't much different than caressing other parts of the body, such as the insides of the wrists and the crooks of elbows. There are a lot of nerves there, and when stroked very, very gently, it feels very good. It isn't done often, but it can be fun in the right circumstances and mood.

"*This* spot," he continued, slipping his thumbs up to the next twist and prying it open, "is what is touched most by a lover, along with the bump just above it. It can be touched by fingertips in the same way the bump is touched, or kissed by a lover's mouth. It even looks a bit like a pair of lips, only they run vertically instead of horizontally, and there are—very thankfully—no teeth. Nor any tongue. But it can be caressed, and it can be kissed."

Tava wasn't sure she wanted to hear these things anymore. She wrinkled her nose, giving Kodan a dubious look. "Isn't that just as bad as . . . as the lower one? Who in their right mind would want to taste *that*?"

"A woman is much like a flower," Kodan told her. "This part, this opening, releases nectar when a woman is aroused . . . and you arouse her by touching and kissing her all over. Well, *I* would arouse her.

You could touch yourself, of course, but you wouldn't be able to kiss most of yourself like I could."

Her cheeks burned again at his words, but not from the same disgust as before. Instead, his words had conjured up an image of him kissing her cheeks, her shoulders . . . and lower. Flustered and feeling like her insides were being twisted up into a grass-log, Tava cleared her throat. "Um . . . right. I'm not sure . . ."

Sensing she was losing her courage, Kodan continued firmly with the lesson. He didn't want her retreating and closing her mind to the things she needed to know. "Tonight, when you retire to the trader wagon, you can touch these things and more, and experiment on yourself. But you must hear the rest of it, so that you understand enough to know what you'll be doing; otherwise you'll fail, and not realize that you're simply doing it wrong.

"This opening can be more than just caressed and kissed. It can be licked and suckled, and you can dampen your fingers and slide them inside . . . like this." Carefully holding the twist open from the back side with the fingers of his left hand, Kodan demonstrated with the fingers of his right hand, first swirling and rubbing the knob of grass poked through the loop at the top, then stroking down the sides of the twist, and finally slipping them in and out through the opening.

It was just a bunch of twisted grass, brittle, scratchy, and threatening to fall apart if he handled it too roughly, but his touch was gentle. It also aroused him, because he wasn't seeing just the twisted bits of summer-bleached straw; he was seeing the flesh of a real woman in his mind. Voice a little rough and unsteady, he pulled his attention back to the lesson.

"I was told that it's a little awkward for a woman to reach deeply into herself on her own. And that for a young maiden, there is often a bit of extra skin around the very opening, making it small and tight, though riding on a horse often stretches or breaks it at an early age. You're an outlander, so you might still have a full maidenhead. Or you might not. Whoever you, ah, choose for a husband will un-doubtedly examine such things while kissing and caressing you down there, and be gentle when proceeding onward. Which would be in-tercourse."

Tava, caught up in the sight of his fingers stroking the twisted grass so gently and soothingly, lost some of her own twisted-grass feeling. "Which is when things will hurt."

"Only the first time, if the extra skin hasn't already been broken," Kodan defended. A moment later, he realized what she meant, and quickly shook his head. He withdrew his fingers, not wanting to touch his impromptu model while they had this particular discus-sion. "*No.* What your mother endured was *not* lovemaking. No one touched her gently, no one caressed her, nor did they try to arouse her in any way. She did not release her nectar, and without the nectar, she was dry inside—here, dry your lips," he ordered.

Puzzled, Tava wiped them with the edge of her hand.

"Now rub the edge of your first finger along your bottom lip, back and forth," he instructed. "Do it about seven or eight times."

Complying, she rubbed her finger across her lip. It was equally dry, slightly callused, and smelling of dried grass from her efforts. After eight strokes, her skin tingled a little and she was glad to quit.

"It felt a little rough after a while, didn't it?" Kodan asked.

"If I'd done it another eight times, I don't think I would have liked it so much," Tava admitted.

"Exactly. Now lick your bottom lip, and lick the edge of your finger, and rub the two together, before the wind can dry them out . . . Easier, isn't it?" he asked.

"Yes, is it," Tava agreed.

"And it feels nicer?" he prompted. "You get more sensations, but they're pleasant ones, right?"

"I suppose so," she said, shrugging.

"Multiply that by a hundred times. If her body is dry and unready, it's going to be unpleasant for the woman. But if she is aroused enough that her nectar flows, she will not be chafed, and she will enjoy it a hundred times more. Whoever attacked your mother, they weren't Shifterai, because Shifterai men are all taught how to arouse a woman, how to make her nectar flow, and how to ensure she enjoys the time spent in her husband's bed," Kodan murmured, holding her gaze. "We may be able to take on the shapes of animals, but you will note that animals wait until their females are in heat and their bodies ripe with nectar before they try to claim their mates. The advantage we have over animals is that we can 'come into season' at any time we wish, by touching and kissing and caressing to excite one another."

That twisting feeling had come back. A little intimidated by it, Tava cleared her throat. "Um . . . men don't need arousing. They just . . . rut. Don't they?"

Kodan stopped, shaking his head, and tugged out the little scrap of grass that had formed the bump. Bracing the knot against his hip, he used it once again to demonstrate. "Men are not like grass-logs. We do *not* go around all day, aroused and ready to rut. If we did, we'd be poking out all the time, and risk damaging ourselves. Not to mention it's difficult to walk when it gets that way. Worse, what if we tripped? The fall might break it off!"

The absurdity of his claim startled a giggle out of her. Covering her mouth, Tava blushed but nodded, conceding his point. "Alright. Men *aren't* aroused every single moment. But . . ."

"It is nothing more than a bit of flesh, Tava. Delicate, in that the pouch at the base needs to be handled delicately," he cautioned her. "And bending it is not a good idea. Unless the male in question is forcing himself on you, in which case I urge you to hit him there. I do suggest you stomp on his foot or hit him in the face or throat first to distract him, as the groin is the first spot a man will instinctively move to defend. But if you want to arouse him, you touch him gently, just as you yourself would want to be touched."

Tava shook her head. "Oh, I don't want . . . I couldn't."

"I think you will. You just haven't thought about it, and you haven't experimented. If you ever *had*, you certainly *would*. But as I was saying, a man has a rod and a sack, and you just caress it—when you're married—as you would want to be touched yourself. With your fingertips, with your mouth, your lips and your, um, tongue." This time it was his turn to blush. Kodan tried not to think about it too much. It helped that he caught her grimacing again. "What?"

"I may not know much about men, but I do know they pass water out of . . . that," she protested, flicking her fingers at the twisted grass.

"Yes, but not all the time, just as your body doesn't pass water all the time. In fact, when a man is aroused, he *can't* pass water. It just all shuts off inside. Sometimes, when a man is dreaming in his sleep, his dreams arouse him," Kodan told her, "and if he wakes up stiff but needs to use a chamber pot or a refreshing tent . . . well, it can be quite painful, waiting for the one need to ease so that he can tend to the other."

"Kodan! You were supposed to gather dried apples!"

The shout startled both of them. Kodan nearly sprained his neck, his head whipped around that fast. Thankfully, his father was closer to the *geome* than to the two of them, though Siinar was striding their way. Flushing until his ears felt burned, Kodan pushed to his feet, muttering, "I am a *multerai* who is about to be named Lord of the Family, and he wants me to gather *dung*?" Raising his voice, he called back, "I sent Kenyen to do that!"

"You should not be spending so much time with an unadopted maiden," Siinar called out, closing the yards of distance between them. "That's why I assigned you that chore, to remind you of your place! Which is *not* to be spent courting an outlander woman. She will not be one of us until she is fully adopted."

"My *place* is leading this warband, Father . . . and I wasn't *courting* her, I was *teaching* her how to twist grass for the fire," Kodan countered, moving forward a few steps to meet his father. He braced his hands on his hips. "I don't know if Medred told you, but your father-in-law sleeps with Mother Earth."

"Yes, and with Chodan's passing, the Councils think to name *you* his successor. Which is why it is vital for you to be circumspect," Siinar chided. "You spend more than enough time with her when you drive her wagon. Running off with her into the grass will not demonstrate the self-control of a leader."

Kodan gaped, then flung out his hands, gesturing. "We are in *full* view of the *geome*, the horses, Mother Earth, and Father Sky! That is *not* 'running off into the grass,' Father. Moreover, with all the misinformation in her background, I am *not* going to pressure her toward such matters."

Siinar held up his hands, coming to a halt a body length away. "I *know* you wouldn't, Kodan. I raised you right. But if you are going to be the Lord of Tiger, our people are going to look closely at everything you do because of it . . . and they'll look sideways at you, too, for being interested in an outlander woman. Thus you must be *more* circumspect than most. I have your best interest in my heart. I am not saying you should not court her, but that you should be a lot more careful in how you follow the laws. In their spirit as well as in their letter. You must wait to court her until her teaching days are through. You can be romantic then, but not one day sooner."

"I would hardly consider the subjects of refreshing tents and chamber pots to be romantic, since that was the topic you interrupted . . . but if you insist that I go spend time elsewhere, then you can teach her how to twist grass-logs while I go gather *rora* vine for the fire." Turning to Tava, he gave her a short bow. "Forgive me for such an abrupt end to your lessons. I hope you will consider the merits of the tips I have given you so far.

"In the meantime, I'm sure my father will continue to teach you the fine art of grass-log twisting in my absence, as well as share many other fascinating tidbits of Shifterai life. Starting with where the refreshing tents are usually dug by custom, in relation to the nearest body of water, to prevent contamination." He gave his father a dry look, and Tava a pointed one, then turned and strode over to where the brown red vines with their heart-shaped leaves could be found.

Siinar watched him go, then looked down at the young woman sitting on the ground. ". . . Refreshing tents and chamber pots? That is what the two of you were discussing so intensely?"

"Yes," she confirmed, glad it was the truth so that she didn't have to lie. It was a slightly stretched truth, but it was the truth. "Though I, um, wouldn't have said intensely so much as, well, embarrassingly— could we talk about something else?"

"Such as?" Siinar asked, settling himself across from her, next to another clump of somewhat longish grass.

"Um . . . all my things. And my animals. If you live in tents three seasons out of four . . . it seems kind of silly to be hauling around all those things. Particularly if it takes most of five wagons to carry it all," Tava admitted.

"Much of that consists of the cages for your fowl. We do not normally take such animals with us," Siinar admitted, adjusting the fall of his tunic hem before plucking several strands of grass. "They stay on the farms ringing the City, since chickens are difficult to herd, and ducks are happier with a body of water nearby. If this were spring or early summer, we would give your animals an escort to the Clan Cat farms; as it is, they will just need to wait a little longer before coming home with all of us.

"When we do get to the Clan farms, your birds will be examined and a value fixed upon them as breeders and layers. Then they will be given to the Clan as a whole to raise, breed, and eat, but you will be given a stipend each year for the value that the birds contribute to the well-being of the Clan as a whole. It won't be much," Siinar warned her, "but a little income is better than none. And they are not bad birds to begin with, plus they have the bonus of being fresh stock, as yet unbred with Plains birds. Most likely they will be reserved more for breeding and laying than for eating, which means you will see a steady amount of income.

"Normally anything gained by the warbands has a one-fifth tax on it, with the tax going first to the Family, and one-fifth of *that* going on to the Clan. But because these chickens and ducks are *your* animals to begin with, you'll get the whole flock listed on your tally. The same with your goats and your gelding, and all the contents of your house. Everything else added to the bargain we made with the village of Five Springs, the extra wagons and horses, the ingots of metal, the lumber, the herbs and the tar-sticks, all of that may be yours in exchange for the sale of your farm, but they were gained after we accepted you among us, so they will be taxed by one-fifth.

"The remaining four-fifths are more than enough to make you either a very cluttered caravaner, or a very wealthy young woman," he finished.

"You're . . . *not* keeping all of those ingots and wagons and horses?" Tava asked, confused.

Siinar shook his gray and brown head, his hair sliding across his shoulders. "Whatever bargain my son may have struck to get you off the Plains, we did not buy *you* with that bandit-slaying contract. Just your presence among us. I would suggest selling most of what you gained because—as you yourself said—it is kind of silly to haul all of that about. Mostly I would suggest selling it to people in the City when we get there. Your furniture does not fold like most of ours does; it is meant to be used in one house in one place, never going anywhere, so it would be better off in the home of a City-dweller. You can trade it for coin or for barter, such as camping chairs and tables, a collapsing bed, a washstand, or anything else that might occupy the inside of a *geome*."

"What about a *geome* itself?" Tava asked, glancing at Kodan, who was tugging thin vines out of the grass a short distance away. "Kodan said it takes hundreds of fleeces to make the felt for one. Do I have enough wealth to buy myself the makings of one?"

Her question made Siinar chuckle. "Hardly. *Geomes* are owned by the men, or by the whole of the tribe, in the case of the Family *geome* and the maidens' *geomes*. It is up to the man to provide the shelter for his family. You could own the sheep, you can own the wood for the staves—you *do* own enough wood for that—and you can own the canvas and the cord, but you cannot own a *geome* as a woman."

Her days among these men made her brave enough to mutter, "That hardly seems fair. At least I owned my own home, in the Valley."

"It is more than fair. A *geome* is nothing more than a shelter . . . and a cold one, in the spring and fall. *You* will own the cookstove and any braziers that may heat it. In fact, tending the hearth is entirely the woman's responsibility. So the first thing you'll want to buy once we get to the City is your own brazier, and the second thing you'll want to look at is a good traveling stove, for knowing what you'll want to buy the day you marry and move into your husband's *geome*—you can get by with a brazier for casual cooking, but a good stove will be a godsend. You can ask my wife, Sinya, what to look for in a really good stove.

"In the meantime, you should start practicing how to twist grass into logs to learn how to keep it in fuel," he reminded her, nodding at the four twists lying on the ground next to her. "You've only made one so far. I see my son had the sense to teach you the three-twist one first; try making another one, and show me what he taught you of it."

She started plucking enough grass to twist, and tried not to blush, let alone think of the *other* things his son had taught her just now.

Off to the side, Kodan eased back on the sharpness of his hearing. His one fear was that she might reveal what their conversation had really been about, but it looked like she wouldn't. His own reddened face could easily be explained by all his stooping, gently teasing up long enough lengths of *rora* vine to burn on the evening fire without breaking the vine and losing some of the precious, pungent sap. But most important, being called to like that had startled the desire roused by their conversation right out of his flesh, allowing him to stand without his father's sharp eyes noticing anything amiss.

Father is right, in that I will be Lord of Tiger and must be more circumspect. But . . . I don't regret sharing that information with her. As much as she needs to hear it from the priestesses themselves, I think it will ease the way, having her hear it from a male first. A nonthreatening, trustworthy male. He nodded to himself as he stripped the seed pods off the vine he had gathered, scattering them toward the south. *Yes, she's better off having heard it first from me. The priestesses will reinforce what I said, but if they'd told her first, she might still have been shy about letting a man touch her, because it would have been shared only by another woman, someone who couldn't possibly force her.*

But I'm a man, I have stated an intent to court her, and so she needed to hear it from me. He paused, glancing subtly at her. *Unless, of course, I'm merely deluding myself because I wanted one last act of rebellion before taking on the leadership of the Family and all its responsibility. Or maybe I just wanted the titillation of sharing something naughty with a maiden . . .*

Kodan stared at her a moment more, listening to her asking his father her questions, and shrugged. *Or maybe I was just sating her curiosity, and nothing more. She even asks about refreshing tents. Blushing, but she asks. I've never known anyone grown, male or female, with as much curiosity as she has—if the priestesses don't answer enough of her questions, I'll gladly answer the rest of them myself, once I'm free to court her again.*

It wasn't until he had four lengths of *rora* coiled neatly around his arm that he recognized the phrasing of that thought. A sharp glance showed Tava was oblivious, focused on twisting the ends of yet another half-mangled grass-log into place. Shaking it off, Kodan headed for the *geome.*

I am not courting her for myself. I'm courting her for the Plains. And anyone would get aroused with such a demonstration. It has little to do with her, herself.

* * *

It had *everything* to do with her.

Unable to sleep, thanks to the dreams that danced through his head whenever he tried, Kodan gave up and shifted shape just enough to grow fur from waist to knees. Leaving his pallet and his neatly folded clothes behind, he picked his way quietly through the others scattered across the floor of the *geome*, sleeping much more peacefully than him. Or as peacefully as one could, given how both the youngest and the oldest members of the warband snored. There was enough noise to cover the sound of him slipping the latch, easing open the *geome* door, and ducking through.

Gently closing the door again, Kodan breathed in the crisp, cold night air, clearing the spicy scent of *rora* smoke from his lungs. The breeze flowed from the north, bringing hints of scents from the herds and braziers of the Family in the distance. Without the brazier in the warband *geome* to keep him warm, Kodan grew more fur across his body, until he was covered from neck to feet, leaving only his head and his hands free.

Facing the other way, he spotted a silhouetted figure a short distance downwind of the trader wagon. Narrowing his eyes, Kodan padded that way. Clouds scudded across part of the night sky, obscuring any glow that might have come from one of the two moons. The starlight was enough for him to pick his way without tripping, but it wasn't until he drew even with the wagon that he recognized the man standing so still as Deian.

It was only after he passed the wagon that he heard the soft, frustrated mutterings of its occupant, and smelled what his friend was apparently inhaling. Biting his lip to keep from growling audibly, Kodan stalked straight up to his friend and glared as best he could, given the very dim light.

Deian raised his finger to his lips. He leaned in close enough to whisper to his friend, ". . . I was wondering if I should go and wake you. She woke with your name on her lips and has since been muttering about not knowing what to touch, or how. Perhaps you know what she means?"

"You should *not* be standing downwind of her, sniffing the breeze as if you were in rut," Kodan hissed back, glad the darkness of the night hid his blush.

Flashing the younger man a grin, Deian tipped his head away from the wagon. "I'll go on a long patrol. You stay here and guard her from anything that might . . . shall we say . . . keep her from a satisfying sleep?"

Shock held him still, long enough for Deian to shift to four legs and lope quietly away. *Deian . . . is* aiding *me in flouting custom?* He glanced at the enclosed wagon, then around the encampment. There were at least three others patrolling, but within a few moments he spotted all of them out at the perimeter, their attention more on the possibility of external threats to the horses, goats, and caged birds than on the activity inside the camp. Duty warred with desire, until he heard another frustrated mutter, ears pricking.

Moving closer to the wagon, he melded with the shadows by the front wheel in time to hear Tava hissing to herself.

"Stupid stupid *stupid* . . . *None* of this works! He didn't seem like he was lying, but . . . ! If this is desire, it *stinks!*"

That didn't sound good. He hadn't told her all those things to make her frustrated and doubtful. His intent had been to reassure her that lovemaking *was* fun, when properly done. Hesitating only a moment, Kodan hissed her name. *"Tava?"*

The wagon rocked a little. A moment later, he heard it creaking, and the sound of her fingers fumbling at the latch holding the forward shutters closed. Unlike the ones on the sides, which opened out, these ones opened inward. She swung one aside and poked her head out, visible only because her face was a paler blot against the dark square of the opening.

"Who's there?"

"*Shh,*" he hissed, switching to a barely audible murmur. "It's me, Kodan."

He heard her sniffing and lifted his arm up over the side of the bench seat, bringing his scent closer to her. She sniffed again, then sighed. "Kodan . . . what are you *doing* here? Are you on night patrol?"

"Shh," he murmured. "Not so loud. You don't want to draw attention from any of the others. I only came out because I couldn't sleep, but then I heard you, um . . ."

She stilled, and he could almost hear her mental embarrassment. He certainly could smell the source of it, faint though it was. She drew in a deep breath and let it out. "Well," she muttered. "Now you know. Either I am so stupid, I can't make heads or tails of your instructions, or I'm as cold to such movements as the surface of the River is in winter."

"You're not cold," Kodan reassured her. He believed it, too. She was too full of life to be as frigid as her claim. "It's just like twisting grass into logs, that's all. It takes practice. You were getting good at twisting logs by the time supper was ready, and you'll learn how to be good at this. I'm sure of it."

She stayed silent several seconds, then muttered, "It doesn't feel anything like a twisted bit of grass. It doesn't work."

"Hold out your hand," Kodan told her. As soon as he saw her limb uncurl itself through the opening, he gently caught her wrist in one hand. "The first thing you have to remember—and which some men forget—is that you *never* start with the loins. That's like dumping raw meat and uncleaned, raw vegetables in a bowl, and calling it stew. You have to prepare the way, divide things into manageable portions, heat them all up, and let it all cook for a while.

"The *first* thing to do is to touch your hands lightly, like this," he instructed, bringing up his other hand so that he could skim the pads of his fingers lightly over her palm. "Slowly and lightly, explore the feel of your skin. Caress it. Only gradually should you move from your fingers to your wrists . . . and only eventually do you stroke your way up your forearm."

She twitched a little in his grip as he trailed his fingers up the outer edge of her arm. "That tickles!"

"Shh," he soothed. "I know. It should tickle, because it feels good, doesn't it?"

". . . Yes."

"Good." Sliding his hands down her arm, he released it. "That is as far as *I* can touch you . . . but if you want to continue . . . I can tell you how to explore yourself. If you want to."

EIGHT

Tava mulled over his offer. It was dark enough that even with her eyes shifted somewhat owlish, she couldn't see much inside the trader wagon. She could see Kodan, but mostly as a shadow along the side of the wagon. Plus the parts she had been exploring were both below the ledge of the window opening, and covered by her nightdress.

She hadn't had any luck touching herself on her own. It just felt weird, and wrong, and . . . well, somewhere between daring and naughty, with a dash of wrongness sprinkled with embarrassment. Those were parts of her body she had only ever associated with things that made a mess, and men causing it pain. *And yet Kodan sounds so sure of himself that there is pleasure to be found . . . and he has been right about other things. So far.*

Her curiosity, mixed with the privacy of the night, prompted her to speak before she was quite aware she had made up her mind. "I want. Um . . . yes. If you think it'll work."

Kodan closed his eyes, both relieved and yet nervous at her capitulation. By the letter of Shifterai law . . . this *was* allowable . . . but not generally considered within its spirit. Stepping closer, wedging himself between the wheel and the front of the wagon, he did his best to meld with the shadows, in case anyone glanced their way.

"Right . . . Sit on your knees and your heels," he directed softly, watching as she withdrew her head and arm from the window opening. "Now, using the same pressure I just used . . . caress the pads of your fingers from the back of your hand up to your elbow. Turn your arm over . . . and trail your fingertips lightly up the soft skin of the underside, all the way up through your palm to your fingers on that hand. Um . . . how does that feel?"

"It tickles," she whispered back, complying. "But . . . I like it. Except it makes my arm feel restless. Is that normal?"

"Yes. Now switch hands and stroke the other one, back and forth, slowly." He couldn't see her anymore, but his ears shifted of their own volition, straining to hear the faint whispering of her fingertips over her skin.

"It doesn't feel quite the same as when you did it," Tava observed, enjoying the soothing yet somewhat enervating touches she was giving herself. "It's still enjoyable, but . . ."

"This is the closest I can be, and still respect you," Kodan reminded her. This was also a very advanced stage of courtship, but she was curious about pleasure. Having read too much of her mother's book, he wanted to erase her fears. "Just . . . imagine that I'm the one touching you."

His words allayed some of her inner fears. Relaxing a little, Tava stroked her arms a few more times, then whispered, ". . . Now what? I feel like my skin is twisting, like a grass-log."

Kodan closed his eyes, remembering how his fingers had stroked the bundled straws. "Now . . . you stroke your upper arms, up over your shoulders, along your throat, and up to your cheeks. You can use your fingertips or the backs of your nails."

"Which would you use?" Tava asked.

She is going to be the death of me. He shifted a little closer, trapping his manhood against the frame of the wagon before it could thicken further. "My fingers up until your throat, and then the backs of my knuckles, with a soft caress of my nails. And then . . . I would cup your cheeks. Tell me . . . how soft is your skin?"

He needed to know. Kodan didn't question why. The painted wood of the wagon lay beneath his own palms, but as she spoke, he imagined the texture of her flesh instead.

"It's warm," Tava admitted, running her fingertips up along the requested path. "The air is cold, so I have a few goose-prickles, but . . . it's warm and smooth, and my cheeks have a very faint, soft fuzz, like the skin of a ripe peach. Only it's softer than that, with more give. It's nicer to touch than my nightdress."

"Good . . . Run your fingers up into your hair. How soft is it?" he asked her.

"Very soft," she reported, raking her fingers slowly over her scalp. "Father always compared it to rabbit fur. Plain brown, but very soft. I didn't braid it, since the night is cold and there's no brazier in the wagon, so it covers my neck and shoulders. I can even feel it keeping most of my back warm, or at least warmer."

"*I would keep you warm.*" As soon as the words breathed free, Kodan bit his lip. *I am* not *courting her for real . . . aren't I?* Dragging his attention back to their lesson, he continued in a murmur, "You have lovely hair. Since it's loose . . . pull some of it down over your front, and stroke it there. Follow the strands down the front of your body, through every curve of each lock."

Raking her hair forward, Tava did as he told her. She didn't have particularly thick hair, and it needed washing, but she had brushed it as best she could, and it was soft and long. A soft gasp escaped her when she trailed her fingers over the tips of her breasts. "Oh!"

"Tell me," Kodan urged, half murmuring, half whispering. "What did you touch? What did you feel?"

"My . . . my hands slid down over my, um, my breasts. And when I got to their tips, I felt . . . twisted, inside. Bound up with something. It felt good," she confessed, and stroked down over her chest again, wanting to feel it again. "Is this . . . desire?"

"It's arousal," he corrected, wishing he could show her the difference in person. "Arousal is contained within oneself. Desire lies within, but it also extends to the other person. You want to give *them* these feelings."

Her hands paused. "Do *you* feel desire? For me?"

He didn't want to alarm her, but he didn't want to lie, either. "Yes . . . but I will stay out here. You are safe from me. I promise you that. Now . . . unfold your legs, and place your hands on your calves."

Puzzled by the odd request, Tava complied anyway, shifting so that she was sitting on her backside instead of her heels. She had to rearrange the skirt of her nightdress, hiking up the hem a little, but managed. "Alright . . . my hands are on my calves. Now what?"

"Rub them, again using a light touch. Rub them in circles that get a little longer with each stroke," Kodan directed her, "until you are cupping your ankles, and tickling the backs of your knees. How does that feel?"

"Nice . . . but the twisting isn't quite as strong as before," she confessed.

"That's alright. Arousal doesn't have to happen all at once," Kodan told her. "Slide your fingertips onto the tops of your feet, and stroke them as you did your hands, and your cheeks."

"Oh! Oh, that feels good. Ticklish, but good." Unbidden, Tava switched to dragging the pads of her fingers up her shins. "I'm touching my shins now. It, um, just felt right . . . and it does feel good."

Good, she's taking initiative. Now, if I can just keep my mind on what she needs to do, rather than on what she is doing . . . Father Sky, preserve me if I go mad. "Circle your fingernails very lightly around your knees," Kodan ordered. "Then stroke just a finger length up along the tops of your thighs, but no more than that from your knees, and stroke back down again."

Doing as she was bid, Tava felt . . . disappointed. "Why only up so far, and no more? It was just starting to feel good up there!"

"Shhh," Kodan soothed, resting his cheek against the painted wood forming the corner of the wagon. "This is called teasing. It builds arousal more strongly than going straight to one's goal . . . and as you are trying to touch yourself as *I* would touch you . . . you may stroke back up onto your thighs, but only as high as two finger lengths. No higher than that, Tava . . . because that is what *I* would do to arouse you."

Yes, it has definitely *been too long since I last visited an earth-priestess* . . . His ears, now elongated and pointed, strained to hear the whispers of skin on skin. His nostrils widened as he inhaled, seeking every scrap of scent he could smell from her, though the wind wasn't entirely in his favor in this position.

What he did smell, listening to her fingers trailing up and down her legs, was his own musk, and he carefully shifted his groin away from the edge of the wagon. The last thing he wanted was to leave the scent of his own arousal all over the vehicle. *Which means . . . dammit . . . I can't do anything about my own needs until I'm well away from this thing* . . . The wind shifted slightly, curling a wisp of feminine musk his way. His instructions were having an effect on the woman in the wagon, stiffening his aching flesh a little more.

"I want to touch more," Tava muttered, switching from fingers to palms and back, trying to evoke more of the shivery-twisty feelings inside her muscles. "Tell me where to touch. Where you would touch."

The Gods have a sense of humor, I see. Smiling wryly, Kodan pictured where her hands should go next. "If you are cold . . . pull the blankets up over your legs. But also pull up the hem of your nightdress. Bunch it around your waist—and try not to touch your flesh in anything but the lightest caress."

Squirming in place, Tava did as he suggested. "Done."

"Slip your hands under the hem of your nightdress and caress your stomach," Kodan directed her, listening to the soft rustle of linen inside the wagon. "Now . . . lie back on your pallet and slide your hands up to cup your breasts, pushing them up. Imagine they are my hands and that I am holding your flesh as gently as a newborn duckling, cupping and stroking them from the base to the tip as lightly as you would pet such soft, downy feathers."

Lying back, Tava paused long enough to tug her old, feather-stuffed pillow under her head, then placed her hands on her stomach. Sliding them up, she imagined they were Kodan's hands, sun-browned and warm. For a moment, she felt a little panicked at the thought of a man grabbing her there . . . but they were her hands, and the words he used said that, even if they were his hands, he *would* handle her flesh gently, not roughly.

He is trustworthy—isn't he outside right now, knowing that he could easily climb in through this window? Yet he stays outside, even though I'm very vulnerable . . . The edge of her thumbnail scraped lightly against one nipple as she stroked her breasts. Her breath caught, triggering his quiet murmur.

"What do you feel?" Kodan asked, clinging to the corner of the wagon with his palms, chest, and cheek at the sound of her faint gasp. "What did you do?"

"My thumbnail . . . against the tip . . ."

He bit his lower lip again, stifling the urge to groan. *"Again,"* he hissed. "Scrape it again, very lightly."

Already puckered from the cold night air, her nipple tightened further. Tava felt an urge to moan, but she wasn't sure how close any of the others might be. There were others out there, men patrolling the edges of the camp to keep it safe from whatever dangers lurked among the grasses of the prairie. But this man was close at hand, and it was his hands she trusted, his hands that her mind substituted for her own.

"*It feels*," Tava whispered, flicking and rubbing first one peak, then the other. "*So good . . .*"

I am going mad, a calm, quiet corner of his mind observed. Right cheek pressed to the corner of the wagon, Kodan brought his left hand to his mouth, biting his knuckle. The window was an arm's length away, open and waiting. He didn't move, save to release his finger and murmur his next instruction.

"With your left hand . . . pluck at your nipple. With your right hand . . . slide it very, very lightly down your belly. Down under the covers," he directed her. "Follow your flesh until you touch your nether-curls—remove any obstacles in your way. If it were my hand, I would not let any scrap of cloth get in my way . . . but I would touch lightly, so very lightly—*yesss!*" he hissed, hearing her gasp, and feeling the slight jiggle of the wagon as her sudden tensing shifted it. He didn't have to be inside the wagon to know how her back had arched, how her muscles had tensed. "Pinch your nipple! Curl up your hips until your fingers can slide down between your thighs, right into the warmth of your nether-lips!"

His voice had started to rise. Kodan bit his knuckle again, silently admonishing himself to keep quiet. Mindful of the shifters assigned to the midnight patrol, he quickly glanced around, but no one seemed to be near. If they hadn't erected the *geome* for most of the rest to sleep in, the two of them would never have been free to do this. But the others were asleep or padding on four feet at the far edges of the encampment. They were alone, for the moment.

Taking his knuckle away, flesh aching from the divots left by his teeth, he asked, "Are you wet?"

The moisture seeping out of her opening surprised her. It was hot and somewhat thick, and very musky, not at all the flowery scent one expected from a more normal sort of nectar. "Yes—yes, I'm wet!"

Again, he bit his knuckle, then forced his hand down. Kodan meant only to free his mouth so that he could speak, so that he could direct her how to touch herself, but his fingers wrapped around his erection. It was pure instinct, and the moment he did so, he could feel his own moisture welling up and seeping from the tip. "So am I . . ."

It took Tava a few moments, fingers gently probing her wetness, to realize what he meant. "*You . . . are wet?*"

Blinking, Kodan stilled the subtle movement of his fingers and gathered his wits. "Uh . . . yes. When a man is . . . very aroused . . . the tip of him weeps its own nectar. Both are, um . . . meant to lubricate the blissful joining of . . . of a man and a woman, to ensure that both of them enjoy it—slide your finger around your middle opening. Gather the moisture, and bring it up to that bump near the top," he directed her. "Rub it gently into your skin up there."

"It's already wet up there," Tava murmured, exploring the folds. The twisting shock that speared through her body surprised her. "Oh! Ohhh . . . oh . . . that feels so good! Why didn't it feel like this before?"

"You, mmm, weren't aroused before," Kodan muttered, resting his forehead against his right wrist. He really shouldn't stroke himself, or let anything more seep from his flesh. The others would smell it if he went any further. Carefully wrapping his fingers around the base of his shaft, he slowly squeezed, focusing more on the compressive pain than on the pleasure of his own touch. "Interest isn't automatically there. Sometimes it arrives on its own, but most of the time . . . it has to be awakened. In both men and women. For a man . . . it's often a sight or a smell. For a woman . . . it's often a sound or a touch. Sometimes it's the other way around . . . and sometimes . . . sometimes it's a *taste* that arouses the flesh."

"A taste?" she asked, eyes widening, though there wasn't anything worth seeing beyond the cloud-scattered sky beyond the half-open shutters.

"*Yesss,*" he hissed, tightening his grip on himself. It wasn't helping. *I'll have to catch it all and scrub my hands in the water, if I go through with this . . . Mother Earth, I don't think I could walk, let alone walk away right now . . .*

Giving in, Kodan shifted his position so that his weight was propped up on his right shoulder. Wrapping his right hand around his flesh, he lengthened the webbing between the fingers of his left hand, cupping the tip of his shaft. The scent of her musk wafted out of the wagon, swirling and mingling with his in the slow night wind. It was too heady a combination to resist.

"Kodan?" Tava asked, feeling his weight shifting against the wagon.

"*Taste* yourself," he urged, stroking his own flesh with a slow, firm pressure. "Dip your finger into your opening, then bring it up to your mouth, and . . . lick . . . ohhh . . ."

"Kodan? Are you . . . You're not coming in *here*, are you?" Tava asked quickly, unnerved by his soft moan and the hints of male musk she could smell.

"No! No . . . I'm staying out here, I promise," he muttered, struggling to keep his voice barely audible. "I respect you. I *desire* you . . . but I respect you, and I will stay out here. Lick your fingers, and circle them around your nub. Dip them down into your nectar and stroke all around, but especially that little bump. That's what I would do to you," he promised, "if you were my wife. But for now, you can do it to yourself as much as you like . . ."

It almost felt like *his* fingers were touching her, circling her flesh. She stroked them lightly at first, then with more pressure. "Kodan . . . ohh . . . it *feels* . . ."

"*Flick!*" he ordered. "Hard and fast!" He switched from his slow stroking to a faster, firmer pumping, pausing only to dampen his fingers and palm with a few quick licks of his tongue. Her gasp and the faint tremor of the wagon told him she was shuddering under his suggested caress. His own muscles trembled in sympathy, and he followed his own instructions. "Faster . . . *faster* . . ."

"*Kodan!*" Trying not to be loud, Tava choked on his name. The rapid strokes of her fingertips had twisted up her insides until they flashed with heat, making her feel as if she were on fire. Her left hand, tucked up under her nightdress and half forgotten, clutched at her left breast, augmenting her pleasure with the squeezing pressure. Her hips bucked, and her finger dipped lower than the stiff, damp nub of flesh giving her so much pleasure. The tip of it dipped into her body, and *that* felt good, enough that she pressed deeper of her own volition, and shuddered with a deeper, hungrier bliss.

A moment later, dazed and falling back down through her bliss, she heard him groaning, too. She felt the wagon shudder slightly in time with his half-choked gasps. Panting, she slowly relaxed, feeling very tired and yet very—even astonishingly—happy with herself. With what had just happened. She could feel her cheeks aching and realized she was smiling. Pleased, Tava slipped her fingers free of her flesh and brought them back up to her lips. The scent of her nectar was salty-sweet and musky, as was its taste.

". . . Kodan?" she asked after her fingers were more or less clean.

"Mmm . . . yes?" he muttered, carefully cradling the mess he had made in his webbed left hand. If he hadn't automatically adjusted the length and thickness of the fur warming his flesh, he would have been sweating from the aftermath of his release.

"What do you taste like?"

He choked at her question, almost slopping the cooling liquid puddled in his hand. "Uh . . . salty? And musky?"

"You haven't tasted yourself?" she asked, wondering at the hesitance in his voice.

"Uh, yes, I have, but . . . I've tasted women far more often, and I like it much better." For a moment, he was tempted to offer a taste of his seed, but they had gone far enough as it was. Still, he didn't want to just end their midnight connection. Licking his lips, he told her what he would have done, if he could have. "If we were mated . . . I wouldn't be out here. I would be in there with you. I would lick your fingers clean, and kiss your sweet mouth. I would stroke your skin, soothing the sweat roused by your pleasure . . . and I would wrap my arms around you, holding you close as we drifted into sleep together."

That sounded . . . nice. Surprisingly nice. The last man to hold her had been her father, and aside from an occasional hug in the privacy of their home, he hadn't held her since she was a young girl. The thought of Kodan holding her was an alluring one.

"Tava?" Kodan asked.

"Yes?" she replied, pushing up on one elbow.

"Don't forget to close the shutter. I can smell the dew beginning to gather in the night air. I wouldn't want you to get damp . . . the wrong kind of damp," he couldn't help adding.

Blushing at his words, Tava sat up and swung the shutter back into place. She paused before closing it completely, whispering, "Good night, Kodan. Thank you . . . and, um, sleep well."

He grinned, resting his cheek against the corner of the wagon. "I believe I will. Good night."

Mindful of the mess cupped in his hand, he headed for the pond. The water would be very cold, but it would be enough to wash the seed from his skin and take most of the smell with it. A quick, wary glance showed the others still patrolling out beyond the edge of the half-dozing, half-grazing horses. Including Deian.

I'll have to thank Deian somehow for allowing me this opportunity. And for keeping it a secret. Not that I broke Shifterai law, not exactly . . . but I doubt I'll have this kind of chance again, once we rejoin the Family. Father is right; the moment I become Lord of Tiger, everyone will be watching me, and watching whomever I choose to court.

That thought was a little depressing, but the rest of him was too satisfied to care. *Now she knows what pleasure is like, and that a man can desire her and not attack. She trusts me . . . and she wants to know what I taste like!* Plus, they hadn't been caught. All in all, he was rather pleased with himself.

* * *

They were almost to the Family, and she still couldn't stop blushing. Not that she was blushing quite so much by now, but every once in a while, she would look over at Kodan, who would be glancing her way, and when their eyes met . . . she blushed. To be fair, he blushed a little, too. He also smiled at her. A lot. He also engaged her in conversation, asking her more questions about her childhood, about the books she had read, and about the things she liked to do.

Right now, they were traveling through herds of sheep, having passed the herds of cattle and horses at the outer edges of the large encampment. Kodan pointed at the tents they were approaching. "The *geomes* of Family Tiger are laid out in a specific pattern. The structures that the whole Family uses are set up in the center: the two Council *geomes* where problems are brought to the two factions for solving, decorated in either horizontal or vertical stripes; the *ageome*, the Lord's tent with its paintings of tigers and nothing but tigers, where those problems the Councils cannot solve are brought and where lawbreakers are brought for Truth Stoning and sentencing.

"Then there is the healer's *geome* with its red and white walls, where the sick and injured are tended; the all-gold teaching *geomes* where the priesthood give our children and young adults their lessons; and the all-white, holy *geome* where one can go to worship Father Sky and Mother Earth. They're all arranged around the great bonfire pits in the center.

"Beyond them in eight spokes stretch the private *geomes*, and the milking stalls—those are the tents with domed roofs but no walls, the ones spaced between the spokes of the camp," Kodan told her, pointing at the canvas roofs in question. "Each one is painted with the animal shapes its owner can take, and here and there will be the red and green refreshing tents. The *geomes* that are all blue are bathing halls—you will use the one's with the red-painted doors, not the green ones, just like the refreshing tents. Close to the center of the camp along each spoke are the eight maidens' *geomes*. You will know those because they are painted to look like a grove of birch trees.

"Farther out are the eight earth-priestess *geomes*, at about the mid-point in each spoke; those are painted with rolling hills. At the very ends are spots reserved for the eight warband *geomes*, which have a diamond painted around the pertinent body part identifying it," he said. "This is why we had to swing to the right a little, since we're aiming for the South Paw site. That's the right hind foot of the Tiger, with the Tailtip warband on the southwest spoke in between it and the West Paw, which is the left hind foot of the Tiger. Most everyone who fights in the South Paw Warband lives in the South Paw spoke.

"Continuing sun-wise, we have the Left Flank, North Paw, Sharp-tooth, East Paw, and Right Flank," Kodan continued, gesturing in a broad circle as he explained. "The herds stretch out in similar spokes, as you have seen, with the long-grass eaters at the very ends, and the short-grass eaters closest to camp. When we travel as a Family, we use the larger *geomes* for communal sleeping each night and eat at communal meals, since it's less work to put up and take down when you have miles to go. But once we reach a suitable spot for pasture . . . which is . . . ?"

"Wherever you have plenty of water," Tava supplied at his prodding.

"Wherever *we* have plenty of water, yes," he agreed. "Once we're at a pasturing site with plenty of water, we spread out and set up all our individual tents. You'll notice that all of the personal tents are painted, usually with the animal shapes that the man who owns it can make."

Tava eyed the trampled, short-cropped grass. "How long do you stay in one area?"

"Depending on the size of the Family herds at the time, the water reserves, the growth of the grass in our absence, and the time of year, we can stay in one spot anywhere from one to six weeks."

"How do you tell which animals belong to which person?" Tava asked, peering next at the sheep they were passing. Children tended them, with the bigger animals being tended by the older youths. Tava craned her neck to look back at the fringes of the herds. Here and there, adults sat on horses, watching for strays and guarding the camp's borders. But none of them seemed concerned about keeping particular groups of animals together, merely types. "They don't seem to be separated in any particular way."

"Those that have ears, have those ears pierced by a thin steel wire, which is strung with a bone bead. That bead is carved with the owner's name, Family, and Clan. Those that do not—like your ducks—will have the bead on a band around their leg. And those that are milked, they know to come to the milking stalls. Otherwise, they are tended as a group. Unless it's their season, in which case we keep very careful track of them to ensure we know what the breeding lines will be—well, all of them but the goats. You can't stop goats from breeding in any season, or at least trying to breed," Kodan admitted, shrugging. He glanced at Tava and smiled slyly. "Much like men and maids, if they're interested in each other."

"You don't brand your animals?" Tava asked, trying hard not to blush. The closer they got to all those *geomes*, the more attention their caravan was drawing. "We never had many goats and only the one gelding, so we never bothered, but I know the richer Alders in the village brand their most valuable beasts."

Kodan shook his head. "We're not barbarians. We may raise them for their milk and their meat, but a tiny earring hole is less painful for the animals to endure than burning a mark into their hide."

She spotted something on the necks of some of the sheep. "What about the ones with the collars?"

"Those are special sheep. They belong to Clan Snake . . . um . . . Family Copperhead. We put the collars on them to make them easier to spot at a distance, to remind everyone—particularly the children— that these are not Family Tiger animals. If they are injured through our carelessness, we have to pay five times their value to their rightful owners in Family Copperhead, instead of the usual twice their value."

"Why do you have . . . ?" Tava broke off as he nodded quickly, anticipating and acknowledging her next question.

"I'm getting to that. Right now, Family Copperhead is having a Farm year. They're tilling the fields and harvesting the crops for Clan Snake this season. As you can see, a Family has a *lot* of herd animals . . . and they must be pastured in different places throughout the three herding seasons, or they'll not only eat the grass to bare earth; they'll wander into the fields and eat the crops before they can grow, trampling everything to dust. Every winter, the Herding Council consults the records of the breeding lines and arranges for the herds of the Families about to start a Farm year to be shared among the other Families.

"Usually that's within their own Clan, but sometimes they hand them out to other Clans and Families, particularly if the lines are getting too closely bred for their health," Kodan continued. "Any calf, kid, lamb, or foal dropped by a female stays with that particular female's herd, and thus with that particular Family. It increases wealth and fosters ties with the other Clans and Families."

Tava mulled that over. "It also shares the burden of extra animals to feed, doesn't it? Preventing overgrazing?"

"Correct. We have sheep from Family Copperhead, Clan Snake," Kodan said, "and one of the five cattle herds from Family Lion—they have almost two thousand people, and it's said the Queen will debate this winter whether they should be broken up into two Families, one to remain Family Lion, the other to take on a new name, or asked to send some of their kin to the smaller Families. Not just in Clan Cat, but in some of the other Clans as well.

"You'll learn a lot more about Clans and Families from the priesthood in your history lessons over the next ten days—all of your questions *will* be answered," he gently teased. "But as we are coming up on the site for the warband *geome*, I will have to focus on other things.

Since I am the warband leader, it is up to me to blow the *an-tak* and officially let everyone know we are safely home."

"*An-tak?*" Tava couldn't help but ask.

Kodan grinned and freed a hand from the reins long enough to point. "If you lean a little to your right, you should see a wrought iron stand in the clearing up ahead and a big, curving ram's horn hanging from it. As soon as we stop, I'll hand you the reins, dismount, and blow three sets of signals. The first one—you'll also learn these from the priests—is to say that South Paw Warband has returned. The second says that no one in the warband died while we were gone."

"Happy news for their waiting family members to hear," Tava murmured, thinking of how she had discovered her own father's absence only when their gelding had returned without him.

"Exactly. And the third . . . if I can remember all the notes right, since I haven't heard them in a long while . . . is that we have brought a newcomer to the Family. That way, everyone will know you are coming to stay among us and aren't merely a guest traveling across the Plains to somewhere else," Kodan explained. "There are also calls for when traders come, and calls to announce a birth or a death, to call for help in an emergency—all the outriders and the older, more responsible children carry a small horn with them, so they can signal for help if they need it."

"That's assuming I *am* going to stay. I might just leave at the end of the year. Or sooner, if I don't like it here," Tava reminded him, though she knew her resolve on that point was weakening.

Kodan gave her a pointed look of his own. "This is your home, Tava. You already fit in with us far more than you ever did with the Mornai . . . and you will see how much you truly belong with us, as you learn more. The priesthood will tell you these things, because you need to know how our culture was formed and why we're so very different from what your mother's book said."

"Speaking of which, where *is* my mother's book?" she asked. "I asked Manolo if he knew which wagon it had been packed into, but he didn't know. Nor did the others."

"I have it. I've been reading it in the evenings, after you retired. I hope you don't mind," Kodan added, guiding the mares so that they pulled the wagon up alongside the one in front of it. "They might be long gone, but these Mongrel shifters might also still exist. From what I've managed to figure out so far from the things your mother related, they seemed to have lurked in the southernmost reaches of the Plains. That's Clan Dog territory, not Clan Cat, so I can't be completely sure, but it also looked like they were on the very fringes of the Plains and often took refuge in the hills bordering the edge of the Correda Mountains, possibly to hide from being discovered.

"Clan Dog might not have known of their existence as a whole . . . but someone might have known of them as an individual, and if they did, and did not report them, I want to know why. Because they were *not* Shifterai," he asserted, halting the wagon a few lengths from the stand bearing the large, spiraling horn. He set the brake with his foot, most of his attention still on her. "I can't be sure, but she describes several of the men as having 'strange marks' on their foreheads . . . which is the one thing we *do* brand. When a Shifterai is such a law-breaker that his punishment is to be banished, we mark his forehead with a brand made of bluesteel, which means the scar will *never* shift shape along with the rest of him, and he will always be recognized as a criminal on the Plains.

"If these men were Shifterai criminals, then it's all the more imperative that we find out if they're still around. No one should go through what your mother endured, and I want to make absolutely sure they're completely gone. One way or another."

Passing her the reins, Kodan stepped over her knees, jumping down from the wagon bench. A few strides got him to the horn, and a deep breath allowed him to blow on the spiral instrument. The notes the ram horn produced vibrated through Tava's chest, echoing out across the prairie. Some of the Valley-raised horses whickered and shied from the abrupt, loud sounds, but the mares hitched to the trader's wagon merely flicked their ears.

The mix of staccato and long notes ended, and he switched to a two-pitch, happy-sounding trumpeting. The third blast added a third note somewhere in the mix, higher than the first two, which he squeaked at first. Kodan played through it anyway, then released the horn with a sigh of relief, hanging it back on the iron stand by its braided leather strap. Coming back to the wagon, he smiled up at Tava.

"There! Now everyone will know we've brought someone new home with us. And you *are* home, Tava," he promised, touching her skirt-covered leg.

NINE

"Hey, no flirting," one of the others said, coming up behind Kodan. Deian clapped his hand on the taller shifter's shoulder and dropped his voice. "She's now officially with the Family, so you need to take her up to the center to present to the priestesses. Do you want me to start the tally of her goods and animals, or have Manolo do it?"

"I think Manolo will want to greet his children after being absent so long, so if you'd be willing . . . ?" Kodan asked.

Deian nodded, then leaned in close, gripping Kodan's shoulder to hold him still for a moment more. "As for last night," he murmured in Kodan's ear, "I'll expect your help in learning a thirteenth shape, in exchange for my silence. I *will* learn a new one. I *know* I can. I just haven't found the right shape for my next beast."

Kodan glanced up at Tava, who was craning her neck, looking at all the approaching members of Family Tiger. "I will help . . . if you'll let Tava watch."

"If I'll let . . . ? Why should *she* watch?" Deian asked, quirking one of his brows.

"Because she doesn't know how we train our shapeshifters," Kodan replied. "Because it isn't something the priesthood would think to teach her, nor could they teach her . . . and because she has a curiosity as boundless as the arms of Father Sky."

Hearing his quip, Tava blushed. Kodan smiled at her in reassurance. Sighing, Deian tossed up his hands.

"Fine! Indulge her every whim! Just get her to the center. Her ten days begin as soon as she is lodged with the priestesses, so the sooner she gets to them, the sooner I can get your help in learning a new shape . . . and the sooner *you* can get back to courting her," the shorter man teased pointedly, clapping Kodan one more time on the shoulder before moving away.

"He has a point. The sooner you get into your ten days, the sooner you'll have most of your questions answered. Come," Kodan urged, holding up both of his hands to help her down from the wagon bench. "Deian will take care of your things, at least until I can come back to watch over them. You won't need most of it for now, anyway."

Letting him take her hand in his once she was safely on the ground, Tava asked one of the questions his words stirred. She *wanted* to ask Kodan how the Shifterai trained their shapechangers, wanted to know how that differed from the undoubtedly haphazard way she had discovered such things, but she was still wary of revealing that she, too, could shift her shape. So instead, she asked something safer.

"Manolo has children?"

"Manolo lost his wife to a plague of wracking-cough that swept through the City two years ago. Almost a thousand of us died before the Healer-priests found the right combination of herbs and spells to heal the sickest among us." Kodan shook his head. "We're usually quite healthy, and careful to isolate those who are ill when we gather in large numbers, but sometimes such things spread too quickly to be caged—yes, Father?"

"I will escort our newest member to the camp center," Siinar stated, holding out his hand to Tava.

"*I* will escort her," Kodan asserted. His father opened his mouth to argue. Guessing what about, Kodan cut him off. "But you are welcome to walk with us, to help observe the proprieties."

"The proprieties include you *not* holding on to her hand for so long," the older Shifterai pointed out.

Sighing roughly, Kodan released Tava's fingers. "Fine. This way, Tava. As Deian said, the sooner we do this, the sooner we'll get to do everything else."

Biting back an urge to smile, Tava contented herself with walking at his side. The whole concept of being courted was still a novel one, for her. Hearing Kodan's impatience, coupled with her memories of the previous night's explorations, made her feel wanted.

Desired, rather, she corrected herself. *I don't think he's actually aroused at this moment, but I do know he likes me.* She wrinkled her nose a moment later. *Lovely.* Now *I want to hold his hand, only I can't.* At least these customs were reassuring, even if they were a bit more restrictive than she had expected.

The sheer number of people wasn't entirely expected, either. The village of Five Springs contained maybe four hundred people, but only on rare occasion had she ever seen all of them gathered together. The men, women, and children heading toward them easily numbered that many.

The members of Family Tiger were friendly, calling out greetings with smiles and upraised hands. Thankfully, she didn't have to greet each and every one. Kodan and Siinar merely introduced her every so often as "Tava Ell Var, formerly of the Mornai" as they walked along. No one impeded their path toward the middle of the camp, either.

Catching sight of her soft, puzzled frown, Kodan asked, "Something is bothering you?"

"They're not asking questions," Tava said. "I thought your people asked lots of questions."

Siinar answered from her other side. "They will, but *after* you have been tucked under the care of the priestesses. At that point, *we* will be interrogated over the next several days, just as you will be taught. Kodan will have to explain his decision to bring you onto the Plains to both the Council of Sisters and the Council of Shifters."

"I won't be in trouble with them," Kodan said, interpreting her swift glance his way. "They will just want to make sure I considered how well you would fit into the Shifterai way of life. Which you will," he reassured her. "Far more than you ever suited Valley life. Once you've learned our history and the basics of our culture, when you come out of the priests' care, then you'll be asked all the questions you can answer about the Mornai way of life. Just as you'll be expected to ask yet more questions about ours . . . unless you're too shy to ask."

She smiled at his teasing and turned her attention back to the dome-roofed tents they were passing. It was easy to tell which ones were common-use by the differences in their decorations. It was also easy to tell which ones were the refreshing tents, since they were small, square, and solid-colored. A blushing request to detour toward one was granted, allowing her to see the inside of the red one.

The front of the tent was divided from the back by plain white curtains strung to either side of the tall central pole, and the back half was divided again by a third curtain, forming two little rooms. The two little back areas each had a wooden box with a lid, a basket of what looked like ashes, and a basket of fresh-picked, broad-bladed grass. Tava recognized it quickly enough as the kind recommended for such needs.

Four more poles held up the corners inside, supported by a short metal shaft caging each pole in place with iron rings, while lines had been strung out to stakes set in the ground from the spikes piercing reinforced holes in the corners of the canvas. In the front half, there was another one of those clever wrought iron washstands to one side, with a scrap of linen, a pot of softsoap, and what looked like recently freshened water in the bowls. On the other side of the entrance in the front half were extra, lidded baskets, no doubt containing more ashes and grass.

I think this just might be more civilized than the old refreshing hut back home, she decided, gingerly lifting the lid on one of the boxes and peering down inside. It was hard to see, with the red walls of the tent lending their scarlet glow to everything, but it looked like the pit dug below the box was well maintained. *Certainly it doesn't smell as bad as I'd have thought, and that washstand is a very nice touch . . .*

Sliding the curtain into place on its rod for privacy, she used the tent as it was intended, then ducked out to scrub her hands in the way she had seen the warband men doing it, first soaping her hands over the graywater bowl, then using the dipper to pour fresh water over her skin. Another woman came into the tent as she was rinsing, an older woman who smiled at her. The woman's smile slipped a little as she dropped her gaze to Tava's dress, and she *tsk*ed.

"Forgive me, I can see you are the outlander the South Paw brought home, but . . . what is that *thing* you are wearing?" the gray-and-black-haired woman asked, wrinkling her nose.

Tava glanced reflexively at her dress, one of her older, pink-dyed gowns. "It's just a dress. A Mornai dress."

"It makes you look like you're wearing a root bag. It is too loose and shapeless. I am Kinedi, one of the Family weavers. I will teach you how to make good Shifterai clothes—you will look very beautiful when you are done, I promise you that," she added, stepping into the other stall and tugging the curtain shut. "Priestess Soukut will no doubt be your chief teacher. I will ask her to let me be your weaving teacher. I think the cloth might be salvageable, but the shape of that dress is not. You are on the Plains now, and you should wear Plains clothes."

"Um . . . thank you," Tava replied politely. She reminded herself that her pride couldn't be stung very much because it *was* an old gown. She supposed, compared to the fitted tunics of the Shifterai, her Mornai dress was rather baggy. But the woman's freely expressed opinion was a bit of a shock, particularly since they were merely in a canvas-walled tent. Anyone outside could have heard her words, including the two men waiting for her. Drying her hands, she stepped outside.

The moment she came out, Kodan studied her clothes objectively. He had heard the weaver's comments, but then, Kinedi hadn't bothered to lower her voice. "She's right. You need Shifterai clothes."

Tava blushed and looked down at her dress again. "I suppose . . ."

"There were plenty of bolts of cloth in the loot we took from the bandit camp. I will trade you, ounce for yard, some of your share of the ingots paid for your farm for some of the warband's share of the cloth we gained," Kodan offered.

Almost agreeing, Tava closed her mouth before she could speak, giving his offer some thought. "Ounce for yard . . . of just the copper, or of the other ingots, too?"

Kodan saw the shrewd wariness in her green eyes and was halfway delighted by it. Not completely, since he did realize he had just awakened whatever bartering instinct she had, but somewhat delighted. He decided to test her trading skills. "Ounce for yard of all."

"Ha! Ounce for yard of the copper, ounce for *three* yards of the bronze, and ounce for *ten* yards of the iron!" She planted her hands on her hips to hide their trembling, since part of her was still nervous that such outspoken daring on her part would bring down the wrath of . . . well, maybe not Kodan, but probably of his father. Or the other men clustering nearby, studying the strange woman in their midst.

To her surprise, not only did those other men grin; Siinar laughed and clapped her on the shoulder. "You, young maiden, have the tongue and heart of a Shifterai woman, not one of those meek Mornai maids . . . but you should have asked for two yards per copper and twelve per iron—and make sure you save enough iron to trade for a good cookstove, almost pound for pound, once we get to the City."

A glance at the men and women around her showed only approval. Even the woman from the refreshing tent, Kinedi, was smiling and waiting to hear her reply. Once again, Tava felt like she were a butterfly, still trapped in its cocoon . . . but with the shell of that cocoon finally beginning to break open.

Facing Kodan, she lifted her chin. "Three yards per ounce of copper, *seven* yards per ounce of bronze . . . and *none* of the iron!"

Laughter roared from the others. It took her a moment to realize they were laughing at Kodan—whose suntanned cheeks had flushed—and not at her. It took her another moment to realize *he* was smiling. That he wasn't offended by her brash raising of the price.

Arms folded across his chest, Kodan rubbed his chin and considered her offer. ". . . *Two* yards per ounce of copper, *four* yards per ounce of bronze . . . and I'll throw in a spool of thread and two metal buttons for every four yards."

Tava looked at the men and women around her and found the weaver-woman pointing at her shoulder, where the front of her *chamsa* tunic was fastened along her right shoulder by three buttons. The older woman then pointed to her hip on that same side and held up four fingers, mouthing the number.

"A spool and *four* buttons. One button per yard," she clarified as Kinedi smiled.

"One button for every three yards, and the fourth is the spool," Kodan countered.

"The *first* is the spool," Tava corrected. "And . . . Kinedi picks out the fabric and the lengths to make . . ."

"To make her six summer-weight and four winter-weight sets of *chamsas* and *breikas*," Kinedi supplied. "Plus two night-tunics, and enough felting for two pairs of *mocasha* and two winter coats."

"Agreed." Unfolding his arms, Kodan held up his palms. He stepped forward when she would have clasped hands, switching it instead to a forearm grip. "*This* is how we seal bargains on the Plains."

"Ah." She gripped his forearms and let him shake and squeeze a little . . . and felt his two littlest fingers lightly caressing her skin on the undersides, where it would be difficult for the others to see the subtle movement. Their eyes met, and she felt her cheeks grow warm with a blush. "Agreed."

Sliding his fingers free of her forearms, he nodded at the weaver. "You should clasp forearms with her, too, to seal your bargain . . . once you've settled on what you'll pay her for her services, of course."

"I'll take one of each of those three metal buttons. That will pay for my part of the labor, the skill and the teaching, and I'll throw in the leather for the soles and toes of the *mocasha*—the winter boots you will need. You will be taught how to make them yourself, to pay for the rest of it," Kinedi bartered. "It is a generous offer, but then, you will need decent clothes to become one of us."

Unsure whether or not that was a good barter, Tava glanced at Kodan. Both he and his father nodded. Nodding herself, she clasped forearms with the woman. "Agreed."

"Agreed! Now go on; the priests are waiting for you," the gray-and-black-haired woman urged her. "Don't forget to tell Soukut that I will be your weaver-teacher, if you want to get your barter's worth!"

"I won't forget," Tava promised, feeling elated at what had just happened. Not the barter itself, for she was used to bartering for what she needed from the other women in the village, but for the fact that she had done so in public, surrounded by men . . . and all of them had approved of her brash counteroffers. She felt light inside, as if she could just leap up and float on the next breeze.

The buoyant feeling persisted all the way to the center of camp, past modest-sized *geomes* painted with animals, wagons covered with heavy tarps, and the occasional animal, usually a horse but sometimes a cat. It surprised her to see the fluffy, striped cats, but she didn't figure out why until the all-blue teaching *geome* came into view. Knowing she had only a few more moments, Tava quickly turned to Kodan with her question.

"Kodan—I see these little cats here and there, and they're clearly pets, but I don't see any dogs. Is it because this is Clan Cat, or . . . ?"

He shook his head. "It's more that dogs don't always get along with shapeshifters, even in the Families of Clan Dog. We don't know why, though some say it could be because our smell changes just enough that a dog thinks of the reshaped shifter as a newcomer and a possible threat to its pack."

"There are a few canine bloodlines that get along, but they're kept more on the farms with the overseers," Siinar explained. "Those are the Shifterai who choose to farm all the time, instead of travel. Those are usually the non-shifter men anyway, so they're probably less of an ongoing threat in the dogs' minds. Besides," the older man added, shrugging eloquently, "who needs to raise and train a herd-dog when you have a shapeshifter at hand?"

"Teaching the newcomer how to suck an egg is *my* job, young man," a new voice interjected.

The strength of the woman's voice made Tava look that way. The sight of the short, sun-wrinkled, white-haired, white-clad woman startled her, for she stood with the posture of a woman in her twenties, spoke with the confidence of a woman in her forties, yet had the body of a woman closer to her seventies. Hazel green eyes studied Tava thoroughly from head to boot and back.

"Well. South Paw brings us a new daughter. Do you come here of your own free will? Do you come to learn the life of the Shifterai, to become one with us and our ways in all things that matter?"

The blunt questions caught her off guard. Tava knew she could answer that she was here only because Kodan was holding her things ransom in exchange for her presence. That she only intended to stay either a month or a year. But a glance at the others, at Kodan himself, at Siinar, at the friendly middle-aged Kinedi, and the other men and women who had followed in her wake, reminded her of what had just happened. That she had been herself—*not* having to bite her tongue and be demure and quiet—and these people, *these* people had approved.

Kodan is right. I was as well suited to Valley life as an eagle raised to think it was a duck. I am not a duck of the Valley. I was meant to soar the skies, not spend my life floating on water. I'm not completely sure I'm an eagle of the Plains, but I do know I am one . . . and I am far better off here than I ever was down there. Squaring her shoulders, she faced the white-clad woman.

"Yes. I am here of my own free will, and . . . I *do* wish to learn the ways of the Shifterai."

"Good! I am Soukut. I am the hearth-priestess of Family Tiger, and still something of an earth-priestess for the older men—you will find out what those things mean in a little bit," Soukut dismissed, flicking her fingers. "You may call me Priestess, Soukut, or some combination of the two. Now, what do I call you, and where were you from?"

"Tava. Tava Ell Var, of Five Springs village, down in the Valley. The Morna Valley," Tava clarified, just in case.

"I figured as much, from your clothes," Soukut muttered, giving Tava's clothes a dismissive glance. "Priest Yemii has been busy finding a selection of clothes for you to try, and Priestess Soulet—she is my daughter, and one of three mage-priests in all of Family Tiger—is heating a bath for you. From the skin out, and from the mind in, we will bathe away your old life and immerse you in one that is new. Come!"

Bemused, Tava turned to look at Kodan. He bowed, pressing his palms together. "I will see you in ten days. I promise."

Tava had the feeling the priestess caught every word. She wanted to reach out to Kodan, to touch him one last time for reassurance, but guessed that it was now forbidden. Nodding her head, she hurried to follow the priestess toward the all-white *geome* a few yards away. As soon as she caught up, she held her tongue for maybe two, three heartbeats, then let her questions spill out.

"Priestess . . . what is an earth-priestess, versus a hearth-priestess? Where am I supposed to stay during these ten days? Who do I pay for the clothes I will wear, until my own can be made? Oh—I'm supposed to say that I made a barter with Kinedi the weaver, for her to teach me Shifterai weaving in exchange for her making me some, uh . . . well, I suppose *you'd* call them decent clothes. You don't mind, do you?"

The aging woman chuckled, opening the door of the holy *geome*. "Patience. All your questions will be answered. First, we pay homage to the Gods: Father Sky and Mother Earth."

The interior of the *geome* was as spacious as the warband *geome*, with a tiger-hide-draped altar set up in the middle of the four ceiling posts and with objects fastened to the latticework walls. But it was the floor and the ceiling that caught and held Tava's attention. The ground had been laid with thick green and yellow felt, matted in such a way that it suggested patterns of low bushes amidst sun-yellowed grass, exactly like the prairie outside. The only spot not covered by the felt was a patch of earth right in front of the altar, where the sod had been moved aside and the soil mounded up so that it was level with the felt flooring.

The ceiling was hung with taut-pulled cloth panels just beneath the roof staves, each panel dyed light blue and painted with the fluffy tufts of white and gray clouds. Instead of four lightglobes hanging from the edges of the ceiling, a huge, pale yellow ball hung from the center, stiffened on the inside with what looked like a long spiral of thin-carved reed. Judging from the bright glow radiating through the thin, oiled paper, there had to be at least three lightglobes inside, if not four.

Tava found herself urged into kneeling in front of the altar and coached into asking the Patron God and Goddess of the Shifting Plains for Their loving protection while she lived among the Shifterai. Then she had to kiss the dirt in front of the altar, but it was no worse than having mud smeared on her forehead for the spring and autumn festivals, or having water dabbed in the summer. Certainly, kissing the soil was far more pleasant than having a chunk of river ice rubbed over her brow in the winter by the village priest back home.

But I'm not back home, Tava reminded herself, discreetly brushing her lips clean as she stood back up. Soukut didn't say anything against it, just said a few more words on behalf of her deities, then led the younger woman through a door in the back of the *geome*. The large white *geome* wasn't the only one that was all white; several smaller ones had been grouped together in a close-fitted circle, forming a sort of private courtyard. Most had their doors facing in, and each door was painted differently from the rest. In the center of the grass, someone had dug a broad fire pit, though at the moment it held only quietly smoldering cinders.

"This is the priests' camp. Unless you choose to become a priestess, this is the only time you will be housed here," Soukut told her. "But that is because you will need to stay here for ten days while you learn the basics of our ways, and we keep you here because you will need to be able to ask questions of any of us.

"As the hearth-priestess, it is my duty to oversee the teaching of all the children in the Family, so that they grow up knowing how to live their lives and tend their homes in accordance with our ways. For this reason, you will share my *geome* as if you were my daughter. The things you will need to learn are the things our children grow up learning over many years, as much by observing and doing and living them as by being taught, but you will need to learn all these things much faster," Soukut warned her.

"So I was told," Tava agreed.

"Good. Now that we have introduced you to Mother Earth and

Father Sky, it is time for you to bathe, which is this blue door here—
priests and priestesses share the same bathing *geome*, but elsewhere
in the camp, you will use the blue *geomes* with the red-painted doors
when you bathe. Red is for the women, and green is for the men," the
priestess instructed, heading for the blue-painted door. "Just like
the refreshing tents. Use only the red ones. Come."

The inside of the bathing *geome* was more like the warband one
she was used to, in that its staves were on the inside and the floor was
scattered with felt rugs, rather than a near-solid circle of felt. It also
contained two bathing tubs, racks draped with toweling cloths, a couple broad benches laid with folded clothes and sandals, and a woman
working at a strange contraption, half brazier and half metal barrel.
She finished pouring a bucket of water into the large barrel at the top
of the object, lowered the bucket, and prodded at the fire in the half-
barrel-shaped brazier underneath, adding two more grass-log twists.
The contraption had arms of a sort, metal pipes that stuck out from
the sides of the water barrel, their ends terminating over the two
bathing tubs to either side. One of the tubs was filled halfway with
gently steaming water.

"The bath is ready and waiting. Welcome," the dark blond
middle-aged woman added to Tava, dusting off her hands. "I am
Soulet, mage-priestess of Family Tiger—do not expect great feats
of power from me, as you may have heard in the old tales. Mages like
that only exist at the fringes of the continent. We are very rare, here
in the heart of the Shattered Empire, so I must save my energies for
when the Family truly needs me."

"Oh, I know they're rare," Tava quickly reassured her. "I've only
ever seen two use their magics in my whole life, and those were travelers headed up the River. My father spoke with both of them, and
I listened as they talked about how the aether is broken this close
to the old capital, and how magic runs in strange ways. One of them
said he thought the men of the Plains had been turned into sort of
magic-sponges and soaked it all up, beyond the normal proportions

of mage-born to common folk, which is why the Valley people have so little of their own."

Both priestesses exchanged bemused looks. Soukut held out her hands. "Come, take off the clothes of your old life. Loose dresses like that are no good for wandering the Plains. There are bushes that hide in the long grass, with twigs that will catch and rip your clothes, if they aren't held close to the body like ours. Sawgrass can cut if there isn't at least some give, which is why we wear gathered *breikas* instead of more fitted trousers, and we need to be free to run and to ride, which is why the *chamsa* is cut up to the hips on both sides."

"The *breikas* are gathered by strings at the waist and ankle, which can be quickly untied by shapeshifters," Soulet continued, helping Tava remove her pink dress, with its loose, gathered skirt and sleeves. She also helped remove the underdress, while her mother made enough space on one of the benches for Tava to sit and unlace her boots. Soulet *tsk*ed at the sight of Tava's footwear. "We also do not lace our boots, again so that it is easier for our shapeshifters to remove. The *chamsa* is fastened by three buttons along the shoulder and one or two at the waist, also easily discarded. There are some differences, though. Men fasten their *chamak* along their left shoulder, and women fasten their *chamsa* on the right."

"And ours are tailored to accommodate our curves, whereas most men have none," Soukut added, taking Tava's boots and socks. "Unless he has a cattle-gut, in which case you should chase him out of the *geome* and make him run around the camp a few dozen times a day, until he becomes fit and lean again. Do not hesitate to insist that your mate be fit and healthy—and make sure you take care of yourself, too."

Stripped of even her underbriefs, Tava blinked at the older woman's words. "That's . . . very different from the Mornai way. Women are supposed to be quiet and demure and *never* yell at their husbands, let alone chase them out of the house."

Both women snorted at that idea. Soukut helped Tava into the hot, waiting bath, and Soulet fetched a pot of softsoap scented with what Tava recognized as the spicy-sweet smell of *rora* flowers. She also fetched a knit scrubbing cloth, which she lathered and rubbed over Tava's back for her.

The mixture of linen and wool scratched a little, but Tava didn't mind; she could tell it was scrubbing away the grime of her travels. The prospect of getting clean felt too good to stop in the face of such a mild discomfort. Laborious though it was to heat enough water, Tava was used to bathing at least twice a week. Taking over the scrubbing, she worked on her arms as Soukut continued.

"I suppose we ought to start with the history of the Shifterai," the older priestess allowed. "One hundred eighty-one years ago, the Aian Empire was destroyed in the Shattering. We don't know the exact cause, other than that it blew up the capital city, flattened most of the surrounding countryside, and changed the bodies of those that survived. Forty-nine of every fifty men suddenly discovered they could change the shape of their bodies, lengthening their arms, growing feathers instead of beards, so on and so forth. This was the reverse of the usual one in fifty people having some gift for magic, but while one in fifty men *couldn't* shift their shape, one in fifty women *could*."

Tava jerked in shock, slipping against the tin of the tub. Water sloshed with the abrupt movement, and the scrubbing cloth floated free of her unnerved fingers.

"The Gods alone know why," Soulet continued, fishing out the rag and dipping it into the softsoap pot to re-lather the material. "It would have made things a lot easier on our beginnings if one in fifty women *couldn't* shift their shape, just like the men. But as things stood, the men with this new magic vastly outnumbered the women who could match it . . . and in the struggle to survive, with broken orchards, blasted crops, and crumbled homes, with no form of government left to impose law and order . . . the men turned into bandits and brigands."

"The strength of their fists and the sharpness of their claws made the new laws," Soukut stated. "For thirty-seven years, the men pillaged, stole, fought, raped, looted, and conquered anything and anyone they could get their paws on. Not *all* of the men wanted to live like that ... but enough of them thought that warbands were the only way they could survive."

Tava was still stuck back on that other piece of news. "The women ... the ones who could shift their shape ... ?"

"We're getting to that," Soukut soothed her, patting Tava on the nearest soapy shoulder before swishing her fingers through the water to clean them. "Naturally, our ancestresses didn't care for the idea of constantly living in fear of being captured and hauled off as a prize, to be taken against our will and forced to bear and raise children who would know nothing but constant war with their brethren. The kinder of the men didn't like it either, particularly the ones who loved their wives. And since it was a war, many of them retreated to the few defensible structures they could find, some of the surviving noble estates, and the great crater that was once the capital, and is now the Shifting City."

"For ten ... no, twelve years, starting with the ... nineteenth year after the Shattering," Soulet lectured, "the people who had moved back to the City built a defensive wall around the buildings they struggled to build at the bottom of the crater, farmed what they could in the fields around the crater's edge, and defended themselves against marauders ... and it was into this defensive refuge of civilization that a shapeshifter woman named Menai came, leading a group of women she had liberated from some of the marauding warbands. There were also some of the non-shifting men who had been treated little better than slaves by their shifter counterparts and several outlanders who had been kidnapped and enslaved by the warbands, who were ranging farther and farther afield, looking for fresh sources of food and wealth to plunder."

"An outlander man, Tikal, had helped her with the refugees' escape. It was he who taught everyone how to make powerful bows and arrows, and learned the secrets of making bluesteel, and together, they told everyone they would declare war on the warbands," the older priestess said, continuing the tale while her daughter helped Tava to stand so they could help scrub her legs. "This made some of the people living in the fortified City upset, because they were small in number compared to the warbands. But Tikal and Menai built a fortress up at the top of the crater. And by the thirty-fifth year after the Shattering, the fortress was complete, and they had taught so many others and led so many raids, that all the warband leaders, the fiercest and the cruelest of all the banditry-minded men, were very angry, and very ready to join together and attack.

"Menai had planned for this, however," Soukut continued. "She first got them to chase her and her warriors this way and that across the Plains, leading them hither and yon, always staying just far enough ahead to avoid a pitched battle, until it was the height of late summer."

"It was a *very* hot and dry summer, too. All the land had baked as bright and yellow as gold, and just as hard," her daughter stated, helping Tava to balance as she scrubbed first one ankle and foot, then the other. "The grass crunched underfoot, turning to dust with each step, and any cloud that dared scuttle across the sky dried up within an hour and vanished. Menai led the combined warbands like a leaf blown at the head of a great, beige cloud, swirling into her fortress of stone not far from the crater's edge. They followed her right up to its walls, too. And *just* as they were about to attack, she finally spoke to them, saying—"

"—Let me, Daughter; I love this part," Soukut interjected, holding up her hands. "She said, 'You men who race upon the ground and fly through the sky and swim through waters of the world, you race and swim and fly only to hurt every person you meet. You are *nothing*. You are not men. You are beasts! You are uncivilized and undeserving of the benefits that come with civilization. If you had any wits, you would be cooperating with everyone you met and gain the greatest wealth and prestige . . . but all you can do is scrabble in the dirt like worms and steal—and you break what you steal and grow mad that it breaks, and you blame everyone but the person who broke it. That person is *you*.

"'Well, you may be the masters of the air and the water and the earth, but you are *not* the masters of civilization! You are thieves, and thieves are *always* caught and punished! In fact, *you* have already been caught, though you don't know it!' . . . And of course, at this pronouncement, all the men in the warbands laughed at her and called out that she was a weak woman, and that they would beat her into submission," Soukut related. "But Menai held up a burning torch and continued. 'Yes, *you* have been caught . . . and *you* will be punished for your crimes. You have only two choices. You will choose to surrender, you will permit yourselves to be bound by a manacle of bluesteel, from which no shifter can shift free, and you will submit to the rule of the very same women you decry . . . or you will die.

"'You say that there is nothing on the earth, in the water, or in the sky that you cannot conquer, nothing that you fear, and you shove your women aside, saying they are fit for nothing more than tending the hearth and bearing your sons. Well, you forget that the hearth is the home of the most powerful element of all, the power of fire . . . and the *entire* ground you stand upon, for two full *miles* in any direction . . . has been seeded with fat and of oil, which your big, shapeshifted feet have trampled all over, spreading all across the ground. As I said . . . you can surrender and submit to *our* civilization . . . or you can die. Choose wisely, but choose *quickly*. I will not give you a second chance.'"

"And it was at *that* point that Tikal's archers appeared over the walls, most of them women, and all of them with oil-rags wrapped around the tips of their arrows," Soulet told Tava, using one of the buckets to scoop up bathwater to carefully wet her hair. "And the young maidens appeared beside them, torches lit and ready for their mothers and their aunts and their sisters to light their arrows if it was needed . . . and *behind* the warbands, the men who were on Menai's side also appeared, from tunnels dug in the ground. The non-shifters lit their own torches and readied their own arrows . . . and the shapeshifters among the defenders took to the skies, men and women both, ready to knock down any who thought to flee that way from the fiery wrath of Menai."

"Most of the men in the warbands saw what their fate would be, a horrible death, and knelt down on the ground with their hands over their heads. Some of them lifted up into the sky, but Menai and Tikal had trained their own fighters well. Some were shot by bluesteel arrows and killed, and a few who had swift bird-shapes managed to fly fast enough to escape," Soukut said, helping Tava lather her hair with more of the spicy-sweet softsoap. "Our ancestors learned later that they flew all the way to the Centa Plains, where they thought to restart their evil ways, but the people who lived there proved too tough for them, and the very evil ones died, and the not so evil ones gave up and submitted to the yoke of Centarai civilization. Which is why, every so often, a shapeshifter is born to the Horse People, and so they trade that shifter to us in exchange for one of our non-shifting men, making us cross-kin."

"But that is a lesson for another time," her daughter pointed out. "To get back to the war . . . Menai and Tikal had each man in the warband fitted with a bluesteel band fastened around his wrist. Bluesteel is the only thing that will prevent a shifter from shifting his or her shape, locking them into their natural form. Without the ability to shift, a criminal does not have the greater strength, speed, weaponry, and means of escape he—or she—would normally have. It is with bluesteel that we also mark our criminals when we banish them from the Plains, when their crimes are too great to make reparations, yet not so horrible that they absolutely must die."

"Kodan told me of that, just today," Tava admitted. "About the bluesteel brands. He thinks . . ." Her words trailed out as she thought about what she was about to say.

Soulet chuckled. "Yes, he thinks a *lot*, doesn't he? It's a good trait for a leader. Many more of our young men could be like him, and we would not suffer the least for it."

Tava shook her head, but more to clear her thoughts than anything. If she told these women about her mother being captured and raped by shapeshifters, they might want to see her mother's book, to read Ellet's words for themselves . . . and if they did, they'd read the part where her mother confessed her need to flee to prevent her unborn child from being raised as a slave.

Kodan was right. I don't *know enough about Shifterai culture yet. I didn't even know they* had *female shifters on the Plains, and yet they clearly do, if one in every fifty women is, or at least was, born a shapeshifter.* "Um . . . about those shapeshifting women . . ."

"We're getting to that," the elder of the two priestesses admonished, though she chuckled. "Once Menai and Tikal won, and their enemies submitted . . . there were a lot of women and men who wanted vengeance for how they themselves had been treated. Menai pointed out—wisely—that to treat these men as they had treated their victims was to be no better than such beasts. One of the strongest shifters to have surrendered then asked her questions about the civilization she claimed to lead . . . and though it took a couple of years to work out the details, they managed to put together a system of government wherein the power of the shapeshifters, with all their power and might, would be balanced with the women's rights to demand a civilized way of life."

"That would be the Council of Shifters and the Council of Sisters, right?" Tava asked.

"Correct!" both women praised, and laughed at their dual answer. Soulet continued for both of them.

"To overcome the wrongful thinking that women were nothing more than chattel, it was decided that women would have the greatest power over our burgeoning society. To honor the strength of our men, most of whom are shapeshifters, it was decreed that any woman who was born a shapeshifter would automatically be given the rank of a princess, and the old Imperial honorific of an *A* being attached in front of her name. Furthermore, that while any man could be a shifter, and anyone with ten shapes or more could become a *multerai*, honored as a powerful lord . . . the only way a man could gain the rank of Prince would be to marry a woman who was a princess. *And* it was decided that the power to ask for someone's hand in marriage would lie solely with a female. Which is why you must *never* hold out your hand to a man, when you—"

"—When I stand across a fire from him, yes. I was warned about that," Tava agreed.

Soukut chuckled. "We have a smart one, Daughter. No, no—don't crouch just yet," she ordered Tava, who had started to sink down to begin rinsing the soap from her hair and skin. "We'll fill our buckets first, so you'll have mostly clean rinse water at the end."

There was a pause in the lecture while they helped Tava to rinse herself, splashing and sluicing the suds from her skin.

"Anyway, to honor the strength of our shapeshifting blood, it was decided that only a Princess of the People could become the Queen of the Shifterai, gaining the *Ai* honorific in front of her name. But only if she displayed great strength and skill," Soulet told Tava, holding out a towel for the younger woman to step into, now that her bath was done.

"Which you will see for yourself this winter, when we return to the City," Soukut agreed. "Every winter, there are shapeshifting contests held. Many are for the men, and some of them can be quite amazing to see, but for the women, it is the contests between the princesses that hold the most interest. These are judged by the purity of one's shape. It's not enough to just lengthen your legs or swap feathers for your hair. You have to take on the shape of an animal so realistically, it would be difficult to tell you from the real thing. *If* you were a shifter."

"Purity of form is very difficult," Soulet warned Tava. "Every detail must be kept in the mind and molded into the flesh, and the shifter must be strong enough to manage not only the differences in shape, but the size, the muscles, and the movements."

"To mimic one of the beasts that fly, swim, or run through the world is seen as a way of honoring Father Sky and Mother Earth. I would say . . . one out of every twenty men can manage as many as five pure shapes. One out of every forty can manage seven or more, and fewer than one out of every eighty can manage ten shapes or more, making them a *multerai*. Those among the men who can become *multerai* are expected to lead the warbands—the *honorable* warbands that they have become—and even to be the Lord of a Family if it has no princesses . . . such as Family Tiger currently lacks," Soukut admitted. "Our last princess, Apeta, died with only sons in her bloodline."

"But . . . that doesn't make sense. There are hundreds of people in this Family," Tava pointed out, accepting a second cloth to rub some of the dampness out of her hair. "If one in fifty women is born a shifter, there should be . . ."

"There should be sixteen or seventeen in Family Tiger . . . *if* such things bred randomly," Soukut agreed. The elderly woman scrubbed Tava's hair with a vigor that belied her apparent age. "But shapeshifting runs more in bloodlines. Four out of five daughters born to a princess will also be princesses . . . but first she must *have* the daughters, and *that* is the random chance of the Gods."

"Clan Cat overall has the correct ratio of shifter women to non-shifters, being one in fifty," Soulet agreed. "Unfortunately . . . right now, most of them were born into Family Lion, which has over two thousand members, and over one hundred princesses, a ratio of one in twenty instead of one in fifty. Mind you, most of them can't take on more than two to five pure shapes . . . but it's not like they're *expected* to ride with the warbands. They have that right if they wish, but not every princess does.

"In fact, every young man gets at least one summer's chance to ride with the warbands if he's a shapeshifter, but only the one summer is guaranteed. The warbands only accept those with five shapes or more for permanent membership, unless they're particularly good at fighting, or tracking, or bartering, that sort of thing."

"What about the ones who aren't shifters?" Tava asked.

"The non-shifter men, like most of the women, can learn any trade they like. A lot of the men settle in or around the City. They take up farming, or blacksmithing, woodwrighting, pottery . . . the sort of crafts that usually work better when kept in one place. We do have blacksmiths, woodwrights, and such that travel with us," Soukut admitted, "but most of the training and all of the large metalworks and carpentry take place in the City. The hardest part of their life is *getting* the raw materials for their crafts. We do have trees on the Plains, but if we cut them all down at once, we'd have no more. Trees take far too long to grow back. And there aren't any significant deposits of metal anywhere, and only so much clay, very little sand, and so forth."

"That explains why Kodan was so insistent about getting ingots of metal and long, straight lumber in exchange for my farm," Tava said, half to herself. Something Kodan had observed earlier came back up in her thoughts. "Kodan said the current Queen has a dilemma regarding Family Lion, whether to split it in half and make a new Family, or to relocate some of its members to the other Families and Clans. You say that Family Lion has too many princesses, while some others, like this one, have none. Why not just break up the excess and send them to the other Families, so that Tiger will have its own princesses?"

Both women exchanged a startled look. Soulet's brows rose, and her mother shrugged.

"She's rather smart, for an outlander," Soukut muttered, giving Tava a small, pleased smile.

"It's not a bad solution, Mother . . . except that it's also a strong tradition that the shifter stays with his *or* her Family, when people marry across the tribes. To lose a princess would be like . . . like losing a tail, or a paw. It's too much a part of that Family's identity," Soulet added, turning back to Tava. "It might be a nice gesture to the other Families to give them extra princesses, but that's assuming a Lion princess would want to be parted from her Family, let alone given to someone else. You cannot *make* a woman go to another Family, though it is strongly encouraged if her husband is a shapeshifter."

"Not to mention, most of those princesses are weak, in the sense that they only have so many shapes they can make . . . and this latest generation doesn't seem to be casting as many shapeshifter daughters as before. If they gave only weak princesses to the other Families, it could be construed as a backhanded compliment, a hidden insult," Soukut pointed out. "Yes, a princess of only two shapes might techni-cally outrank a *multerai* that can shift twelve . . . but the *multerai* with twelve shapes will have a great deal more experience in leading a Family than a princess who is at the bottom of her particular kinship hierarchy. It might just be better to break up the Family by creating a new one."

"They *could* invoke the Five Year law," her daughter argued. "They do it with the top five princesses each winter—you cannot shift more shapes than the current Queen, and expect to be instantly crowned," Soulet explained. "You have to undergo five years of apprenticeship to the Queen and her Councilors—which includes the Council of Princesses and the Council of Crafters, as well as the Council of Shifters and the Council of Sisters. At the end of the five years of apprenticeship, if you are the strongest heir, *and* have shown good judgment, the Councils can declare whether or not you are qualified to be the next Queen, and the current Queen can decide whether she wishes to remain in place for another year, or abdicate in favor of her top successor."

"You'd be surprised at how many do wish to step down, at least for a few years," Soukut revealed. "They don't have to go through the five years of apprenticeship all over again, but they do go into the pool of the top five princesses for reconsideration if they wish it. This helps ensure that a bad Queen can be ousted fairly quickly and replaced by someone provably competent, and gives those that need a rest from all the pressures of the job the chance to have that rest, without vacating the leadership of the nation."

"That sounds very complex," Tava murmured, thinking it over. "But it does make sense. Um . . . what are those?" she asked, distracted by the scrap of fabric the younger priestess had plucked from one of the benches.

"Undershorts. The long-legged kind you were wearing are the kind we reserve for winter, when we need the extra cloth for layers. These are much more practical to wear with *breikas*, since they don't bunch up," Soulet told her, handing over the legless scrap of linen. "Well . . . they *can* bunch up in back, but all undergarments do that. Try them on, to make sure they fit. Then we'll try the *breikas*, though it's more about fitting those to your leg length than to your hip size."

"What shall we talk of next, Daughter? Ah! The Grieving Day. When we don't have a princess to lead us," Soukut explained, "we have a Lord of the Family, being the strongest male shifter. Well, our strongest shifter, Chodan, passed away a few weeks ago. A Family is best run by a single person to make the best decisions, based on the many choices the two Councils, the crafters, and the priesthood can bring to her or him, so we've all agreed that the warlord of South Paw—your escort, Kodan—shall become the new Lord of Tiger.

"Chodan was well liked as our Lord, and so we held a Grieving Day for the majority of the Family three days after his passing. When the last warband comes back, which will be the Tailtip Warband, we'll hold another Grieving Day about three days after their return. It'll be a little hard on the new Lord, since he is one of Chodan's grandsons, but Kodan is a strong young man. As for what happens on a Grieving Day," Soukut continued, "we take the whole day to remember the one who has passed on into the arms of Mother Earth. We tell stories, we remember words, and we allow ourselves the chance to miss them and to cry.

"A special hole is also dug," the mother of the pair added. "Into this, our grief is shouted, our anger screamed, our final words whispered. We give ourselves the opportunity to say the things we never had the chance to say while the deceased was still among us. It makes a good release of our emotions, so that we can let go and move on. It's not too good to let the grief wait too long before it can be fully expressed, but it's also not too good to have too much mourning. Animals must be milked, children must be minded, and everyone must be fed."

"Life flows on," Tava murmured, remembering her own recent acquaintance with grief. "The waters come and the waters go, for the River flows on and on . . ."

"Is that a liturgy from among the Mornai?" Soukut asked, while her daughter held up a couple different sets of gathered pants next to Tava's hip, trying to gauge their length.

"Yes. My father . . . my father died from a bandit attack, just a few days before the South Paw Warband showed up at my village," Tava confessed. "They avenged his death . . . but with his death, the Alders of my village wanted to steal my home. It's a good farm, up on the second embankment, so it has good enough soil, but doesn't flood very often. Kodan bartered for the cost of my farm plus a few other things in exchange for destroying the bandits. If he hadn't convinced me to come here, I'd either be a servant in the Aldeman's house or traveling on my own, trying to find work as a scribe."

Soukut patted Tava on her bare arm. "You're much better off up here, trust me. We may not have much need for scribes, in the sense that we teach all of our children to write, but that doesn't mean all of us *like* to write. Or have the time or the health for it. One of Kodan's aunts is the record keeper for the Council of Sisters, but her fingers are starting to cramp from arthritis. You may not have the herds a

Shifterai woman normally inherits, but you should be able to make a good living."

"Speaking of which, that is a good segue into inheritance laws," Soulet pointed out, handing Tava the darker blue of the two *breikas* in her hands. "Here, try this on, and we'll go into an explanation of inheritance and lineage. By the time we have you dressed—if you continue to be as sharp as you've proven so far—we'll have you able to figure out lines of leadership, kinship, and fellowship by the time lunch is ready."

"Yemii isn't cooking it, is he?" Soukut asked her daughter quickly. "He puts too much cheese in everything."

"It was either him or Tanali, and she's busy helping the other earth-priestesses greet the men of the South Paw."

"Pardon, but . . . what *is* an earth-priestess?" Tava asked. "You've explained what a hearth-priestess is, a teacher of knowledge, and a mage-priestess is equally obvious, but . . ."

"An earth-priestess is a widow who has agreed to serve the needs and urges of the men of her Family. This ensures that the men always have a safe outlet for their urges, that our maidens remain maidens, and that our men are given proper instruction on how to be considerate, skillful lovers . . . which our maidens appreciate in turn whenever we choose to marry. Or remarry. A widow is given one year in the maiden's *geome* to grieve, at which point she is free to either remarry or become an earth-priestess for at least a year. I myself was widowed when my husband fell from his horse while trying to divert a cattle stampede," Soukut explained. "Soulet was only four at the time. I grieved for a year, then agreed to be an earth-priestess . . . and I'll admit I enjoyed it enough that I agreed to continue being one."

"Whereas I didn't think about becoming a priestess, period, until I realized I was able to do strange things just by thinking hard, and was brought to the City to study with the mage-priests. That's where I met Yemii, my husband," her daughter told Tava. "He's a Healer-priest, and a very, very minor mage, most of which he uses to augment the effects of his herbs and potions. I help him as much as I can, though my powers are attuned more toward other applications. I was lucky in that I had the choice to come back to Family Tiger and that my husband could come with me; mage-priests are often assigned where they are needed most."

"You will meet Yemii at lunch," Soukut said. "In fact, you can't miss him. He's the tallest non-shifter in the Family, with hair almost as pale as the grass outside. He's also a very good Healer-priest. A lot of the men who feel called to serve Father Sky and Mother Earth end up as Healer-priests, since so many of the women end up as earth-priestesses."

"How do you get picked to be a hearth-priestess, then?" Tava asked. "Is it only the women, or . . . ?"

"Men can be picked, too. But you do have to be able to fool others into thinking you know everything," Soukut joked. "In other words, be old enough. Come, finish getting dressed, and we'll talk about inheritances next."

Knowing there was a lot more ahead for her to learn, and relieved that her many questions *would* be answered, Tava gladly complied.

TEN

❦

It wasn't until late that night when, tired and head reeling with information, she finally had the chance to *think* about what she had learned.

Lying awake in the dark of the priestesses' *geome*, Tava listened to the aging woman's soft snores, and the occasional squeak from her own bed as she shifted, trying to get comfortable. Soukut had shown Tava how to set up a Shifterai bed, with its woven web of ropes that needed to be pulled tight, particularly on a damp night when the ropes threatened to stretch, but which was easy to transport. It had more give to it than the platform-style bed she was used to sleeping on. Between that and her whirling thoughts, the younger woman just could not sleep.

Why didn't Kodan tell *me about Shifterai princesses? Did he want to keep it a secret, or was it just forgetfulness? No*, she decided, curling her hand under her cheek. She wasn't in her own bed with her own duck-feather mattress and pillows; those were probably still back with the wagons somewhere. Currently, she was sleeping in a narrow bed reserved for guests of the priesthood, with a thick wool pallet and fluffy goose-feather pillows, which didn't give the same thick support she was used to. *No . . . Kodan does think things through. He doesn't seem to forget much.*

So why didn't he tell me? The blankets were felted wool, a little scratchy against her chin where the linen sheet didn't quite overlap the upper edge. Tava wanted to curl up her knees, since she was lying on her side, but there wasn't room on the frame. Twisting onto her stomach—listening to the ropes squeak softly as they rubbed against the holes carved in the wooden frame—she tried to puzzle it through. *Take it back to the beginning. He said . . . he said I shouldn't tell the others that I was a shapeshifter because . . . I didn't understand their culture.*

But it was more than that, she remembered. *He said the others would react to that news, and react in a way that could frighten, alarm, or confuse me. That they wouldn't think of me as an outlander, but as a Shifterai . . . and would expect me to be a Shifterai princess, right from the start. Which, given the reverence Soukut and her daughter placed on women shapeshifters, would be understandable from their point of view, and would have indeed confused and frightened me. Women just aren't given that kind of authority in Mornai culture. Some of the women had status because of their husbands, like Abigan, but only among the other women, not among the men.*

So the question is, did he secretly think I would react out of proportion to suddenly having status? Tava hadn't really seen women doing such things, because of the patriarchal attitudes of the Valley folk, but she had seen men letting a sudden elevation of status go to their heads. *Half the time a man gets elevated to the status of an Alder, he struts around, giving orders to the women, the children, and even to his own friends. And in that one village to the north, when I went with Father to watch him scribing a marriage contract . . . that girl . . . I can't remember her name, but she was getting married to one of the widowed Alders up there, and she*

took on airs in private while we stayed in her family's home overnight, ordering me about like she was twice my age, instead of only four or so years
older.

I can see why Kodan might hesitate to tell me I'd gain status. I wouldn't
want to deal with anyone that obnoxious, either. Restless, she twisted onto
her back, draping one arm over her head, partly to bunch up the
goose down so that it supported her neck a little better. It would be
even worse. That girl in that village knew how far she could press, and what
she could get away with around me. She grew up in the Valley, the same as
me. But I don't know what I could "get away with" here on the Plains.

They can fill my head with all the facts and figures—and in some
cases, gossip—that they know, but you can't teach a culture in a single day,
nor learn it by rote. It has to be lived, with adjustments made for each new
situation.

So here's another question, she thought, staring up at the faint light
coming down through the smoke hole in the cone-protected roof.
How long would Kodan want to keep my abilities a secret? I mean, I know
why I would want to keep them a secret. First and foremost, I'm still holding
the chance I might need to escape in reserve . . . though I must admit I like
these people. The only time Soukut . . . no, sorry, Soulet, the daughter, told
me to be quiet and stop asking questions was when I was letting my supper
grow cold.

That memory made her smile. I think I've talked both of those women
sore; no wonder Soukut is snoring! Her daughter said something about how,
given how fast I'm absorbing and retaining information, they shouldn't
throw me into a more formal sort of class just yet. That instead, I should just
ask as many questions as they can tolerate—if Kodan had a book on the
plants of the Plains as an instructional aid for their children, I should ask if
they have any other, similar books, just so I can read those instead and give
their poor voices a rest . . .

But back to the problem of being a princess. Do I want to be a princess?
That was a serious question for her. I've had some minor status as a

scribe, and concomitant responsibilities. But it's not the same thing at all. If Family Tiger has no princesses, and my shapeshifting abilities are revealed . . . they'll expect me to be a Shifterai princess. To take over the leadership of the Family.

One of the ladies—I can't remember which—said that a poorly trained princess is a lousy substitute for a competent multerai *lord. And Kodan did emphasize just how much responsibility a* multerai *is supposed to handle. Himself in particular, since he is now the strongest shifter in Family Tiger. I think he would make a good Lord of Tiger, at least based on what little I know. He certainly thinks ahead about things, which Father always said was important. To think, and then act.*

I think it best if I continue to hide my shapechanging abilities, at least for a while more, she decided. *I don't know enough about this culture— though I've had an earful in just one day! A brief overview of their history, inheritance laws, taxation, and tithe structures, an overview of their seasonal migration behaviors, an introduction to their worship practices, what to expect when we pack up camp and start heading for the City . . . but it's not nearly enough knowledge to risk letting anyone presume I can be a Shifterai princess just yet.*

Inhaling deeply, she stretched both arms over her head and arched her back, tensing everything, then let out her breath in a heavy sigh, relaxing her muscles. It didn't work. She was still wide-awake. *Nothing for it but to keep thinking, I suppose . . . If they knew I was a princess— adopted or not—I don't think Family Tiger would be eager to let me go. Not if we're as rare as all that.*

And I think, if a woman has that much status, she'd be eyed by these Shifterai men like the girls of the village eyed the Aldeman's two sons. Like prime beef fattened for the fall. They'd not be so bold as to squabble in public . . . but in private, when we were all picking berries in the summer, they'd argue as to which would make the better husband, and whose father would be able to make the better marriage offer for their daughter.

I, of course, was ridiculed as being too "manly" as a scribe to be a good, proper prospect for a wife . . . but they never said it to my face. I had status, a craft, a way to earn my living above and beyond their farming and gathering. But it was as much a millstone tied to my feet as a platform to stand above them, at least in Valley life. Up here, on the Plains . . . women can have status. Very high status. And all I know about it is that I'm not ready to even think about whether or not I want to grasp it.

The tight cocoon of my old Mornai life is cracking, but it still constricts me, Tava acknowledged. *I'm still something of a caterpillar, inside. But only because I haven't fully figured out how to shape myself a set of huge, beautiful wings.*

Soukut *snork*ed and shifted on her own, broader bed, making the ropes creak and the bedding rustle. Tava sighed and shifted onto her other side. She could hear padding footsteps somewhere beyond the lattice and felt walls, and in the distance the bleating of a goat. Other sounds could be heard, along with the fluttering of something cloth-ish being rustled by the night wind.

There's another problem. There are so many people here. Back home, I didn't live in the heart of the village, but on its outskirts. I had lots of privacy to be myself, and when I discovered I could wriggle and lengthen my toes that one day, I had lots of privacy to learn how to shift the rest of my body. Here . . . everyone lives in each other's pouches, practically. If I keep my abilities a secret, I won't be able to shift my shape. Not without the risk of being seen and caught.

I miss being able to shift my shape, but for all that, there are no restrictions on a woman's status in Shifterai life . . . There does seem to be quite a few restrictions on a young woman's freedom. I have to be circumspect around men, I have to stay in the maiden's geome at night . . . Even Soukut admit-ted that, by letting me stay with her in her home, I was treated more like a son than a daughter, since daughters of my age stay with the other unmar-ried women.

Are the freedoms gained by being able to say whatever I want—within the bounds of general politeness, of course—worth the losses of not being able to go wherever I want? They have all these customs that give the women great status and power, and are very civilized because of it, but the trade-off is making sure the women do nothing to excite a man into forgetting his civilized side. Not that I'm complaining about how careful these people are to avoid anything that could lead a man into the temptation of forcing himself on a woman! Mother's memoir is enough reason to be glad of that. But it just seems . . . restrictive.

So is living here worth that restriction? Twisting to get more comfortable, she stifled a yawn with the other one, finally feeling sleepy. *I don't know . . . mainly because I don't yet know. I'm seeing their culture through eyes that are only a few days old. Kodan is right about a lot of things. I do need to stay for at least a month, if not a year. I have questions that can be answered by asking and questions that can only be answered by observing, and observing takes time.*

Her right hand brushed against her breast as she tucked it back by her side. That reminded her of his instructions. Idly, Tava rubbed her thumb against her nipple. It did feel good, better than her first attempts at self-arousal, but not quite as good as when he had been there, just out of reach, whispering instructions to her in the night.

A smile spread across her face. *That's another reason for sticking around. I liked what I felt last night. I didn't even know it was possible, until he showed me. Just like I didn't know it was possible to live a completely different life, before he came along. I wonder . . . is one of the reasons why he wants me to keep silent on my shapeshifting abilities because he wants to keep my status all to himself? Like I'm a gold coin found washed downstream with the spring mud, something to be plucked out and tucked away quickly, before the others could try to claim it for themselves?*

For that matter . . . do I want him to pluck me out for himself?

That was something she hadn't really considered yet. Growing up with just her father, she had considered living alone as an adult a normal option. Particularly since being placed under the patriarchal thumb of some Valley man hadn't appealed to her independent mind.

Kodan says he wants to court me, but not once has he tried to stifle anything about me, save for keeping the secret of my shapeshifting abilities.

Well, that, and he insisted I come onto the Plains with him, she allowed honestly. *But do I want to be courted by him? All the power for picking a mate rests in the hands of a Shifterai woman. It's not a matter of the eldest men of each family arranging the match, with only a minor amount of consultation between their respective daughters and sons.*

If I don't *want him interested in me, would it be fair to let him . . . No, I can feel parts of me protesting at that thought,* Tava admitted, smiling a second time. *I do* like *him, very much so. He's different from the Mornai men I know, yet in some ways he's very much like Father. Intelligent, thoughtful, bookish . . . even if his father complains about it. I don't know yet if I'd actually hold out my hand to him . . . but I do know I'm willing to let him court me some more.*

Once I'm done having my head stuffed with the Shifterai way of life, of course . . .

It was hard, waiting for her ten days of instruction to end. Kodan caught glimpses of her as the priestesses led Tava around the Family, introducing her to people, showing her how various tasks were completed, and explaining in general how things were meant to be done on the Plains. It didn't help that his own days were quickly filled with all manner of distractions.

He did get to see Tava when she was brought out with the others to witness the simple ceremony acknowledging him as the new Lord of Tiger, which basically consisted of being given a coat made from stripe-cat fur, accepting the fealty of the two Councils pledging as a group to follow his lead in whatever decisions needed to be made, and the fealties of those individuals who wanted to show their support personally. But though both of them were now housed in the center of the camp, neither of them had much contact with the other.

Being a leader, Kodan discovered, was rather lonely. He had plenty of attention from what felt like half the maidens in the Family, but they just giggled and blushed when they saw him, or asked trivial questions solely so that they could engage his attention. It was true that several of the maidens were prettier than Tava, with fuller figures and thicker hair, and more of the confidence that came with the self-awareness of their own beauty. Many were energetic and opinionated, as a Shifterai woman should be, but it wasn't quite the same as Tava's quiet but still fiery spirit.

The closest he could get to her were the inquiries he was allowed to make regarding the progress of her instruction. As Lord of Tiger, it was his right to know how well a newcomer was adapting to Shifterai life. Kodan wasn't fooled into thinking Priestess Soukut had missed his interest in her, but at least the elderly priestess was willing to give him a glowing report each day on how fast Tava was learning and adapting to her new home.

In fact, she complained that Tava was thinking *too* much, making it difficult for her instructors to keep up with her at times. That revelation had made Kodan laugh, but it also made him feel wistful, since he wasn't one of the ones answering her questions. Instead, he was kept busy settling the arguments and disputes that had accumulated in the weeks since the passing of the previous Lord.

By the eighth day, Kodan had finally caught up on all previous complaints. A few new ones had arisen, but the greatest concern on everyone's mind was that the Tailtip Warband had not yet returned. There was still plenty of water in the cellar-reservoirs off to the east of the camp, but there was a debate as to whether they should move the camp to the east side of the cisterns so that fresh grass would be within reach of the herds while they waited a little longer, or just start heading for the farms around the City so that they could arrive in time for the late harvests, in the hope that the warband would catch up with them eventually.

As Tava's sponsor into the Family, it was his responsibility to care for her belongings while she was undergoing instruction. Naturally, the hearth-priestess had taken Tava around the encampment, showing her how the Shifterai cared for their animals and giving her opportunities to practice on the animals of others as well as her own. Kodan still managed to be on hand for the milking of her three goats each morning and late afternoon, and on the eighth day, they almost had enough privacy for him to speak with her.

Almost, except that just as they both settled down on the stools kept under the roof of the milking stall, one of the older children drove a group of nanny goats into the other half of the covered area, bringing the animals out of the misting rain. The youth's family converged on the tent, ready to help with the milking. Mindful of the curious looks cast his way, and the fact that his every move was now scrutinized and discussed, Kodan resigned himself to a bland inquiry or two about her progress.

Tava immediately chatted about all the things she had been learning. Half his attention on the teats of the goat in front of him, Kodan listened and nodded and remembered to ask a few questions of his own. It didn't matter what she said about the mixture of herbs needed for soothing the sores on a cow's udder, or the latest chapter in the book on how to hunt the wild animals that roamed the Plains; he just liked listening to her voice.

He also liked looking at her, enjoying the sight of her clad in brand-new clothes, a *chamsa* cut from some of the blue linen from the trader wagon and golden tan *breikas* tucked into her boots. She wore a lighter yellow undertunic beneath the blue one, visible at the cuffs, collar, and panelskirts, and he liked the combination on her. A nip from the nanny he was milking pulled his attention back to what he was doing. With her udder milked almost dry, he gentled his touch, pausing to pinch her ear when the goat tried to nip him again.

Tied to one of the posts hammered into the ground, the goat went back to nibbling on the straw scattered over the ground as he finished milking her. Kodan shifted his stool to the third of Tava's little herd. She did so on the other side at the same time, making him smile. A quick glance at the others under the protective awning showed they were focused on their own animals.

"Here," Kodan murmured, reaching under the goat's belly, "let me see your milking technique."

His hands covered hers as they grasped the nanny's teats, and their eyes met above the creature's back. He smiled at her, and she blushed and smiled back. Kodan didn't bother to actually guide her fingers in the rippling squeeze that milking required. Instead, he caressed her hands, subtly stroking the backs of her fingers as she worked.

"You have a good technique." Another quick glance toward the others, and he dropped his voice to a whisper, one barely audible over the light pattering of rain on the canvas roof and the hissing of the milk hitting the pail. "With a nanny goat, you squeeze and pull . . . but with a man, you rub and stroke . . ."

Her green eyes widened, and another blush crept across her cheeks. Kodan grinned.

"I just want to make sure you're fully instructed in all things."

She blushed even harder. Leaning closer to the animal's flanks, Tava whispered back, "Soulet called her husband, Priest Yemii, into the teaching tent yesterday. She had him strip, and . . . pointed out everything on him, including how to touch him. I wasn't sure if I'd rather have had your Mother Earth open up and swallow me down, I was that flustered—I know I would have died from shock if she'd asked *me* to touch him. You didn't warn me they'd do *that*, you know!"

"That's usually the duty of any male priest, to be used as a model for instruction," Kodan returned under his breath. "But no, you wouldn't be asked to touch him. I didn't even think about it, because the earth-priestesses encourage the men they teach to learn right there and then what things are and how they should be treated. It's a different method of instruction. Very, um, hands-on. But you *can* always refuse if something makes you uncomfortable, Tava. You do have the right to say no."

Grateful that she could have a reprieve, Tava confessed, "I'm glad I can say no. It was bad enough Soukut wanted me to touch myself, to practice . . . things . . . on myself in front of her. But it just isn't the same. It was even less interesting than, um, in private, though at least since that night, it's been much nicer than my first few attempts. But . . . it's not the same on my own." Green eyes peeked up at him as she stroked and squeezed rhythmically, then darted toward the others and back. ". . . I miss you."

Pride and pleasure welled up inside of him. "I miss you, too."

This isn't about courting her into wanting to stay on the Plains anymore, he acknowledged silently, watching her every move. *It's about courting her for my own reasons. I've met many Shifterai women over the years, many of them beautiful and intelligent, but none of them interests me the way she does. Just two more days, and then she'll be formally adopted into the Family, and I can openly—*

The blaring notes of the *an-tak* startled both of them. Turning his head, Kodan pinpointed the sound as coming from the center of camp and the pattern of notes as the call for a general assembly. That confused him, and disappointed him, too. As the Lord of Tiger, it was his responsibility foremost to respond to such a call, though he didn't know why anyone from either the Shifter or the Sister Council should have sounded that particular pattern.

"That's . . . the call for the general assembly, right?" Tava asked, puzzling it out for herself.

Kodan nodded. Pulling back, he checked the nanny's udder, sliding his hands from hers to the goat's tender skin. "This is the one with the kid, so she's almost done anyway. Always leave a little milk for the offspring to suckle at night."

"I know . . . and thank you for helping me with them," Tava added.

"Thank my little cousins, who get paid in honeycomb and other sweets to tend your goats on top of the rest of my kin's herds," he quipped. "I'll untie and send them back to the fields while you carry the pails to the priests' camp."

"Ah, go on, Kodan!" one of the middle-aged men milking the other goats called out. "We'll take them back to pasture with ours. You need to answer the *an-tak*. Just take my son Jemak with the two of you, so we'll know what's happening at the center."

Nodding, Kodan gestured for the teenaged boy to come over and join them. "Jemak, you take the lighter pail, and I'll take the heavier one."

"I *can* carry my own pails," Tava reminded him.

Kodan quirked a brow at her. "Yes, but why should you have to work that hard, when you have two strong men to order around?"

About to protest, Tava caught the teenaged boy pulling back his shoulders and lifting his chin, smiling a little. He was skinny and young, no more than fifteen, but it was obvious he took pride in being included as a fellow "strong man" by Kodan. Unwilling to deflate the boy's pride, she nodded, acceding Kodan's point.

They weren't the only ones headed toward the center of the sprawling encampment. Tava had learned the various horn calls the Family used to keep itself informed. There were calls to announce the return and the condition of a warband, alarms sounded for when strangers approached or wild beasts were spotted stalking the herds, and variations for summoning the leader of a Family, the two primary Councils, a general assembly consisting of a few people from each kin-family, and a grand assembly of everyone who could walk, save for the outermost herd watchers.

This was just a general assembly. Instead of more than eight hundred people converging on the center of camp, the numbers that assembled ended up being closer to about one hundred and fifty, though there were enough bodies making their way into the *ageome*, the largest domed tent in the whole of the camp, that Tava couldn't be completely sure of the actual number. Many were the older members of the Family, with gray salting at least half the heads that she counted. A good number were also teenagers, those who bordered the ages between being old enough to tend the herds responsibly and old enough to tend some other, more skill-dependent chore.

Since she didn't know why the assembly had been called, Tava focused more of her attention on the construction of the *ageome*. It had an outer ring like the warband *geome*, but the outer ring required eight stout poles to support its staves, for it also had a second, middle ring requiring four more poles, taller than the outer set. The roofstaves were also painted, some dark brown, others ginger and tan; the effect on the white roof made it look like a stylized stripe-cat hide.

Across from the front door—which was a double door with both panels pulled wide—a normal, single door sat at the back. Two braziers had been set off to either side, currently smoking lightly from grass-log embers draped with a couple coils of *rora* vine. The felted carpets covering the ground held scattered cushions and low tables suitable for small group projects, games, and other reasons people might want to gather in a large, sheltered area, particularly on a damp day like this one was. All in all, it was a pleasant place to gather, she thought. It was a pity she had been too busy with her many lessons to have entered the *ageome* until now.

Some of the bodies in the tent were clustering around a figure near the center, embracing and exclaiming. It took Kodan a few moments to pick out the name of the person being greeted. When he did, he winced. But it was too late; the influx of bodies had carried him right up to a familiar, dark-haired, hazel-eyed woman. He didn't even have the excuse of holding a pail in his hands, since the three of them had stopped by the holy *geome* to deliver the milk. Forced by politeness, Kodan grasped the woman's forearms—more to forestall her from attempting an unwanted hug than because he wanted to touch her.

"Rahala," he acknowledged simply.

She smiled broadly at him, her fingers flexing on the undersides of his forearms. Caressing him secretly. "Kodan! I understand you are now the Lord of Tiger. Congratulations—my condolences on the loss of your great-father. Chodan was a good leader for the Family. But I knew you'd be his equal, if you ever had the chance. Of course, circumstances have changed once again, but I know I'll rely heavily on you for your good advice in the days to come."

He didn't know what to make of her strange comment. Pulling his arms free, suppressing the urge to scrub away the ticklish, unwelcome sensations her fingers had left, Kodan glanced around the tent. The only faces he saw were the ones he recognized, the members of Family Tiger who had been sent by their kin and their neighbors to see what was going on here.

"You came back alone? Where is your escort?" Kodan asked, frowning at her. "Was it you that blew the *an-tak?* You know that such a thing isn't done unless there's a very good reason, Rahala, and returning safely from a trip isn't reason enough to call an assembly. You have taken several people away from their tasks."

"I came alone because I no longer *need* an escort . . . and yes, I sounded the call for this assembly. I happen to have the best of reasons. People of the Tiger!" Rahala called out, turning away from him slightly so that she could address the others in the broad, tall *ageome*. "I bring you the best of news. Once more, Family Tiger has a princess!"

Kodan stared at her in shock. Reflexively, he glanced at Tava, who also looked startled by Rahala's news. It seemed impossible that she should know Tava was a shapeshifter, and even more improbable that she could sound so *happy* about it—but she continued.

"That's right. While I traveled westward, stretching my experiences and my horizons . . . somehow, I finally figured out how to stretch myself! And I have learned very quickly—look!" Running her hands through her thick, dark locks, sweeping them back over her shoulders, Rahala unbuttoned her green *chamsa*. Pulling it open, she bared her torso to the gathered waistband of her *breikas*.

Kodan flinched, not wanting to see any part of her skin . . . but a different dismay filled him. Her chest was covered in a pelt of dark brown fur the exact same shade as her hair. It wasn't a trick, either; he could see where the hairs started growing out of her skin up by her collarbone, and the overall contour matched too closely to her curves to have been some sort of cleverly crafted animal hide.

". . . I have already mastered *five* shapes . . . and I just know I'll be able to master several more. At the rate I have been learning, I know I'll master them very soon," Rahala boasted, raising her voice above the exclamations of the others in the *ageome*. Tugging the folds of her tunic straight, she refastened it at waist and shoulder, hiding her furred chest. "I hope to have enough learned for it to be worth Family Tiger's while for me to enter the Princess Challenge! Of course, I realize I may not win . . . but I do plan on bringing back to life the last, missing traces of prestige and power our Family deserves. Rejoice, Family Tiger! You have a princess to rule over you once again!"

Oh . . . Gods . . . Disgusted, Kodan started to turn away. Rahala quickly caught his hand, holding him close.

"As I said, Kodan . . . I *know* I can rely on your good, sound advice in how to best rule Family Tiger. We'll have to go over what needs doing very soon. I don't want the Family to suffer from the slightest neglect anymore. Together, we can restore its full glory." She squeezed his hand and smiled warmly at him again.

Kodan tugged his hand free. Rahala's revelation was distasteful to him. Technically, he *had* to advise her; he was the Lord of Tiger, even if he had been so for barely a week. It was his duty to transition the reins of power into her hands, now that she was a princess. That fact alone continued to bewilder him. Rahala was twenty, and he couldn't remember if he had ever heard of a maiden that old suddenly developing shapeshifter powers. As old as eighteen, but not twenty.

Thankfully, the others moved forward to congratulate Rahala on her new powers, giving her little chance to recapture his fingers. Someone else touched his hand—his other hand. It was Tava. She tugged him back out of the knot of men and women swarming to chatter with the returned maiden in their midst. Stopping near one of the braziers, she beckoned his head down into range and whispered in his ear.

"Kodan, I have to know. Did you bring me onto the Plains so that *I* would become a princess of your people? Did you want *me* to rule this Family?"

She would ask those questions. Turning his head, Kodan murmured his answer in her ear, careful to keep his reply equally as private. "Yes, and no. Yes, I wanted you to come onto the Plains, because you're a shapeshifter. Because you *are* Shifterai, even if you were raised elsewhere. You are a princess because it is your birthright.

"But no, I didn't think specifically of you becoming the Princess of Family Tiger. Nor would you have to rule if you chose otherwise. I wouldn't expect or demand it of you." He pulled back just enough to meet her gaze. "I just want you to be *you* . . . and to have the chance to court you. Once you're free of your ten days."

She blushed a little, but smiled. "Two more days . . ."

"Kodan?" Rahala asked, moving closer. Her eyes were on Tava, her expression filled with curiosity. "Who is this woman? I don't recognize her."

"This is Tava Ell Var, formerly of the Mornai. She'll be adopted by the Family in two more days," Kodan explained. Mindful of the others watching them, he continued the introductions politely. "Tava, this is Rah . . . Arahala Jen Liu of Family Tiger, Clan Cat."

"You must feel very lucky, having the honor and privilege of being adopted among the Shifterai," Rahala said, holding up her arms in a greeting.

Glancing down, Tava realized the other young woman was offering her forearms palm-down for clasping. That was considered more of a dominant stance than a gracious one when offered first, at least as Soukut had explained it to her. *Whoever this woman is, Kodan doesn't like her, and she makes me think she's trying just a little too hard to claim her status.*

Since the other woman was patiently waiting, still smiling in a friendly manner, Tava lifted her own hands. She had always been viewed as an outsider back in Five Springs for her unusual origins and her unfeminine ways. There was little this woman could do to make her feel more uncomfortable than that, though Tava guessed it would be prudent to keep an eye on the differences between what this other woman said and what she did.

"Welcome to Family Tiger . . . or rather, welcome in a few more days. I look forward to presiding over your petition for adoption. Who is your sponsor into the Family?" Rahala inquired, releasing Tava after a brief squeeze.

"South Paw Warband sponsors her," Kodan stated, hedging around the fact that it had been more his own idea than anyone else's in the warband. *Somehow, I don't think it's wise to let Rahala know just yet that I intend to court Tava, instead of her . . . like she's still clearly hoping I will.*

"South Paw Warband?" Rahala repeated, raising her brows.

Kodan nodded. "We came across her while she was being threatened by a Mornai Alder, who was trying to steal her property and turn her into a servant. Naturally, we couldn't stand by and watch a woman being beaten. We negotiated for the sale of her property, rather than its theft, and brought her and her goods back to the Family."

"Tava is already a blessing for Family Tiger, above and beyond the tangible wealth she brings," a somewhat hoarse voice interjected. It belonged to Priestess Soulet; she smiled wryly at Tava, though her comments were addressed to the newly returned princess. "She's been asking a *lot* of questions for us to answer, keeping us talking from dawn to dusk and beyond . . . as you can hear. Tava has also learned far more than is normally expected of anyone for their ten days of instruction—as much in these eight days as I've seen most others learn in two full turnings of Brother Moon. And she's learned it well enough that we're now hard-pressed to find something new for her to learn."

"That's . . . good to know. That's *very* good," Rahala praised. "It's wonderful to know that a newcomer is so eager to learn, and hopefully just as eager to contribute. As I said, I look forward to reviewing your petition for adoption."

"Your own petition to be declared a Princess of the People must be reviewed first," Kodan stated firmly, annoyed at her phrasing.

"What do you mean, my own petition?" Rahala countered.

Kodan didn't back down. *If she's going to demand that Tava goes through a formal petition, then so will I. She probably wants to review Tava's adoption personally in case I'm the driving force behind her presence on the Plains. Apparently I was right to want to hide just how much my hand ensured Tava's relocation.*

He folded his arms across his chest, continuing before Rahala could fully protest. "I have never heard of any female shapeshifter developing her powers at your age. *Male* ones, yes, but we all know men finish maturing at a slower rate than women.

"I will also not accept a display of fur on your chest as proof, when I did not see you shape it into place on your bare flesh. I have heard of certain potions and mage-crafted amulets that can simulate such things. In order to quell all doubts about your abilities, you will be expected to demonstrate those abilities to the Family as a whole . . . in four days' time," he stated.

"Four days?" Arahala protested. "Why wait so long? Why not call a full assembly today? I'm ready and willing to prove I'm a shifter right here and now!"

"Because we are busy with other matters . . . and because Tail-tip Warband has not returned. By delaying only four days, we will hopefully give them time to rejoin us. You *do* want the doubts of everyone in the Family to be firmly laid to rest, don't you?" he asked pointedly.

From the hint of irritation in her hazel eyes, his point had been driven home. She didn't lose her smile, however. ". . . Of course. But surely we don't have to wait four whole days? Why not tomorrow?"

"I'm busy tomorrow. The day after is Tava's adoption day, which I'm sure you'll not want to overshadow your own glory," he stated, struggling to keep the sarcasm out of his tone. "After that, we'll need at least a full day to prepare a second feast to honor you—presuming you do pass your petition with flying feathers." He smiled as he said it, making his words sound more like he was implying a jest than a challenge to her claim. "Consider it three extra days to practice trying to master a sixth shape . . . since I'm sure you'll want to impress everyone."

"This is fair and reasonable," Priestess Soulet stated. "We may not be Family Lion, with plenty of princesses to spare, but it would be nice if we had a *multerai* princess. Or at least someone close to it."

Glancing around at the nodding Family members, Rahala returned her attention to Kodan. She gave him a strange half smile, one that looked part bitter, part smug. "Then I'll try my best to impress you, Lord Kodan. Perhaps I'll even manage it, now that I'm a princess."

Managing a polite nod, Kodan strode for the back door of the *ageome*, leaving her to the others. He carefully did not look back at Tava, in order to give the impression that she was not important enough to still be on his mind. He didn't want Rahala on his mind, either, but her parting comment lingered as he retreated to the privacy of his own *geome*. He had erected it behind the *ageome*, in the position that had once been reserved for his own great-father's home, which meant a short trip through the increasing patter of rain.

Once the door was shut, all he had to do was stir up the embers in his brazier, add a couple tufted grass-logs to bring up the blaze, and rap one of his two lightglobes to life. Dropping onto his bed, Kodan lay back and stared at the single row of staves forming the spokes of his roof. So long as he was in here, Rahala—*I won't call her Arahala in my thoughts*—couldn't disturb him. A pity he couldn't hide in here forever, though.

That last quip of hers, "now that I'm a princess . . ." Is that *what she* thinks has been holding back any interest in her? I don't care if a woman is a princess! I just care if she's smart, and witty, and charming, and *not* status-hungry . . . all of which Tava is. She knows what a princess is by now. I know Soukut and the others have taught her everything they can think of regarding such things. If she wanted the status and rank of a princess, she would have revealed herself as a shapeshifter by now! But she doesn't . . .

Unfortunately, he acknowledged, grimacing, *Rahala does. Mother Earth . . . whatever possessed You to give* her *of all women the power to shift her shape? Gods . . . I hope it's just a trick. If it is, I can declare her a shame to her people and cast her out of the Family.* Another grimace pulled his lips back from his teeth, from the urge to bite something. *Unfortunately, she seems so* smug *about her abilities, so sure of them . . . I don't think it* is *a trick.*

If Rahala is *a real princess . . . I don't know what she'll do to the Family once she starts to lead us. She certainly won't like the fact that I'm courting—or will be courting—Tava. Which is why I have to get Tava adopted* before *Rahala can prove anything formally. Before she's fully adopted, she's just a guest, and the Princess of Family Tiger can send a mere guest packing, if she so desires. Technically, I could, too. But I don't want to. Rather the opposite.*

Part of it, he decided, lying on his bed and listening to the pattering of the rain on the roof of his *geome, is that Rahala seemed to set her sight on me from the very moment she turned into a maiden . . . Alright, maybe a turn or two of Sister Moon after she went into the maiden's* geome. *But she's always tried to catch my interest over the years. She went into the* geome *when she turned, what, twelve? Thirteen?*

I remember I was twenty, maybe twenty-one when I first noticed her attempts to spend time in my company. I was already a multerai, *too . . . which might have compounded her interest,* Kodan allowed. *But I was too busy worrying over my future, as a fledgling warlord and a potential future Lord of the Family. I didn't have the time to spare for courting the older maidens, and I certainly wasn't interested in a fledgling girl. The hearth-*

priestess and the earth-priestesses caution men to avoid courting the younger maidens, because they're still so young and don't know their own minds. There are plenty of tales of older men marrying young maidens, only to find both parties regretting it later on, when she finishes growing up and changes her mind.

Of course, the irony of it all is that Rahala hasn't *changed her mind regarding me.*

At first, he hadn't actively discouraged her, though he hadn't exactly encouraged her interest, either. The Shifterai knew that young love was simply a phase one went through. Even Kodan had suffered it for a little while in his youth, though it had been a much older maiden when he was about fourteen, a maiden who had met a man from another Family when they were wintering in the City that year. She had ended up marrying him and moving to that other Family, and Kodan had gotten over his crush within a short period of time. It helped that he had known at the time that he was too young for her, leaving him philosophical at best about love.

Now here I am, trying to avoid the attention of one woman while wanting to court another, and worried about what the first one will do to the second if she decides the second one is a serious rival. Rahala is already suspicious. The longer I take in courting Tava, the more time Rahala will have to think up some way to spoil things for us. She's done it before with other maidens who tried to catch my eye. She's also clever enough to think of ways to harass Tava without openly displaying bad behavior . . . though she's never had to avoid the level of attention that being the leader of a Family entails.

But that brings up another worry. I know *most of the Family knows I'm the one behind Tava's adoption. And that I'm interested in courting her, even if she is an outlander.* His mind turned over the possibilities of that situation. *Someone is bound to let my interest slip . . . if not by accident, then possibly quite deliberately. Tava is an outlander . . . and Rahala is not just a Shifterai woman, but potentially a shapechanger, too.*

Which brings me back to her parting comment. Does the rest *of the*

Family think that the only reason I've been turning down her interest in me, and the interest of all the other maidens in the Family, is because there haven't been any princesses in our encampment until now? If so . . . that's a stupid line of reasoning, he decided, frowning. *If I wanted a princess, I could've courted any of the ones I've met over the years, wintering in the City. Gods know Family Lion certainly has several to spare. Of course, most of those are barely able to take on three or four shapes . . .*

A moment later, he stiffened, then smacked the heel of his hand into his forehead. *Stupid! Stupid stupid! Do you realize you have never once asked Tava how many shapes she can shift into? She doesn't* have *to reveal herself as a shapeshifter if she doesn't want to—in fact, if she would rather move to another Family, I think I'd follow her—but if Rahala tries to make her life unpleasant, it's possible that Tava can make enough pure shapes to out-shift Rahala!*

The only problem with that line of thought was that Kodan had seen her shifting only that one time in the forest, and that had been a rapid flow from one shape to the next. A bearlike shape, a furred, muscular humanoid, and a tigerish creature. The stripe-cat had looked the most realistic, about as real as his own had been, but there hadn't been enough time to be *sure* she could shape herself into a pure animal form. Not to mention that combat was a free-for-all in more ways than one, since battling an enemy successfully meant shifting whatever sort of limb, claw, or muscle would best get the job done.

Unfortunately, there's no telling how many or how few pure forms she can shift. Rahala hasn't been gone that long, and if she could learn five *shapes in such a short time . . . she could be a very powerful shapeshifter, indeed. Which means she might be able to learn twice that many . . . and I don't even know if Tava can shape a third form beyond a bear and a tiger, never mind as many as Rahala might.*

But . . . if she can . . . She may have learned a lot more than most new adoptees learn in just eight days, but she'd still need to live in our culture for some time before her judgment as a leader would be readily accepted. Rahala could argue that, as the native-born, she'd be the better princess, at least to start out with . . . and then find some way to drive Tava away, maybe. Unless . . . unless if Tava held out her hand to me, and I leaped across to her . . . then she'd have me to back her up, and the combination of a power-ful princess and an experienced warlord as her closest counselor should be enough to tip the balance in our favor, where the Councils are concerned.

The problem being, if Tava is powerful enough to out-shift Rahala, if Tava wishes to reveal her powers as a shapeshifter, and if she'd be willing to hold out her hand to me in marriage . . .

His thoughts had spiraled back to his original, pre-Rahala prob-lem: Getting Tava interested enough in him to *want* to hold out her hand to him. The mage-priestess' comment about talking her-self hoarse in order to satisfy Tava's boundless curiosity reminded him of his own method of sating it. Pushing himself upright, Kodan glanced around his *geome*, seeking the chest of books he had brought, the one containing a sample of his City-stored collection.

I still owe her at least one new book . . . and all the rest of them that I can find, as lures for her attention. Plus, since she's an adult maiden, as soon as the adoption ceremony passes, there will be an opportunity for all the bachelors in the Family who might be interested in her to give her courting gifts. Nothing lascivious as a first-gift . . . but a book could hardly be consid-ered inappropriate.

Rising, he crossed to the chest he wanted and knelt in front of it, unlatching the lid. *Let's see . . . She already has my book on plants. I didn't think to bring the one covering the animals of the Plains; that one would have made a good, thoughtful companion to the first, but I left it back at the City.*

She might be interested in this book on bow-carving and arrow-fletching, and the use of archery in hunting and warfare throughout known history. Soukut said she's coming along very well in her archery lessons—in many ways, Tava is shaping up to be the perfect Shifterai maiden. Or at least perfect for me, he acknowledged, smiling to himself. *I think other men might find her mix of long, thoughtful silences and excessive, probing questions a bit of a headache, whereas I find it fascinating.*

Or maybe I should give her my copy of Tales from Troya. *It's a book of adventures, fictional stories of heroes and heroines getting into and out of trouble, triumphing over evil, and many of them romantic in nature. Perfect for relaxing in the evening. Of course, most of them deal with stories from a mountainous terrain, hardly evocative of the Plains . . . but she did live somewhat close to the Correda Mountains. And we did meet first among the foothills of those mountains, even if it was a very, very brief meeting . . .*

For another maiden, one who was equally interested in reading, he might have chosen the book of adventurers. But Tava was different. She had clearly delighted in the tales he and the others in the South Paw Warband had related, but she had also shown equal delight in learning practical things. It took Kodan several minutes of dithering over which one to give her before it dawned on him that he could give her both.

That, more than anything, will show her how interested I am in her, he decided. *She's a scribe by trade. She not only understands the value of books more than most, she* values *books more than most. True, I haven't read* Tales from Troya *in a few years, but there are other copies floating around the City, or there were, last time I visited the shops of the booksellers . . . No, better yet*, he thought, inspired. *I can make it a condition of giving the books to her that she* read *some of them to me! Yes . . . that'll be perfect.*

Or rather, make the suggestion *that she reads the stories to me. I'd rather she read them to me of her own free will, that she showed her interest in spending time with me of her own free will. I'll suggest the idea, but not make it a condition. I did coerce her into coming to the Plains in the first place; I'll not compound it by coercing her into spending time with me if she really doesn't want to. Particularly since she* seems *to want to spend time with me of her own volition.*

So . . . the book of archery first. It isn't often done, since the Lord of a Family is usually already mated, but it would be my duty as the highest-

ranking bachelor to present a courting gift first, if I am so inclined. And I am so inclined, he asserted mentally, extracting the parchment-spined tome from among the others resting on end in the chest. *Then, after the other bachelors have had their chance to present their gifts . . . I'll give her the adventure book. I'll mention how I'd be delighted to listen to her reading them if she cares to share any of the stories, and how I'd be honored to read some of them to her in turn.*

It'll twist Rahala's tail—shifted or fictional—to see me giving her two first-gifts. Now that I've finally met the one woman who actually interests me, I do want to make it clear to Rahala that she'll never be that woman, no matter what she does, or how hard she tries. I never have been interested in her, and I never will be.

Tava is the one woman I want. A rueful smile twisted his mouth. *Even if I didn't realize it back when we first met. Thank you, Father Sky, for opening my eyes.*

ELEVEN

Despite her training, Tava couldn't keep up with the names and faces of the whole Family being paraded past her as a part of her welcoming ceremony. She was accustomed to keeping track of the constantly shifting offers and counteroffers of contracts, yes, but seven hundred eighty-three men, women, and children were a bit too much to memorize. They did group themselves according to which branch of the sprawling camp they were associated with, which was somewhat helpful, though the naming of kinship ties coupled with the occasional listing of occupations and skills clouded the details in her mind.

It was with a dazed sort of relief that the long greeting line finally came to an end. At least she had been given a bench seat to rest upon, and she wasn't expected to do more than smile, murmur a particular person's name, clasp forearms with them, and occasionally allow someone to hug her in greeting—usually an exuberant child, though Kodan's father and mother also hugged her in welcome. But the line came to an end and she was allowed to sink back onto the bench and wait for the next stage of the ceremony.

The heat of the roaring bonfire in the great pit was far enough away that it was pleasant, not overbearing. It was also necessary, for the last rainstorm had brought a distinct nip of cold wind with it. She wasn't the only one wearing a long, woolen overtunic, though hers was undoubtedly the newest, for the bright blue wool, trimmed along its edges with linen dyed a lovely shade of lavender, had been given its last few stitches by the weaver Kinedi just that morning. The outer coat went well with her light blue linen *chamsa* and matching lavender *breikas*.

Even her boots were new, calf-high *mocasha* made from felted gray wool and black-dyed leather. Several members of the family had commented on how the colors suited her, and many of the women had admired the Mornai-style plaiting of her hair, with its woven and pinned loops decorating the nape of her neck. Between that and the admiring glances of some of the younger men, Tava felt pretty as well as welcomed, two things she'd never quite felt this strongly back down in the Valley.

The warm appreciation visible in Kodan's light brown eyes warmed her almost as much as the fire did. In contrast, the hints of displeasure in the shapeshifter woman's eyes chilled some of the air between her and Rahala. The other woman did smile at her, and greeted her properly enough, but Tava couldn't quite bring herself to trust the genial-seeming curve of those lovely lips. Even now, Rahala hovered close to Kodan, her smile still there despite the length of time it had taken so many people to come forward, herding their children and minding their elders.

She was also acting the part of the gracious hostess and ruler-presumptive. Tava had to admire Rahala's deftness, even as she disliked it. The other woman never quite overstepped Kodan's authority . . . but she did play up her status as a shapeshifter . . . and appeared wearing a thin, sleeveless linen *chamsa* that exposed the dark brown fur coating her arms, sheltering her flesh from the wind in much the same way many of the men were doing.

More than that, Rahala had first appeared with bare skin, had rubbed her upper arms dramatically in front of the others . . . and then grew the fur into place. Much as Tava herself would have done, if she didn't have such nice clothes to wear, and wasn't still hesitant about exposing that aspect of herself. She certainly didn't want to copy the attention-drawing aspects of her rival.

The smells of cooking food wafting from the *geomes* placed upwind of camp center were beginning to make her hungry. Wondering when the promised feast would arrive, she turned to ask Kodan, but he was listening to something Deian was whispering in his ear. The other shapeshifter gestured, and Kodan nodded.

Raising his hands, Kodan sought to recapture the attention of those still gathered around the great bonfire. Many of the women and some of the men had slipped away to tend to those wonderful smells, or to return to their duty in watching over the various herds in the distance, but the rest had gathered into groups around the fire, talking and laughing among themselves. Many of the children were laughing and shrieking, enjoying a chase-me game not too dissimilar to the dozens Tava herself had played at that age back in the Valley. They dodged among the benches, chairs, and cushions strewn around the clearing between the largest *geomes* at the center of the camp, leaping like mountain goats over the obstacles in their paths.

A few of the adults thankfully noticed Kodan's gesture and nudged their nearest neighbors, who in turn caught the attention of still more, catching and quieting the children with admonishments to pay attention.

"Family Tiger!" Kodan called out, raising his voice to be heard above the crackling roar of the fire. "We have greeted our newest member and made her feel quite welcome. But before we can start the feast, there is one more greeting that should be given. Tava Ell Var is a maiden of suitable age. With that in mind, I invoke the rite of First-Gifting . . . by being the first of many undoubted admirers to give her a courting gift."

Tava flicked her gaze to Rahala. The other woman's smile had stiffened, along with her posture. Tava quickly pulled her attention back to Kodan, who had plucked something from a cloth bag tucked under one of the folding chairs brought out for the adoption ceremony. Approaching her, he knelt on one knee and presented the book.

"This book covers the history, construction, and use of the bow and arrow. I give it to you so that you will know how much I want to ensure you remain safe from all that would threaten you," he stated, placing the book in her lap.

His words were formal, but his gaze was warm. The way he carefully folded her fingers around the tome was equally warming, for it reminded her of the way he had caressed her hand and forearm the night before arriving at the camp. Blushing, Tava curled her fingers around the corners of the book, mindful of all the eyes upon her and unsure if she was free to caress him back. It might be acceptable by the customs she had been instructed in, but everyone was watching them, including Rahala. She settled for a subtle shift of her thumbs, permitting her a subtle caress of her own.

". . . This is where you say something polite to your suitor," Kodan added in a murmur.

"Uh . . . I accept your gift, Kodan Sin Siin, and thank you for your caring thoughtfulness. I will treasure it well and treat it gently . . . particularly as it will always remind me of you," Tava said, speaking up so that the others could hear her reply. Squeezing her hands, Kodan rose and backed up, gesturing for someone else to take his place.

Deian came forward, kneeling in front of her as smoothly as if he had rehearsed. "I do realize you only have eyes for my friend, but I hope you will enjoy my gift anyway," he murmured, before raising his voice loud enough for the others to hear. "I give you this bracelet of amber, each bead carved like a stripe-cat, so that you will always feel protected by the men of our Family . . . and hopefully by this tiger in particular."

"Thank you, Deian; your protection on the journey here was noticed and appreciated," Tava told him. His pleased smile told her that her response was the right one. Rising, he pressed his hands together, bowed politely, and stepped back. To her surprise, Manolo took his place.

"I offer you this wreath of flowers, made of prairie roses, forget-me-nots, and *rora* vine . . . so that you will always think sweetly of me, no matter what life may ask you to burn in your hearth." The grin he flashed her startled her even more, for the older man had seemed as sober as his middle-aged years. He leaned forward a little and murmured an explanation. "You'll be getting a *lot* of these wreaths, judging from the way the hills and folds for a couple miles around have been denuded. That, and the Family does need to move camp soon."

Tava blushed at the older man's claim, unsure of what to say in response. Thankfully, he didn't seem to need one.

A light caress of the hands now holding the wreath on top of the bracelet on top of the book, and he gracefully rose and backed away, leaving the venue free for someone else. Kenyen flung himself into Manolo's place, his arms draped with a small but beautiful blanket made of pieced-together squares of creamy white and silvery gray lamb's wool.

"I give you this lap-throw so that you may stay warm wherever and whenever you sit. Hopefully, you will sit and think fondly of me with it." Nudging her other gifts up off her lap, he draped it over her legs and tucked it in, then spoke quietly. "I realize my brother thinks he has the first claim to court you, but I do hope you will consider my own courting as equally sincere. He was right to rescue you, and I am very glad that you are one of us now. I hope to show you *how* glad someday very soon."

Before she could think of a reply, he bounded to his feet, bowed gracefully, and backed up. Torei hesitantly came forward, knelt on one knee, and offered her a wreath. Accepting it along with his stammered praise of her loveliness, Tava realized that an actual line had formed behind him, a line that was a good thirty or more men long. Many were close to Torei and her in age, including a good number who were clearly still in the awkward stages of puberty, while some were a little older like Kodan, and a few were Manolo's age.

Just as the older shifter had quietly warned her, many were carrying wreaths in their hands, though some had brought other gifts. Soukut had explained that this would probably happen, but Tava had dismissed it. There was still a part of her that didn't think she was all that attractive, based on how little attention the young men of the Valley had given her. Bewildered that so many men *would* want to give her courting gifts, Tava didn't know quite how to respond, other than politely. All she could do was accept the gifts handed to her, piling them on the expanse of bench to either side, and murmur her thanks for their thoughtfulness.

Behind and to one side, ostensibly presiding over the gift-giving ceremony as the Lord of the Family, Kodan carefully hid his displeasure. Part of him knew the other men had noticed her intelligence and her beauty, and had been prepared for it . . . but part of him had *not* expected his own brother to give her a gift as semi-intimate as a lap-throw. The only more telling gesture Kenyen could have made of his affection would have been to give her a piece of clothing. Or worse, a blanket for her bed, not just for her lap.

Apparently he hadn't hidden it well enough. Moving up next to him, Deian leaned in close and murmured in his ear, "So . . . would you like me to go fetch a blanket from your own bed, so that you can top your brother's intentions in the eyes of all? Or are you going to take the more prudent path, and not give her any further gifts under the watchful eyes of our subtly seething princess-to-be?"

Torn between prudence and passion, Kodan almost stayed his

hand. The sight of Tava absentmindedly smoothing her hands over the soft lambskin throw in the brief pause between suitors made up his mind. "On my bed is a foxfur blanket."

He didn't have to say anything more. Nodding, Deian vanished from his side. Kodan couldn't exactly leave to fetch it himself; it was his responsibility to oversee the celebrations. His duty to make sure no one caused a scene, started a fight, or drank too much from the skins of wine that would be passed around later, once the actual feasting began. His duty to make sure the single men of the Family treated their newest maiden with respect and courtesy.

A brief pause came in the gift-giving, as the courage of some of the youngest men, barely more than boys, faltered. Taking advantage of their hesitation, Kodan fetched out his second gift. Before the youths could goad the foremost among them into approaching Tava, he stepped into their place, dropping once more to one knee.

"This is my second courting gift to you," Kodan stated calmly, as if he hadn't just caused a stir of renewed interest in the men and women idly watching the gift-giving. "It is a book of adventure tales from the kingdom of Troya, which lies on the far side of the Centa Plains from here, off to the east. I hope you enjoy its many stories, as I have enjoyed the many hours in which I have come to know you."

Her surprised stare melted into a warm smile. Covering his hands as he cradled the book, Tava caressed his skin, then squeezed it. "Anything you give me is a joy, Kodan."

"It's been a while since I last read this book," he remembered to say, though the soft strokes of her fingertips were very distracting. "If you like, we could take turns reading it together sometime."

"I'd like that. I have a book of my own," Tava added impulsively. "A book filled with tales from distant lands, many of them from the far side of the world. My father inherited it from his father, all the way back from before the Shattering. We could read that one together, too, if you like."

Triumph mingled with pleasure inside of Kodan, making him grin.

I was right! he silently crowed. *Books* are *the perfect way to court her!* "I would be honored and delighted to spend any time with you, Tava . . . but sharing a book would triple my delight."

This time, her smile spread faster than her blush. "As it would mine."

Rising, he spun and gestured for the next youth to take his place. The others pushed the young man forward, one of Kodan's teenaged cousins, and the boy stammered much like Torei as he glanced between his cousin and his target. Moving back so that he wouldn't seem quite so proprietary, Kodan checked the urge to fold his arms across his chest. Looking intimidating wouldn't help, either.

Rituals like this one were a good chance for young men to practice their courtship approaches. From the gentle way Tava was smiling and accepting each wreath presented by the younger men, she was making sure it was a pleasant, positive experience for them. Only a few hesitated now, with the rest turning eager to fling themselves at her feet, some of them even attempting to wax poetic about her presence among them, egged on by the competitive presence of their peers, and Kodan's own example. Aside from a few lingering blushes, Tava seemed to be taking it in stride now.

Soukut probably told her what to expect, and she's taken it to heart, treating them with politeness and courtesy. Barely fledged men have tender egos, and my Tava is making it easy for them to approach her. We all know it isn't all that serious—young love never is, though I'd wish Rahala would've remembered that—but she's giving them a chance to express themselves . . . not quite like that, though.

Stepping forward, Kodan folded his arms across his chest and loomed over the current emboldened, impassioned youth. The teenaged boy had seized Tava's hand and looked like he was going to kiss it. Catching sight of Kodan's approach just as he puckered his lips, he lifted his head, his eyes wide, much like a deer scenting a predator. Kodan lifted one brow, glancing briefly at her hand, then at the young man's still-pursed mouth. The moment the youth stopped puckering and started blushing with shame, Kodan nodded and stepped back, unfolding his arms. No words needed to be spoken; it was enough that the boy's enthusiasm had been reined in before custom and courtship law were broken.

The impetuous boy was replaced by a slightly older, more controlled youth who confined his praise to verbal expressions, though he did offer Tava a soft kerchief made from cotton as a courting gift. The fabric was rare and expensive, since cotton grew only down in the kingdoms along the southern coast. Kodan wished some of the bolts of fabric salvaged from the bandits had been cotton. He would have gladly given Tava most of his share to ensure she had comfortable garments to wear, but the salvaged materials had just been wool and linen.

An impatient sigh reached his ears. Rahala had moved up next to him on his right—he still couldn't bring himself to think of her as Arahala, Princess of the People. Arms folded across her chest, Rahala lifted her chin at the last of the youths competing for Tava's attention.

"For the love of Mother Earth, they're starting to line up for a second time. This is for the *first*-gift, not the second, third, or fourth, and their antics are going to delay the feast," she muttered, furred arms making a dark line across the front of her pink sleeveless *chamsa*. "For that matter, why didn't you just hand both books to her at once, and be done with it? You've encouraged them to go beyond custom with that little slip, Kodan."

Kodan stared at Rahala, wondering when the woman would get the point. With perfect timing, Deian slipped up on his left side. He smiled at Rahala and held up the bundle of linen-backed fur. Accepting it from his friend, Kodan gave Rahala a warm smile. Her gaze dropped to the lush quilt, and her eyes widened a little. A petty part of Kodan gloated over what he guessed was going through her mind, that the bedfur was for *her*. It wasn't unknown for others to take the opportunity of a first-gifting ceremony to give gifts to other women, not just the one or ones directly honored.

"You're right, Rahala. This *has* gone on long enough."

Just as she swayed forward, unfolding her arms in the undoubted belief he was going to hand her the fur quilt, Kodan moved away. Striding up to the straggling line of youths, he fixed them with a chiding, firm look.

"Enough. This is a ritual of gift-giving intended to make a maiden feel welcome. Not a competition to see who can give her the most extravagant compliment. Save such things for the winter gathers and dances, when you can practice your charm on *many* women . . . some of whom might actually appreciate your competitive efforts on their behalf. If you have no more gifts to present to her, go help your kin bring the food into the *ageome*."

Most of the half-grown men scattered. Aware that the others in the Family were now watching him again, Kodan turned and dropped to one knee a third time. The sight of the large bundle in his hands had quelled a lot of the nearer conversations, allowing his voice to be heard.

"I have another gift for you, Tava," he said, resting the bundle of furs on his bent knee. Gently, he plucked up the edge of the lap-throw his brother had given. "The sheepskin throw which my brother gave you is a good gift, one suitable for keeping you warm as you sit in a chair. I, however, would give you *this*. It has been taken straight from the warmth of my bed . . . in the hopes that my fur will keep you warm in yours."

A choked noise off to the side told him that Rahala had heard every word. The gifting of a bedfur was an intimate gesture, both physically and verbally. *Fur* in this case meant not just the pieced-together hides forming long stripes of reddish summer and silvery winter foxfur, but the fur he himself could shape from his own hide.

Kodan hoped he had finally made his intentions clear to the other woman.

Tava couldn't remember either Soukut or the others in the priest camp mentioning anything quite like this, but she could tell it was a significant gift. A lot of the Family were staring at the two of them with surprised, curious, and thoughtful expressions on their faces, with one notable exception. The woman Rahala looked livid, eyes narrowed, mouth pinched tight, and furred arms folded tightly across the fitted linen front of her *chamsa*.

Furred arms . . . oh! Tava's brain finally caught up to the innuendo in Kodan's words. Part of her was suddenly preoccupied with blushing, but another part was busy mulling through the ramifications of this particular gift. *He's implying that, if he can't spend the night with me directly, this fur blanket will be the next best substitute . . . and he's doing it in front of everyone. If I accept it, then I'm making it clear—not only to him, but to everyone else—that I would accept him that intimately.*

Pleasure shivered through her nerves at that thought. *Father often said that, if I really liked a particular man, I'd not be afraid to let him touch me. That it would be the exact opposite of what my mother said of her experiences. He also told me that it would have to be with a man who could interest my mind as much as my body . . . and Kodan does do both.*

Wanting to accept the fur, but aware of the quilted sheepskin draped over her lap, Tava picked up the sheepskin. She folded it carefully and found a place for it on the bench, since it was too nice to just drop on the ground, but she did set it aside deliberately. *Kenyen is a nice man—they're all nice men—but he isn't his brother.*

"I accept your gift, Kodan." She started to say more, but he quickly stood and shook out the striped fur and linen quilt in a silent invitation to wrap herself in it. Rising herself, Tava turned so that he could drape it over her back.

Kodan carefully wrapped the folds around her shoulders, wrapping his arms around her as well. The pelts were ones garnered from the foxes that had threatened the flocks of fowl tended on the Clan Cat farms. Some of them, he himself had hunted and caught, though most had been traded for other goods. It was his favorite piece of bedding, but he had no qualms about giving it to Tava. Unfortunately, he couldn't let her linger in his embrace, even if the thick fur protected her body from his. The rules of Shifterai courtship were strict about such things, and he did have to uphold them as Lord of the Family.

Withdrawing his touch, he watched her turn to face him. She had caught the folds of the fur in her hands, and was sniffing at the long strands.

". . . It smells like you," Tava murmured, inhaling again. "I'll think of you all the more when I curl up under this."

She recognizes my scent! Flushing with pleasure, Kodan gestured for her to reseat herself. He lifted his chin at the *ageome*, addressing the watchful crowd with the same words he had heard his late greatfather say so many times before. "Bring out the food, and let the feasting begin! Bring out your instruments, too—let us enjoy music and dancing, and celebrate the joys of today!"

Some of them scattered, making their way toward their own encampments to help bring the dishes their kin had been preparing and cooking for half the day. Others started fetching musical instruments, ranging from simple reed-pipes and drums to eight-stringed lutes meant to be laid across the knees and plucked with blunt-shifted claws. Some just stood and stared, giving the trio of Tava, Kodan, and Rahala puzzled, thoughtful looks. A few, mostly some of Rahala's kin and some of the maidens she had lived with in the Right Flank maiden's *geome*, were giving Tava less than welcoming looks.

No doubt they, too, expected me to give in to Rahala's wishes and dreams, particularly now that she's a princess. But I won't. Not to please them, and certainly not to please her. For that matter, it's never been about a woman's status for me. It's always been about the woman herself.

It took the sight of Tava's hand held out to him to realize she had not only sat down on her bench again, but had cleared a spot on it for him. Pleased by her invitation, Kodan settled himself on the long, carved plank next to her, but refused her silent offer to share the fur. So long as the bulk of it was kept between them, it would be a tangible, visible sort of proof that he wasn't going to take its place in her bed. Not until she held out her hand to him, allowing them to wed.

Noticing some children wriggling around even as their parents fetched their instruments, Tava pointed at them. "Is that the twist-dance you talked about? Soukut said I was too big and too old to bother learning how to do it, when I could get any child in the Family to help me patch felt."

Following her line of sight, Kodan smiled. "That's a version of it. There will be casual dancing as the musicians warm up their instruments, playing songs and such while the food is brought, then everyone will be more interested in feasting and listening than in moving around. But as the afternoon goes on, we'll start forming dancing groups, and you'll get to practice some of those dances the priestesses taught you."

"If I can *remember* the steps, I'll dance," Tava joked. "I can't believe how much they managed to teach me, but it's so much, I'm hard-pressed to sort out the finer details. Particularly with dancing. That's something you have to *do* a lot, to memorize it—is the food going to be ready soon?" she added plaintively. "I haven't had anything but water and milk since Soulet cooked us porridge for breakfast."

"You'll be well fed," Kodan reassured her. "All manner of things will have been caught, fished, dug, plucked, hunted, and found for us to eat, from roasted cattail roots and wild onions to game birds and smoked lamb. I found and dug up some of those cattails myself, yesterday . . . though I wisely gave them to my mother to cook. I always end up scorching them in the brazier embers." He flashed her a grin. "One of the advantages of being a warlord is that I can always assign someone else the cooking chore . . . but one of the drawbacks is that I never get enough practice at it."

"My father cooked a good number of our meals himself. He did teach me, and it was expected of a Valley woman to do most of the cooking . . . but he liked doing it. I miss him."

Kodan touched her hand, which rested on the folds of his blanket. "When the Grieving Day comes for my great-father, you can use it to honor your grief for your father. We all do, for those we still miss over the years. Even if no one has died for a long while, we still hold a Grieving Day twice a year, just so we can remember the ones who have gone on before."

She smiled wistfully. "Yemii was my instructor on basic healing techniques, which he said included how to set a broken heart as well as a broken bone. He told me about it."

"What are you doing still sitting out here?" a feminine voice called out. His mother, Sinya, stopped next to the two of them, hands on her hips. "The guest of honor needs to be in the *ageome* now, so she can start sampling our food! Pick up her things, and move her bench into the Family tent."

Despite the fact that he now outranked her, Kodan rose automatically from years of respectful obedience to his mother. Tava did as well, though he guessed she moved more from politeness than from the same habit. The sight of his mother opening her arms and embracing the younger woman as soon as she was on her feet pleased him deeply. Rahala was popular with many in the Family, and even a little influential before her recent revelation, but so was his mother. More so, in some ways, for she was one of the top ten females on the Council of Sisters. If Sinya accepted Tava, then most of the others would follow her lead. He hoped.

His mother's words stirred several of the others into action. Kodan quickly grabbed his and his brother's furs, the two books, and the amber bracelet before they could be jostled onto the ground.

Manolo came over and looped several of the wreaths onto his fore-arms, as did Deian, and Kenyen hefted the long bench itself, carrying it toward the *ageome*.

Entering the large, domed tent, Tava saw it was now as brightly lit inside as the world outside, thanks to the many lightglobes dan-gling in their rafter-hung bags. The bright globes illuminated the food-laden tables set against the curving latticework walls. Someone pressed a plate into her hands, and someone else gave her a nudge to the left, where the platters held freshly roasted meats. Beyond those were pots with steaming roots and vegetables, bowls of greens, bas-kets of fruits, kettles of dark rice and savory soups, and slices of vari-ous breads and cakes.

There wasn't enough room on her plate for everything, by any means. Tava did her best, taking small chunks of this and dabbing spoonfuls of that onto her plate. By the time she reached the sweets, she was hard-pressed to find a spare scrap of pottery for the tempta-tions that still awaited sampling—there were even clever little domes made of bent bamboo and loose-woven cloth covering bowls of drip-ping honeycombs, to keep stray insects out of the sticky-sweet treat.

Both braziers were still in the *ageome*, though they had been fit-ted with grills that supported kettles of boiling-hot water for Corre-dai tea and gently steaming pots of spice-mulled wine. The short tables were still scattered around the broad, round tent, though there weren't any projects or games in sight. A normal-height table had been settled prominently near the center of the tent, along with one of the canvas-slung chairs the Shifterai favored when they weren't using a felted ground cushion.

Kodan's bedfur had been draped over the chair, telling Tava where she was supposed to sit. The table was small, and no other chairs had been settled next to it, though there were two short benches to either side. No sooner did she approach the table, ready to set down her plate, than Kenyen appeared at her side, a mug in either hand. He offered both to her, one from each of the brazier pots. Tava was grateful he didn't seem upset at his older brother's extra gifts, and grateful he didn't linger too much, gracefully giving way when Kinedi approached, admiring her handiwork on Tava's body.

The two of them talked for a bit; then Kinedi was replaced by the woman who had been selected to be her riding instructor, since Shifterai riding was different in several ways from the Mornai style, starting with the expectation that Shifterai women would ride astride rather than sidesaddle. As that conversation ended, Tava idly wondered if the gathered trousers they wore had something to do with granting them the freedom to ride astride, or if the freedom to straddle a horse had led to the popularity of the practical garment.

She didn't have much time to reflect on it, however, for yet another person came up to talk with her, and another, barely giving her time to sample each new flavor on her overcrowded plate. One of them was a young woman about her own age of twenty or so. She seated herself on one of the benches and held out her hands palm up, reintroducing herself as Tava clasped them.

"I don't know if you remember me in the sea of faces earlier, but I'm Kelsa. I'm the lead maiden for the South Paw maiden's *geome*, and I've been asked by our fearless Lord over there to make sure you have room among us." Kelsa tipped her head in Kodan's direction, where he was busy discussing something with an elderly man. "I say fearless, because *she* is glaring tooth and claw at you. She hides it fairly well, but I do know her, and she is doing it."

Kelsa didn't bother to tip her head at the *she* in question. Tava knew the other woman meant Rahala. "So long as she doesn't actually *shift* paws and fangs, she can glare all she likes. So . . . if you're the one in charge of the *geome* I'll be housed in, when do I move my things into it?"

"When the sun gets down to a fist length above the horizon. And you don't do the moving," Kelsa added, grinning. "You make the men do it, particularly all the men who gave you courting gifts just now.

The challenge is for them to set up your bed and arrange your furnishings in your section before the sun touches the horizon, because we're not allowed to have any men inside the maiden's *geome* after sunset.

"Do feel free to fuss and order them to move your bed this way and that; it's all part of the fun," Kelsa added, chuckling. "You should've seen little Nama ordering them about, the day she turned into a young woman—imagine a short little eleven-year-old girl bossing around big, tall, muscular men as if she had all the authority of the Sister Council at her back. Which of course she did; the day we turn into a woman is a very important one for us Shifterai girls. That's why we have these welcoming ceremonies for former outlanders, because most of you don't get to celebrate your first day as a woman among us."

"The priestesses did mention something about that," Tava agreed. "I know the others have been tending my animals while I've been trained, and storing most of my goods, but I have so many wagons of things from the sale of my farm, I don't know how much of it I can unpack for the *geome*, nor who will be looking after it in the days to come."

"You won't have much room for your belongings; your bed, a chair, and a couple of chests, and maybe a pair of work baskets are about all you can fit. Knowing Kodan, he'll continue to make sure the rest of your goods are well guarded. Knowing Kenyen, for that matter. And Deian, and even Manolo," Kelsa teased. "But don't worry that you'll never see the rest of your things. Once we get to the City, there will be plenty of room in Family Tiger's maiden halls.

"Of course, I've heard rumors that Kodan has an entire wall lined with books in his personal quarters, which is no doubt why he felt free to give you two of the few he brought with him . . . Wait a moment. Are you *actually* drooling over the thought of all those books? When there's honeycomb and almond cake to drool over instead?" Kelsa demanded, mock-astonished.

Warmed by the other woman's friendliness, Tava felt like yet another crack had formed in the cocoon of her old, restrictive life. It gave her enough room to daringly retort, "Why should I drool over cake and honey, when I could be drooling all over the men wanting to court me?"

"*All* the men, or just the one?" Kelsa quipped back, and laughed as Tava blushed. "There's nothing wrong with admiring a man's looks, as well as admiring his books."

"Thank the Gods," Tava muttered, glancing at Kodan again. He had finished his conversation and was looking her way. Their eyes met, and both smiled at the same time. Kelsa chuckled again, recapturing Tava's attention.

"I think we'll get along fine. Just be glad Rahala's expected to return to the Right Flank *geome*, now that she's back. You've managed to do what she's dreamed of doing for the last eight years—what many of us have dreamed of doing. Capturing the attention of one of the three cutest *multerai* in the whole of the Family."

Unbidden, Tava's gaze went back to Kodan. "I'd still like him even if he weren't a shapeshifter."

"That's one of the reasons why he's so cute. Deian is better-looking, but Kodan is sweet. Nice and manly when it counts, and very successful as a warlord, but also quite sweet. Anyway, eat up, and enjoy the dancing. I'll come back for you when the sun is a fist and a finger above the horizon, so we can herd the men off to help set up your new home—just don't be so impossible in bossing them around that they're still inside when the top of the sun sinks below the horizon."

"I know; they told me all the rules," Tava reassured her.

The customs for traveling across the Plains were stricter than those for a full encampment like this one. Maidens in an encampment were allowed to roam around past sunset, with one exception: They were forbidden to go into any private *geome* other than that of a close relative, either their parents' or that of a blood-related aunt. They could enter any holy tent, teaching tent, bathing tent, refreshing tent, one of the other maiden *geomes* scattered around the camp, or the *ageome* itself with impunity, and they were allowed to stay outside as much as the weather and their own common sense demanded. Provided they didn't wander off somewhere private with a man, of course.

Before Kodan, Tava hadn't understood how some of the young women in her home village could be tempted by such thoughts. Her mother's book had been part of the reason behind such thinking, but part of it had been the Mornai menfolk themselves. These Shifterai men were much more tolerant, even encouraging, of her inner spirit. *They* want *me to stop being a caterpillar and turn myself into a butterfly. Kodan was definitely right. I do belong here, far more than I ever did back there.*

When Kelsa left, others took her place, forming a stream of bodies that flowed into and out of the *ageome*. She found the time to visit the refreshing tents and to nibble on a little bit more of the delicious foods brought from all across the camp, food which kept getting changed out and replaced as various dishes and pans were scraped clean. But it was the infectious, cheerful melodies played by the musicians that eventually lured her back outside.

Benches had been scattered across the trampled grass of the clearing, filled with people eating and talking and enjoying the music. One particular patch of grass in their midst was being trampled further into the earth, as the Shifterai swirled and stomped, spun and danced. Sometimes they clapped their own hands, and sometimes they clapped the palms of those across from them, depending on the pattern of the dance.

Remembering this one from her ten days of lessons, Tava let herself be swept up into the whirling, grinning, rhythmic figures. She fumbled a few of the steps and kept trying to spin the wrong way, but her mistakes merely made her laugh, for the others encouraged her efforts to do better. No one scoffed at her errors. For the first time in her life, she felt like she *belonged* in a group of people.

The exercise eventually combined with the heat of the bonfire and the wool of her outer *chamsa*, making her quite warm. Unbuttoning the blue and lavender garment, Tava retreated to the *ageome* long enough to drop it on the fur-covered chair, drank the rest of her now-lukewarm tea, and returned to the dancing outside.

There were a lot more people dancing now, crowding the area left open for such things. The dances where everyone did the same thing had given way to somewhat more random movements, though most everyone still followed the driving beat of the hands slapping their rhythms on the various drums.

A whole clutch of young men seemed to be engaged in a rhythmic jumping contest, thrusting as high as they could every fourth bounce. The young women had congregated closer to the bonfire, doing some sort of graceful, slow spinning dance, alternating with a sort of wiggle from their upraised hands down through their toes and back up again, before circling around and around again. Urged closer by a gesture from Kelsa, Tava joined them, giving herself up to the heat and the music as soon as she felt she could approximate the others' moves.

The closer she came to the fire, bumped and jostled by the crowded dancers, the more Tava felt like they were trying to celebrate its moves—the boys were the leaping of the sparks and the girls were the writhing of its flames. The idea intrigued her, so she let herself get closer still to the edge of the bonfire pit, studying the flames with the intent to copy their natural, fiery grace.

Women are the keepers of fire in this society, she reminded herself, staring at the blazing logs. They were real wood logs, too, augmented by many tightly twisted grass-logs, piled chest-high in a pit dug as big as a private *geome* in diameter and more than a forearm length in depth. This close, the heat was intense, a firm counter to the cold

wind that whipped the flames higher than their heads. She was glad
she had removed her woolen outer tunic

*It's only fitting that I try to emulate a flame, now that I'm one of them.
There is something sensual about moving like this after all, something sort
of like the first time I figured out how to stretch and shift my body—*

Someone stumbled into her from behind, hard enough to knock
Tava off her balance. She staggered forward . . . and the edge of the
bonfire pit crumbled under her foot just as that same someone, splut-
tering apologies, bumped roughly into her again. Unable to stop herself, Tava tumbled face-first into the pit.

TWELVE

Someone screamed her name as she fell. Heart pounding, muscles burning, Tava flung herself forward, her only escape route. She dove and twisted, dodged, rose, and backed up. The heat was too intense, the spears of burning light too unpredictable, too deadly. Whirling, she darted away from the mountain of flames, dodging sparks as she fled. A sea of shocked faces and jostling bodies met her, including the stunned, wide hazel eyes of the pink-clad Rahala . . . right behind where Tava had been dancing.

There was no place for her to land, no room for her to relax out of the fastest, tightest shift of her life. Rising up, Tava saw what had to be most of the Family crowding the clearing, including a frantic-looking Kodan pushing and shoving his way through the others. More were streaming out of the *ageome*, summoned by the screams of the dancers. Even the musicians had stopped their playing, leaving only the snapping of the bonfire and the yelling of Family Tiger.

Her muscles, straining to keep her aloft, cramped in deadly warning. She had shifted into this form more than a dozen times before, but the first time had nearly killed her, for she hadn't known the hidden dangers involved. Well aware of them now, Tava raced for the wide-open doors of the *ageome*. Zooming inside, dodging the last of the people escaping the structure, she lost the energy to stay aloft.

Giving up on her shape, Tava dropped roughly to the felt-strewn ground next to the table of sweets. One of her knees buckled when she tried to stand, and her hand shook so badly that she sent the cover of her goal tumbling over the back of the table, but finesse didn't matter at this point. Thrusting her hand into the bowl, she didn't bother grabbing any of the waxy yellow lumps in her way, just smeared her fist in the golden residue at the bottom before shoving her fingers into her mouth.

Sugar, sweet, *sweet* sugar flooded her senses. Tava almost devoured her hand, shifting her tongue just catlike enough to scrape as much honey off her skin as she could manage. Smearing her fingers in the bowl again, she scooped more of the sticky treat into her mouth, desperate to get enough of it before her body went into shock.

The first time she had shifted that shape, she had wisely had her father on hand, ostensibly to guide her transformation. Seeing her control break and her flesh expand back into her natural form, only to collapse on the ground, had sent Varamon scrambling to catch her. Realizing she was desperately hungry, Tava had tried to convey her need, but thinking she was thirsty, her father had snatched up the nearest thing. Thankfully, it had been a cooling pot of barley water, brown and sweet, ready for him to infuse it with the starter yeast needed to brew it into ale.

The barley water was exactly what her starving body needed. Very cautious experimentation had proven that honey was the best cure for the sudden, overwhelming depletion of energy in her veins that came with that particular animal form, though anything suitably sugary would do in a pinch, as the barley water had done. Here and now, naked and trembling, Tava was deeply grateful the children of the

Family hadn't already scraped the bowls of honeycombs dry. There wasn't much honey left, but there was enough to replace the energy she had lost.

Outside, she could hear a babble of shocked, uncertain voices, and several people shouting her name, including Kodan. Sucking the last of the sticky honey from her skin, Tava rose on still-trembling legs and made her way to the small table near the center. The air in here, now that bodies no longer filled the structure, was growing cold enough to make her skin prickle and her muscles shiver from a new reason. Summer was definitely over for the year.

Just like her secret.

Aware that someone might turn back to the *ageome* and see her standing there naked, Tava tugged the foxfur blanket off the chair with her left hand, dislodging her wool *chamsa*. She could have put on the garment, but her right hand was still a little sticky, and she didn't think her energy-depleted fingers were up to the finicky task of dealing with buttons just yet.

Swinging the linen and fur quilt around her body, she managed to tuck it under her right arm and gather it up over her left shoulder, shrouding her body with the fur against her skin so it could keep her warm. Past experiments had proven it was wiser to wait several minutes for the sweets to soothe her taxed flesh before shifting shape again, otherwise she would have just cloaked her body in a layer of fur, Shifterai-style.

At least I can do something like this and not run the risk of being called—and treated like—a harlot by the village Alders for daring to be unclothed in a public place. I've destroyed my secret in saving my life, but here on the Plains, it's not an unnatural ability.

"—Tava? *Tava!* Father Sky, you're *alive!*" Kinedi rushed into the oversized *geome*, gaping at the sight of the younger woman. Her shout drew the others, who poured into the *ageome*, crowding it until Tava was forced to retreat to the back door just so she wouldn't feel like she was about to be trampled alive.

The middle-aged weaver clung to her exposed arm, barely pausing for breath in the babbling of her questions. How did she escape her clothes, how did she survive, how did she end up here in the *ageome*. The men and women who had followed her added their own confused demands, until the panel at Tava's back swung open, and hands cupped her bare and fur-covered shoulders.

"Enough!" The deep-roared word cut through the confusion, quelling the barrage of questions. Relieved beyond words that Tava was alive, Kodan glared at the members of Family Tiger. "This is *not* the place for such things. There is not enough room in the *ageome* for all of you. Everyone, *outside!"*

A tug on her shoulders got Tava to move backward with him, though she almost tripped over the bottom edge of the doorframe when the edge of his blanket-gift caught on it. As soon as she was safely clear and steady, Kodan swung the door shut and spun to put his back to it, holding it closed with his weight so no one else could follow. Pulling her into his arms, he held her tight, burying his face in the soft brown locks that had come undone during her shifted escape.

He didn't have to guess how she had escaped so miraculously; he knew what she was, and was deeply grateful for it. Hearing her name screamed, seeing the shock on the faces of the others, he had feared the worst when he had shoved his way to the edge of the bonfire pit. Seeing only her empty, burning clothes and one of her abandoned felt boots slumped on the edge of the pit, the other tumbled into the ashes at the edge of the embers, Kodan had instantly realized she was still alive, somewhere.

Whatever form she had taken to *survive* the fall outlined by her burning garments, he couldn't begin to guess. But she was alive, and he couldn't stop the need to hold her, to feel her against him, to *know* down to his bones that she was very much alive. He held her scandalously close, stroking his shaking hand over her hair, and felt her clinging to him in turn, her own limbs trembling.

Knowing they didn't have much time left before someone would come around the broad curve of the *ageome* to look for them, Kodan acted on pure instinct. Tugging her head gently back by her hair, he pressed his mouth to hers. The kiss—any kiss given by an unmated man to a maiden woman, whether it was on her lips, or her hand, or anywhere else—was completely forbidden by Shifterai law. It was utterly wrong, and at the same time utterly necessary.

It was also utterly returned. Tava clung to him, kissing him back as best she could, though she hadn't really ever kissed a man before. It wasn't at all like kissing her father on the cheek. In Kodan's arms, she felt safe; in his arms, she knew she didn't have to rely on her own strength to see her through some crisis. In his arms, she felt cherished beyond words, because this action—however forbidden—was clearly the only way he could express it.

However, it didn't last much longer. Mindful of the overwhelming shock and curiosity of the rest of the Family, Kodan ended the kiss after just a few seconds. A quick survey of her expression reassured him that she wasn't offended. He hugged her one last moment, then released her from his embrace. "Come," he murmured. "I'm sorry your secret is out, because they *will* demand to know how you survived . . . but I'm not sorry you're alive."

"Neither am I," Tava said, catching his hand in hers, hoping she had removed the last of the honey from her skin. "I'm *very* glad I'm alive."

Several of the Family came into view on either side of the curving, tiger-painted walls. Kodan held up his free hand, gesturing them to stop. He was glad they hadn't approached in time to see their illicit kiss, but this wasn't the place for the coming discussion.

"Back to the center!" he ordered. "Someone sound the full assembly on the *an-tak*, and make a place where we can stand and be seen! All of our questions will have to wait until then, so that *everyone* can hear and understand."

The nearest of the Shifterai started turning around, passing along his instructions to the others crowding up behind them. Kodan and Tava followed them, hands still clasped in the only public intimacy they were allowed. Someone blew the low-high, low-high notes on the spiraling horn, signaling a full assembly, and by the time the pair reached the front of the *ageome*, following the shuffling crowd, the clearing had been organized.

The benches and several folding chairs had been dragged into close-packed rows, with the elderly and nursing mothers given preferential seating upon them. Hundreds more—particularly the children—curled up cross-legged in front of them on the ground, and the rest found places to stand behind the seats. Though "behind" wasn't entirely accurate; the benches and chairs followed the arc of the large, broad clearing at the center of the encampment, curving around the bonfire pit that had almost killed her.

A space had been left open near the edge of that pit, ironically right next to where Tava had fallen. The scent of charred linen and scorched wool wafted across the clearing, making several of those who smelled it rub their wrinkling noses, triggering a few sneezes. Seated bodies squirmed out of their way, making a narrow, meandering path toward that patch of empty, trampled grass.

Once they neared the fire, her exposed arm no longer felt the cold of the late-afternoon air, but that meant the fur blanket she was still holding around her naked body was also becoming increasingly warm. Ignoring it for the time being, Tava focused her mind on figuring out what she wanted to say, and how much she wanted to reveal.

Waiting until it looked like most of the Family had gathered, Kodan held up both of his hands for attention, then lowered them, stepping to the side and turning so that he faced the blanket-wrapped woman next to him. "Tava . . . please tell us what happened, and how you survived."

Dropping gracefully, he settled cross-legged on the ground, leaving the attention of the Family focused fully upon her. Lifting her chin a little, wrapping her dignity around her like the fur quilt, Tava kept her explanation simple.

"I was dancing with the others, but near the edge of the bonfire pit. Someone bumped into me, we both stumbled, and when they bumped into me again, I fell into the pit. Not wanting to get burned . . . I shifted my shape and flew away from the fire."

Her confession startled the gathered Family, though the adults seemed more surprised than the children. Tava could guess why easily enough. Children rarely paid attention to the finer details and nuances. The adults knew she was an outlander from the kingdom of Morna, and they knew the Mornai weren't shapeshifters.

"Not to spoil your adoption into Family Tiger," Rahala called out, "but everyone knows the Mornai aren't shifters. Either you're lying . . . or you're a mage. And if you're a mage, it's rather insulting that you'd use a spell to try to be a princess."

"Careful, *Rahala* . . . since 'everyone knows' shapeshifting abilities develop right alongside puberty," Kodan countered. "Either *you're* lying . . . about your age," he conceded dryly, "or *you're* a mage."

The other woman flushed with anger at his words, but Tava could tell that Kodan's rejoinder wouldn't quell the doubt spreading across the Family. She hadn't wanted to reveal her past, but it looked like the best choice at proving her words.

"My father was, is, and forevermore shall be Varamon Vel Tith, the Mornai scribe who raised me . . . but my mother, Ellet Sou Tred, of the kingdom of Zantha, was already pregnant with me when she escaped her captors. She had been kidnapped and held captive for two years by a group of shapeshifting men calling themselves Family Mongrel . . . and she never knew *which* of the men constantly forcing themselves on her was the one that sired me." Tava had to wait until the exclamations of shock, disgust, and horror died down before she could continue. "I didn't even know I *could* change my shape until I was about thirteen, which was eight years ago. That was the year I became a young woman.

"All I knew about shapeshifters was whatever my mother had told my father of her ordeal, which he had written down in one of his books. I didn't even know what a Shifterai princess *was* until Priestess Soukut told me about them during my very first day of instruction. 'Family Mongrel' didn't have any female shifters, according to my mother. Just violent, cruel brutes who could alter their shapes." She glanced at Kodan. "It took a lot of effort by Kodan and the others to convince me that *they* weren't violent. That I could trust them, instead of fear them. I know now that whoever or whatever brutalized my mother, they may have been shapechangers, but they were *not* Shifterai."

"What shape did you form to escape the fire?" someone else asked. Tava couldn't remember the name of the man, though she tried. "We never saw anything!"

"I turned myself into a hummingbird," Tava said. That caused another stir. She waited for the mutterings to die down and elaborated on her reply. "I knew I had to escape my clothes before they could catch on fire, which meant taking on a very small shape. I also knew I had to fly, so that I could avoid having to land on the coals. But though I can also form the shape of an owl and a raven, I knew the owl was too big to escape my clothes, and the raven not deft enough to escape the flames. Unlike any other bird, a hummingbird cannot only fly swiftly, it can hover in place and even fly backward if necessary. Which it was."

"If your shifting powers are so closely attuned to birds . . . then you rightfully belong somewhere in Clan Hawk, not in Clan Cat," Rahala stated dryly.

Tava didn't have to think twice about it to know the other woman was trying to get rid of her. She would have planted her hands on her hips if she hadn't needed to keep holding the foxfur blanket in place. Instead, she lifted her chin a little. "I was informed by the priestesses that one's affinity for true forms as a shapeshifter was *not* a requirement for maintaining residence in a particular Clan and Family. A transfer might be suggested for aesthetic reasons, but it *isn't* required."

So there; you're not getting rid of me that *way*, Tava added silently. Aloud, she continued, keeping her tone rational and calm, though she couldn't quite stop the slight bite to her words. The Mornai might have thought even a hint of irritation was disrespectfully insolent, but these Shifterai didn't seem to give it a second thought.

"I was also told that one's first shape is considered the most significant whenever there's a possibility of changing Clans and Families. My very first shapeshift was a housecat, qualifying me for Clan Cat. And I have since successfully turned myself into a stripe-cat, which even by the most narrow-minded definition means I *can* be considered a suitable candidate for Family Tiger."

Abandoning her chair, Rahala pushed to her feet, lifting her own chin. "Well, I can take on *more* than five forms! I have managed to learn two—*three* more in the last few days, and I know I'll be able to learn more. It takes more than five shapes to lead *this* Family."

"It takes more than learning *any* number of shapes to lead a Family," Tava countered, struggling against her rising dislike of the other woman. Showing that distaste openly wouldn't look good in the eyes of the others. The more she saw of Rahala, the less she liked the woman. "And I never said I've only mastered five pure forms."

"Why didn't you tell us you were a shapeshifter?" Siinar called out.

"At first, because I was still influenced by my mother's perceptions and didn't know how badly you male shapeshifters would react to the thought of a woman having similar powers. I also wanted to hold it a secret in case you proved to be just as cruel as I'd feared, and needed a means of escape," Tava admitted bluntly. "But once I learned the truth of the Shifterai, I realized I didn't want anyone thinking I was power hungry, or boastful. I also kept silent because I wanted to be liked for myself, not for what I could do."

A glance in Rahala's direction showed the other woman silently fuming, no doubt pricked by Tava's verbal jab.

"I didn't come here to be a princess. I didn't even know I *was* a princess, by Shifterai standards," she pointed out. "I came here because Kodan and the others were nice to me, and because they earnestly wanted to show me that the so-called Shifterai I'd read about from my mother's accounts were *not* the real Shifterai. I came here because I wanted to know the truth."

Grateful she hadn't mentioned his bargain regarding her belongings, Kodan decided he would also keep to himself the fact that he had known all along she was a shapeshifting princess. At the edge of his vision, he could see the sun starting to sink down below the domed roof of the blue teaching *geome* and remembered the next step in the disrupted adoption celebration. Rising, he recaptured the attention of the others.

"As much as I'm certain all of us could spend the rest of the day and well into the night asking Tava . . . Atava plenty of questions," he amended, giving her the honorific prefix to denote her newly revealed rank, "it is almost time for the moving-in ritual. Kelsa, you are the chief resident of the South Paw maiden's *geome*. I want you to—"

"—*I* want to see her change her shape," a voice called out, interrupting him. Several others quickly agreed.

Someone else added their own opinion. "*I* want to see Rahala fully shift, too."

"The Council of Sisters agrees!" he heard his own mother assert. Sinya continued tartly. "You cast doubts upon Arahala's abilities, and *she* casts doubts upon Atava's. The Council is willing to permit the delay in settling our newest member into her quarters by a few minutes past sunset . . . so long as the questions of *both* their abilities are satisfactorily answered. And we do have questions."

Seeing both agreement and curiosity on far too many faces in the Family, Kodan gave in. Lifting his hand, he gestured for Rahala to join him and Tava. *It's just as well, I suppose, though I could have used at least a day's reprieve to consult with Tava. And I still don't know how many shapes Tava can shift into, nor how pure her forms might be, considering she didn't learn them under our tutelage and standards.*

He'd gladly take her as his wife even if she never managed a truly pure form. Such things didn't matter to him. Unfortunately this wasn't about taking her as his wife; this was about accepting her as a Princess of the People.

"Rahala, you were the first to make the claim of being a Princess of the People. You will therefore go first. You will be judged on their purity by the Council of Shifters . . . so try not to make any mistakes," he reminded her. "I call upon Sakro, Casten, Tofris, Jumaj, Tekelis, and Kamar, the other warlords of Family Tiger, to come forward and represent the Council of Shifters as the judges of her true shapes."

All of the warband leaders were *multerai*. There were a handful more beyond the eight warlords—though Tailtip Warband technically wasn't present—but Kodan figured six would be enough to thoroughly reassure the rest of the Family without unduly crowding either of the two women during each examination.

"Begin with your first shape," he instructed Rahala as soon as the men had assembled.

Nodding, she unbuttoned her linen *chamsa*, peeling back the pink fabric to reveal a chest as heavily furred as her arms. She toed off her *mocasha* and untied her *breikas*, letting them drop to the ground before nudging them to one side with her foot. It looked like she had donned a tightly fitted fur suit, rather than having grown it, but it did cover her decently. Smoothing her dark locks back from her face, Rahala shifted herself into a tawny, brown-striped tigress.

The transformation was startlingly fast for someone who had supposedly learned how to manage it only in the last few weeks, but it was also a thorough one. Kodan didn't have to poke at her coat to check for underhairs, nor run his hands over her flanks to know that her muscle structure was accurate. Rahala had managed to turn herself into a very convincing stripe-cat on the first attempt. She even sat on her haunches and groomed her shoulder like a cat would, smoothing her fur with her broad, rasping tongue.

Once the other warlords pronounced themselves satisfied with her first demonstration of skill, she shifted back to her fur-covered self, then shifted again into the bulk of a dark bay mare. From there, she took on the form of a bear, a goat, a sow, a sheep, and a deer, each time returning briefly to her human form before transforming into the next. Her last—eighth—shape was a rabbit, requiring the warlord to pick her up and display her in her mottled fur to the rest of the Family so that they could more easily see such a small shape.

Returning to her bipedal form, Rahala smoothed back her hair, accepted her *chamsa* from the warlord of North Paw, and spoke. "... I realize I haven't mastered any flighted forms just yet, but I have faith I will succeed. I was thinking maybe I should try for a duck next, so I could shape myself into something that can swim, or at least float."

She shrugged back into her *chamsa*, then smoothed her hair back again ... and the fur covering her arms and her legs, the latter visible through the slits down either side of her tunic, retracted back into her skin. She lifted her arms, displaying her lightly tanned flesh to all, then carefully stepped back into her *breikas*.

The other warlords turned to Tava. Sighing, she shifted fur of her own for modesty and unwrapped her gift blanket. Despite the thick pelt she had grown, Tava felt rather naked without clothes to conceal her figure.

As soon as the foxfur was folded and set aside, she shrunk herself down into the body of a calico cat. Like Rahala's rabbit, she had to be picked up to be displayed to all, as well as gently poked and prodded. As soon as they set her down, she shifted into a nanny goat without bother to return to human form as her rival had done, then shifted herself into a barn rat, which again required her to be scooped off the ground and held aloft.

Next, she shifted into a chestnut horse, then a bigger, paler version of the black and cream pig that Rahala had formed, following it with a smallish brown bear. For her seventh form, she chose her river turtle form. That seemed to confound the warlords, for they spent extra time examining her, poking and prodding, and even turning her over. Disliking the helpless feeling of being on her back, Tava squirmed and tried to talk, but her vocal cords were inadequate for speech in this body. She endured the torment of being manhandled belly-up until she was set down again. The moment she was done, she shifted back into her human form.

"Did you *have* to poke and prod me so long?" she demanded, irritated into speaking her mind. "And *never* turn me on my back when I'm shaped like that! It's *very* uncomfortable."

"We've never seen a tortoise that looked like that," Warlord Tofris stated, folding his arms across his middle-aged chest. "I'm not sure it should count as a pure form."

"It is *not* a tortoise form," Tava corrected him, still uncomfortable inside from the helpless feeling of having been held belly-up. "It is a river turtle. I spent several weeks practicing it a couple years ago. I even passed the scrutiny of my father, who compared me to some of the real river turtles we had found on the banks of the Morning River, and *he* found no significant differences."

"The shapes of natural-born animals not found on the Plains are still accepted by the Council of Shifters as valid for purity, even when they're not forms familiar to the rest of us," Kodan reminded his fellow warlords, speaking up for the first time since the evaluations had begun. "It is the function of the muscles, the proportion of the limbs for each of their given functions, and the overall naturalness of the appearance which is judged in such cases. Under *those* guidelines, did she pass for a real animal?"

Tofris and the others nodded. Kodan turned his attention back to Tava. "You have shown us seven forms. You have also mentioned two more which you have yet to display, the forms of a tiger, and a hummingbird. If you wish all nine to be counted, you must assume your last two shapes for scrutiny and judgment."

"I would prefer not to form my hummingbird shape again. At least, not for today," Tava stated. Noticing the dubious look on Rahala's face, she defended her decision. "The metabolism of a hummingbird is not the same as a human. When I fly as a hummingbird, I look and act and fly just like a real hummingbird, but doing so devours all the energy in my blood.

"I can only manage the shift for short periods of time because of this, before I have to shift back and eat a lot of sweet things to ensure I don't collapse . . . and I already ate most of the remaining honey in the *ageome*. Unless someone has a fresh honeycomb for me to devour, I'd rather not risk my health with a second shift of that form today," she told the warlords. "I'd gladly do it another day, but not today, and not without a pot of honey or a cauldron of barley water close at hand."

"What about your tiger form?" Kodan prompted her. "Can you shift into that?"

Tava didn't bother to speak. She just melded her flesh from two feet to four, and recolored her light brown bodyfur into a striped pelt of orange, black, and white. The warlords prodded her muscles and ruffled her fur until her ears went flat and her tail snapped, but they eventually pronounced her indistinguishable from a real grass-cat.

From there, she shifted again, this time into her barn owl shape. One of the other warlords, Jumaj, shifted his own flesh, toughening the skin of his left arm from fingers to elbow in stout reptilian scales. With his reshaped limb serving as an impromptu gauntlet, he offered it to Tava, who stepped from the ground to his wrist, letting him lift her up so that she could be displayed and examined. His precaution was wise; her talons were long and sharp, and the poking and prodding and manual spreading of her wings forced her to clutch at his arm a couple of times for balance. From owl shape to raven was easily managed, though again she disliked having her wings man-handled.

As soon as she was lowered back to the ground, Tava trans-formed back into her human self, shifting from feathers to fur. It wasn't enough to make her feel decent, though it was more the ex-posing of her shifting abilities that left her feeling naked than the lack of clothes. Stooping, she picked up the foxfur quilt Kodan had given her and wrapped it around her body. Not for warmth, given the heat of the bonfire at her back, but just to give herself some mental privacy.

". . . Atava Ell Var has displayed ten pure forms," Warlord Jumaj stated as she tucked the fur and linen blanket back into place. "Arahala Jen Liu has demonstrated only eight. Atava is the superior princess."

"—I'm still learning my shapes!" Rahala protested. "Give me a few more days, and I *will* surpass her! I know I can learn at least two more shapes, if not more. *I* am the superior princess, and the rightful ruler of Family Tiger!"

If she had still had cat ears, Tava would have laid them flat against her skull. "You would have to learn *five* more shapes. I have three shapes I have not yet displayed for judgment, including my humming-bird form, which for safety's sake, I should not reshape for the rest of today. One of the other two is also out of the question at the moment, as it is the body of a river eel. A *water*-breathing creature. I'd have to transform in a pond or a tub, or even in a bucket, provided it held enough water for me to breathe."

"And the other form?" one of the other warlords asked.

"It's a creature called a pseudo-tree. I ran across a description of it in one of my father's books, and decided I'd try to master its shape. It's a carnivore that lives on the west coast of Aiar, but it disguises it-self to look like a plant, and barely moves at all until a suitable animal comes within reach of its branch-tentacles. The book speculated that it was left over from the old mage wars, prior to the unification of the Empire a thousand years or so before it Shattered, but couldn't prove that it had been manufactured by any one particular mage. Because of its rarity and unusualness, I doubt you'd accept it for those reasons alone."

"You're right. We wouldn't," Jumaj agreed. "Not without looking at this book, and maybe even finding a far-traveler or two who has seen one of these creatures for themselves."

"Strange creatures or not, Atava has proven she can take on more forms than Arahala," Tofris reminded them. "Arahala claims she can learn more, but she hasn't actually done so, yet . . . and many of us have often boasted we could learn more shapes if we only tried . . . only to fail when we do try. Unless and until Arahala can shift more shapes, Atava is the superior shifter, and thus should be the Princess of Tiger."

That caused another stir of conversation among the members of Family Tiger. Tava opened her mouth to say she wasn't actually interested in being the leader of an entire Family, particularly when she was so new, but Rahala beat her to it. The other woman raised her voice to be heard over the muttered speculations of the Family.

"You can't be seriously considering giving the leadership of Tiger to *her*!" she protested, poking her thumb at Tava. "She's an outlander! Yes, she's passed her ten days of instruction, but it takes years to actually understand our ways, and years more to gain the training a true leader needs! *I* am the native-born and native-raised shapeshifter. *I* am the better choice to lead our people."

"*Enough!*" As before, the single, shouted word silenced everyone. Kodan gestured for the other warlords to sit back down, now that their examinations were through. "Arahala, I concede your point. Atava *is* still new to the Shifting Plains and does not yet fully grasp our culture. As such, she cannot lead Family Tiger at this time."

The Shifterai woman all but preened under his acknowledgment.

"I'm glad you see the wisdom in my words and have chosen what is best and right for the Family."

"Which is why I do not choose *you*." At her shocked look, Kodan permitted himself a slight, tight smile. "You are just as ignorant as she is, in your own way. It is true that you were born a Shifterai, but *you* have not been a shapeshifter long enough to grasp all that it entails. You have not yet grasped what shapeshifters can and cannot do. Nor have you fought as a shapeshifter. Atava knows very little of what it means to be a Shifterai, this is true, but *she* has been a shapeshifter for many years.

"Because of these things, it is my judgment as Lord of Family Tiger that *neither* of you have enough experience to lead Family Tiger as it should be led. Not at this point in time." He met the gazes of both women levelly, hoping that Tava—Atava—at least would understand why he was saying these things. From the faint nod she gave him, he knew that she understood. Rahala—and he still couldn't bring himself to think of her name with the honorific—folded her arms across her chest, looking like she was barely restraining herself from arguing her case.

"Thankfully Shifterai law has an established precedence for circumstances like this. For the next full year, I will remain the Lord of the Family, and *both* of you will be apprenticed to me."

Both women blinked. Tava looked more taken aback by his statement, but Rahala looked stunned. Kodan could guess why. The mere thought of Rahala being made his apprentice was not something he would have cared for under other circumstances, but it was the price he had to pay for being a *good* leader. That meant thinking of the needs of the Family over his own preferences and wishes. Even if it meant working closely with a woman he couldn't otherwise stand.

On the one hand, Rahala had expressed an interest in working toward being recognized as worthy of the Sister Council, and some of the things she had done in the past had suggested an aptitude for it. And on the other hand, she just might slip up at some point and show a side of herself that neither Council would accept in a leader. *Or as the saying goes, hand her plenty of rope, and wait to see whether or not she trips herself with it.*

Kodan continued. "In many respects, this will be very much like a miniature apprenticeship to the Queen and her Councils, save that it will last only one year, not five, and you will be apprenticed to me and not Her Majesty. In all other regards, it is similar. You have passed the initial Princess Challenge and will now undergo the necessary period of instruction. The Council of Sisters and the Council of Shifters will train you in the ways of both shapeshifting and leadership, and as you progress, you will both be given greater and greater responsibility in managing the Family.

"This apprenticeship year will have a dual purpose. You will not only learn how to manage this Family . . . you will *both* be given enough time to fully learn your shapeshifting abilities. For you, Arahala, you may have lived among shapeshifters all your life, but you are only just now stretching your powers. For you, Atava, you may have stretched your powers for many years, but you have done so almost entirely on your own, and you may find yourself benefiting from the wisdom the Shifterai have gained in all our practice over the years.

"At the end of the apprenticeship year," he continued, "you will each display all of the shapes you know, including any you may have learned in the interim. The Councils will review your progress and pass judgment as to whether or not one or both of you need a second apprenticeship year. If the Councils approve of your training and consider each of you fit for leadership, whichever woman has the greater number of shapes will be made Princess of Family Tiger.

"If you have any objections to my ruling in this matter, *now* is the time to air them," Kodan finished. His attention was more on Rahala, who opened her mouth, then closed it, so he was surprised when Tava spoke. More than that, he was surprised by what she said.

"I do not have any objections; what you suggest sounds just and fair. I do, however, have a question," she said, meeting his gaze steadily. "Given that you yourself have only just become Lord of the Family, what reasons would you give to Family Tiger for remaining its Lord and leader while we undergo this proposed year of training?"

For a moment, Kodan felt betrayed by her question. It was an open challenge to his authority over the Family, and with it, his solution to the problem at hand. Tava gazed at him steadily, patiently, but without the slightly sullen challenge in her eyes that Rahala held. It was obvious Rahala thought he was just trying to withhold the power she wanted. Tava, on the other hand . . . was waiting patiently for him to answer.

Not to justify myself to them, he realized, looking out over the rows of children, women, and men waiting for his reply, *but to* answer *the doubts she has raised. The doubts a lot of them might very well be having . . . particularly those who like and support Rahala. Clever, clever woman.* Resting his fists on his hips, he answered her calmly, making sure his voice was loud enough to be clearly heard.

"I have three things that neither of you have in full. I have a lifetime of experience in living on the Plains and following the Shifterai laws. I have many years of experience as not just a shapeshifter, but as a *multerai*, for I have mastered more than ten pure shapes. And I have led the South Paw Warband on many of its expeditions for the past seven years," he listed. "For these reasons, I am better suited to lead this Family for the next year than either of you.

"For another reason, I *have* undergone an apprenticeship of sorts, working within the Council of Shifters for many years, cooperating with the Council of Sisters, studying the writings of past leaders, and helping to represent Family Tiger at the Clan Cat Council of Shifters each winter. I have more direct experience in the means and methods of managing this Family than either of you. Family Tiger is both wealthy and powerful in Clan Cat *because* it is well managed . . .

and I will not see it mismanaged by an inexperienced fool, nor hand it over to someone who only cares about the power and prestige of such a position and nothing about our people.

"If anyone objects to *that* . . . they are free to find another Family."

Only the crackle and hiss of the bonfire at his back and the rustling of the wind through the camp broke the silence following his words. The Family absorbed his answer, studying him with thoughtful expressions. A few of the older members actually looked pleased, which contrasted with the boredom on the faces of some of the younger children.

Tava dipped her head in a partial bow. ". . . Thank you for answering my question. I will submit myself to the proposed year of apprenticeship."

"As will I," Rahala added firmly.

"Good." Craning his neck to peer past the teaching *geome*, Kodan gauged how much time was left. "Now, if we hurry, we can get our *newest* princess settled into her new home. The bachelors of the Family will assist Atava. Report to Kelsa for instructions. You have just enough time to arrange her quarters in the maiden's *geome* before the sun sets and still see your way back to the *ageome* for the rest of the festivities, if you hurry.

"Those of you who brought food, do not forget to take back your dishes by the end of the night . . . and *everyone* be more careful of what they're doing whenever they're near the bonfire pit. Now, let's have some music again," Kodan ordered, nodding at the instruments that had been abandoned. "As you have all just seen, we now have *several* things to celebrate."

THIRTEEN

❖❖❖

Once again, Tava found herself contemplating the night-shadowed ceiling of a *geome*. This one was much bigger than Priestess Soukut's portable home, though not quite as large as the *ageome*. Just a little larger than the warband version, it had the same cloth partitions used to give the men on night watch some privacy in which to sleep. The two main differences were, the middle ring had six support poles instead of four, and the area between them and the lattice walls had been curtained off into nine sections, two per gap between the poles, not counting the gap at the door, which was left empty for a sort of entryway, but including the double-wide space across from it, which she had been given.

Three lightglobes hung from the ceiling in net-woven bags. Two of them had been double-rapped sharply to extinguish their magical glow, while the third had been very softly tapped by Kelsa, and now provided the faint light allowing Tava to stare at the ceiling and count the staves radiating out from the middle ring. Her bed was still a narrow Shifterai cot, though her own feather-stuffed bedding had been pushed and shoved and squished into a thicker shape to fit on the tightly interwoven ropes. She could still see the fingers of the men as they deftly passed the stout cords back and forth through the holes in the frame, weaving them into a sturdy cross-hatch that could support her weight.

None of those fingers had belonged to Kodan, however. Nor had he been one of the men arranging her other belongings: her chest of books; her trunk of clothes—Shifterai clothes, her Mornai ones having been picked apart to salvage the cloth—one of the benches from her former home, which served partially as a night table; and her father's scribing table and chair, which she still had to remind herself were now hers.

Many eager hands had made the work pass with unbelievable swiftness. From the declaration that, as she was a princess and this particular *geome* had the room, she would get twice the space of the others, to the final settling of her father's . . . of *her* chair in front of the writing table, the work had barely lasted longer than it took for the sun to slide from a thumb length above the horizon to less than halfway below it. No sooner was it done than Kelsa had shooed the men out of the *geome* and given Tava a brief reintroduction to the other occupants, young women who ranged in age from two fourteen-year-old cousins to Kelsa herself at twenty-four.

After that, they had all returned to the center of the encampment for a few more hours. Kodan had been around, and he had been polite, but he hadn't approached Tava for an actual conversation. It was the thought of his actions and his distance which kept her awake now, staring at the dimly lit poles supporting the complex roof of the rounded, domed tent.

He can't have been too upset at what I did . . . can he? She knew he was smart and thought things through. From the moment she realized how he was going to outwit the Alders of Five Springs, Tava had known he wasn't a man to be underestimated. *And his answer to my question—bold though it was—did come out very eloquently. I know he quelled a lot of the doubts I could see in the others' eyes regarding his own leadership abilities. That's why I asked it, and I'm positive that's why he replied so well.*

Outside, she could hear someone walking between the felted structures.

But . . . was I too bold in asking it? I tried to ask it politely, tried to do it in a way that showed some faith in him, some courtesy for his position . . . but did I offend him anyway for openly voicing all those potential doubts?

Such thoughts made her want to tuck herself firmly back inside her cocoon. *The last thing I want to do is to lose his esteem . . . and his affection for me.*

She twisted onto her side, trying to get comfortable . . . and the feather-stuffed pallet slumped beneath her, part of it spilling over the edge of the narrow cot. Sighing heavily, she climbed out of the bed and stripped back the sheets and foxfur quilt covering it. *I'm going to have to restitch the mattress cover to fit. Thankfully all I have to do is grab it along one side and shake all the feathers to the other, then measure the width of the cot and stitch down through the emptied bit.*

. . . Actually, if I grab it and give a good shake now, then tuck the emptied bit under, that might work. At least for one night. Gripping the sturdy canvas cover, Tava heaved it up, emitting a grunt, trying to shake the feathers down. A whisper startled her.

"Tava?"

Giving up on heaving the pallet onto its side, Tava moved closer to the bench, which had been placed along the curving lattice wall. She couldn't see through the thick layers of canvas and felt, but a quick, subtle shift to sharpen her hearing let her pick up the sounds of someone breathing just beyond the barrier of wood, linen, and wool. "Who's there?"

"It's Kodan," he murmured. Standing in the near-dark outside her tent, clad in wool garments lined with his own fur, he wasn't physically cold. But there was something that prickled at his conscience, chilling him, and he needed to discuss it with her. "Could I see you outside for a few minutes?"

Tava knew he couldn't come in to see her. Soukut had confirmed that an unrelated man and a maiden could not be in the same private, enclosed space between sunset and sunrise. She also didn't know how lightly or heavily her fellow maidens slept at night; a half-murmured conversation through a wall tent might wake the others. There was also the fact that if Kodan wanted to chastise her for her brash question, Tava didn't feel like letting anyone else listen.

". . . I'll be right out," she whispered. A glance down reminded her that she was still wearing one of the few Mornai garments that hadn't been scrapped, but her nightdress was hardly appropriate for wearing outside. Finding the blue and lavender wool *chamsa* she had been wearing earlier, the only garment to have survived the fiasco with the bonfire, she buttoned it over her loose, linen shift.

Despite the rug cushioning her from the grass, the ground was a little chilly beneath her feet. Rather than bothering with trying to find something to wear, Tava simply shifted the skin of her soles into something thicker, more insulated. She could do that now, without having to worry about it being noticed.

Padding as quietly as she could over the rug-strewn ground, she slipped through the door of the *geome*, catching the spring-hinged panel before it could bang against its frame. Once it was shut quietly, she turned to find Kodan standing less than an arm's length away. He didn't hold out his hand to her, but he did tip his head, silently asking her to join him in moving away from the *geome*. Nodding, she walked beside him all the way back to the center of the sprawling camp.

The bonfire had long since died down to a bed of coals. Two elderly Shifterai men were still up, sitting in a pair of canvas-slung chairs and talking companionably, if quietly. Picking an unclaimed bench left behind at the end of the celebration, Kodan and Tava sat down on it. They were far enough away from both the men and the various *geomes* that their conversation would remain private, but were still in an open, public place.

For a long moment, silence stretched between the two of them. Then, simultaneously, they both said, "I wanted to—"

Both broke off, and Kodan gestured for her to go first. Tava looked down at her hands, clasped tightly in her lap. "I wanted to . . . to apologize for being so brash, this evening. For challenging your authority so openly. I wasn't *trying* to challenge it, but . . ."

"Shh," Kodan soothed her. "I figured it out within moments. You were being your clever self. You realized there would be doubts along those lines in the Family, and you wanted to make sure I reassured the others that I am qualified to lead them. Particularly when we do have two princesses, and one of them clearly superior to the other." He reached for her fingers with his left hand, covering them with a little squeeze. "I wanted to apologize myself for seeming to ignore you afterward. After bringing down such a firm but fair judgment, I didn't want anyone to see me favoring you right away once again, for fear they'd think I'd try to favor you during the selection process."

Tava frowned at that. She glanced at him, quirking her brow. "But you have no *say* in who is selected as the chief princess. The way you phrased things, it is the two Councils who decide whether or not each of us has learned enough about how to govern this Family to be entrusted with its leadership."

"*You* have thought of that, and *I* have thought of that, but that doesn't guarantee everyone *else* has thought of that," Kodan pointed out. "I . . . also wanted to apologize deeply for putting you on the spot like that. I shouldn't have presumed that you *want* to be considered for the leadership of Family Tiger. The others will assume it simply because you're a princess, but I shouldn't have."

"Aside from the fact I don't know what kind of a leader I'd make, because I've never been *allowed* to lead . . . I'm not offended," Tava confessed. This, too, she had thought about while lying in bed. "I was startled, and uncomfortable, but no worse than anything else I've felt since you bargained with me to come here. I'm glad you did convince me to come."

The dim glow of the bonfire embers and the faint radiance from the stars couldn't hide his pleased smile. Kodan gently squeezed her hand again. "I hope you stay longer than a month. In fact, I hope you choose to stay longer than a year. A lot longer . . . but that brings me to my next apology," he added, letting his smile fade in exchange for a sober look. "I shouldn't have kissed you. I'm sorry."

Tava blinked at him. Their kiss, stolen behind the back door of the Lord's *geome*, was one of her favorite memories of the past night. *But if he's regretting it . . .* She looked down at the hand still covering hers and swallowed her disappointment. "Oh."

"Are you *disappointed* that I'm apologizing?" Kodan asked her.

"Well, yes," Tava admitted, glancing at him again. "I mean, *I* enjoyed it. I just thought that you, um . . . But if *you* didn't enjoy it, then . . ."

"My enjoyment isn't the point . . . though I did enjoy it very much," Kodan corrected her. His hand gently squeezed hers. "The point is, I *shouldn't* have done it, and I'm apologizing for my unbecoming behavior."

"Oh! Right . . . the courtship customs. You're forgiven," Tava stated firmly. She looked around quickly to make sure they were still verbally private, even if they were in view of the two elderly Shifterai watching the dying embers of the bonfire. Glancing at Kodan, she offered him a shy smile. "Even if you should transgress custom quite a bit more . . . I'd still forgive you."

He gave her a mock-glare. "You're tempting me into wanting to do things that would bring shame upon us both, if anyone found out. Things that shouldn't take place outside the bounds of marriage . . . a marriage which is literally in *your* hands. Not that I'm asking you to reach for me right now. Not if lust is your only motivation."

Tava looked at him sharply. He met her gaze steadily.

"I would want you to reach for *me*. Not for my body, not for my status, not for my shapes. I want you to know your own mind when it comes to your future, and for you to know your heart." Moving his hand, he twined his fingers with hers. "If you continue to learn as well as you have, and to think just as fast . . . in a year's time, you will most likely become Atava, Princess of Family Tiger. *If* you choose to stay with us at the end of our bartered year. But I would still want *you*. Not the princess, not the shapeshifter, not the leader everyone would expect you to become. Just you: Tava. Even if I must now call you Atava in public, I would leap to you if you were just Tava, and you wanted me to."

His quiet admission touched her. Leaning against him, Tava rested her head on his shoulder. "I'm glad you found me when you did, and I'm very glad you brought me here. The more I learn of the *true* Shifterai, the more I want to stay here. But as much as I feel like I finally belong somewhere . . . a good part of that is you. I may have lost my physical home down in the Valley . . . but I still feel it inside whenever I'm with you. My sense of home. Some of it comes from your people—"

"—*Our* people," he corrected her, freeing his hand so that he could wrap his arm around her shoulders.

"Some of it comes from *our* people," Tava agreed, daring to slip her own arm around his waist. "But more of it comes from you. The men of the Shifting Plains might be more . . . mm . . . relaxed, I suppose, when it comes to how they behave in public, compared to the men of the Valley, but even so, very few of them like all the same things that I do. They don't *think* like you and I do—your brother giving me that lambskin blanket, for one."

"I'll admit I wasn't happy to see him giving you that," Kodan admitted, tilting his head so that he could rest his cheek on her hair.

"Do you want me to give it back?" Tava asked. "I don't *think* I've encouraged his attention . . ."

"No, you can keep it. Kenyen is impulsive, and he likes you. It's very easy to like you," Kodan added. "He just needs to find the right woman for himself. Someone *other* than you."

Smiling, Tava dared to tease, "Feeling a little possessive of me?"

"A little. But my brother is more interested in being a warrior than a scholar. He wouldn't share your love of books, like I do," he said.

"That reminds me. You owe me a new book to read. You promised when we first came here that you'd lend me a new book," she reminded him.

Kodan craned his neck, peering at her. "I gave you *two* of my books, woman!"

"Yes, but you *gave* them to me. You said you would *loan* me a book when we got here—and you gave me those two books several days later, not as soon as we arrived," she added tartly.

Chuckling, he tucked her closer at his side. "I see you will make a great law-sayer someday . . . I couldn't *lend* you a book since you were being instructed in other things and wouldn't have had time to read it. I didn't want to torment you with something you couldn't immediately enjoy."

"Like doing the things men and maidens shouldn't do outside of marriage," Tava sighed.

"All it would take is for you to hold out your hand," he murmured, "and I would gladly leap the largest fire for you."

The combination of his words and the sight of the still-smoldering bonfire pit made Tava wince. "The *smallest* fire, if you please. I still remember what my mother went through. What all those women went through, being treated like that."

Kodan hugged her. "We'll go looking for them, next year. I myself want to make sure such filth aren't still around. We can afford to spare a few warbands from seeking income and trade. I'll put Deian in charge; he's traded off being warlord with me over the years."

"The position of warlord is offered to all suitable men at least twice, so that they may know what responsibility feels like and how

to apply their lessons in strategy to real situations," Tava recited dutifully. Sighing, she added, "Part of me wants to go right now to look
for them. To confront my fears that this Family Mongrel is still
around and still torturing women and abusing children. But . . . I
wouldn't know where to start, other than in the mountains to the
south, and winter will be here soon."

"It's something best started in the spring," Kodan agreed. "My
intent is to take your book to the City to show to Her Majesty and
the Councils. They might ask the heads of the other Families to lend
a warband or two of their own, enough to blanket the southern border. With enough shifters searching, even if this Family Mongrel is
long gone, we should find traces of where they used to hide . . . and
with enough shifters searching, if they do still exist, we'll be able to
crush them and rescue their captives. I would like to look for them as
much as you, but winter is coming, and winter on the Plains is not to
be treated lightly."

"Nor would it be easy to find those caves in the mountains where
they took shelter," Tava agreed. "Between the winds and the snow . . .
I was always grateful we lived on the west bank, sheltered by the edge
of the Valley, whenever we'd hear word of how bad the winds would
blow across to the east bank."

"We'll be safely sheltered in the City by then," Kodan promised.

A comfortable silence settled between them. Tired from the long
day, Tava closed her eyes. She snuggled a little closer, enjoying the
warmth and scent of the man next to her. He cradled her close for a
little bit, then yawned. Sighing, Kodan gently nudged her.

"Come. You need to return to your bed," he murmured, nudging
her up onto her feet. "I need to retire to my own, too. We'll both need
our rest. We can stay here another five days at most, if we shift the
long-grazers to the east. If Tailtip hasn't returned by then, we'll have
to head for the City and hope they catch up before the first storms of
late autumn."

"Is it normal for warbands to be out so late?" Tava asked, curious.

"Sometimes. If they've been hired for a lengthy job, or a distant one, it can take a while for them to return," Kodan said. "Mata is the one in charge of Tailtip this time. He's my father's age, with plenty of experience. He'll be able to get his men safely home, whether that home is here, or all the way to the City. We'll just have to wait and see whether they join us in time or not. *You* need to sleep. There are a few things I still need to oversee in the next few days, but I do owe Deian assistance in trying for a new shape, and you need to know how we Shifterai do it. Not to mention I'm interested to hear how you managed it."

"There wasn't much to it," Tava demurred. "We had a barn cat several years ago. One day when I was thirteen, I was watching her stretch after getting up from a nap, and imagined how nice it must feel to stretch like that. When I gave it a try myself . . . my body lengthened. It startled me, but it didn't frighten me . . . so I tried it again.

"I ran and told my father, showed him what I could do, and he cautioned me not to tell anyone else, since the Alders would think a display of magic in a girl was unnatural and might treat me cruelly instead of merely with indifference. But I did practice, mostly by imagining what it would *feel* like to be a particular animal, and by having my father on hand to tell me if I was getting it right. I think a mirror might have helped more," Tava added lightly, "but the best I could do was either a still pond during the day or a windowpane at night."

"That's actually not very different from the way we do it," Kodan agreed as they walked among the tents of the South Paw section. "We help each other to learn new shapes by watching and making corrections. If the person helping is a *multerai*, sometimes we can sort of . . . *lend* our magic to the other person, by laying our hands on the other shifter and *feeling* the new shape ourselves. Only without actually shaping it, just sort of pushing that feeling into the other shapeshifter.

"That's what Deian wanted me to help him do, since it's more effective when it involves two *multerai*. Once they learn the new shape—if they haven't reached their limit on shapes they can learn— then they can usually manage it on their own. But we do reach a point of limitation," he admitted. "I can take fifteen shapes, which is three more than Her Majesty, and which makes me the tenth or eleventh best shifter in all the Clans. But every time I try for a sixteenth shape . . . I lose the sense of it, and it eludes me."

"I don't know yet if I've reached the limit of the shapes I can learn," Tava admitted. "I couldn't always practice new shapes, without the risk of being caught. And I had to find a new shape, and track it, and study it so that I could get a sense of what it was like to *be* that kind of animal. The hardest one was learning how to be an eel. Breathing water is *very* different from breathing air."

"I know. I learned how to be a trout just two years ago. It was part of a dare, since true water-breathers are so hard to emulate." Knowing their parting was inevitable, he slowed his steps as they approached her waiting *geome*. Turning to face her, he cupped her cheeks, warming them in his palms. "Know your own mind, Tava. Particularly when it comes to me."

Wanting to kiss her but knowing—despite her invitation—that he shouldn't, Kodan contented himself with a gentle caress of her skin. It pleased him when she lifted her own fingers to his face. A twitch of his skin made sure his jaw was as smooth as if it had been shaved, permitting her fingertips to glide over his skin without being scratched.

"Sleep well, Tava," he finally whispered.

A daring thought crossed her mind. She knew he could feel her face warming from it, but whispered it anyway. "I know I'd sleep *very* well if we—"

He cut her off with his forefinger, silencing her suggestion. Shifting to her side, he nodded at the door, and swatted her lightly on her rump when she didn't move. "Good night."

Disappointed but knowing he was right—and knowing that he

respected her—Tava retreated to the maiden's *geome*. The disarray of her bed reminded her that she had to restitch her mattress narrower in the morning. Doing her best to shake it down and tuck under the extra fabric, she lay down and covered herself with his foxfur gift.

This time, it didn't take her nearly as long to fall asleep.

T ava bent her head once more over the thumbnail-sized arrowhead she was patiently gluing into its shaft. Unfortunately, the formerly gummy tip of her birch-tar stick had cooled and solidified again. Leaning forward, she extended the lump over the flames of the nearby brazier.

"I could do that for you," Medred offered.

The Shifterai, whom she had first met the day before her arrival and adoption, extended his hand to take the stick from her. Annoyed, Tava swayed out of his reach, but that put her within reach of another would-be suitor.

"She wants *me* to do it," Tedro countered, reaching for the stick.

"*No*, thank you. I can do this myself," she asserted, dodging his hand as well. Hoping the resin had softened enough, she quickly brought it back to the arrow shaft, dabbing on the dark, tacky glue. Pressing it into place, she waited until it set, then double-checked to make sure the second scrap of sharpened metal would fit into its notch.

Shifterai arrows were made with a primary arrowhead for the initial penetration and a second blade which was set about a thumb length back from the first and slightly rotated from the cutting plane of the first arrowhead, making it stick out something like a fin. They were made that way for two reasons: for one, to induce extra bleeding in whatever animal a hunter might hit, which would bring down the game animal that much faster; and for another, to make it that much harder for an attacking shifter to shift away the injury. Shifters could heal their injuries faster than normal, depending on their strength, but pain was still pain, a deterrent against unacceptable behavior.

Soukut and her daughter had explained that it wasn't really *necessary* these days, since the men of the Shifting Plains were now civilized, but Shifterai women were taught to carry on the traditional modification made by their nation's founding Queen and her Consort "just in case." The only wound a shifter couldn't heal was one caused by bluesteel, but the process to make the cobalt-hued metal was laborious and secretive. It was considered too expensive in terms of materials, magic, and labor to waste on common hunting arrows, though it was forged into manacles, brands, and blades.

The hearth-priestess had also told her that her instruction in Shifterai ways would continue well past the original ten days, though it wouldn't be nearly as intense. Tava's current task was to practice making arrows of her own, rather than just borrow them from someone else's quiver. Her skills with a single-headed target arrow had been deemed good enough. Soukut had told her to make hunting arrows, since there would likely be a chance to hunt game on the journey northwest, toward the City.

"You don't *have* to do this," Medred told her. "You *are* a princess. You can choose to stay back and direct the fighting from a distance."

"At-t-tava is very b-brave," Torei stammered. "She j-just might-t choose t-t-t-t . . . to *fight!*"

Startled by his loud statement, the result of straining against his verbal ailment, Tava jumped just as she removed the second arrow blade to leave room for the birch-tar glue. The back of the blade caught on the end of the groove, and the edge of the metallic triangle sliced across her fingers. Hissing at the pain, she dropped the arrow on her lap and gingerly uncurled her fingers, gauging the seriousness of the cuts.

Blood welled up freely from her first and middle fingers, though not as much from the third. Medred grabbed her hand without warning, jostling and pulling on the injury even more. "She's injured! Someone get Yemii!"

"Stop that!" Jerking her hand free, Tava frowned and concentrated.

Her hand from wrist to fingertip rippled and swelled into a stripe-furred, claw-tipped paw. Shifting it back again, she checked the cuts, which were still bloody, but no longer actually bleeding. A second shift to cat paw and back smoothed out the gaping edges. Lifting her hand, she wriggled her reddened but undamaged fingers.

"As you can see, I am quite capable of healing myself. I don't need the Healer-priest—and I *don't* need the lot of you hovering around me! I *can* make arrows by myself, and I *don't need your help!*" Twisting to include Torei in her pointed glare, she fluttered her unbloodied hand at them. "Go away!"

Exchanging wary looks—and a few pointed glares of their own—the trio of men got up and moved away. Picking up the stick with its lump of birch tar, she held it over the flames in the brazier to soften it, and carefully glued the second arrowhead into place. Not until she finished did she realize her fingers had smeared blood on the shaft, staining the pale wood in slowly browning blotches. Sighing heavily, Tava set her arrow-making supplies on the bench where she had been sitting and headed off to find one of the wrought iron washstands these Shifterai favored over the bowl and pitcher arrangement used by the Mornai.

She didn't get more than three body lengths from the brazier and bench before yet another single Shifterai male trotted up to her side.

"Are you going to fetch something? Would you like me to carry it for you?" the smiling, dark blond male asked solicitously.

"No. Thank you," she added, clinging to a scrap of politeness. *I suppose it's a sign of just how far I've come, that I don't flinch at the thought of being so openly nearly rude to these men,* Tava thought, bemused. Then she winced as another man broke off what he was doing, coming over to join the queue of potential suitors wanting her attention. *Or maybe I'm just too annoyed to care . . .*

I *am way too annoyed to care!*

Glaring at Kenyen, Tava unleashed her anger on the latest of her suitor-pests. "And *another* thing—I *do not* need an escort to the refreshing tent! I am *quite* capable of farting on my own!"

His wasn't the only face that flushed at her blunt assertion, though some of those whose cheeks flushed also suffered from shaking shoulders and hastily raised hands. Not everyone was amused, however. Some of the nearer members of Family Tiger were startled by her language. One of the older women dropped the stack of pottery bowls and metal cooking utensils she was carrying. Two of the bowls cracked, and the implements clattered noisily, tumbling across the trampled ground.

"What do I have to *do* to get it through to you that I am *not* interested in you like that? *Any* of you?" she added, swinging around to include the other half dozen of her too-earnest suitors.

Kenyen touched her arm. Tava rounded on him, fist lifting in aggravated warning, but he merely released her and held up his hands, his normally lighthearted expression sober. "There *is* one thing you can do to discourage our interest in you."

"*What?*" she demanded.

He flashed her a grin. "All you have to do is choose one of—"

"—What's with all the shouting? I could hear you from halfway across the—aaaah!" Tripping over the fallen utensils, Rahala stumbled and dropped to the ground. Part of the broken pottery *crunch*ed further under her, making her cry out again.

As much as she disliked the other woman, Tava didn't want to see her injured. She started forward, intending to help Rahala up, but several of her would-be suitors got there first. Once on her feet, it was obvious the other woman hadn't survived her fall unscathed.

Blood smeared her *breikas*, and a hesitant exploration extracted a sharp shard of pottery from her flesh.

Teeth clenched, Rahala accepted the arms offered to support her. "—I'll be fine! Just help me to my *geome*—whoever dropped this mess, clean it up! This isn't Family Pigsty!"

The woman who had dropped the bowls and utensils flushed with shame. Strangely enough, it was Rahala's own acerbic words which quelled Tava's temper. Mostly out of shame that she could have acted like that herself. Unfortunately, she still had the problem of her would-be suitors to deal with.

Out of the corner of her eye, she saw Kodan and Deian approaching. Kodan looked at the tableau of the limping Rahala, supported on either side by two men, the woman picking up the broken pottery and scattered spoons, his brother, Tava, and the other men, all clumped together in the clearing in front of the South Paw maidens' *geome*.

He slowed to a stop and lifted his brow. "Is there something I should know about?"

"Yes," Tava stated, making up her mind. She moved away from Kenyen and the others, placing the nearby brazier between her and the Lord of Family Tiger. "I want to make it perfectly clear to everyone here that there is only *one* man I am interested in as a suitor . . . and that man is *you*, Kodan Sin Siin."

Looking straight at him, the tripod-held brazier between them, she lifted her hand.

Kodan glanced quickly at Rahala, wanting to see her reaction. He would have bet half his wealth that her pinched expression came more from her anger at this little scene than from the pain of her wound . . . but she *was* a witness to it. Looking back at Tava, he eyed the wrought iron tripod between them, the peak of which came up to the middle of his chest. It wouldn't be the easiest obstacle to clear, but there was a fire crackling softly in the metal pan hanging from the tripod.

A quick shift to make stronger leg muscles was all that was needed to allow him to leap over the obstacle in his path. Landing with a *thud*, barely conscious of having sprinted and jumped, Kodan caught Tava's outstretched hand. Tugging her close, he did what he had been longing to do for days, and what he should not have done just three days ago, before it was legal for him to do so.

One moment, he was on the ground across from her; the next, he seemed to float over the brazier with impressive ease. The moment after that, his lips were on hers, thrilling her with their firm, fervent warmth. A shout rose up from most of the people witnessing it, but he didn't stop kissing her. Tava clung to him, learning quickly how to tilt her head and nibble, returning each caress of his tongue and lips.

The clearing of a voice broke them apart. Deian folded his arms across his chest and gave both of them an amused, patient look. "... I take it our plan to practice shifting another shape is about to be set aside?"

"Ugh—take me back to my *geome!*" Rahala ordered Medred and his cousin, beckoning the bachelors over to her side of the brazier. "Kodan . . . *A*kodan," she acknowledged with gritted teeth, "I'm sure it will be no surprise to you that I have decided I will *not* apprentice to you. As soon as we reach the City, I plan on entering the Princess Challenge. At the rate I am learning shapes, I shall probably surpass Her Majesty's twelve pure forms . . . and will become her new apprentice before winter is over. Take good care of Family Tiger, once I'm gone. *I'll* have a kingdom to run."

A curt gesture from one hand directed her escort to help her away from the newly mated pair. The sight of her hobbling away, supported on either side, made Tava frown in puzzlement. Before she could more than wonder why Rahala hadn't shifted her wound away, Kodan recaptured her attention.

"I believe there are some belongings of yours that need to be relocated, yes?" he asked her. "After that, we can help both of you strive for a new shape. Deian, you wanted to try for an eagle form, correct?"

"I wouldn't want to interrupt your chance to celebrate your newly wedded bliss," his friend demurred.

Kodan gave the other shifter a sardonic look. "I'm Lord of Family Tiger. *Everyone* will want to interrupt my newly wedded bliss." Turning, Tava tucked against his side, he caught sight of his brother's grinning face. ". . . What?"

"It's about *time*, that's what," Kenyen said. He winked at Tava. "I was afraid I'd actually have to seduce you, just to get you to make up your mind about him. Now, can I have my sheepskin lap blanket back?"

Kodan whapped him on the shoulder. "No, you cannot! That was a first-gift, Kenyen!"

"*Yes*, he can," Tava countered, resting her hand on Kodan's chest. Her husband's chest. It wasn't the baptised-in-the-River wedding she was used to seeing, but she knew the Gods didn't care which kingdom's customs were used, so long as the couple's intent was pure and there were witnesses to the marriage rite used. She smiled at Kodan. "After all, *yours* is the only fur I'll ever need."

The warmth in his gaze was broken only by the approaching argument of a middle-aged woman hauling a youngish boy of about eleven or twelve into view, pulling him by the collar of his woolen *chamak*. "Lord Kodan, I want you to punish this *miscreant* immediately! I caught him with his sticky fingers on my honey buns, trying to make off with three of them while I was off at the refreshing tent!"

"I was just brushing the flies off them, I swear!" the boy protested.

"Liar!" the woman snapped, shaking him a little.

"I'm not lying!" He squirmed in an effort to get free, but her grip was too sturdy.

Kodan groaned. He heard a giggle and glanced down at his bride. She smiled and patted his chest.

"You go do your Lord-of-the-Family things. We'll have plenty of time later for *other* activities," Tava promised.

Almost agreeing with her, Kodan narrowed his eyes in the next moment. "Oh, no, you don't, *apprentice*. You're going to *help* me adjudicate this dispute."

Sighing, she studied the boy and the woman. Inspiration struck as the youth protested once more that he was innocent and not the liar his captor claimed. "Fine. I'll go get my Truth Stone. *That'll* be the quickest way to see whose version is the truth."

"Ha! I'll have you as a pot-scrubber for half a turn of Brother Moon!" the woman crowed as the boy in her grip froze.

"Alright, I *did* want to eat one of them," he confessed grudgingly. "But there *were* flies buzzing around, too, and I didn't want them to be spoiled! I'll swear it on a Truth Stone!"

Someone else came riding up on a horse, calling out as he approached. "Lord Kodan! Lord Kodan! A rattlesnake startled some of the cattle on the northeast side and several have bolted. We need a half dozen riders to go after them!"

"Gods, it never ends," Kodan muttered under his breath to Tava. "You handle the woman and the boy; fetch the Truth Stone and be reasonably fair. I'll organize the round-up party and bring back the cattle. We'll move your things and practice shifting new shapes after these problems—and no doubt several others—have been settled."

FOURTEEN

‿‿❊‿‿

She heard him coming before the door to his *geome* ever opened.

"... and if it is *not* a genuine emergency, as in fire, flood, invasion, or murder, I will be *very* upset at whoever causes the interruption. *You* are the next-ranked shifter, Deian. *You* keep the peace of the Family tonight. And *yes*, Kinedi, I will give her the new clothes. I will also give her the temporary pectoral the Family carvers made, and *no*, I don't think she wants any sweets this late at night, Mother, but thank you for the offer. Supper was delicious, as always. Good night, everyone ... *Good night*."

The door swung open, and Kodan ducked through the opening. One arm was loaded with a bundle of lavender-dyed linen, no doubt a new set of *chamsa* and *breikas* to replace the ones lost in the fire a few days ago. The other arm pulled the door firmly shut, if not quite banging it. Flipping down the lever that locked it against outside intrusion, he straightened, sighing.

Tava bit her lower lip, but it was no good. She couldn't prevent the smile that curved her lips. Carefully fitting a scrap of ribbon into the pages of the book on her lap, she watched him cross to one of the chests she had arranged along the right side of the *geome* as one entered.

"A new *chamsa* . . . and *breikas*," Kodan confirmed, unfolding the garments and the webwork bundle of pale beads they had sheltered, displaying each item in turn, "and a bone pectoral, since that's what the carvers had the most of on hand. Once we get to the City, the Family artisans will have access to metalworking and gem-cutting supplies and will make you a proper collar."

"Every shifter gets at least one pectoral for free, usually carved from wood or bone, or painted ceramic beads," Tava recited, remembering her lessons. "Anything fancier than that, and they have to pay for it themselves. The only exception to this is for a princess. Since she is a noble treasure for a Family to possess, it is considered only fitting that the entire Family should contribute to the material costs and crafting of her pectoral."

He smiled and crossed to the broad bed, leaving her things piled on her book chest. "You remember well."

"I'm a scribe. A trained memory is an asset. But having remembered that, and thinking of Family Lion having all those princesses," Tava continued, shifting to set her book on the night table beside the bed, "I feel sorry for how much all those collars must have cost."

Kodan chuckled. "Maybe that's why Family Tiger has been so wealthy, not having had any of our own until now."

"And now you have two," Tava agreed.

"And now *we* have two," he corrected, settling onto the edge of the bed next to her. "But I'd rather not think about the other one right now. I am sorry I took so long coming back from the final round of inspecting the camp for the night. Can you forgive me?"

Smiling warmly, she said, "It's one of the things I like about you, the fact that you honestly *care* about everyone in this Family. *Our*

Family," she added, mock-teasing him. It thrilled her to be able to do so, and pleased her when he smiled back. Reaching out, Tava patted the cover of the book she had been reading. "Besides, I had a good friend to cuddle up with while I waited for you."

"Careful, you'll make me jealous," Kodan mock-warned her. Reaching for the book, he picked it up. The leather was dark with age, the embossing worn and slightly scuffed, but the title was still legible. "*Legends of the Painted Warriors: Volume III.* A book on the Painted Warriors of Mendhi?"

"Yes. My father inherited it from *his* father, and from *his* mother, and from . . . so on and so forth," Tava dismissed. "It predates the Shattering of Aiar. Before the one you gave me, this one, and my copy of *Father Fox's Tales*, were the only two books of adventure stories I owned. The rest of them are either books of information or of discussion. When I want to relax and fall asleep, I'll open my copy of *A Discourse of Proper Exchequery Practices Using Arithmantic Accounting.* When I want to relax but stay awake . . . it's either *Legends* or *Father Fox's,* but I wasn't in the mood for children's fables."

"May I?" Kodan asked, lifting the book in his hands.

Tava nodded, giving him permission to open it. Curling her legs, she sat forward to peer at the pages with him, abandoning the pile of pillows she had made against the modest headboard of the broad, rope-strung bed. He flipped slowly through the pages, randomly skimming the text and the occasional illustration.

Pausing at one, Kodan tapped the image of a man dressed in a short vest and a strange combination of abbreviated skirt and loincloth, his body covered in a dozen tattoos. Some were inked on his calves, others on his forearms; one had been drawn around his navel, just visible peeking above the waistband of his pleated skirt-thing, while another wrapped around his throat like an abstract collar. Flipping back to another illustration, Kodan tapped the stomach of a woman clad in a similar outfit, though her vest was fastened snugly across her chest. Her tattooes ranged from her calves and thighs to her biceps, one on her forehead, and another circling her belly button.

"I remember the old man who came at midsummer, the one with that west-bound caravan that Rah . . . *A*rahala was so interested in. He had various marks on his thighs, his biceps, and his hands, something on his cheek, and this one particular mark on his stomach," Kodan said. He flicked ahead to another illustration, but that one didn't show the stomach of the figure, so he tried another. Tapping the page, he nodded. "If these drawings are accurate, I wonder why each one has this tattoo right here on their stomach? It's a little bit different between men and women, but all the men have the same one, and all the women have the same."

"I've read this book dozens of times, maybe hundreds, and it doesn't ever say why they all share that similar mark," Tava confessed. "It doesn't actually contain anything on *how* the tattoos are made, just that certain styles of marks in certain locations have certain effects, acting like permanently inscribed spells. It's a book of adventure tales, after all, not one containing instructions on how to re-create a Painted Warrior's powers. For that, I suspect you'd need a Mendhi mage to tell you what to do."

"I used to wonder what it would be like to be a mage," Kodan admitted. "To be able to do more than shift my shape. To wave my hand and make things happen. After I grew up, I realized I prefer being a shapeshifter." Leaning forward, he returned the tome to the night table, then swerved and kissed Tava lightly on the lips. Pulling back, he smiled at her. "Most of all, I prefer being right here, right now, with you. Barring fire, flood, invasion, or murder, *nothing* is going to interrupt us."

"Nothing?" Tava teased, leaning back onto the pillows as he leaned forward, looming over her.

"Nothing, if it has any wisdom at all," her husband promised. He started to kiss her again, then pulled back, wincing. "Ah . . . wait. I forgot to put a few more grass-logs on the fire. It's growing rather cold outside, and we're not going to be using the blankets just yet. Pardon the interruption," Kodan apologized, backing off the bed.

"So long as it's grass-logs and not dried dung, I'll be happy," Tava quipped. "The *rora* flowers do make it smell nicer, but *nicer* isn't always enough."

"I'll put one of your first-gift wreaths on the fire anyway. The scent of burning grass isn't that much better than dung," he admitted.

It didn't take long for him to stoke the fire in the brazier pan, or for the spicy-sweet scent of burning *rora* vine to spread through the tent. Crossing to one of his own chests, Kodan began removing his clothes. Watching him, Tava realized she should be doing the same, and started unbuttoning her top.

"We'll have a Washing Day before we break camp. There's just enough water here for us to do that, which is why we like picking this particular pasture site as our last one before heading in for the winter," Kodan told her, folding his *chamak*. He pulled off his boots and unlaced each ankle cuff in turn. "There won't be enough water for laundry on the journey north, until we get to the City. They collect a lot of rainwater in its cisterns—if we hadn't dug deep pits and piled up the resulting dirt and rock across half the crater floor, the crater would have gradually become a lake.

"In fact, there *is* a lake, though most of us only see it in winter, when it freezes over." Turning, he flashed her a grin. "We like to skate on it for fun, though not everyone can shift bone skates on their feet. You were getting very close to mastering the body of an eagle earlier, so I think you might be able to figure out the trick of ice skates, too. If not, they're not that expensive to buy. The best bone-skate carvers are in . . . Clan . . ."

His gaze dropped as she peeled back the folds of her *chamsa*, letting the material fall onto the bed behind her. Tava hadn't shifted fur to cover herself. The appreciative heat in his gaze as it slipped down over her bare breasts warmed her more than the cheerfully crackling flames in the brazier. Glad she had been so bold, Tava loosened the ankle drawstrings of her *breikas*, then slipped off the bed and untied the one at the waistband.

The slithering of the material down her thighs impelled him to move. Rounding the end of the bed, Kodan checked the urge to pull her into his arms and kiss her senseless, to feel every part of her against every part of him. This wasn't an earth-priestess experienced in the needs of men, but a woman who had initially thought Shifterai men were nothing more than ravaging brutes. Glad he was still wearing his *breikas*, though the gathered folds did little to hide the tenting of his arousal, Kodan knelt on the felt-lined floor in front of her and gently caught her hands in his.

She blushed when he lifted them to his mouth, and blushed harder when he didn't just kiss, but also licked and sucked on her fingers. She remembered his descriptions of what to do with herself, of what *he* would do with her, and felt tingles of desire rising in her blood.

His hands left hers, allowing him to skim his palms up her arms and then down her ribs. Tava giggled and squirmed, ticklish. She batted his hands away, only to have him catch her wrists and tuck her arms behind her back. Leaning forward, he licked her stomach. That tickled her, too, but it also aroused her.

His grip wasn't strong; she knew she could pull away, but being lightly restrained also made her feel vulnerable. That Kodan kissed and supped his way around her navel and up to her ribs, treating her gently, made her feel cherished. The combination aroused her even further. She wanted to run her fingers through his soft, dark hair, to return each touch. Yet at the same time, she longed to stay the center of his attention like this.

It's just like Father said, she acknowledged, sucking in a sharp breath when Kodan licked the curve of her breast. *When a man and a maiden truly trust each other, everything they do together is pleasure . . . and I truly trust Kodan. I love him . . . and I really desire him.*

Needing to caress more of her skin, Kodan released her hands. She shifted them to his scalp, stroking her fingers through his hair in counterpoint to the stroking of his palms along her back. The sensual caress pleased him. Leaving her hands free for whatever else she might desire, he smoothed his own down to her calves and back up to her thighs.

The feel of her hand catching one of his, of her guiding his fingertips to the damp folds of her flesh, shocked him. Not that it was unwanted, but he hadn't expected her to be so bold. Nor did he anticipate her words, soft and husky-voiced.

"Touch me," Tava urged him, cupping his fingers in place. "Like you said you would, that night."

Arousal spiked through his blood. Biting back the urge to groan, Kodan nudged her closer to the side of the bed. "Then sit, and part your thighs. Lie back, if you want."

Turning a little, Tava perched on the edge of the bed. It was somewhat low compared to the shelf of a Mornai bed, but it did put their heads at almost the same level. She watched him shuffle closer, then rise up a little once he knelt between her thighs, bringing their lips together. It also brushed his body against hers. The warmth of skin and the slight rasp of fabric teased her flesh. Wanting more of these wonderful feelings, wanting to share them, Tava slid her hands over his shoulders and down his chest.

Her touch thrilled him. Kissing her thoroughly, Kodan coaxed her tongue into play, suckling it as he had suckled her fingers and breasts. He stroked her skin all over, enjoying the freedom to touch her wherever he pleased, to caress, rub, and tweak. Tava drew his fingers back down to her loins after a little while. The moisture that greeted his fingers encouraged him to rub and stroke her flesh down there, until her hips were rocking and circling into his touch in the quest to intensify her pleasure.

Breaking off their kisses, Kodan gently pushed her back. Disappointed, Tava reluctantly complied with his urgings. She lay back on the rumpled bedding, hips barely resting on the bed. Kodan stroked his hands down her torso, skimming over her shoulders, breasts, and belly to her thighs. He stroked again and again, first swerving to the middle of her body, then dipping to the outside, before spiraling around her breasts until her back arched up in the need for more.

"Please . . ." she breathed. She tried to catch his hands, but Kodan sank down onto his heels. Dipping his head, he licked the seam of flesh bared by her parted limbs. Pleasure rushed through her as he did it again and again, doing with his tongue what she had expected him to do with his fingers. "Kodan! Oh . . . Kodan . . ."

Encouraged by her gasps and her sighs, by the fingers raking through his hair and the tensing of her limbs, Kodan loved her with his mouth until she spasmed and cried out. He gentled his touch, but didn't stop kissing her flesh. Once her panting eased, he renewed the firmer strokes of his tongue, adding gentle nips of his teeth to her nether-lips.

The feel of her hands returning to his hair pleased him. Untying the drawstring of his *breikas*, he freed his own flesh. Kissing his way up onto her abdomen, he ignored her wordless noise of protest. Rising onto his knees, Kodan guided his manhood into position.

Tava felt her flesh stretching, and shifted automatically to accommodate him. A slow push was followed by gentle rocking. This was far more than the single finger she had used on herself. Far better, too. Tava pushed up onto her elbows, wanting to see as well as feel him loving her this way. Catching her hands, Kodan helped pull her upright, then resumed his gentle thrusts.

"Look at us," he murmured, his own attention more on her face than on the conjoining of their flesh. "Working together . . . moving together . . . *being* together. You and I . . . husband and wife . . . woman and man . . ."

Tava pulled her gaze up from the hypnotic sight and sensation of him pleasuring her. She met Kodan's dark eyes. The emotion in them matched her own intense feelings.

"Loving each other," she whispered, not quite making it a question.

"*Yes,*" Kodan growled, shifting his hands to her hips. Pulling her closer, he thrust powerfully.

Her pleasure intensified, but the position threatened to slide her off the bed between bounces. Dropping back, Tava let herself fall onto the bedding. Kodan rubbed his palms along her stomach and up over her breasts. On the return stroke, he slipped his thumb down between her folds, massaging her flesh as he continued to stroke.

"Remember this?" he asked her, panting. "Remember how I said I would touch you? All of this, and so much more!"

His words released her pleasure. Arching her back, Tava moaned as she fell, a quavering note of bliss that morphed into his name at its end. He picked up his pace, prolonging her desire, until he fell as well. Shuddering for several seconds, he finally stopped and slumped, resting his sweating face on her stomach. Tava gently stroked his hair as they both rested.

She felt . . . free. No longer restricted by anything in her life, other than her desire to please her husband and the whims of her own will. *Like I've finally escaped the cocoon of Valley life that confined me for too long.* A whimsical thought struck. *I wonder . . . should I try to shapeshift myself into a butterfly? I certainly feel like one, and even the Shifterai say that* feeling *like the animal you're trying to imitate is an important part of getting that animal-shape right . . .*

Gradually, Kodan became aware of the sounds of the night. The crackling of the burning grass-logs had been joined by a pattering on the roof. Drawing a deep breath, he rose from the ground and scooped up his wife. Turning her a little, he laid her on the bed, tugged the covers out from under her.

Tava sat up and helped, pushing the bedding down with her hands and heels. Underneath was the feather pallet she had brought from her home. Unstitched to its normal size, it was narrower than his own wool-stuffed mattress and now might need extra fabric to extend its width properly, but the extra softness was worth it. So was the extra warmth; the night air was now damp as well as chilly, enough that she didn't mind cuddling close to Kodan. Helping him pull the blankets up into place, she curled up against him and grinned.

"Mm?" he asked, eyeing her almost smug expression.

"I *like* being married. I'll never have to shiver in a cold bed all on my own anymore," she said.

Kodan chuckled and pulled her closer. "I can think of several ways to keep you warm."

"I hope so," Tava muttered boldly, sliding her hand from his hip to his backside. From his sigh of appreciation, she guessed he liked her touch. "I hope I can come up with a few ways to keep you warm, too."

"I have no doubt," he agreed. "Do you hear the rain on the roof?"

"Yes," Tava said, wondering at the change in subject. "What of it?"

"Father Sky is smiling on our marriage. Rain on a wedding night is said to be a blessing on the union from the Gods, because rain is how Father Sky kisses Mother Earth, and wind is how He caresses Her. Sometimes He gets overly passionate, but we never doubt that He loves Her, even during the fiercest of storms."

"I'll settle for just rain," Tava told him. "I'm not too keen on the thought of all these *geomes* blowing away in a strong wind."

"They're *very* stable, Tava," he reassured her patiently. "*Geomes* don't blow over in the wind."

"What about a whirlwind?"

"We have several priestesses and even a mage, all of whom can pray and even cast a spell or two to avert such things. You needn't worry, wife," Kodan stated. Then slid his hand down to the junction of her thighs. "But I can see I'll have to work harder at distracting you from all your worries and cares."

Lifting her knee to give him more room to work, Tava kissed her husband.

* * *

"If you can find one, you'll want to get a camp stove with the pipe hole offset to one side," Sinya lectured her daughter-in-law. "That gives you more cooking surface. My sister swears by the round-bodied ones, but I prefer the octagonal fireboxes. It's easier to find a water tank that can fit flush against the side. You get less water overall, true, but the replacement tanks are cheaper and easier for the City smiths to make when the original one rusts through. Are you done stirring the dough?"

"I was thinking of adding some wild chives," Tava said, setting down the bowl full of biscuit dough. Now that Tava was no longer being fed either by the priesthood or by her fellow maidens, Kodan's mother had offered to feed her until she could set up a camp kitchen of her own, just as the older woman still often fed both of her sons despite the fact that they had *geomes* of their own. Moving over to the washstand, Tava rinsed bits of flour and dough from her fingers. "I saw some growing next to the cistern just north of the Right Flank earth-priestess *geome* and thought it might be nice to have. That's what we do with our biscuits down in the Valley, either add chive or small onions. Sometimes we even add cheese."

Sinya eyed the stew she was making. She stirred it, sniffed at the steam, and covered it with a lid. ". . . I think chives and cheese *would* taste good in the dumplings. Go and fetch some chives from the cistern. Extra cooking time never harms a stew, so long as you keep adding water now and again."

Tava smiled. "That's what my father said. Well, he said it more about soups, but a stew is like a thickened soup."

Sinya laughed. "I have two boys and a girl, plus my husband to feed. Soup's a bit thin for a shapeshifter; they expend a lot of energy when they shift, so they need food that will stick to their bones. There's a small bowl in that chest over there, and the scissors I use to cut food."

"Where is your daughter?" Tava asked, moving to fetch the implements. "I haven't met her."

"She moved to Family Bobcat when she picked her husband. You'll get to meet her when we get to the City. Bobcat's a bigger Family than Tiger, so she often brings her kin-family to stay with us in our tenements where there's more room. Bobcat also has five princesses—oh! That reminds me, the full of Brother Moon is coming up in just two more days. That's when the Council of Sisters traditionally pays our princesses their Family fee. The Council of Shifters does it on the new of Brother Moon."

"It feels strange to be paid money just for existing. I mean, I haven't really *done* anything for the Family, yet. You don't even need me as a scribe, since all of you can read and write," Tava said as she shut the chest lid, bowl and scissors balanced in her other hand.

"If my son hasn't thought of it yet, I'll strongly suggest appointing you as the scribe for both Councils. You'll learn a lot more about how a Family is governed by sitting in on both Councils than you would in a hundred days of listening to the hearth-priestess," Sinya asserted. "Arahala will undoubtedly want to sit in on both Councils, too. She always wanted to sit in on the Sister Council, though we told her she just wasn't experienced enough—in other words, *mature* enough—but then, that girl never learned to keep her mouth shut.

"Mark my words, you'll learn more by *listening* and thinking everything through than you'd ever learn by flapping your lips with your half-formed opinions," Sinya added. "Now that she's a princess, we can't by law keep her out, but I doubt she'll remember the law that she's supposed to shut up and listen for the first two turns of Sister Moon. Make sure you don't take after her."

My, these Shifterai women are blunt at times. Tava shook her head. "My father bribed the Alders into letting me sit with him during the various village meetings, even the ones the women weren't normally allowed to attend. I don't know what he did to blackmail them, but for *my* part, I had to keep utterly silent and very still, save for whatever notes I was supposed to be taking. I learned the value of listening and thinking things through for myself long ago. Particularly since some of those graybeards didn't seem to think before they 'flapped their lips,' as you so accurately put it."

"Good. Then you'll be miles ahead of the other girl. I wondered if Kodan was thinking right when he said he wanted to pursue an outlander woman—don't just stand there!" his mother half scolded. "Even a stew won't cook forever, and that dough needs to be dropped into the pot! Go fetch the chives while I grate some cheese. I should have some sharp cow's cheese left—oh! You'll want to get a cold chest for your kitchen goods, too, for storing delicate foods. The spells are depressingly expensive, though thankfully they only have to be renewed once every few years. But the convenience is utterly worth it in the long run, and since you will be paid a tithe every two weeks, you should be able to afford it . . ."

Quickly ducking out through the door, Tava let it shut behind her. Kodan's mother was intelligent, opinionated, and talkative . . . and thus a little exhausting for the Valley-bred woman to deal with. Kind, though; Tava would be the first to admit Sinya Trei Dan was kind. She was glad to get away from the chatty woman, if only for a little while. Tava just wasn't used to the presence of so many adult women in her life. It was one of many changes she was still getting used to, here on the Plains.

A stray thought made her chuckle. *No wonder he's so quiet and thoughtful! His mother "flaps her lips" more than enough to carry a conversation by herself, though at least what she says is worth listening to. The same can't be said for everyone, alas. She's also right in that I'll learn far more if I keep my lips shut and my ears open. These are my people now. And being born a female shifter, they'll expect me to be a Princess of the People . . . which means becoming a leader. Particularly if Arahala plans on apprenticing to the Queen this winter. Everyone here will be looking at me to be the Princess of Family Tiger.*

At least getting married to Kodan seems to have cut off the annoying flood of suitors, she thought, smiling at Torei as she passed the front of his *geome* on her way to the cistern. The youth stuttered a greeting, but didn't get up and chase after her, thankfully. Tava nodded politely in reply. She suppressed the urge to chuckle as she reached the center of camp. *I can't believe I yelled what I did about using the refreshing tent yesterday. Back home . . . I probably would've been whipped for such vulgarity, and by my own father . . .*

I think I'll want to avoid being so vulgar in the future. It's hard enough trying to think of myself as a princess, but I should try my best to live up to the honor these . . . my people are now giving me. After all, the princesses from the stories in Father Fox's Tales *are kind and courteous young women. They may be fictional stories, but they do make a good example.*

I just wish my own father was still around to see me now. To know I've found a place for myself at last . . .

Thinking about her father didn't hurt quite as much anymore. She still missed him, but the pain of her grief had eased. With the sun shining through the broad gaps in the clouds, with everything freshly washed from the rain and drying out in the bright light, Tava felt refreshed and renewed herself.

Ready to try being a butterfly, in fact . . . but I think I'll want a fellow shifter and some food and water on hand, just in case becoming a butterfly is like becoming a hummingbird. And I do have to fetch that wild chive and get back to Siinar and Sinya's geome before the stew cooks dry. Yes, I'll ask Kodan to help watch me this afternoon. I think we can get a free hour in which to practice . . .

The grass around the cistern had been trampled down to bare earth, testament to how many people had come and gone in the weeks the Family had camped in this one location. It was also a bit muddy, thanks to the overnight rain. Picking her way carefully down the slope to the bushes outlining the docklike covering of long timbers, she found she wasn't the only one wanting to descend the former cellar steps.

A line of four other women had formed at the top of the steps, while the sounds of splashing water echoed up from the opening. Tava detoured around the women so that she could reach the wild chive growing near the planks covering the cistern walls. Some of the planks looked brand-new, taken from the lumber traded from the villagers back at Five Springs, while others were old and weathered, though not quite in need of replacing just yet. Her lessons from Priestess Soukut had included instructions on how to repair and plaster similar such cisterns across the Plains, as well as how to dredge new retention ponds, and which bushes to plant around their edges for both food and shade, limiting how much water might evaporate on hot summer days.

"Hurry up down there!" one of the older women ordered as Tava stooped to start snipping off choice stalks of chive.

"Have patience!" a familiar voice snapped.

Tava recognized it belatedly as Rahala's voice. She emerged a few moments later with two full buckets. The other shifter also limped slightly as she mounted the worn stone steps. The sight of her uneven footsteps made Tava frown thoughtfully.

Odd . . . she's a shifter, like me. Admittedly, I hadn't realized for the first few years of experimenting that a shapeshifter could shift a wound healed, but if she's strong enough to assume all of those shapes, surely she's strong enough to shift her thigh whole and sound again? From what I was told, even the weakest of shifters can manage partial healing, but the strongest ones can heal themselves very quickly. Even I picked up the trick of it quickly enough, once I knew it could be done.

It didn't take more than four or five body lengths from the path to the cistern before two young men showed up, asking Rahala if she needed help. Tava watched the other shifter princess hand over the buckets. Without their burden weighing her down, she walked normally enough that Tava wondered if Rahala had faked the injury just to ensure she'd have such offers of help.

Be charitable, Tava, she admonished herself, snipping a last few pieces of chive into the bowl she had brought. *Just minutes ago, you were telling yourself to be kind and generous, like a true princess of old. Or at least the kind found in adventure tales. At least the men of the Plains do offer to help their women with such chores. Father stopped helping me fetch water from the well once I grew big enough to carry a full bucket on my own, and I never had a young man courting me, back in the Valley.*

Let her enjoy her suitors. She didn't get the one she wanted for a husband, and she has to help feed the maidens of her geome, just one more unmarried woman among the rest. I have a mother-in-law and a new kin-family waiting for me, as well as the husband I wanted.

"Kodan?" Tava asked.

"*A*kodan," Siinar corrected her as his eldest son looked up from his bowl of stew and dumplings. "He did marry you, you know."

"Akodan," she corrected, rolling her eyes slightly. "How long does it take a new shifter to get the hang of shift-healing their wounds? Not speed-healing in the midst of battle, just regular healing."

"Not very long at all," Kenyen answered before Kodan could. Like the others, he was seated on the cushion-strewn floor of Siinar's *geome* at a low, rounded table. The older couple kept the table stored under the frame of their rope-bed, a practical solution for the limited space they possessed.

"Even the weakest of shifters, like Torei, can pick up the trick of it within a few hours," Siinar agreed. "Why do you ask?"

"Well, I never really got injured as a child, not seriously, so I never really thought about changing my shape to change the state of any wounds," Tava admitted, shrugging. "But then, I didn't grow up a Shifterai, and didn't realize it was possible for the first few years. I was thinking about it just now because I saw Arahala limping up out of the cistern when I went to get the chives for the dumplings, and I wondered how long it should take her to learn how to heal the cut she received yesterday."

"She's Shifterai. Even a non-shifter knows the basics of how we heal ourselves," Kodan said, scooping up another spoonful of stew. He paused and frowned. "Are you sure she was still limping? I saw her walking in the distance earlier this morning, and she seemed fine."

"She stopped limping once a couple of her suitors came by to carry her buckets for her," Tava admitted. "She may have been exaggerating her injury to get their sympathy . . . but I think she was still limping a little bit anyway as they headed back to her *geome*. Or at least she was walking slower than those two men were."

Kodan almost dismissed her concern. He had to remind himself that Rahala *was* a fellow shifter and a member of Family Tiger. If she hadn't mastered the art of shift-healing herself, it was the responsibility of the other shifters in the Family to make sure she learned. That meant the ultimate responsibility for such instruction was his, particularly if no one else had thought of instructing her yet. *I really should go over the basics with Tava, too, to make sure she also understands how we do it.*

"We'll go visit her after lunch, and make sure both of you have lessons in how to shift-heal," he decided. "It's mostly instinctive, but sometimes the pain can overwhelm the body's memory of how it normally should feel when whole and well. Sometimes a *multerai* can use the same hands-on techniques for shift-healing as for shapeshifting."

"That reminds me, I wanted to try a new shape this afternoon," Tava said, scraping up the last of the stew in her bowl.

"You're still working on an eagle, and you want to try a new shape?" Siinar asked her.

"Which shape?" Kodan asked, curious.

"A butterfly."

Four sets of brown eyes stared at her. Kenyen lowered his spoon. "A . . . *butterfly?*"

"Yes, a butterfly," Tava agreed. "I've always felt like I've been trapped for most of my life, back down in the Valley. Like I was a caterpillar stuffed into a cocoon for years on end, bound and restricted by the ways of Mornai society. But up here . . . I finally feel free. I feel like I can flutter my wings and fly, and go wherever I want. Do whatever I want. I can say and *be* whatever I want. I no longer have to restrict myself to being drab and blending in with the leaves of the forest. Up here on the Plains, I can be as colorful as I want. I *feel* like a butterfly—and isn't *feeling* like the animal half of a shape-shifter's battle?"

Siinar blinked. "It's . . . not a particularly *practical* shape to shift . . . but then, neither is a hummingbird. And yet I've never heard of any-one successfully shifting into something as small as a hummingbird, yet clearly you could."

Kodan reached over and rested his hand on her forearm. "If you really want to try, I'll do my best to help you. I've never even consid-ered shifting into an insect, but I can at least watch what you do and make suggestions as you try. We can do it after we've visited R . . . Arahala."

"Arahala, Atava—it's *not* that difficult to say!" Sinya scolded her son, whapping him on the shoulder. The blow was a light one, but pointed all the same. "Show your respect for others, *A*kodan! You're not just the Lord of Family Tiger, anymore; you're *also* a Prince of the People now. You have a responsibility to lead the way in courtesy as well as in everything else."

"Yes, Mother," he replied, attempting to sound meek. Sinya whapped him again for rolling his eyes. Letting it pass, Kodan glanced at his wife. "Are you finished, Atava?"

Tava ate her last spoonful of stew and nodded. "I'm ready."

"You are *not* leaving me to wash the dishes on my own," Kenyen protested as his brother rose.

Kodan smirked at his sibling. "As our beloved mother has just reminded me, I *am* the Lord of Family Tiger . . . and I delegate *you* to wash the lunch dishes for me."

Tava bit her lip in the effort to suppress her giggle, but earned a dirty look from Kenyen anyway. Ducking out of the *geome*, she caught

Kodan's hand and laced their fingers together. He smiled and matched his stride to hers.

It took a while to get from the South Paw to the Right Flank. The distance wasn't actually all that much, but Kodan's time and attention were in demand. Every few lengths, one or more people would come up to him, wanting to talk with him.

Some of them wanted to talk to Tava, too, ranging from elderly men and women wanting to give her a piece of advice to young children who would blush, giggle, ask a question or two, then skip off to attend to some early-afternoon chore. It felt strange to be the center of such friendly, admiring attention, and yet it wasn't unpleasant. She felt even more grateful to Kodan for rescuing her into this new life, even if she hadn't thought it was one at the time.

All the more reason to make sure I repay the great favor he's done me, by being the best Shifterai I can be . . .

". . . I said *no*! I don't want your help, and I *don't* want you in my quarters! Now, *get out!*"

The owner of that particular strident voice was easily discerned. A young woman of about fourteen or fifteen ran out of the maiden's *geome*. She spun once she was clear of the door, poked her thumbs in her ears, waggled her fingers, and raspberried the hidden occupant that had banished her from the canvas-wrapped structure. Turning around again, she pulled up short at the sight of Kodan just a few feet away.

"What was that about, Dannika?" he asked, hands going to his hips.

The girl folded her arms defensively across her yellow-clad chest. "Oh, she was just being stupid because I saw some paint on her stomach and asked her if she wanted me to bring a wash bowl," Dannika muttered. "And then she *yelled* at me for it."

"No, I meant the rude . . . Wait. *What* did you say?" Kodan asked, abandoning his disapproval of the girl's unseemly gesturing.

"I offered to bring her a wash bowl, and she yelled at me," the

Shifterai maiden repeated, glancing briefly at Tava. "Just because she's a princess doesn't give her the right to be mean when someone offers to help."

Tava narrowed her eyes. "You said you saw *paint* on her stomach?"

"Yes. Right about here," Dannika said, gesturing at her abdomen. "She was changing the bandage on her leg."

Exchanging a quick look with Kodan, Tava held out her hand. "Come with me."

The girl eyed the two of them and shrugged, accepting Tava's hand. ". . . Okay."

Since they seemed to be on a mission, only a few people approached Kodan, delaying him only a moment or two each time while Tava and Dannika waited for their business to finish. The three of them headed for the center of camp and the spot behind the *ageome* where Kodan had set up his own quarters. Leaving the younger woman outside, Tava fetched the book from the night table. She found some of the illustrations as she returned to the doorway, and turned the book so that Dannika could read it.

"Did the paint on Arahala's stomach look like any of these marks?" Tava asked, tapping one of the tattooed figures in the drawing.

Peering at it for a moment, Dannika nodded and touched the oval one circling the man's belly button. "Yes. This one. Or . . . more like this one, actually," she corrected herself, pointing at the female figure next to him. "But it's hard to tell, since the drawing doesn't show all of it."

Kodan approached, waving off another questioner before they could divert his attention again. Tava quickly flipped a few pages farther into the book as her husband stopped and peered over Dannika's shoulder. The younger woman nodded, tapping the next illustration that showed a bared female middle.

"That's it. That's what I saw. This curlicue bit here kind of reminds me of the petals of a greenthorn flower," the girl offered.

"Yemii was just teaching us yesterday how dried greenthorn petals can be brewed into a tea that helps ease the pain of a toothache, and that's why it caught my eye. Now, why do you ask?"

"I thought I'd seen something similar myself," Tava replied smoothly. She didn't have to look at Kodan to know this was something that had to be handled delicately. There was a chance her suspicions weren't true, which meant it would be wiser to keep gossip to a minimum.

"Thank you for answering my wife's curiosity. I'll have a word with Arahala about her rudeness, don't worry," Kodan promised the young maiden. "Go and tend to your afternoon chores now."

Nodding, the girl headed off.

Tava closed the book and hugged it to her chest. She spoke softly, moving closer to Kodan. They weren't surrounded by others, but she didn't think talking loudly about their discovery would be good for the Family. "This is a delicate matter, isn't it?"

"Very. Rahala is popular with at least half of Tiger. To suggest that she isn't . . . well, she doesn't *smell* like a mage, because mages smell like pepper to me, and I would have noticed that. But then, most Painted Warriors technically *aren't* mages, from what I've heard."

"No, they're not," Tava agreed. "At least, they're not born mages, though how they empower their tattoos isn't widely known. So, what do we do about her?"

"Go find my brother," Kodan instructed her under his breath, mindful of how close they were to the center of the camp and the people passing through it. "Tell him to start with South Paw and work his way west and north. He needs to find the members of the Shifter Council one at a time and tell them to gather quietly and privately in the Shifter *geome* within the hour, and that they are *not* to let anyone else hear about the meeting, including *A*rahala. I'll head east and south from North Paw, covering the rest of the camp. Bring your Truth Stone, as well as that book, and wait for us in there.

"We'll summon her for questioning *after* this matter has been brought before the Council, so that she doesn't have time to conceal the truth somehow. Or flee."

Nodding, Tava returned the book to their quarters before heading off to find Kenyen, guessing it would be better if she avoided making people think about why she might be carrying it around, until it was actually needed.

FIFTEEN

◦⟫⟪◦

Rahala stepped into the vertically striped *geome* and stopped for a moment, looking around at the thirty-plus men gathered inside, with Tava the lone female in their midst. Like Tava, she was wearing a bone-carved pectoral collar draped in an arc from shoulder to shoulder. Unlike Tava, who wore her blue replacement *chamsa*, Rahala was wearing a rose pink tunic cut from linen, not wool.

"Oh . . . you're already assembled." She continued forward, clearing enough room for Siinar to enter behind her. "What is this meeting about? The Shifter Council doesn't meet for another two days."

"An allegation of misconduct on the part of a shapeshifter has been raised. Please have a seat," Kodan added, gesturing at the empty chair on his right.

Siinar politely offered his hand, assisting Rahala into her seat. His other hand came up just as she seated herself, clamping a hinged bracelet around her still-outstretched wrist. Rahala blinked and started.

"What the . . . ? You're using bluesteel on *me?* I've done nothing wrong!" she protested. "I'm a princess!"

"That remains to be seen," Kodan told her. "Please cooperate with the Council's inquiries. Your compliance or lack thereof will be taken into account, should their findings result in the need for a judgment."

"—A judgment that could be biased?" Rahala scoffed. "Just because I was *persistent* in the past regarding my pursuit of your affections is no reason for you to persecute me here in the present!"

"There will be no persecution in this hearing," Deian stated flatly. He held up the white marble disc of a Truth Stone. "Merely a vigorous pursuit of the truth. If you are innocent, the Stone will prove it, and you will have nothing to fear."

Her eyes widened at the sight of the Stone. Mouth tightening, Rahala glared at Kodan. The Lord of Family Tiger merely gestured for his friend to begin.

"Hold this in your hand—your *other* hand," he corrected as she turned up the palm of the one with the cobalt-hued bracelet on her wrist, "—and state that your name is Agatha."

Taking it in her other hand, Rahala complied. "My name is Agatha."

"Display the Truth Stone, please." He waited until the blackened marks made by her fingers faded from the purified marble, then asked, "Did you proclaim to this Family a few days ago that you had discovered you could shift your shape while you were off on your trip west across the Plains?"

"Yes." Flicking the stone, Rahala displayed its unblemished sides. "I can shift my shape. I don't see what my being a shapeshifter has to do with an allegation of misconduct."

"Did you, or did you not, announce to several members of Family Tiger your intentions to apply your sudden, new shapeshifting skills to the Princess Challenge this winter, in the specifically stated hope of becoming Ailundra's own apprentice?" Kenyen asked, speaking up from his seat on one of the benches scattered around the tent.

"Of course I did," Rahala stated, eyeing him warily. She paused, then drew in a deep breath and admitted, "I'll admit I was jealous that Akodan chose someone *else* over me, when I had tried for so many years to ensnare his affections. I felt humiliated, and I didn't want to stay in a Family where I'd be constantly reminded of . . . of my failure." Lifting the Stone, she showed its all-white sides, then let it drop back into her palm, gripping it. "Is there something *wrong* in wanting to remove myself from a source of pain? Is *that* suddenly a form of misconduct? I would think you would be dancing happily at the thought of being rid of me, Akodan."

He opened his mouth to reply, but before Kodan could speak, the blaring of an *an-kat* sounded in the distance. Everyone held still, listening to the pattern of the notes. Tava frowned, not quite catching all of it, but Kodan nodded.

". . . Good. Tailtip has returned, with no deaths." Rising from his chair, he glanced at Rahala, then looked at the other shifters gathered inside the vertically striped tent, many of them *multerai*, the rest elders. "You've already heard my opinions on the points still waiting to be discussed. I think it best if I remove myself from these proceedings and go welcome our last warband. I wouldn't want my past interactions with the accused to have any bearing or influence on the outcome of this hearing.

"I leave Atava in charge of sentencing, with the provision this Council advises her on the appropriate Shifterai laws and precedences, whatever the outcome may be. *She* has no history of dislike for the accused." Bowing, Kodan strode out of the *geome*, letting the door bang shut behind him.

"I still would like to know what I have been accused of," Rahala stated in the silence following his departure.

"Deian, please continue," Tava directed her husband's friend. She shifted the book on her lap to a more comfortable position, checking to make sure the title was not visible from the other woman's position, seated on the far side of Kodan's empty chair.

"Did you travel earlier this summer with the West Paw Warband, accompanying a trading caravan headed west across the Plains?" Deian asked Rahala.

"Yes, I did. And farther west with a warband providing further escort from Clan Dog, Family Malamute," Rahala added. She displayed the disc in her hand, showing her honesty.

"Did you converse at any point in time with a certain Painted Warrior of Mendhi who was traveling with that caravan?" Deian asked.

Rahala gripped the Stone for a moment, then smiled. "Of course I did. Everyone spoke with him. He was an affable fellow with many amusing stories to tell."

"Did you at any point in time ask bribe, coerce, or in any other way convince him to bestow upon you any sort of variation of the tattoo-based magics of a Painted Warrior of Mendhi?" Deian pressed as soon as she gripped the all-white Stone once more.

Her fingers tightened until her knuckles were as white as the marble they curled around. If Tava hadn't been looking at the Truth Stone, she wouldn't have noticed the other woman's display of distress, for Rahala's smile hadn't slipped. Even her voice was calm when she spoke. Not quite lighthearted, but not tense, either.

"Why would I do such a thing? I am Shifterai, not Mendhi."

"That doesn't answer the question," Deian reminded her. "Did you in any way request, coerce, or otherwise convince the Painted Warrior to give you Mendhi tattoo magics of your own?"

"I will admit that I questioned him about how Mendhi tattoo magic worked, but a lot of other people asked him about it, too," Rahala stated, shrugging. Again, the Truth Stone was unblemished when she displayed it. "Is it suddenly illegal to try and satiate one's curiosity about foreign ways and foreign lands?"

Deian folded his arms across his chest. "You didn't answer the question I asked."

"How about a different question?" Kenyen offered. "Arahala, do you currently possess the power of Mendhi-style tattoo magics? Whether or not you are actively using any, and regardless of what kind they may be, do you possess Mendhi tattoo powers?"

". . . Yes, or no?" Deian prompted her when she didn't answer. "Yes, you possess Mendhi tattoo magics, or no, you do not possess Mendhi tattoo magics. The answer is simple; we await your reply."

This time, her fingers weren't the only thing that tightened. Mouth pinching, brow furrowing, Rahala glared at Deian. She didn't answer. Unfolding his arms, the *multerai* braced his palms on the armrests of her canvas-slung chair, bringing his face within a hand length of hers.

"Be *mindful*, woman, that the *honesty* of your answer will correlate directly to the *leniency* with which this Council will judge your actions. You sit accused of using *foreign* magic to duplicate natural-born Shifterai shapeshifting magics. As is the law in *many* a land, including this one," Deian reminded her, "failure to answer a direct, Truth Stone–verified question will be considered a tacit admission of guilt."

He stayed there a few moments, then straightened.

"As the second-ranked *multerai* in Family Tiger, I accuse Rahala, self-styled Princess of the People, of using foreign magic to duplicate natural-born Shifterai powers. I further accuse Rahala, self-styled Princess of the People, of plotting openly to use her foreign-bought powers to subvert the rightful place of true-born Shifterai princesses, and thus overthrow the rightful government of the Shifting Plains, an act of treaso—"

"—Alright!" Rahala shouted, cutting him off. "*Yes*, I paid that Painted Warrior to give me Mendhite tattoo magics. Because I *love* this land, and I have every right to see it ruled *properly*. If it is a *sin* to want the best possible woman to rule over the Plains, then *yes*, I have sinned!"

"You're not the best."

Rahala looked at Tava, her glare shifting into a sneer. "Oh, and like *you* are? You're a *foreigner*! I, at least, am native-born! Where do *your* powers come from?"

Rising from her chair, Tava crossed to Rahala. She held out her hand, waiting until the other woman dropped the disc into her palm.

"My shapeshifting powers are inherent and natural-born, and are not triggered by spell, rune, tattoo, amulet, potion, or other external force. They came to me in puberty when I fancied what it would be like to *be* a cat, and found myself, my flesh, shifting shape from the strength of my imaginings . . . in the exact same way that a native-born Shifterai imagines a new form into his or her flesh." Uncurling her fingers, she held up the Truth Stone, displaying its all-white sides not only to Rahala, but to the others on the Council of Shifters. Gripping it again, she added, ". . . *My* name is Agatha."

This time, the sides of the disc were mottled with the blackened imprint of her fingers, proving the Stone was still working perfectly. Dropping the disc back into Rahala's hand, Tava returned to her chair. But she didn't stay silent, nor did she seat herself. Lifting the book she had abandoned on the fabric seat, she opened it and displayed the pages to Rahala.

"This is a book of stories following the adventures of Mendhite Painted Warriors. It contains several illustrations. When you yelled at young Dannika, she came out of the *geome* and encountered Akodan and me. We were on our way to see you because we were concerned that you hadn't yet shift-healed the wound you received yesterday when you fell on that broken pottery. Dannika said she had offered to bring you some water to wash your wound . . . and to wash the paint from your stomach."

Flicking through the pictures, Tava pointed at one of the female figures.

"Dannika identified *this* mark, which has been drawn identically on every female Painted Warrior illustrated in this book, as being the same mark she saw on your stomach. We have proof enough that you lied about your powers, between what she saw, the sudden manifestation of your powers, your inability to shift-heal a simple cut, and your refusal to speak." Closing the book, Tava seated herself. "As a *true* Shifterai princess, it falls to me to decide what to do with you. Give me a reason to be lenient, *Rahala*.

"Give me a reason *not* to ask you other, more dangerous questions, further compounding your transgressions."

For a long moment, Rahala stayed silent. Then she lifted her chin slightly. Proudly. ". . . I confess. I deliberately accompanied that caravan, seeking to gain Mendhite tattoo magics in order to simulate shapeshifting powers and thus promote myself as a Shifterai princess. I did so because I love the Plains, and believed I could rule it better than any other . . . and I confess I did it in the hopes that Kodan Sin Siin would finally pay attention to me, believing that he was holding out for a Shifterai princess as his future bride . . . which he did."

She paused between each statement, displaying the Truth Stone.

"I confess I intended to use my Mendhite tattoo magics to apprentice myself to Ailundra, for the express purpose of becoming the next Queen . . . but *not* to overthrow our government. I am loyal to the Plains and loyal to its people, and *that* is the truth."

A final display of the disc proved her words were as pure as the enchanted marble.

"Your loyalty may not be questionable, Rahala," Kamar, one of the warband leaders stated. "But your ethics are. The law is the law. The Queen must be a natural-born shapeshifter, and by correlation of the laws of inheritance, all Princesses of the People must be natural-born shifters as well. You may be native-born, but you are not natural-born. By *faking* your powers, you have lost the right to claim you are a Shifterai, because you have insulted our laws and our ways. Your betrayal of our people deserves the sentence of banishment from the Plains. So say I, Kamar Lu Tieth."

"So say I, Deian Bar Shou," Deian stated, stepping back from Rahala.

"So say I, Siinar Sid Quen."

"So say I, Jumaj El Sui."

"So say I . . ."

Rahala kept her chin up as the members of the Shifter Council voted, but her eyes glittered with unshed tears. Watching her struggle to maintain her composure, Tava wondered what price the other woman had to pay to gain her ill-advised abilities in the first place. She thought about it while the men around her stated their agreement on the proposed verdict in turn.

"The Council is unanimous. Rahala Jen Liu's actions deserve banishment from the Plains," Deian stated. "Atava, it is up to you to decide what her punishment is to be. Akodan asked that we advise you in this matter, so I will tell you that banishment is standard for acts of treason and other high crimes . . . but the *kind* of banishment varies."

"The most lenient of banishments simply casts the accused out of the Family and Clan to which she would normally belong," one of the older men stated. "She would then be free to travel with all of her belongings to another Clan and Family. I do not think she deserves such leniency."

Several of the others nodded. Kenyen, the youngest of the men inside the *geome*, explained the other end of the spectrum. "The harshest sentence casts her out with nothing but the clothes on her back, the shoes on her feet, and a single waterskin for sustenance . . . but no coins, no cloak, no animals, nothing but those few things permitted by law . . . and a brand burned in bluesteel upon her forehead, scarring her permanently with a rune proclaiming to both the Shifterai and our cross-kin the Centarai that she is banished and cast out forever from living on both Plains."

"She did confess her crimes . . . eventually," Jumaj pointed out. "So the harshest punishment should not be applied. But she did confess an intent to fake shapeshifting powers in order to claim the Shifting Throne. I do not think she should be allowed to continue to live on the Shifting Plains, even in some other Clan. She doesn't deserve it."

"I say, give her a horse, some food, some clothing, and half the coin she is due in payment for her in-camp goods . . . but brand her forehead so that all who see her know she can never return to the Shifting Plains . . . and will find no shelters on the Centa Plains, either," someone else said.

From the nodding of the men around her, Tava gauged they thought it was a fair punishment. Her itch of curiosity wouldn't leave it at that, however. Tapping the book on her lap, she addressed Rahala.

"Tell me what price you paid to gain these magics, and how they work, when everyone knows you weren't born a shifter and weren't born a mage . . . and I will be more lenient than that with you. Use the Truth Stone," she added as Rahala narrowed her hazel eyes in speculation. "Speak the truth, satisfy my curiosity with your honesty, and I will be more lenient. Stay silent, or lie, and get no more than your deceit deserves."

Rahala blushed, but spoke after only a moment. ". . . I paid two prices. He wanted . . . intercourse . . . in a manner which would not ruin my virginity. That was the price he demanded for tattooing my skin. As for how they work . . . I had to pay a second price. The same price that all Painted Warriors who were not born mages must pay. I had to sacrifice my fertility so that the life-energy that would normally go toward such things would instead be channeled into empowering my . . . shapeshifting ways."

Resisting the urge to squirm at both pieces of news, Tava asked, "And how did you hide all the tattoos necessary to be able to take on so many shapes?"

"With another tattoo, of course." Lifting her left hand, which still had the bluesteel bracelet clasped around her wrist, Rahala ran her fingers over her hair. "It was hidden on my scalp, and in turn, it hides all the rest across my body. The only one it cannot hide is the empowerment tattoo centered around my navel. If I hadn't grown lax, if I had kept my stomach covered in fur, *none* of you would have known."

"Actually, your disguise slipped the moment you fell and injured yourself," Tava told her. "Even I, who hadn't realized it was possible until a few years after my first shapeshifting experiments, learned just how quickly and easily I could shift-heal my injuries. This you should have known as a native-born. You should have included the request for a tattoo that would rapidly heal your injuries."

Rahala clenched her teeth. "He didn't *know* that one. It had been applied by another Painted Warrior on his back, and without having learned it, he could not duplicate it for me. I didn't think it would matter, because a Princess of the People is never asked to fight. She may choose to do so, but she does not *have* to. Now, is *that* honest enough for you? Or is there more you wish to know?"

The question of her tumble into the bonfire hovered in the back of Tava's mind. She kept it there, however. "There are many questions we could ask you. Some of them might be even more damning than an accusation of treason . . . but you have satisfied enough of my curiosity, and I thank you for it.

"I agree with the others on the Shifter Council that you do not deserve to live among the same Shifterai you tried to deceive. Nor should you be free to take shelter among the Centarai, for I will not inflict your arrogance upon our cross-kin," Tava added. It was odd that she finally felt comfortable saying *we* and *our* in regard to the Shifterai at this moment in time, but she did. With the eyes of the men upon her, silently awaiting her judgment, she gave it. "You will therefore be branded with bluesteel. But you will be given a covered wagon with two horses, and all your personal belongings that you can pack into it to carry off the Plains.

"I know what it is like to be forced to flee the only home you've ever known. I will not treat you like the Alders of Five Springs treated me. I will not steal away your belongings, nor will I beat you for your insolence . . . and you *have* been insolent, Rahala," Tava added bluntly. "You may take whatever of your belongings you can fit onto that two-horse wain. If you do not own two horses and a wagon, I will gift them to you out of the ones I gained when I left the Valley . . . because I want you *gone*. You have lost the right to claim the Plains as your home."

"What of my things in the City?" Rahala dared to ask, lifting her chin just a little bit more.

"They are forfeit to the crown, as payment for the harm you would have done through your deception, had you succeeded. You may take only what you possess here in this encampment—and Rahala, if you try to flee or disguise yourself before you are branded and packed off . . . you will be stripped of everything but the clothes on your back and a waterskin for your survival. This is my judgment for your punishment," Tava finished firmly.

Deian cleared his throat. "How long will she have to pack?"

"She will be considered packed by sunrise tomorrow. Hobble her in bluesteel chains and set guards to watch her every hour she remains so that she cannot flee . . . but give her assistance in loading her things. She will sleep in the *ageome*, too, so you can keep an eye on her all night long. Just in case."

Jumaj rose from his chair, his expression grim. "I will go heat the branding iron," he stated. "She is of the Right Flank, and its members are my responsibility this year."

"Fetch Yemii while you do so. She'll need a potion for the pain," Tava explained. "This may be a justly earned punishment, but there's no need to make it excessively cruel." Rising from her own seat, Tava tucked her book under her arm and plucked the Truth Stone from the other woman's hand. "You brought this upon yourself, Rahala. You chose to deceive your own people. You chose to fake the things which you knew by law had to be natural. You made the wrong choices. I hope you will learn to make the right ones, wherever you go in the future."

Kodan found her in their *geome*, sitting at her scribe's desk with the Truth Stone in her hands. Closing and latching the door, he crossed the felt-strewn floor and gently cupped her wool-clad shoulders.

"Are you all right?"

Tava lifted the disc. "This is what sent me into exile from the only home I'd ever known . . . and I'm happy that it did. This is also what is sending *her* into exile. I don't know if she'll ever be happy. Period. I know that telling everyone the news of the hearing and my judgment made a lot of people in the Family unhappy with me . . . but if I hadn't had *this* on hand to prove my words were true, it would have been that much more difficult to send her away."

"She was popular, in her own way. It's possible all the admiration she garnered from her kin and her friends went to her head at an early age, and so she just craved more," Kodan offered. "More recognition, more admiration, more power. But her worst offense wasn't craving more. It was craving it for her own selfish ends. If she *had* made it all the way to being our Queen, we would have suffered as a whole. We need people in charge who honestly *care* about others. Rahala mostly just cared for herself."

"I still can't help but feel sorry for her. Particularly after watching her scream when Jumaj . . ." Tava shuddered.

Taking the polished marble from her hand, Kodan set it on the flat top of the angled desk. Tugging her to her feet, he enfolded her in his arms. "You need to forget for a few hours. Now that Tailtip is back, we will have a Grieving Day tomorrow. You can grieve over what happened because of her tomorrow, or even what happened *to* her, if you like. The day after that will be a day for laundering and packing our belongings, and the day after *that*, we will depart for the City.

"The *nice* thing about living in the Shifting City is that the leader of the Family won't be quite so heavily in demand for every least little thing. *Somewhat* in demand," Kodan allowed wryly. "But everyone will be so busy with helping bring in the last of the harvests, then settling in and meeting with their old neighbors, catching up on the various news and returning livestock to the various Families and Clans, you and I will be quite bored. Or we would be, if I couldn't think of several things we could do to fill all the hours and days where we'll be blissfully ignored."

Lifting her head from his shoulder, Tava glanced at the waiting bed. "Like . . . ?"

"Like *read new books?*" Kodan teased her, giving his wife a little squeeze. "Or at least they'll be new to you. I have almost fifty of them back in my winter quarters, packed with bay leaves and rune-stitched ribbons to keep away mildew and insects. I think—"

A knock on the *geome* door interrupted them. Groaning, Kodan dropped his forehead against hers. Tava giggled and squeezed him in sympathy.

Whoever it was on the other side spoke up, projecting his voice through the wooden panel. "Lord Kodan? Tailtip Warband wishes to distribute its tithe, now that they've finished putting up the warband *geome* and have unpacked their own homes. They also wanted to meet the new Princess of Family Tiger."

"Say the word," Kodan muttered, "and I will tell them all to go away. Even *we* deserve some privacy as newlyweds."

"We'll have time later," Tava reminded him. "Later this afternoon, if nothing else. You can order Deian to handle anything the Family requires. But I really should meet with the last warband. These are the kind of people I've always wanted to care about, and I need to show them that I care. That I *am* one of you, now that I'm free to be with you. Besides, if we don't show up together, the bachelor ones might not realize we're married and pester me with courtship attempts—I can see now why you cautioned me not to say a word about my abilities."

"... Lord Kodan?"

He opened his mouth to reply, then shut it and shook his head. "No ... I'll give my time and effort to this Family, but I'll also keep some of it for you." Raising his voice, Kodan called out, "Tell Tailtip we'll meet with them in an hour!"

Tava muffled a giggle behind a quickly raised hand.

"In an *hour*?" the man repeated through the door. "But they're bringing the tithe up to the *ageome* now for distribution!"

"I said an hour!" Kodan called back. "We *are* newly wed, you know!"

"I say it, too!" Tava added boldly, glad whoever it was couldn't see how hard she was blushing. "Come back in an hour!"

"*Ah*. Um ... yes, Your Highness, Lord Kodan. Of course. In an hour ... or two."

Both of them choked on their laughter. It was hard to hear the man moving away from the *geome* door because of their mirth, but it didn't really matter. Tava grinned at Kodan, who grinned back. Then he kissed her. It was an awkward thing, half smile-bared teeth and half laughter-stuttered breath, but it was fun all the same.

Tava nipped her way to Kodan's ear. If they had an hour—or two, but probably just an hour—she knew of the perfect way to get her mind off the thoughts that had been troubling her. For once, it didn't involve a book, though it did involve burying herself between the covers. Unfortunately, just as she started exploring the sensitivities of his earlobe, Kodan twitched and squirmed free. Spinning her around, he wrapped his arms around her from behind and began tugging on the fastenings of her *chamsa*.

"No, you don't, *wife*," he growled. "It is *my* duty to arouse *you* first. You will have the chance to make me mindless with lust *after* I have done the same to you."

"So I *wasn't* imagining things last night," Tava said, leaning back into his embrace as he first bared her breasts, then covered them with his warm, gently kneading palms, sliding his fingers beneath the bone-and-cord network of beads the Family carvers had given her. She sighed happily, enjoying his touch. "Or rather, this morning. You *do* like having your ears licked."

"Very much. *Too* much." Nudging aside her hair, Kodan nipped her neck gently with his lips and teeth. The sensations he stirred aroused her. Tava arched her spine, pressing her backside into his loins and her breasts into his fingers. She trusted his dominance because she trusted him. It was a heady addition to her desire, knowing he *would* ensure she enjoyed their interactions.

"Show me, Kodan," she murmured, lifting her hands behind her head to caress his hair. "Show me *everything*."

"We only have an hour," he pointed out dryly, before nipping at her nape again. "But I'll try to show you a little more, at least."

She groaned and pressed into him again. Her eagerness gave him an idea. It was a daring one, since he still wasn't completely certain how comfortable she was about living among shapeshifters. It was also an arousing one, at least for him. *With luck . . . it will be for her, too.*

". . . Tava, do you trust me?" Kodan asked, stilling the touch of his lips and his hands.

Tipping her head, she smiled up at him. "Completely."

Her answer was humbling. Resolving to never break such a gift, Kodan swallowed and cleared his throat. "Then strip off your clothing . . . and shift yourself into a stripe-cat."

Tava's eyes widened. She didn't know what to make of his request, save that she *did* trust him. Blinking, she pulled free and found the clasps holding the carved pectoral on her shoulders. "Alright."

Kodan brushed aside her fingers, unfastening it with the familiarity of practice. His own, made from gold and carved gemstones, was dispensed with as well, both abandoned in a tangle on the seat of her chair. They parted long enough to remove the rest of their clothes. Then his wife, trusting him implicitly, dropped gracefully to all fours, her beautiful naked skin turning into a thick, soft pelt.

Shaping her words carefully in spite of her muzzle, as she had learned to do long ago in order to communicate with her father, Tava asked, ". . . Now vhat do ve do?"

Lowering himself to his knees at her side, Kodan gently raked his fingers through her fur. "Now you learn why Shifterai princesses are prized above all other females . . . because you can become *any* female you want. And as any man in Family Tiger can tell you, being a cat can be a *very* pleasurable thing."

With that said, Kodan raked his fingernails through her fur, scratching around her ears and her chin, fluffing and combing her fur all the way to her tail. The feelings were pleasurable enough, but it wasn't until he deliberately kneaded the muscles at the base of her tail that Tava realized just *how* pleasurable being a cat could be. She dug her claws into the felt floor and bowed her spine, pushing her haunches greedily up into his touch. A rumble escaped her throat, the closest a tiger could come to a purr.

Hearing it, Kodan chuckled. "You like that, do you?"

"Mmmm, *yessss*. More!" she demanded, kneading her claws. Until she realized they were now stuck in the felt rugs covering the ground. Dismayed, Tava shifted quickly back to her human form and stared at the holes she had made. "Gods . . . if I hadn't realized . . . I wanted to knead *you* like the floor!"

"Shh," Kodan soothed her, stroking her back like he had stroked her fur, though his extra little massage was bestowed on her buttocks, not the base of her spine. "I was about to shift shape and join you. Then your claws wouldn't have bothered me, because of my own thick fur. The way cats mate is perhaps a little rougher and quicker than humans . . . but I'm told by a reliable source that it can be *quite* pleasurable between two shifters."

"By a reliable source?" Tava asked, distracted.

"There are a couple of widowed princesses from the many in Family Lion who have chosen to take up the roll of earth-priestesses for a few years. Deian was lucky enough to be granted time with one last winter. He said it was . . . quite stimulating. Very erotic, in fact. And quite an honor. Princesses who choose the path of the earth-priestess are rare and are often more selective in whom they decide to comfort than the average earth-priestess."

"Well, you now have *me* for all such comforts," Tava asserted, pushing aside her small twinge of jealousy at the thought of him visiting someone else.

He smiled at her. "Yes, I do . . . Shift, and make love with me."

"You first," she coaxed.

Nodding, he altered himself into a tiger. Rather than joining him, Tava boldly ruffled his fur, then massaged his ears. He rumbled and kneaded the felt carpeting the *geome* and stuck his rump in the air when she raked her way down to the base of his tail. Golden brown eyes studied her, then a furry foreleg swept out, knocking her gently to the ground. Lowering his head to her stomach, Kodan nuzzled her naked flesh with his fuzzy face until she giggled and clutched at his fur.

Smelling her, hearing her, feeling her, and thus unable to resist, he licked her. Just the tip of his tongue, but he rasped her flesh all the same. Tava gasped, and Kodan pulled back, eyeing her warily.

"That was . . . um . . . a bit rough," she offered, hoping her honesty wasn't going to offend him. She had to say it, though; his tongue had felt like sandstone on the underside of her breast.

He twitched his tail. "Svitch to fur like me, and hyu vill not mind it zo much."

Hesitating only a moment, Tava rolled over and shifted her shape once she was on hands and knees. Kodan immediately began grooming her fur, starting with the shorter hairs behind her ears. That felt really, really good. So good, she started kneading the carpeting again.

By the time he licked his way down to her tail, her haunches were in the air and she was rumbling at the pure sensuality of being groomed by her mate. Carnal instinct filled her, and she twitched her tail to the side in feline invitation. But rather than the strength and power of a male tiger mounting her, she felt her mate shifting his shape back to his human form.

". . . Kodan?" she asked, shifting back as well.

"If I start this as a tiger, it will be over far too soon. It's in their nature to be quick," he told her, crawling half over her. He pressed kisses to her spine and nudged his erection against her damp flesh. "We may have only an hour . . . but it is an hour."

Kissing his way down to her rump, he lapped at the seam between her nether-cheeks. Tava quickly lowered her head to her wrists, sealing her mouth with the back of one fist to stifle her moans. It felt so good, she spread her knees, inviting more of the same. He obliged her for a while, before kissing his way back up the length of her spine.

Just as he pressed himself into her, a knock at the door startled both of them.

"Lord Kodan?"

For a moment, embarrassment warred with irritation. The irritation won. Raising her head from her arms, Tava yelled at whoever it was. "Go away!"

"But I need to talk to—"

"—Go. Away!" she asserted. "He's *mine*."

"But I—"

Pleased by her claim and yet irritated by the untimely interruption, Kodan gave in to both of those feelings. The shifting of his shape made his wife gasp, but it also gave him the chance to literally roar out his displeasure. From the yelp on the other side of the door and the sound of whoever it was scurrying away, his point had gotten across. About to shift shape again and apologize to Tava, Kodan stilled as she moaned.

She couldn't help it. Her Mornai upbringing hadn't even *covered* something this exotic, and her Shifterai instruction had been little more than Soukut saying, *If your husband wishes to add shapeshifting to your lovemaking, you do have the right to say no at any point, but if you say yes, you might be pleasantly surprised. But that's something best left to be negotiated between the two of you.* The feel of all that soft, warm fur was unbelievably sensual, but it was the thickness filling her that made the surreal experience erotic.

His comment about claws and fur made her shift her shape, too. Kodan grunted, then rumbled in the stripe-cat equivalent of a purr as she fluffed herself out beneath him. She felt his breath whuffling along her nape, then the tugging of his tongue grooming her fur. A moment later, his teeth nipped at her nape, holding her in place as he thrust.

It was quick, but it was also excitingly different. Both roared out as their striped bodies strained. Tired from so many rapid shifts, Kodan was the first one to change. He slumped over her soft-furred back until she shifted, returning to her naked, natural state. Sliding to the side, Kodan braced himself on one elbow and used his other hand to stroke her light brown hair back from her face.

". . . Are you all right?" he finally asked as she just blinked and stared at the lattice walls of his portable home.

Tava blinked again. A smile curved her lips. A blush heated her cheeks, too, but she definitely smiled. Shifting her gaze to his face, she swayed close enough to rub her nose against his. Then licked it. Kodan spluttered and she *mrraowrrl*ed, pushing him over as if she was still some sort of cat. Within heartbeats, he found himself sprawled on his back next to her chair, panting and squirming as she attacked his ear with all the fervor of a cat licking the flavor off of a fish. It didn't help when she straddled his stomach, pinning him further to the ground.

Thankfully, she took mercy on him. Switching to his mouth, Tava kissed him with equal fervor, nipping at his lips and suckling his tongue. Re-aroused, Kodan pulled her down a little farther on his chest and positioned her over his lap. It didn't take much more effort than that to position himself, nor did he have to do anything else; his wife sank down onto him with more of the same enthusiasm, and there was nothing short of a grass fire that would make him stop her from having her way. Whoever had come to the door of their *geome* would just have to wait a little longer before either the Lord of Tiger or his bride would be ready again for visitors.

Indeed, with the first edge of their hunger sated, it was at least a full hour later before the two lovers felt ready to rise and dress. Gently kissing the nape he had licked and bitten, Kodan finished fastening the clasps of her temporary pectoral in place. Switching his attention to her hands, he kissed the fingers holding her hair up out of his way.

Turning in his arms, Tava stroked his dark locks back from his face. She smiled shyly at first, then smugly, and bit her lip. "I, um, suggest . . ."

"Yes?" Kodan prompted her.

"That next time . . . we fly somewhere far away, far from where anyone could possibly hear us. Because we now have to go out and meet with the Tailtip warriors . . . and I just *know* they were listening to the two of us yowling away. I'm not sure I can bear it if they stare at us," she muttered.

Laughing, Kodan hugged her close. Kissing her cheek, he said, "You shouldn't be embarrassed, Tava. Rather, you should be flattered. I know I will be, because they'll all be muttering what a lucky man I am, and envying me for my good fortune. Of course, they'll also get it wrong in doing so."

"Oh?" Tava asked, pulling back a little. "How so?"

"They'll be envying me because they'll be thinking I had the good fortune to marry the most talented, beautiful princess in the kingdom. But the truth is," Kodan confessed, resting his forehead against hers, "I had the good sense to win the hand of a woman as smart and kind as she is beautiful. If not more so."

"You mean you had the wit to blackmail me into following you home, where you promptly stole my heart," she teased.

"That, too," he agreed. "But I didn't steal your heart. I merely exchanged it for mine." Catching one of her hands, he brought it to his lips for a kiss. "Come. Our people are waiting for us."

Blushing yet feeling smug at the same time, Tava let him lead her outside.

Her face flushed harder as they entered the back of the *ageome* through the normal-sized door, for they were met by more than the twenty or so warband men she expected. At least twenty more were there as well, including several members of both Councils and Kodan's parents. There was also a pile of fabrics fit to rival the stash liberated from the bandits, carved chests filled with semiprecious stones, and bags of what smelled like fresh-dried Corredai tea.

Stepping close and turning slightly, Siinar held out his hand toward her, introducing her to the returned warriors.

"This is Atava Ell Var, formerly of the Morna Valley, and now Princess of Family Tiger. She is an apprentice to my son Akodan, Lord of Family Tiger, and my new daughter-in-law. Your Highness, these are Warlord Mata and his men of the Tailtip Warband."

The middle-aged man eyed Tava. "Please forgive my skepticism, but . . . we've already heard about Rahala's deception. It is said your own abilities were proven true, but . . ."

"You wish me to fetch the Truth Stone?" Tava asked, guessing what he wanted.

"I'll take the Council of Shifters' word," the warlord corrected quickly. "I'm certain they questioned you thoroughly in light of what happened. I just want to *see* it."

"We haven't had a princess in the Family for too many years, and to hear that you're actually from the Valley lands . . . It's kind of hard to believe without seeing it for ourselves," one of the men behind Mata said apologetically. "We hope you understand."

Some of the others nodded, echoing the sentiment.

"I think I do understand," Tava reassured them. Turning to her husband, she asked, "Akodan, would you hold out your hand?"

Bemused, he did so. Tava smiled and shifted, as fast and tight as she had shifted just days before. This time, she merely hovered in midair for a mere moment while her clothing and pectoral dropped free, then alighted on his fingers, resting her jewel-feathered body.

"A . . . bird?" Mata asked, looking from her to her husband.

"Not just any bird, but a hummingbird," Kodan corrected, giving his tiny wife a proud smile. "She has mastered many other shapes, including a stripe-cat—in fact, she's mastered more than enough to apprentice herself to the Queen, should she ever want to rule."

Obliging him, Tava jumped off his hand. She landed on four large, clawed paws, her brightly colored feathers exchanged for somewhat duller stripes. The feel of the thick felt under her paws reminded her too much of what she and Kodan had just been doing. Embarrassment warred briefly with pride, until she glanced up at her husband.

The warmth and the approval in Kodan's dark eyes made her feel buoyant instead of bashful. Buoyant enough, she let go of the tigerish feelings that had shaped her flesh and embraced the new feeling within her. The newest feeling, of all the shapes she had mastered. Bunching her muscles, Tava leaped up and transformed.

Relatively huge wings flapped hard against the air, great sails of striped brown and cream, black and gold. It was an awkward way to fly, and she was grateful to land on the hand Kodan hastily extended beneath her bobbling body. Not that she could see it well, for her vision seemed to be fragmented and fuzzy. Her sense of smell was equally skewed, and every little vibration of sound and breeze made her wings want to tremble. Being a butterfly was even stranger than being an eel, for all that she didn't have to breathe water.

Mindful of how it wasn't too wise to stay in a vastly different body for long, particularly the first few times around, Tava crawled awkwardly to the edge of her husband's hand and spilled her flesh out and down. Between one breath and the next, she re-formed herself as a fur-clad human, and shared the words she herself felt.

"Welcome home to Family Tiger, gentlemen," she told them, smiling at their awed expressions. Glancing at Kodan, she squeezed the warm hand clasping hers. "I know that I'm finally home, too."